A
LION
NAME

L. D. MUSSELL

MussellWorks Publishing
mussellworks.com

A LION NAME
This book is a work of fiction. Any reference to historical events, real people, or real places are used fictitiously. Other names, characters, places, and events are products of the author's imagination, and any resemblance to actual events or places or persons, living or dead, is entirely coincidental.

First paperback edition March 2023
First Ebook edition March 2023

Book and cover design, cover art Copyright © 2023 by L. D. Mussell
mussellworks.com

For all of you
Rebels and dreamers
Young at heart and free of mind
For those hiding in the shadow
of your own Lion Name
This is your time, this is your world
It is from your imagination
That our reality is born
So dream beautiful
Dream BIG

The Boys

Don't sneeze, Jimmy. I'm telling you, bwana, you'll wake her up, and then you'll have no chance."

The boys were belly-down in a field of wild African grasses at a place where the savanna meets the bushlands.

"And you know what happens if she wakes up…"

"Ya, I know, Toots. *Shplap*! We'll be the chapatis at Mandaha's next dinner, flattened!" Jioba interjected with a wild glint in his eyes. Then he appeared distracted by his own thoughts and, with a boyish grin, added, "That might actually not be such a bad thing, Mandaha dipping me in stew and eating me all up..." His words trailed off as his fingers danced around his lips like he was eating some imaginary delight.

"Oh please, that's my sista we are talking about. Besides, now is not the time." EnKare clasped Jioba's round cheeks in his hands. "Look, Jimmy," he whispered, then turning his friend's head towards the slumbering rhinoceros he continued, "Look at her sleeping there, like a big, white mountain. I did all the hard work. I put the mucuna seed on her rear end. Now all you have to do is go get it and bring it back—without waking her up, or getting yourself killed. Just please," he paused for a moment and widened his eyes for dramatic effect, "please don't wake her up, whatever you do."

He could see tiny beads of sweat forming on Jioba's temple and upper lip, and for a moment a look of doubt crossed the boy's face. Jioba glanced down at the grass and let out a quiet sigh. When he looked up again the wildness was back in his eyes.

"OK, bwana, I'm going, but only because you said that this would make me a man, tu sabes?" And without waiting for a response Jioba popped up into a crouching position and tip-toed towards nine tons of slumbering mountainous flesh with a mucuna seed perched delicately on its backside.

EnKare spectated from the safety of his hiding place as his best friend in the whole world, his crazy, mischievous, fearless, best friend who ever was, moved closer and closer to a sleeping white rhino not more than thirty paces away.

When Jioba reached spitting distance of the beast he glanced back with an expression that said, *are you sure this is a good idea?* EnKare shot back a *you got this* look of encouragement and then gave him a big thumbs up and a wide, all-teeth-showing, grin. Jioba turned and faced the rhino again. He slowly stretched out one hand, appeared distracted for a moment by the sight of his own limb trembling, then took the last two steps.

EnKare wondered if perhaps this wasn't such a good idea after all. But all he could do at this point was watch and hope for the best.

Jioba reached out and took hold of the mucuna seed between his first finger and thumb. Then, with the focus of a thief plucking a bun from Mrs. Tulu's bread stall, he lifted the seed from its resting place. Looking back, triumphant victory ablaze in his eyes, he held the prize over his head in a clenched fist.

While Jioba was busy doing a silent victory dance, the rhino woke from its siesta and swung its sleepy head over to look at him. Seeing this,

EnKare jumped up from his grassy sanctuary and began waving his arms frantically.

"Jimmy, don't look now," he yelled, "but she's awake. Run, bwana, RUN!"

Jioba's eyes grew to the size of custard apples. His feet remained grounded while his torso and neck made a painstakingly slow pivot towards the rhino, where he found himself face to face with the beast's colossal snout. The two appeared to lock eyes for one brief, intense moment. Jioba let out a high pitched scream while his arms shot straight into the air, sending the mucuna seed flying. Then he turned and broke into an all-out run for dear life.

Seeing his friend flying towards him, EnKare sprang to the side to get out of the way.

The earth thundered.

The ground quaked.

All manner of bird and small critter came flittering from hiding places, darting this way and that.

Jioba's gait more resembled an ostrich with sand in its eyes, than a fifteen year old boy running for his life. The distance between the boy and the alabaster beast was closing fast, and he wondered how much longer Jioba's legs would hold up.

Then he found out.

A small, seemingly innocuous, strand of creeper grass caught Jioba's foot and, through a crack between the fingers of his hands, EnKare watched the boy's body sail through the air, complete a full somersault, then clatter down in a pile of arms, legs, and dust. No sooner did his body hit the ground then Jioba grasped his head and curled into a little ball.

A moment passed.

Then another.

"Psssst. Eh, bwana, you OK?"

Jioba opened his eyes ever so slowly, and EnKare watched the expression on his friend's face shift from blind fear, to confusion. The Rhino was standing over him, one bone-crushing, flat-padded foot on either side of his body. EnKare stood by her side, an arm thrown over her neck, looking down at the heap of boy.

"Hey, Jimmy, I'd like you to meet Oldoinyo. She's one of the family." The gentle giant opened her mouth and a slobber-coated mucuna seed dripped out and landed on Jioba's bare chest.

"Uh, thanks," Jioba grimaced.

"I swear, Jimmy, your face! You should have seen your face, bwana!" EnKare sputtered. "And now," he finger whip-snapped the air, "you are a MAN!" Despite his laughter he had the composure to help Jioba to his feet. Oldoinyo's mammoth head bowed down gracefully. "Grab hold of her horn. She'll pull you up."

With caution, Jioba took hold of the beast's lethal spear, and with an effortless tug of her head the rattled boy popped off the ground like a glass fishnet buoy surfacing from the deep.

"Are you OK, Jioba?"

"I'm fine, Toots, but for a minute there I thought it was lights out, kwisha kabisa, el fin de la calle! Tu sabes mon ami?"

"So…I guess you could say that we are *even* now, eh?"

"Even! EVEN! You crazy, bwana?" Jioba shrieked. "I almost got eaten by this…THING. This was ten times worse than the stingray incident."

"Oh, I'm not talking about the stingray incident. I'm talking about the man-eating giant sea anemone incident!" EnKare retorted.

In a hushed voice, Jioba dropped his head, stretched his lower lip thin in a gesture of guilt, and said, "Oh…Hector!"

"'Just dive down there a short ways,' you said. 'Just reach into that nice colorful blanket of soft tentacles and grab that pretty little gray pearl,' you said."

"Ya, bwana, but your friendly giant here could have crushed me! Just by accident! One misplaced step…"

"Pearls don't even grow in sea anemones!" EnKare cut him off. "I couldn't use my whole right arm for half a day, not to mention the tactical challenge and emotional indignity of trying to pee on my own arm while getting tossed about on your little dingy in the middle of the harbor. Not exactly the best move for attracting the ladies back on the beach, tu sabes? And does that even work? Does urine really do anything for the anemone poison, or did you just tell me that so I'd make an even bigger fool of myself?"

"No no, it really does work. I'm not *that* mean." Jioba took a deep breath in and then surrendered. "OK, OK, bwana. I suppose you're right. Even!"

They stood in silence for a moment. Then, glancing up at each other, burst into laughter.

"Awǫn ǫrẹ?" EnKare probed.

"Marafiki?" Jioba suggested.

"CHABALANGUS!" they both proclaimed, and then broke into one of their famous handshakes. This one started with a standard shake, then they grabbed thumbs, then thumbs and first fingers, then palms slid back and fingers locked momentarily, followed by the four finger snap. From there the back of the palms slid all the way along the forearms, followed by a front-back flip-flop hand slap, culminating with grabbing the other's head and touching foreheads together.

"Ya, Toots, you got me good, bwana! So, this is the legendary Oldoinyo? I probably should have figured that out. I thought she'd be bigger," Jioba teased. "Didn't your baba find her as a baby in the back of a cave?"

"Yep. She's like a great aunt to me, or something. A member of the family. And don't worry, she'd never hurt a hair on your head."

"Ha! Very funny," Jioba said, running his hand over his short, well groomed curls.

Grabbing his lower lip with his thumb and index knuckle, EnKare sucked in air, creating a whistle, then called out, "Pilipili, twendeni, let's go."

There was a rustling in one of the nearby trees, then a tiny creature sprang from a branch, sailed through the air with all four legs spread wide, and landed on Oldoinyo's back. From there it darted along the rhino's spine and leaped up onto EnKare's shoulder, touched her little nose to his, then pulled a handful of his braids over her back and fell asleep.

Pilipili was small, even for a galago, and she could nap comfortably in the palm of his hand. She was a fluffy gray and white nocturnal primate with large, glassy eyes, even larger ears, and a tiny pink nose. With her powerful hind legs she could leap great distances from tree to tree, which she did to search for insects or to escape predators. She used her long, bushy tail to steer as she flew through the air, or to curl up with as a pillow. The lives of her mother and father had been taken by a green mamba, and she was alone when he found her, half starved to death at the bottom of a hole in the trunk of a tree.

It had become clear early on that Pilipili considered *him* to be a fellow bushbaby, and as such, he was subject to her constant grooming. Rest assured that if so much as a tick found its way onto his body, it wouldn't last long on her watch. He had raised her to live in the wild in hopes that one day she would leap off into the night to go be with her own kind again. But she had her own plan and had adapted to living in both worlds. She'd come and go as she pleased, disappearing at night to feast on insects and to keep a watchful eye on the family compound, then lounging around the house during the day, napping wherever her little heart desired. Like Oldoinyo, he considered Pilipili one of the family. The smallest member, but family all the same.

Laughing and chewing on tender grass shoots, an arm slung over the other's shoulder, the boys bade Oldoinyo farewell and wandered off through the savanna, heading for home.

Quite the pair of misfits they made, and as different looking as any two boys could be from one another. Coming from a Himba mother and Maasai father, EnKare was tall and slender with high cheekbones and a long nose line. His skin was dark cacao butter with a touch of red chili mixed in, giving him a deep, warm radiance. Being a Morani, a junior warrior in the Maasai tradition, he wore his hair in long, ocher-stained braids that flowed down onto his shoulders and back. Cylindrical plugs made of rhino horn adorned his ears, and around his neck, upper arms, and wrists he wore colorfully beaded straps of leather. Today he wore a pair of softened cow hide shorts, and a red shuka cloth draped over one shoulder and cinched to his waist with a leather strap. At his side hung a rungu and a simi, weapons of the Morani, though he frequently had his spear with him as well. He had carved the rungu, a short handled club, from the root of a mighty baobab tree—but the simi, a handmade, double sided short-sword with a cowhide-wrapped handle, was handed down to him from his father, who had received it, in turn, from his father.

Jioba, on the other hand, was stout with a muscular build, of the seafaring Bube people who had lived in the region long before Iworo. He kept his curly black hair cropped close to his head, and today he was wearing nothing more than a pair of canvas shorts that he had fashioned from an old piece of hemp sail cloth, and a braided sinew necklace with a fish hook pendant that his father had carved from a piece of whale bone. Jioba's face was round, with full cheeks, a prominent domed forehead, wide, flat nose, and plump lips that were either talking, smiling, or usually both. In contrast to his skin, which was the color of charcoaled mahogany, his teeth glistened like polished elephant tusks. Despite what the rest of his face was doing his eyes were always smiling. They had a sparkle to them, like the sun's rays reflecting off a happy ocean's face.

Soles as hard as elephant skin, the boys' bare feet carried them nimbly over the variegated West African landscape. From the grasslands of Hornbill Hill, where Oldoinyo was busy nibbling on tender whistling-thorn, they dropped down into the lowland mangrove forest flanking the Benito River.

Sobaco, the townsfolk called it, taken from the old Castilian word for armpit—so named in reflection of the town's sentiments towards the forest. To them it was a place where not much of anything good happened, or lived. But to the boys, Sobaco was a land of hidden secrets, mysterious caves, and wondrous and terrifying beings. This was where EnKare could go to get away from it all, where no one, except Jioba of course, dared set foot.

They plotted a course through the mangrove forest, moving across it as adroitly as if they were strolling down a dirt road. The trick to not getting eaten alive by the giant carnivorous mud-toads, or by the mud itself, was to hop from stone to stone and stuckmuck to grassy-tufted stuckmuck, staying just above the brackish swamp water.

Presently, they arrived at the edge of Elephant Rock, an assemblage of giant granite boulders that rose up abruptly out of the sea of mangroves— completely out of place, a forgotten pile of dice or dominoes cast down by the hand of a colossus. That's how the story played out in EnKare's imagination anyway. What else could explain such an anomalous outcropping?

"Come on, Jimmy, race you to the top," he shouted, then sprinted off before his friend had a chance to respond. But Jioba was not one to back down from a challenge, no matter the disadvantage, and he let out a Bube war cry and gave chase.

Pilipili, on the other hand, who was used to having her naps interrupted by her giant bushbaby friend, woke up and leaped to a nearby rock.

Centuries of wind and rain had left the stone coarse and rugged, and the skin of EnKare's feet bit eagerly into the mineral matrix. Higher and higher he ran, until the mangrove forest below was nothing more than a blanket of moss covering the earth.

This was a place of power, a place where he could come to seek answers to questions that lingered in his heart. This was a place where he could view the world through new eyes.

At the top they sat down on the domed surface and took in the view. From this height one could see all the way across their little town to the Bight Of Biafra and to the magnificent Atlantic Ocean—where the sun was steadily marching towards the horizon, towards Nchi Mbaya, towards the badlands.

After Iworo, Mbini was nothing more than a ghost town. But as survivors came up from the caverns and caves, the town slowly filled with life once again.

He could see the pathway leaving the mangroves and lacing its way past the houses and shops. He could make out his own home, on the outskirts of town, and the market place, right in the heart of the village.

From the market his eyes followed the roadway that led out to the west side of town, to the ocean beaches, and to Jioba's house. Then, as his eyes gazed far out to sea, his mind began to wander.

"Hey, Jimmy, you ever wonder what's happening out there beyond the waves, in Nchi Mbaya? Do you think maybe somewhere out there are two boys, like us, climbing rocks and messing around?"

After a contemplative pause, Jioba responded. "Toots, if there is anything left out there, it can't be any good, bwana. Besides, we have everything, everything we need right here in Africa: freedom, radiation-free skies, peace, abundant resources…" By this time he was standing, hands reaching out and arms waving in grand sweeping passes, as though speaking to a crowd of cheering citizens at a political rally.

EnKare laughed and blurted out, "Mrs. Msoke, seriously Jimmy, you sound just like Mrs. Msoke lecturing us in social studies class." He finger whip-snapped the air and added, "I don't know how you do it, bwana. You're the master of impersonations."

Jioba took a deep bow and sat down again. "Asante sana, bwana. A man's gotta be good at something, tu sabes?"

As they sat and looked out over their home, EnKare's mind found its way to a question that had been gnawing at him as of late. How was he ever going to earn his Lion Name. He was no hero like Olubi, his older cousin. The man had pretty much saved their entire village. A crash of native black rhinos were defending their territory from the white rhinos that had come over with Baba from the east, and the fighting between them threatened to level Mbini. Olubi blended the rhino scents and marked key spots throughout the area with the mixture, effectively bringing the herds together and saving the village from annihilation. No, EnKare was no great warrior. And he certainly didn't have the brain power of Olubi. He wanted to travel, to explore the world and to see what lies beyond—to be an adventurer, like Abu Bakari, Sacagawea, Marco Polo, or Nellie Bly. *Even if it is forbidden, it can't be as bad as they say, traveling to Nchi Mbaya, it just can't be.*

His thoughts were interrupted by the sensation of Pilipili's soft fur as she climbed up his arm and resumed her napping among his braids.

And here they say that Africa is a land of freedom, and yet I'm not even free to explore the world, because it is…forbidden! His thoughts weren't taking him anywhere positive, and he knew it. But would he be stuck with his birth name forever? He pictured himself as an old man still dressing and behaving like a child. It was a bleak image.

"What's buggin' ya, Toots?" Jioba's voice sliced through his growing wall of self-pity.

He let out a sigh. "I don't know. I mean I do know. It's my Lion Name."

"Ah. You mean that rite of passage where you have to do something great and then you get a new name and become a man?" Jioba sure knew how to cut right through the goat fat to get to the meat of an issue.

"Ya, that one. I mean, what did you have to do again? You know, to become a man?"

"I had to build my own boat, then sail it out around Ilha Do Príncipe and back again by myself. I've built the boat, but haven't done the island loop yet. So I guess I'm half a man. Ha."

"You see, at least you were given specific instructions, a plan that you could follow. Me! I don't know what to do. What if nothing 'worthy' ever happens in my whole life and I never become a man?"

"Ya, personally I don't know about this whole 'becoming a man' thing. Seems like all of a sudden you get all the responsibility and burden of life dumped on you—your free time, and time with your friends vanishes, and poof, you're suddenly supposed to be a man!"

"You know, you're right, Jimmy! Who needs to grow up anyway. We can stay young and free forever."

Then suddenly, like two bananas from the same bunch, they jumped to their feet, pumped their fists into the air, and yelled, "Young and free FOREVER!"

Family

They returned to the village just as the last rays of the day illuminated the underbellies of the water-laden clouds that hugged the coastline. Thunderheads such as these looked like bloated goat's entrails—purple, twisting, and bulbous—weary of their burden and ready to submit to gravity.

"Think it's gonna rain, bwana?" Jioba inquired with an upward glance.

Before EnKare could respond, a drop the size of a field mouse splattered across his face. "Chabalangus, Bwana! That answer your question?"

Pilipili must have sensed what was coming next, because she leaped to the ground and disappeared into a thicket of trees. The boys took off sprinting along the trail, whooping and hollering as the water fell across the land in diagonal sheets.

When they reached EnKare's boma, the family compound, he yelled out, "Jimmy, come inside till the rain passes."

"Sounds good, bwana!"

There was no *typical* Mbini home. After Iworo, city and country folk, and people from tribes all across the continent came to settle in his sleepy seaside town. Some lived in small shacks made from recycled materials and driftwood scavenged off the beach, while others made their home with mud walls and palm thatched roofs.

Three families lived together within EnKare's boma, and the entire estate was surrounded by a giant thorn hedge with one small entrance. At night, a cluster of thorned branches was dragged across the opening to protect the people, cattle, and goats from predators.

Built within the wall was EnKare's family home, his manyatta, where he lived with his parents, sister, and occasionally Pilipili. His Auntie Naserian and Uncle Wafula had their home on the opposite side of the boma, and then off in a distant corner, Cousin Olubi was working on his own place.

The boma was a busy place, like a small town of its own, filled with meandering chickens, ruminating goats, and cattle basking at the mud hole. When his parents first moved there, Okuruwo, his mother, had planted over thirty fruit and nuts varieties from her collection of seeds. EnKare spent countless hours hanging out in the trees and eating the fruit, which came in an endless harvest throughout the year. If he and Jioba weren't tossing down avocados from the highest branches, they were slurping up tangy passion fruit, popping loquats in their mouths, or smashing open almond fruit to get to the nuts. If this thing called *paradise* existed, the boma was it!

Of all the trees in the boma, his favorite was a true giant of a baobab named EnKishón. EnKishón was so big around at the trunk, that if half the people in the village joined hands at the base, they still wouldn't meet up. EnKare had built an extensive fort in the tree and could walk the girthy branches like he was strolling through town.

The expansive canopy was home to three types of monkey, all claiming their own barrios among the branches; the Vervets, the Red Colobus, and the Patas monkeys. Most of the time they lived peacefully enough, keeping to their own neighborhoods; however, at least once a year, a Vervet would conveniently forget the unwritten code and sneak into Colobus or Patas territory to steal a piece of fruit. This would result in a three way screaming match that lasted through one, and sometimes two, sleepless nights.

Safely sheltered under EnKishón's prodigious canopy was his manyatta, the home he was born in and where he had lived his entire life. The manyatta was like an extension of the tree itself, like a burl growing out of its side. The home was built into a natural depression in the tree's trunk, its walls curving with the flow of the giant's base roots.

According to the elders, the house was a perfect blend of ancient and contemporary systems working in harmony. Built as they had been for thousands of years, the inner rooms had thick mud-straw-dung walls that were cozy and protective—thermal mass that acted like a cave, keeping the inside of the home cool and pleasant. Wooden shutters at the windows and doors allowed the inside to be flooded with light, or cloaked in darkness—perfect for sleeping in; a fifteen year old's favorite pastime.

Beyond the inner rooms were patios, decks and an outdoor kitchen, wide open spaces where the family spent most of their time.

Outside the kitchen window was a bio-gas digester that converted food waste into a gas used for cooking. The digester's byproduct was a fertilizer slurry used on the family gardens. The toilet in the house composted humanure into a rich humus that was also used in the gardens.

Like most of the structures in Mbini, a solar membrane on the roof, paired with the town's central solar plant and water-powered generators, provided a moderate flow of electricity to the home. The water generators also created steam, which was pressurized with wind turbines and pumped to homes and buildings where hot water was used.

EnKare understood the principles of plasma cold-fusion and voltage magnification through series resonance circuitry. It was standard physics taught in schools across Africa. Mrs. Msoke taught that oil barons, from the old time, had hidden this technology in order to keep people dependent on fossil fuels—dirty energy that was poisoning the air, water, and soil of the world.

Whenever the old timers spoke of it they'd shake their heads, scrunch up their faces, and spit on the ground in disgust. But then they'd proudly remind you that the new tech had been designed and perfected by Dr. Amelia Wangari, an East African physicist who had survived Iworo and then gone on to perfect the water generator design.

The boys came bounding up the steps to EnKare's manyatta, looking like a pair of soggy street mongrels. The whole family, including a perfectly dry Pilipili, was gathered on the covered patio, watching the rain fall from the sky.

"Hi everyone. Sorry I'm a little late, Mama," EnKare confessed, as he bowed his head to show respect and beg forgiveness. Then, claiming a pardon which had not been offered, he added as a footnote, "Can Jioba stay till the rain stops?"

The brow on his mother's face dropped and she pushed her lips out and made a quick, inward kissing sound. To the uninitiated ear, the tone might be dismissed as a harmless pardon—but to EnKare, it delivered the full force of a reprimand, ripe with scrutiny, scorn, and disapproval.

They sat on the deck and watched as the sky emptied itself. The spent clouds moved east unveiling a moonless black canvas brushed in stardust. Out over the ocean, to the west, strokes of blood orange and grapefruit lingered.

"OK, bwana, you better get home before it gets too dark. See you tomorrow?" Like there was any chance he wouldn't see his friend tomorrow.

"Ya, bwana, kesho." Jioba replied.

The boys slapped out a handshake, then Jioba looked up to say goodbye to the family. His eyes met Mandaha's and his face instantly grew pale.

"Bye... OK... tomorrow... thank... see..." he managed to stammer, then he smiled nervously, turned around, and stepped straight off the edge of the deck, landing face first in the mud.

"Ah, you OK, Jimmy?" EnKare gasped.

Jioba popped up off the ground in a flash and waved sheepishly towards the family. "Ya. All good, just, em, missed the step is all."

At this point the family was laughing, and even EnKare couldn't help but giggle at the spectacle. Pearly teeth and the whites of eyes beamed up at them from the mud monster that now stood in his friend's place.

"Boys, why don't you go get washed up. Jioba, you can borrow one of EnKare's kikois. And then why don't you stay for supper. I'm sure Bötébbá won't mind." Okuruwo was not a very talkative woman, but when she did speak everyone paid attention.

"That sounds great. Thank you," Jioba sputtered through mud.

"C'mon, bwana." EnKare stretched out a hand and pulled his friend onto the deck. They headed into the house, giggling and warthogging about.

When they came back out into the living room the space had been prepared for the meal. Fine carpets from the north covered the oil-swept earthen floor, and in the center of the room was a low, round table, hand-carved from a single slab of mahogany. On the floor around the table were assorted cushions covered in embroidery, tiny sequins, and small circular mirrors, peyote stitched into the fabric. The adobe walls arched overhead to meet a ceiling of tightly woven branches that gave the room a forest canopy feeling. Suspended over the center of the room was a chandelier made of elephant tusks interlaced in a spiral. The elephants were never hunted, as they were considered Elders that possessed great wisdom and timeless knowledge. Any elephant tusks and bones, found scattered across the land after Iworo, were collected and used as tools, in jewelry making, and to decorate homes—a somber reminder of difficult times in the not so distant past.

"Come on, boys, grab a cushion. The food is ready." The sweetest words to grace a growing boy's ears came from Mandaha's affable command, as she appeared at the archway to the kitchen, carrying in one hand a plate stacked tall with chapatis, and in the other, a large, steaming bowl of peanut and raisin rice. Baba followed close behind with a pot of curried goat.

As the spicy sapor reach his nostrils, all thoughts instantly vanished from his mind, save those of food and of its glorious consumption.

Once the family was seated there was a moment of silence.

"Thank you, EnKulu and Mandaha, for preparing this meal for us." Okuruwo's voice broke the silence. She looked down at the food on the table as one might look at a grandparent, with deep fondness and appreciation. Then speaking directly to the food, "Your spirits return to your ancestral homes and your bodies remain here to become part of us. We are one and the same. Thank you."

EnKare listed in his mind all the different plants and animals that went into the meal and then thanked each one individually. He did it rather quickly, because, well, he was hungry. More like starving.

"Let's eat!" announced Baba.

Once plates were piled high and hands were busy scooping up food with pieces of chapati, the dinner table banter began.

"Everything OK with the herd of rhino today, EnKulu?" inquired Okuruwo.

"Oh yes, just fine. Though Oldoinyo was missing for a while. She showed up eventually, so no worries."

EnKare shot a quick glance at Jioba, who was cramming his mouth with a rice and curry filled piece of chapati. Jioba gave his acknowledgment with a subtle wink back.

"And how were your classes today, my love?" Okuruwo asked Mandaha.

"I love it. Oh, I love it so much! Today we started working with Solomon's Seal, Polygonatum Biflorum…"

"Oh no, do we have to hear about another herb right now while we're eating? And why are we still using the Latin names for things?" EnKare voiced his protests loudly.

Jioba interrupted, "Actually mind not please hear it I'd like to."

Mandaha looked at Jioba like maybe he had chewed on one too many Datura Inoxia seeds, and teased, "So you'd like to hear about Solomon's Seal?"

Jioba stared wide eyed at her and nodded.

Turning to her brother, "You see, Toots, some people here *do* want to hear about it."

"Chabalangus, bibi. My name is not…ugh, you know I don't like it when you call me that."

"EnKare, watch your language, please."

"What, 'Toots'? But Jimmy calls you that all the time."

"Ya, and only Jimmy gets to, understand?"

"OK, kids, that's enough. So, Mandaha, you were saying, about Polygonatum Biflorum?"

EnKare tuned his sister out. *Who cares about Solomon's Seal anyway? Apparently Jimmy does, but she could be talking about pretty much anything and he'd find it interesting. Why couldn't I have been born into a normal family? This,* he looked around the table at his family members, *this is not a normal family.*

His mother was a Wenye Hekima! In old Swahili this meant 'Wise Ones.' She was one of the nine founding elders of Unified Africa. Tales of her birth in Mezumo Cave, and how she became the living embodiment of the Sacred Fire of the Himba by the time she was four years old, were told to children as bedtime stories all across the continent.

And then there was his father! The man who answered the call of the Wenye Hekima and volunteered to take on the life of a nomad once again. With Oldoinyo at his side, he and a small group of Maasai traversed the continent for years, moving with a crash of white rhinos and helping to bring their kind back from the brink of extinction. Thanks to Baba, the great rhino herdsman, white rhinos had repopulated the continent and balance had been restored to countless ecosystems.

And Mandaha, though he would never admit it out loud, was amazing! She was only seventeen and already a nurse, a midwife, and currently training to be an apothecary. Talk about a high achieving family.

"Toots!" Mandaha's voice evaporated his thoughts. "If you and Jimmy take care of the dishes you can have an extra large piece of the passion fruit crumble."

"Passion fruit crumble?" His face lit up. He hardly even noticed his sister's 'Toots' jab.

"An EXTRA large piece?"

The Hunt

With a crisp snap the arrow let fly. Without waiting to see if it hit its mark, she disappeared silently into the thick underbrush and listened attentively.

A muted crunch.

Neck vertebrae giving way followed by a quick shuffling of leaves as the tȟáȟča's body fell to the ground.

A soft thud.

She made a small clicking sound with her tongue and motioned to Níškola to remain perfectly still.

Slowing her breathing and heart rate so as to not drown out the forest sounds with her own, she remained motionless.

Dusk was approaching.

She had set up the kill so that the deer's body would fall into a thick brake of bush ferns. Making the kill was the easy part. Everything living in those woods would want a piece of that deer.

And of her.

And right now monks were her biggest concern.

Crack! A branch snapped overhead.

Monks!

She trained her ears on the canopy above. *A small band of them, maybe five or six.*

She could hear their soft chatter, and, though she didn't speak their language, she had learned to elucidate meaning from their tones and inflections.

A scout dropped to the forest floor. From a crouching position the monk cautiously rose up on two legs and began walking awkwardly in the direction of the fallen deer. If he discovered her, both their lives would be at risk.

Monks were aggressively territorial and unabashedly omnivorous, snacking on whatever showed up for dinner, including humans and other monks from rival clans. As he passed by her hiding place, she could see his hand-like feet. The big toe-thumb was an asset in the trees, but on flat ground it made him slow and clumsy.

There was nothing she could do now but watch in silence and hope he passed by the deer without looking into the brush. The monk reached the ferns and, using his wooden spear, parted the foliage and stepped forward.

The deer is lost.

Suddenly the monk let out a scream and flew backwards out of the underbrush, landing on his back. From his thigh protruded a black and white quill the length of an atlatl spear. He struggled for a moment to remove the quill and failed. Then he staggered to his feet, and from one leg leaped for the nearest branch.

She watched as the monk caught hold of the branch with one hand, catapulting himself upward through the lower foliage, pulling and swinging arm over arm, injured leg dangling behind. The rest of the group had already moved off through the forest top, shrieking, shaking branches, and making a commotion. With the injured scout trailing behind, soon the whole clan vanished in the sea of green.

When Wakíŋyaŋ was certain the monks were gone, she rose from her hiding place and moved slowly towards the bush ferns. A p̌ahíŋ, a giant porcupine standing almost as tall as her at the shoulders, was responsible for the attack on the monk. It had found the deer and was intent on keeping it for herself.

Reaching into her wóphiye, a tanned skin medicine bag that she wore over one shoulder, she retrieved a small gourd filled with puma urine and pulled off the corked top. She dipped a small piece of buckskin into the gourd and wiped the rank liquid onto her neck and arms, then put the gourd and cloth back into her wóphiye.

With an arrow nocked and drawn she moved toward the ferns. When she was just a few paces away she gave a low guttural hiss, mimicking a large cat announcing its presence. The pȟahíŋ, whose eyesight was minimal at best, heard the hiss, caught whiff of the puma's scent, and sprinted away in the opposite direction, recklessly crashing through the underbrush as she went.

"*Phreeeet*! Níškola, uší!" She gave a short whistle and called to her friend to come. "Come help me, we have to move quickly."

With a hand on one leg, and Níškola's strong jaws clamped around the other, the two pulled the deer from the bush ferns and into a small clearing. A calloused palm over the stag's heart, she took a moment to thank him and apologize for cutting his life short.

Níškola put his wet nose up against her cheek and whined softly.

"You did good, Níška." She spoke tenderly as she scratched behind his ear. Then from a sheath on her belt she drew her knife, a steel blade that she had fashioned from a piece of washed up beach scrap. With deft skill and efficiency she opened the deer from sternum to crotch and removed its entrails.

Next, she snapped the deer's front legs at the knee joint and sliced down towards the hoof between the bone and tendon. She then interlaced the broken front legs through slits between the tendon and bone of its back legs, turning the deer's body into a backpack. Her father, Maȟpíya, had shown her this technique when she had seven winters.

She then placed the heart, kidneys, and liver back into the deer's body cavity, wiped her bloodied hands on the bush ferns, and hoisted the carcass up onto her back.

"Níškola, uší," she called out, and they began the journey home.

Following animal paths through the forest lands they navigated the steep terrain until they came to the edge of the river. Níškola ran straight to the water for a drink while Wakíŋyaŋ sat on the ground and disentangled her arms from the deer.

"Good idea, Níška. I'll be right back." She followed a trickling rivulet back up into the underbrush to the head of a spring and dug a small depression. While the sediment settled and fresh clean water percolated back into the cavity, she cut a thistle stalk at the base, shaved off the thorns, and fashioned it into a straw. Carefully keeping the tip of the straw out of the sediment, she drank in the cool, life bringing effusion. Her thirst quenched, she rejoined Níškola on the river's edge and washed the dried blood from her forearms and hands.

The encounter with the monks had taken up precious moments that they didn't have. A cloud of skeets was forming out over the river and heading for the shore, and soon the worms would be coming to the surface to feed. Being out after dark was not an option.

"Look, Níška, skeets! Quick, let's get you tethered up." She approached a thicket, lifted a few branches and leaves out of the way, and pulled a drag sled from its hiding place. She loaded the deer onto the sled and secured it with leather straps.

"Níška, uší. It's your turn now."

Níškola positioned himself at the front of the sled, and she used more strapping to attach the two arms of the contraption to either side of his enormous rib cage.

Smack! She retracted her hand from the back of her neck and glanced fearfully at the smashed body lying crumpled and bloody in her palm. *I'm sorry, skeet.*

"Itóhekiya! Home, Níškola. GO!" Heading with the river's flow Níškola took off running through the reeds and grasses, the loaded sled bouncing along at his tail. She ran behind to make sure the tȟáȟča's body didn't come loose.

The skeet cloud reached the bank and veered downriver, following the scent of flesh and blood. Skeets could fly faster than even the swiftest of runners on an open field, and she knew they would soon be overcome by the cloud before they could make it home. Their only chance was a diversion, some other hapless creature that was still out at dusk, which might capture the blood thirsty skeets' attention.

In the distance, at the confluence of a side creek and the main river, she could see the log bridge that crossed the tributary.

We'll have to take the bridge.

Crossing at this time of day was unwise, but they were out of options.

She could run like the wind could blow, and keeping up with Níškola was not a problem, so long as he was hauling a large stag behind him. She had been running over sand and rock, down paths and through forests, over creeks and along river banks since the time she could walk. You learned to run early in life or the land devoured you. That was the way.

As they approached the bridge, three fallen tree trunks lashed together and spanning from one bank to the other, the sun's fiery orb dropped below the horizon.

"Inážiŋkhiya! Stop, Níška!" He came to a stop at the edge of the bridge. She picked up the end of the sled poles and called out, "Itóhekiya."

Moving slowly, Níškola started across the logs.

Glancing back, she could see the skeet cloud approaching fast.

Perhaps we just aren't meant to have this kill. When we reach the other side of the log I'll cut Níška free. The skeets will be diverted by the deer carcass long enough for us to escape.

She pushed on the poles to let Níškola know it was OK for him to pick up the pace. Reaching the far side of the log, she pulled her knife and was ready to cut the deer loose, when a ripple in the water below the bridge caught her eye. Instincts taking over, she sheathed the blade and pulled her bow from her back. In the same instant a worm shot out of the water, head first, caught hold of the underside of the logs with his claws, and hoisted himself onto the bridge.

She nocked an arrow as the worm dropped onto all fours and charged directly at her. Knowing that a head shot would only ricochet off its thick skull bones and break the arrow, she held her ground and waited.

Then the worm was airborne, teeth gnashing, claws protracted, hurtling towards her with deadly intent.

In a single fluid motion she leapt sideways, out of the worm's path, simultaneously drawing her bow and letting the arrow fly.

She hit the ground, rolled, bounced up into a crouch and nocked a second arrow.

It wouldn't be needed.

The first had passed between two of the worm's ribs and struck the creature in the heart. He was dead before he hit the ground.

She placed a hand on the worm's chest. "I'm sorry for cutting your life short. Today you picked the wrong prey." Then, moving quickly, she braced her foot against the translucent pink skin of the worm's body, and with two hands jerked the arrow from his flesh. She sheathed the arrows and returned the bow to her back, then drew her knife and made two quick slices along the worm's wrists.

"Itóhekiya Níška! Go!"

They were off and running again.

She glanced back to where the worm lay dead. The plan had worked. The swarm of skeets descended on the carcass and was feasting on the blood that flowed from its opened veins.

They ran swiftly and silently, without stopping and without tiring, moving over the terrain as though one spirit flowed through them.

Approaching the entrance to the village, Wakíŋyaŋ pierced the sky with a whistle burst, and a guard from inside opened the gate and closed it again as they crossed the threshold.

"Cutting it a little close, Wakíŋyaŋ," the guard cautioned, as she came to a halt just inside the village walls.

"Ya? Well, I made it, so..." She shrugged and shot the guard a sly smile.

Returning home always felt good—the smoke from burning skeet-grass and eucalyptus leaves wafting through the air, the sound of children and dogs playing, the steady percussive rhythm of grain being ground by hand in stone mortars.

As they walked across the open center of the village, children ran up to her, chittering and chattering, asking questions about where she had been, how the hunt went—was it fun—could she come play when she was done, —could she teach them how to be a brave hunter like her. Then they'd run off again without waiting for the answers.

Níškola received the same treatment from the village canine population. Grown wolf-dogs greeted him, tails wagging, sniffed the deer then licked him on the nose. Puppies approached, tails tucked, heads bowed, falling onto their backs under his legs and kicking and squirming, until something else caught their attention and they went running off yipping and yapping.

One of Wakíŋyaŋ's friends, a young man named Leaf, stopped them as they passed by. "Hi, Wakíŋyaŋ. Oh nice. That's a pretty good kill you got there." Then, glancing up at the darkening sky, "Looks like you were cutting it a little close though."

She smiled. Leaf was a good kid. He couldn't hunt a maštíŋska if his life depended on it. But he could turn a skin into anything!—from a bowstring to the softest fur jacket. When it came to tanning hides, he was a master.

"Ya, I know. Don't tell Uŋčí, OK. You know how she worries about me."

"I never do. Let me give you a hand?"

"No thanks. This is the easy part. But why don't you come by later if you want, and have some of the heart meat with me."

"Sounds good. See you later."

Leaf took off in the opposite direction as they brought the deer across the common ground to the hut where game was hung.

She untied the sled from Níškola's back. He stepped out of the contraption, walked to the entrance of the hut, and peered back at her. She gave a subtle lift of her head, *thank you my friend,* and he turned and bounded off.

To hang the deer, she threaded a wooden dowel between the tendon and bone of both its back legs, pulled a rope down from an overhead beam, and attached it to the center of the dowel. Then she threaded the rope around the dowel and threw it back up over the smooth, rounded beam, creating a pulley mechanism. She hoisted the deer's body off the ground and secured the rope to a cleat on the wall.

In the morning, one group would skin the deer, scrape and flesh the hide and prepare it for tanning, and another group would process the meat and distribute it among the villagers.

She retrieved the kidneys, liver, and heart from the deer's body cavity and headed towards her hut. These organs were highly prized for their dense nutrients, distinct flavors, and association with the animal's power. According to the traditions of her village they belonged to the hunter, a solemn recognition of the deep connection, the contract between predator and prey. Tradition or not, she always shared the good bits with friends, and of course, with Grandmother, who she couldn't wait to tell about the monk—and the pʰahíŋ. She figured she might as well leave out the part about the worm and the skeets.

What Grandmother doesn't know about, Grandmother can't worry about.

Grandmother

U ŋčí, I'm home," she called out as she pushed aside the tanned skin door-flap and entered the cottage.

"Come here, precious one. Tell me, how was your hunt?"

Grandmother spoke from the center of the hut where she was busy preparing food over an open fire. To the rest of the village she was known as Wakȟáŋ Kiktá, Awakened Spirit, but to Wakíŋyaŋ she was Uŋčí.

"It was good, Uŋčí. The tȟáȟča died without pain or fear."

"Good, my love. Good." She formed acorn tortillas with her hands and laid them on a large, flat stone at the edge of the fire to cook. In an earthen pot she prepared deer steaks by rubbing them with salt and a mixture of dried xalapa, cayenne, and habanero pepper flakes. "It's late. You worry an old woman, you know?"

"I'm sorry, Uŋčí. Here, these are for you," she offered, handing Grandmother the organs. "You take a break and let me finish the cooking."

Wakíŋyaŋ flipped the tortillas on the hot-stone and started the next batch from a fresh ball of dough. "We ran into a monk, which slowed us down. I know I shouldn't have been out so late, but I just couldn't let the deer go to waste."

Wakȟáŋ Kiktá circled the fire until she was standing behind her, then began slowly unraveling Wakíŋyaŋ's braids and affectionately combing them out with her fingers. "There is no such thing as letting a tȟáȟča go to waste, my love. Had the deer stayed where it fell, you would have fed the forest this night. And had your arrow missed that worm, the forest would have fed on you."

Wakíŋyaŋ remained quiet for a moment, perplexed. *How could she have known about the worm attack?*

"And I see you encountered some skeets as well." Grandmother took a small gourd from a wooden shelf, dipped her fingers into it and rubbed the oily concoction all around the welt on the back of Wakíŋyaŋ's neck. "Oh my, Little Thunder, you'll be the death of this old woman one of these days. You'll have to remember to apply this ointment to the bite, morning and night…

"For the next quarter moon. Ya, I know, Uŋčí," she finished Grandmother's sentence.

"*Hmph.* There'll be no bot larvae growing in that strong, beautiful neck of yours, do you hear me?" Grandmother's voice was firm, loving.

She turned the steaks over in the pepper flakes and then threw them into the pot. "Yes, Uŋčí, you're right. I shouldn't take such risks. And don't worry, I'll remember to put the ointment on. Now, as soon as I flip these steaks we can eat."

Smoke rose indolently up through the center of the hut and escaped through a hole in the thatching, while the two women sat on woven reed mats eating the peppered deer meat rolled in acorn tortillas.

She didn't realize how depleted she was until the first bite, and as she nourished herself on the bounty of the forest she looked fondly at Grandmother through the wisps of smoke that spiraled through her long, silver hair.

She must be seventy or eighty winters, though she isn't at all frail or weak like she pretends to be sometimes. How does she do it? Sit on the Council of Elders, is one of the village Wíŋyaŋ Wakȟáŋ, does her part in all the village chores—and she still manages to take care of me while putting up will all my nonsense. Thoughts shifting, *and how does she just know things? Like the fact that I was attacked by a worm today and shot it with my bow? Or the swarm of skeets?*

"One day you will learn to release your mind's attachment to your body."

She nearly choked on the piece of meat she was chewing. Could Grandmother read her thoughts too? "What do you mean, Uŋčí?"

"The four physical elements currently occupy the four corners of your medicine wheel," Wakȟáŋ Kiktá continued. "In order to survive in the world around us, the world after the burn, one must master the physical elements, or perish. Will you pass me another tortilla, sweetheart?" She smiled at Wakíŋyaŋ then continued. "From the time you could walk, this gift has guided you, and with it you have acquired teachings from Earth, Water, Fire, and Air. Through these elements you have developed a mastery of the physical world."

She hadn't really given it much thought. The world was the way it was. You hunted. You were hunted. Being faster, smarter, quieter, more invisible, and more accurate meant the difference between being predator or prey. But was there something more? She saw it in Grandmother and some of the other elders of the village. They understood things beyond the world she knew. But how?

"The answer to the question in your heart doesn't lie here in the physical world, my love. Your mind is strongly attached to your body, as it should be. Daydream, or lose your concentration, for even a moment, and it's your lifeless body trailing behind Igmúthaŋka, or disappearing into a worm hole, never to be seen again. But the wisdom you seek lies in a different realm, and its gateway will become known to you when you learn to release your mind's attachment to your body."

"How do I do that, Uŋčí?" She chuckled at the image of opening up the top of her own head, like a trap door, and literally releasing her mind. *Ha, there it goes now, floating up through the thatch.*

After a pause, Wakȟáŋ Kiktá replied, "I will teach you."

Wakíŋyaŋ's eyes widened. "When will you teach me?"

Grandmother smiled at her with a glint in her eyes. "When you are ready, Little Thunder, when you are ready. One day you will guide our people, and to do that you will need to walk in both worlds; this one—" She reached over and pinched Wakíŋyaŋ, who promptly swatted her hand away. "—and the world of Wóniya."

Restless

Questions drifted around in her head as she lay on her back watching the firelight dance across the thatch. What was this spirit world that Uŋčí spoke of? How could one detach their mind from their body? What did that even mean?

A hollow feeling in the center of her stomach drew her attention away from her thoughts. She had felt this sensation before and wondered if it was this thing she had heard others describe as *loneliness*. But how could she be lonely? Uŋčí was always there for her, and she had Níškola.

"Níška! *Tssst.*" She called out with a soft tongue-click so as not to wake Grandmother. The enormous wolf-dog rose from his usual spot in front of the hut, stretched, yawned, and then pushed the flap open with his nose and peered inside.

"Níška, uší," she called softly and patted the ground beside her. Her bed was a cinnamon-brown fur from a bear her father had hunted many winters ago. A little too warm for Níškola's liking, but a spot on the cool earth next to her would do just fine. He lumbered over to the head of her bed, sniffed the ground, paced in a circle two or three times, and collapsed in a heap.

"The hunt really wore you out, huh, Níška?"

A long exhale through his nose was all he had to say on the matter.

Pushing her head up against the fur of his chest, she scratched his belly and smiled to herself, thinking about her wolf-dog companion.

His name meant *tiny*. She had named him that because at their bonding ceremony, when he was just a pup and she was only seven winters, he was the runt of the litter. He was just this little feisty ball of fur. But he grew up to be anything but a runt. He was almost the same size as the wolves in the Crater Bay Pack that patrolled the area. When standing beside her he could rest his chin on her shoulder. He was, however, still a big ball of fur and the best pillow she could imagine.

The lonely feeling dissipated, and she drifted off to sleep, reflecting on the day's hunt and imagining what the world of the spirits was like.

Taken

A muffled scream woke her from a deep sleep. "Uŋčí, is that you?" A long exhale, followed by a staccato nasal rumbling from Grandmother's side of the hut answered the question.

Then who…?

She looked around to see where the sound might have come from, then quickly realized that she must have made the noise herself.

Bits and pieces of the dream she was having clung to the walls of her consciousness. The hollow feeling in her abdomen returned. She felt restless, like a residual disquietude had followed her back from the dreamworld.

She pulled a fur ruana over her head and stepped out of the hut into the cool, night air. Níškola whined softly but didn't get up.

"Stay there, Níška, I'll be back in a little while."

She walked around the back of the hut to the village barrier wall, pulled aside one of the poles and slipped through the opening. She had created this secret hole so that she could come and go as she pleased, without having to deal with the gate guards.

Once outside the village, she moved silently down an overgrown footpath to the ocean's edge.

When the sun went to bed, one world ceased to exist, and another germinated to life in its place—the nightworld, with its long shadows, cicada concertos, and cool, moist air.

The sand felt soft to her bare feet, and each time she took a step, a fireprint was left behind. To Wakíŋyaŋ, firesand was one of the many mysterious splendors of the nightworld.

She took off running across the beach, looking back to see her prints light up. She danced and did cartwheels, made sand balls and tossed them out into the waves and watched them burst into infinite sparkles, then suspend in the water, undulating like giant, glowing jellyfish swaying in the tide.

All along, she imagined that a magical being of light was running after her, playing with her, dancing with her, spying on her from out beneath the waves. The night didn't judge. It had no expectations. She could be silly, act irrationally, say things that didn't make any sense—in the nightworld she could be anything!

Coming to a small outcropping of rock at the shoreline, she sat down to rest. As she gazed at the diagonal lines of starlight playing across the bay, she recalled parts of the dream that had woken her. She remembered being surrounded by what looked like shiny metal, like the pieces she would find along the beach that had been polished by sand and waves.

And there were people in the dream who appeared as dark shadows. She couldn't distinguish their features. At one point she had approached one of these strange shadow people, and then a worm had grabbed her around the waist and pulled her down into its tunnel. An arm reached down into the hole, but was just beyond her reach. Was it to help her? To push her deeper into the hole? She screamed, and that's when she woke up.

Forms and images such as these had never come to her in the dreamworld before and she found them perplexing, and a little disturbing.

As the thoughts faded she turned on her seat to face the forest, her back to the sea.

She listened to the gentle song of the cicadas in the treetops. Their cadence and intensity told her that daybreak wasn't far off. She wasn't tired yet, but decided she would head back to the village to get a little more sleep before dawn.

Turning to hop down from the rocks, she found herself face to face with one of the beings from her dream.

For a moment she froze—too dumbfounded to think or move.

A sharp blow struck the back of her head.

Firesand burst before her eyes.

The world evaporated.

Crossfire

A warm African breeze drifted lazily over the sleepy ocean, coaxing tiny ripples to the glassy surface and causing the morning sun's rays to shatter into a million fractals of light. Palm trees along the shore shook off the last of the evening rains while a pod of bottle nose dolphins plied the mouth of the Benito River in search of sardines for breakfast.

He was having second thoughts as he balanced on the bowsprit of Jioba's sailboat. Since there were no waves to speak of on this particular morning, Jioba was simulating a rough ocean by flinging himself from one side to the other, giving the hefty wooden craft a good rocking. For a moment EnKare prevailed, though he felt like a juvenile secretary bird alighting on a flimsy acacia branch.

"I got this, bwana," he yelled. "No no no no no no nooooooooo!"

Seconds later he bobbed to the surface, dog paddling beside the boat.

"Ya, you got this, Toots. Ha!" Jioba's infectious smile beamed over the side rail.

He felt like a hippo in a palm tree, out of his element. Grabbing the side of the boat, he hoisted himself onto the deck. "OK, Jimmy, you show me how it's done. But I'm not gonna go easy on you, bwana."

Jioba leapt up on the bowsprit while EnKare rocked the boat. At first it looked like he wasn't going to last more than a minute, but it soon became clear that his seafaring friend was just toying with him. So he doubled his efforts until the boat thrashed about, like it was caught in a game of cat and mouse with a Kraken.

Jioba yelled, "That's the best you got?" Then he started walking around the outer edge of the boat, balancing on the strip of wood along the railing. A couple of times it looked as though he was going to take the plunge, but then somehow he'd manage to pull out of it, relaxing into what appeared to be a fall only to have the boat swing his legs back under him at the last moment. He made it look so easy. So effortless.

Jioba made it all the way to the stern, waited for just the right pitch, and then launched himself into a back flip.

Letting the boat come to a rest, EnKare peered over the railing. There was no sign of Jioba. He looked in the water all around the boat, squinting back the sun's reflection to see if Jioba was swimming somewhere under the surface. Just then, Jioba sprang out of the water, grabbed him by the arm, and pulled him overboard. A water fight ensued the moment they hit the water.

"OK OK OK I give up, bwana," he sputtered after a minute or two of nonstop splashing. Climbing back up onto the deck, he inquired, "So how is all of this," waving his arms wildly in front of his face, "supposed to make me a better swimmer anyway?"

With an extra wide grin, "It's not...I just like seeing you flop around like a beached whale."

"Jimmy, I'm serious. You know I..."

"Sea legs."

"Ya. They're nice. Congratulations."

"No, *sea* legs, bwana. It's what we call it when you can move around out here on a boat just the same as on land. Sea legs." To illustrate his point he popped up into a handstand on the boat's side railing.

EnKare chuckled. "Technically, wouldn't those be sea arms?"

He hadn't thought much about it before, but Jioba was really becoming a master sailor. He cut and stitched his own sails, made his own fishing line from intestine, fashioned fish hooks from bone, wood, scrap metal, seeds, and fabric. He could catch anything that lived in the ocean, and he could swim like a fish—or more like a sea turtle.

He built the boat they were sitting on with his bare hands, using nothing but material that he scavenged off the beach, and wood that he harvested and hewed using the same tools and techniques as his ancestors. For the ribs of the boat he used actual whale ribs from the remains of a Mama Bulu that washed up on the sand during the previous monsoon. It wasn't the most attractive vessel on the water, but every last detail, down to the hinged rudder that was carved from a single piece of baobab, was created by Jioba's hands. This made it a work of art, a masterpiece.

Of course he wouldn't tell any of this to Jioba. If that boy's head got any bigger, it might explode.

They had been relaxing on the boat for a while when EnKare said, "O Capitán, my Capitán, what's next? I'm not gonna get better at swimming by lounging around on the deck all day, now am I?"

"OK, bwana. We'll pull in closer to shore and work on some drills and some breath control exercises. Grab the anchor."

While he hoisted the anchor, Jioba raised the mainsail and held the boom out perpendicular to the boat to catch the breeze and fill the sail. The fabric billowed as they glided over the water towards the beach. He loved the feeling of moving over the surface of sea, propelled by the wind's gentle breath and nothing more. As long as the wind blew, what was to stop someone from sailing to the ends of the earth, and beyond.

A hundred meters from shore Jioba gave the order to throw out the anchor while he dropped the sail, bunched it up around the boom, and tied it off with the tail end of the mainsheet.

The boys spent the rest of the afternoon practicing different swimming strokes, messing around on deck, and distance-flirting with the young ladies sunbathing on the sand—a two man comedy show at its finest.

"OK, bwana. Now let's get serious for a moment," Jioba insisted as their third water fight simmered to a low boil. "We're gonna swim along the bottom carrying this stone. We each have to keep one hand on it, and use the other hand to swim. Then one of us at a time gets to surface for a breath while the other stays with the stone. Then we keep swimming, and so on. Sabes?"

"That sounds easy enough. So, how far do we go like that?"

"Not far, Toots. Just from here to the beach."

EnKare's eyes grew as wide as a bush baby's, and his jaw dropped open. Cocking his head to one side he asked, "Is that even possible, bwana?"

Jioba smiled. "Let's find out."

For the first set of breaths things were easy enough. By the third time he surfaced, however, matters had taken a turn for the worse. He pushed his breath out as best he could, sucked in a gulp of air, and swam back down to where Jioba waited with the rock. As he took his turn at the bottom, he could feel his diaphragm contracting, straining to expand his lungs and bring in fresh oxygen. By the time Jioba returned, thin-lipped panic had completely taken over his body and mind. He was certain he didn't have enough air to get back to the surface. At any moment his heaving diaphragm would prevail, expand his ribcage and allow the water to come rushing in to his lungs.

Kicking off the bottom he fought for the surface with all his strength.

Jioba was waiting for him when he bubbled to the surface, gasping and floundering.

"Chabalangus, bwana!"

"Not as easy as you thought, eh, Toots?" Jioba heckled.

Sputtering between breaths, "No. Not easy. At all!"

"Come on," Jioba nodded towards the beach, "let's go take a break."

Adding a dramatic flair to their arrival, the boys dragged themselves up onto the sand like shipwrecked sailors clinging to life. The charade didn't last long, however, as a ball of sand hit EnKare *smack* on his back. He lifted his head to see Jioba, ear to ear smile, packing another projectile tightly between his hands.

"Oh you DEAD, bwana!"

They took off sprinting down the beach, sand-balls flying indiscriminately, chickens, young children, the occasional sunbather caught in the crossfire.

Ice Cocos

It was a typical day so far. A day of sand battles and water fights, swim lessons and aerial acrobatics on the beach. They lay splayed out on the sand, breathing heavily, beads of sweat streaming down their faces.

"I could eat an elephant right now!"

"Vamanos!"

After a quick dip in the ocean to clean off the sand, they headed to the boardwalk and the seaside shops, tummies growling. As they danced passed the leather shop EnKare called out, "Jambo, Mr. Bioko."

Mr. Bioko's gravelly voice called from the back of the shop, "Hujambo, EnKare. Tell your father the halter is ready for him."

"Ms. Rita, I must say, you are looking as beautiful as ever," Jioba cooed as they passed the flower shop.

Ms. Rita smiled and handed Jioba a small potted plant with vibrant orange leaves. "Give this buganvilla to your mother, and tell her I'll pop by this evening for some tea."

As they passed by the entrance to the bakery, Jioba called out, "A good afternoon to you, Mrs. Tulu."

A heavenly aroma drifted out of the shop, and they paused for a moment at the doorway, breathing in the delightful smell of warm baked bread and pastries. Mrs. Tulu appeared from the back wearing a colorful apron around her waist and a floral patterned bandana on her head.

"Here you go, boys. Try a piece of my latest creation." She smiled as she handed them a warm, doughy, honey-basted roll. They received the gift like they'd just been handed a map to the secret location of a limitless supply of wild honey—staring at it with half-lowered eyelids, humming softly, rocking gently on their feet. Then the spell broke, they ripped the roll in half and devoured it instantly.

"Fanksh Mishish Tulush, It'sh sho good," EnKare muffled through a mouth full of bread.

Waving goodbye, bellies partially satiated, they continued their stroll along the boardwalk. The sidewalks and roads, once suffocated in cement and asphalt during the time before Iworo, had eroded away. Soft grasses and woven reed mats now covered the rough and crumbling surfaces, reflecting the sun's heat and keeping the streets cool—a much more agreeable surface for bare feet to walk on.

Presently, they came to Concha's Café. They were met at the entrance by a booming figure that filled the doorway. Her braided hair fell in long, tightly woven cornrows, tied off with colorful bits of beach glass and little shells that bounced around her shoulders and back. She wore large, dangly, hoop earrings fashioned out of bamboo rings, and across her breast hung a necklace of stone-sized amber beads that flowed over her stout shoulders and disappeared between her robust bosoms. Her blouse was a bright red, hand knitted, frilly affair that inadequately contained all that it was designed to. Two wide, flat bare feet peeked out from under her skirt, which was an aqua marine batik splashed with images of sea turtles, whales, fish, and corals.

"Señora Concha, how..." Jioba's words were cut short as the flamboyant woman pulled him in for a hug.

"Jioba, ma boy! It's been a whole day since ya came round to see me, and that's too long! You hear me?" Señora Concha's voice boomed as she squeezed her arms around his relatively small body.

There's no way he can hear you. And it's a good thing Jimmy can hold his breath for so long 'cause I can't imagine he can breathe in there.

Señora Concha pulled Jioba from her bosom, turned to EnKare and said, "It's your turn. Now come give ya Auntie Concha a hug."

While smothered in embrace, all he could think about was the pleasant scent of rose water and amber.

Greeting formalities survived, the boys took a seat under the awning in front of the café on stools made of coconut trunks, and watched the people go by as they waited for their food to arrive. There was no menu at Concha's Café. You just sat yourself down, and she brought out whatever she had prepared that day. And if you ever asked her what she was serving, she'd respond with something like, "Oh just a little a dis, and a little a dat. But don't ya worry, ma darlings, Señora Concha will make you fat."

The tinkling hair chimes announced the arrival of the meal. Soon the table was covered with a steaming mound of cornmeal ugali, bowls of fish stew, a plate of fried plantains, and two coco waters.

"Señora Concha," EnKare sputtered between mouthfuls, "you are the greatest chef in all of Mbini!"

"And don't ya eva forget it," she sang as she made her way back into the café, tossing a dishrag over one shoulder and swaying her hippo-hips from side to side.

Until now he'd been too busy eating to notice that they weren't the only customers at Concha's Café that afternoon. Sitting on the other side of the doorway were a couple of men in their mid-twenties. They had finished off their meal and were sipping on coffee and chatting excitedly. He didn't recognize them. Perhaps they were from Bata, or one of the other nearby villages. The boys gave each other a quick look; one that said, *let's eavesdrop on these guys for a while.*

"Bwana, I'm telling you. Capitán Kodo has the most advanced ship ever built, from the yards at Tema. Solar sails! Electric engines! A central desalinator, jet propulsion. Hydrofoils, bwana!"

"Ya, Tomobo, but do you really think it's wise..."

"You are such a worrywarthog, Jafra. We have a guaranteed spot on the boat. My uncle Kodo is the capitán, remember? This is the chance of a lifetime!"

"I suppose you're right. One small problem, though. We still have to find a way to get to Accra. They set sail on the next full moon, which is in fourteen days."

"I know. It will take at least a month to get there over land. We need a boat. A fast boat."

Jioba's eyes widened, and he got that look on his face. Then, before EnKare could do anything about it, Jioba stood up and announced, "Gentlemen, I've got just the boat for you!"

The men looked at each other and then turned towards Jioba.

"I'm sorry. I couldn't help but overhear that you were in need of a boat to take you to Accra. I'm the capitán of the fastest boat in all of Mbini. I can get you there before the next full moon." He just blurted it out.

"So... I'm sorry, who are you?"

Jioba leaned over and extended his hand. "Jina langu ni Jioba. This is my best friend, EnKare. A su servicio."

The man reached out and shook his hand. "I'm Tomobo. This is Jafra."

EnKare waved to the men from where he sat.

"Come, join us," Jafra beckoned with a hand gesture, "and tell us about this boat of yours."

They moved over to the young men's table, and EnKare sat back and watched with amusement as his friend sweet-talked the two strangers. *That boy could sell a blind man a lantern.*

The men were full of questions. How big is the boat? Is there a cabin for sleeping? A place to cook? Is there enough cargo space to carry three or four hundred pounds of provisions? Could they really get there before the next full moon?

"Gentlemen, let me assure you, I can get you to Accra with days to spare. Come. My boat isn't far from here. You can see her for yourself."

Tomobo gave Jafra a look that that said, *well, we don't have a lot of options right now so...what the heck.* "OK, let's see this boat of yours. We'll have to take care of our exchange for the food and coffee first, then we'll be ready to go." Then calling out to Señora Concha, the man said, "Señora, we're ready to chop that fire wood for you now, just..."

"Wait a minute," Jioba interjected. "Gentlemen, your meal is on me today!" Then turning to Señora Concha, he bubbled in a sweet boyish voice, "Señora Concha, would it be alright to put these good men's trade on my account? I'll settle up with you tomorrow when I bring in a fresh catch?"

Señora Concha put her hands on her hips, pursed her lips, and gave Jioba a sly look. "What mischief ya gettin' yaself into now, boy?" Walking up to him and pinching his cheek, "One of these days that smile of yours is gonna get you into all manner of trouble. You hear me, boy?"

Kissing the woman's hand as he backed out of the café, "Yes, Señora Concha. Thank you, Señora Concha, you're the best, Señora Concha." Turning, "Gentlemen, if you'll be so good as to follow me."

As they walked along the sidewalk, EnKare couldn't help but chuckle to himself. He couldn't believe his friend sometimes. Always getting into some crazy situation or another. Always getting in way over his head. Like the time he offered to carry Mrs. Msoke's daughter across the floodplain of the river so she wouldn't get her feet muddy. Chivalry was not dead, but Jioba almost was! Or the time he tried to 'fly' from the top of the old radio tower with pieces of scrap metal strapped to his arms as wings.

These men will take one look at the boat, thank him for the offer, and that's the last we'll see of them. One thing he knew for certain was that his friend's heart was always in the right place.

They stood on the beach looking out at the craft. Tomobo's eyebrows were lowered, a deep look of concern on his face. Jafra's nose was slightly wrinkled, eyebrows lifted high on his forehead, and he shook his head slowly side to side.

"Well, gentlemen, what do you think?" Jioba enthused, gesturing towards his boat with an outstretched arm, oblivious to the serious concern on the men's faces.

After a moment or two of silence, the men looked at each other, and then Tomobo turned to Jioba. "She's a nice boat. Jafra and I will have to think about it. Talk over details. Finalize plans. Thank you for taking the time to show us. We'll be in touch if we decide to take you up on the offer." Then the two strangers turned to leave.

"Remember! She's the fastest boat in the Bay of Biafra!" Jioba's voice trailed after them.

EnKare slung an arm over his friend's shoulder. "C'mon Jimmy. You gave it a good shot. Now let's go down to Mama Sana's place for an ice coco."

As they walked along, toes digging in to the cooling afternoon sand, they talked about the two strangers and the events of the afternoon.

"You're crazy, you know that?"

"Yes, I am. But what does that have to do with anything?" Jioba shot back from behind a grin.

"I mean, have you ever been to Accra? Do you even know how to get there?"

"Hmm…No. I have no idea. But if it's in Africa then I can get us there. At home we have my father's collection of maps and charts for the seas all the way around the continent. Tides! Currents! Reefs! Everything, bwana" He finger whip-snapped the air with each point on his list.

They arrived at Mama Sana's, ordered a couple of ice cocos, and walked out onto the sand to watch the sun setting over the bay. Pelicans glided past with wingtips inches from peeling waves.

"But do you really think they'll come back?"

"Bwana! Does a hyrax start sunbathing at sunrise? When they can't find anyone else willing to take them, they'll come running."

"And you're sure you can make it? I mean, do you even want to go?"

"Chabalangus, Toots!" Jioba shrieked, "Think about it. This is the chance of a lifetime, bwana. We've always wanted to see Accra..."

EnKare cut him off mid-sentence. "*WE*! No no no, Jimmy. There's no *we*, bwana. This one's all YOU."

"C'mon, Toots. I know you've dreamed of walking through the garden streets of Old Town, and sampling foods from all over the world, some even from the time before Iworo! And going to Aye Market, which is so big that it has no beginning and no end! Just imagine, Toots, you and me, taking on the town that never sleeps. What do you say, bwana?"

"Take it easy, Jimmy. Let's just see if those men ever come back. Then we can talk business."

He was doing his best to maintain some degree of levelheadedness. But deep down he couldn't help but do a little dreaming of his own. *First Accra, then the world!* Why not? After all, hardly a day sneaked past without him dreaming about being a world explorer.

As the ocean drank up the last of the sun's fiery orb, his mind was ablaze with visions of stepping onto distant shores, exploring new and exiting worlds, going where no one—at least no one from small-town Mbini—had ever gone before.

Giant

She stood at the entrance to Grandmother's hut. It was midday, and the sun beat down from the heavens casting the world around her in a purple haze. A voice from inside called out, "Wakíŋyaŋ, is that you? Come inside, won't you sweetheart?"

She recognized Grandmother's soft-spoken voice. "Coming, Uŋčí."

She ducked her head and stepped through the doorway. After a blink or two her eyes still didn't adjust to the low light.

That's odd.

The windows were shuttered, and even the smoke flap in the thatched roof was closed.

That's really odd. That flap's almost never closed.

Squinting into the darkness, she called out, "Uŋčí, where are you? It's so dark in here."

"Give your senses time, Little Thunder. For now, just listen to my voice. You have stepped into the veil for the first time. Your spirit walking has begun, and for this I am filled with joy."

Then her voice turned somber. "But there will be no celebration today to mark this rite of passage for you."

"I don't understand, Uŋčí. What do you mean, I have 'stepped through the veil for the first time?' What veil? What are you talking about? And why won't my eyes adjust? I still can't see you."

Then gradually things started to come into focus, though something was still off—like she was looking through a piece of white birch bark scraped thin. Níškola was curled up on the floor in one of the corners of the hut. This, too, was off. Why wasn't he out running around with the other wolf-dogs, and why hadn't he rushed up to greet her with his usual face licks and nuzzling?

"Níškola," she called to him. "Uší, boy. Come say hi."

Níškola didn't move. He lay motionless, his snout resting woefully between his front paws. He whimpered softly and then let out a long sigh.

"Níškola, what's the matter? Uŋčí, what's wrong with Níška?" She moved towards the wolf-dog.

"Wakíŋyaŋ. Inážiŋkhiya!" Wakȟáŋ Kiktá's voice hit her with the force of a heavy, flat-faced wave. Uŋčí had never spoken to her in that tone before. Something was wrong. Something was very wrong. A slight dizziness came over her, and, for a moment, the room began to blur.

"What's wrong with me, Uŋčí, I don't feel well?"

Grandmother was sitting cross-legged on the bearskin rug on the far side of the cabin.

"And why are you speaking that way? Did I do something wrong?"

"Try not to stare at me, Little Thunder. You don't have the personal power to sustain my image. Look at me in short glances. You are in danger, brave one, and you must—" Her words were cut short.

"Uuŋčííí!"

The scream escaped from her own lips, though it sounded like the cry of someone on the other side of a canyon, distant and stifled.

The room pulsed, and receded into a muddy gray.

Níškola raised his head off the ground and whined, then disappeared into the obscurity of the earthen floor.

The walls, windows, and thatched ceiling, the fire pit, all faded away. She looked at Grandmother, now the only remaining effigy, suspended in front of her, floating cross-legged in a silvery haze, her long white hair flowing down her shoulders and over the colorful embroidery of her ruana.

"Be strong now, Little Thunder. And remember…"

Then Grandmother evaporated and the familiar voice was replaced by a sharp metallic ringing in her ears.

She blinked repeatedly in an attempt to bring things back into focus. Throbbing pain emanated from the back of her head and drove forward to her eyes. She couldn't feel any other part of her body.

Nothing.

Panic welled up inside her, followed by a fierce desire to lash out, scream and kick.

But Father's teachings came back—*in moments like these it's always best to take three deep breaths.*

Breath

Sensation returned to her body...

Toes and fingers...

Arms and legs...

Slowly reanimating her core. Was she still dizzy, or was the whole world rocking?

Breath

Blinking cleared the sting from her eyes, and her vision pulled into focus. She was face down, staring at dark, wet wood, half submerged in a reddish liquid. The muffled sound of water sloshed and gurgled all around.

Breath

She attempted to move, but the effort shot pain through her wrists and ankles.

Through a confused mind thoughts came slowly. The last thing she remembered was going for a walk on the beach at night. Looking out at the firewater.

Then nothing.

The here and now materialized incrementally as each of her senses fired back to life. She was lying face down on the bottom of a boat with her wrists tied together behind her back and lashed to her ankles, which were hoisted up towards her head—a most painful and effective binding. She couldn't move a muscle without the ropes digging deeper into flesh.

Straining her ears—*oars slapping the surface of water.*

Craning her neck—*bare feet. Human.*

The predicament was clear. She was a captive. *But who? Why? And where are we going?* She knew one thing for certain; these were not monks or worms, or she'd already be dead. And the feet she could see were human. Most likely one of the bands of rogues that Uŋčí was always warning her about.

There wasn't much she could do in her current state, so she remained as still as possible to minimize the pain.

The bilge water sloshing around her face, had a distinctive, red hue. A pain throbbed in the back of her head, and a slow-moving droplet trickled from her hairline, tickling her cheek as it traversed her face and dripped into the water by her nose.

Exhaustion and pain.

Fading in and out of consciousness.

When awake, she listened to her captors' conversations. They spoke a dialect she had not heard before, filled with foreign words and expressions. Still, she could pick up most of what they were saying, and, from the sounds of it, she wasn't the only captive on the boat.

Their leader had a deep voice, and she heard one of the others refer to him as Bronx. They were clearly afraid of this man. When speaking to him directly, the pitch of their voices rose sharply, cracking with stress. She heard so many amusing titles of respect for this man, that, despite her miserable condition, she quite appreciated the entertainment. When one of the rogues addressed him as "Your Highest-Upness," she almost laughed out loud, but the boat rocked and sent blood-filled water down her throat instead.

There's more than one boat. Perhaps two or three others.

How long have I been unconscious?

The way the sun beat down on her back, it was close to midday.

It was early morning when they took me. But was that last night or has it been two or even three days since then?

From the pain, monotony, dehydration and hunger, she drifted in and out.

It was late in the afternoon when the boat violently ground to a halt, sending her sliding forward and scraping her chin along the swollen bilge boards. Someone cut the rope that connected her wrists to her ankles, and her lifeless legs clattered down in a pile.

"Nuf sleepytime, wormbait! On dem feet n-off boat, all'ya!" One of the rogues from another boat was yelling.

A voice above her, "Ya heard, skeetjuice. Gitup na."

Then bony hands grabbed her by the armpits and yanked her to her feet. Pȟahíŋ-quill pain shot through her legs as she swayed back and forth, struggling not to fall over.

Once steady, she looked around. Her boat was run up on a beach. There were two other boats with rogues offloading cargo and captives. Each boat had a leader, but the captain of her boat, Bronx, appeared to be in charge of all of them.

Bronx rose from his seat and stood in front of her, the boat swaying under his weight. Like a child standing at the foot of a cliff, she stared straight ahead at abdominal muscles rippling to the rhythm of breath.

Treetrunk legs.

Oakbarrel arms.

Black hair that grew from his head in serpentine, matted clumps that jutted out in all directions. Around the burnt-osage skin of his neck hung a collar made of woven hair with bits and pieces of dried scalp and skull still attached.

Human!

He was clothed in bearskin—one draped over his shoulders and another secured around his waist with a leather strap. But one weapon hung at his side, fashioned from pieces of iron rod, like the ones she had seen in the ruins of burnt out cities. The iron was twisted into a long handle, then knotted at the top to form a bristling, rust covered mace.

And the man smelled. The potpourri of rotting flesh, feces, and layer upon layer of fetid body odor stung her eyes, causing them to tear.

Father's words came again: *When you are most afraid, that is when you show no fear.*

She tilted her head back and stared straight into the giant's hard, stoic face. After a moment or two Bronx lifted an arm. Startled by the smell, as much as the action, she stumbled back a step.

"Drink." He had the voice of a leviathan.

Deep.

Final.

Unnerving.

She broke her gaze and looked down at the man's outstretched hand. He was holding a transparent, smooth gourd filled with liquid.

"Drink," he repeated.

"Untie my hands."

Bronx nodded, and a rogue standing behind her removed the binding, crossed her wrists in front of her, and retied the rope. She lifted her hands, took hold of the strange gourd and tilted it up to her lips. *Thank you, Water.*

The first sip felt like drinking hot sand, as it burned and scraped its way down her withered throat. She coughed and grimaced at the pain. It must have been days since she last drank water, she thought. She drank until the gourd was empty and then handed it back.

The giant stepped off the boat and joined the other captains on the beach.

A grating voice barked, "Off boat, wormbait, n git wit dem others."

Wakíŋyaŋ stepped off the bow, her feet dropping down into the cool, shallow water. The soles of her bare feet welcomed the gritty sand between her toes.

Once empty, the boats were pulled across the shore and hidden under the thick canopy of coastal forest. She was standing in a line with five other captives. There were two young boys, čhekpá, identical twins, no more than six winters, whimpering and shivering. The other three were girls, two around her age, sixteen or seventeen winters, and the third no more than eight winters. They were all bound at the wrists and ankles.

"Ooooooooooweeee! Lookie lookie lookie yer Highest-Bossman. We done good. Ooooooooweeee!" One of Bronx's subordinates was screeching. He was a wild man who looked more like the remnants of a burnt manzanita bush than a human being. His face and body was covered in blotchy burn scars that extended up onto his head, leaving him without eyebrows or lashes on one side of his face. Tufts of hair sprouted randomly from the top of his skull where the skin was healthy enough to grow it. His jaw was stuck open and cranked off center and his tongue dangled out to one side of a large, gnarled tooth that rested on his lower lip. One eye squinted nearly closed while the other bulged abnormally wide.

Walking up to one of the girls in front of her, the gnarled man lifted a handful of her hair, pressed his nose into it and breathed in deeply.

"Ooooooooweeee, an they smells sooooo good," he inhaled the words through his chattering teeth.

"*Grrunk*!" Bronx grunted loudly.

The wiry man cried out, throwing himself at the giant's feet. "OK, OK, OK. Fritz gives ya his deepest-est apologies, yer Lordness." Then, without pausing for air, he leapt up and barked an order at the whole assembly. "K french fries, feet walkin', no talkin', worms and monks be stalkin'. Now home-it y'all!" And with that the whole group set off walking along the beach.

Moving with the hobbles on was cumbersome and tiring work. The ropes cut in to her skin, chafing and blistering her ankles. That, and the fact that they where walking on sand and fine pebbles, made for a slow journey.

The wild man who called himself Fritz walked in a continual circle around the procession, arms flapping like a bat with injured wings. As he passed by Bronx she heard him say, "Yer Highest-Upness, 'haps we needs cut our precious cargo down now, 'fo dat sun dry up, an all worms come a-lookin' fo a nibble." Then, responding to a look that Bronx gave him, he followed with, "Yer right, yer Greatestness. I, I, I don't know what Fritz was thinkin'. OooWeee C'mon, wormbait," he yelled at the group. "This pace…is a dis-grace…Boss don't wanna waste…the pretty face…so make haste."

Wakíŋyaŋ was grateful when Fritz called out for a rest. By now it was late afternoon, and the sun had dipped down beyond the coastline forest.

I hope these rogues have a plan.

With her legs shackled and arms tied, and with the sun only moments from bedding down for the night, she felt vulnerable.

One of the other captives, the skinny little girl with ratty hair the color of straw, and freckles on her nose, sat a short distance away, resting on a log. Wakíŋyaŋ shuffled over and took a seat beside her.

"Are you OK?" she asked.

The girl didn't respond but shook her head slowly. Her lips were dry and cracked and her face was emaciated and pale grey. There was no spark of life in her sky blue eyes.

She's just a child.

"Excuse me, Fritz," she called out to the gangly man who was on the other side of the group, screeching at one of the other rogues. "This girl isn't well. She needs water. Maybe some food if you have any." She figured she risked a beating, but this child would die without help.

Fritz jostled and bounced his way towards her, arms flapping. "Not touchin' dat fleabag. Feeder yerself, skeetjuice."

And with that he threw a transparent gourd at her and walked off. She unscrewed the top and lifted the gourd to the girl's lips.

"Drink slowly, it might hurt."

The girl managed to take in a little water without coughing it up.

"There. Does that feel any better?"

The child nodded slowly and drew her lips back slightly in an attempted smile.

"Don't worry. I won't let anyone hurt you. Here, try to drink a little more."

At just that moment a horrific scream shattered the tranquility of the forest. The sky overhead filled with the barks and chatter of zitkála, giant flying foxes with six-pace wingspans, capable of plucking a grown man from the face of the earth in their dagger-long talons. Zitkála were known for launching vicious aerial attacks and catching victims off-guard, or circling above a battle or hunting party to scavenge off the remaining carrion.

This feels wrong. We aren't hunting. There's no battle going on.

"Wait here," she said to the straw-haired girl.

"WORMS!" Someone screamed.

Now the zitkála make sense. Whenever a group of worms rose to the surface to feed, there was bound to be a swarm of them circling overhead, waiting to drop down and pick off the scraps.

It so happened they had stopped to rest right above a nesting clew of worms. Chaos spread through the band of rogues as the translucent-skinned creatures wriggled out of the sand and emerged from the layer of rotting leaves.

Bronx roared like an angered bear, barking orders at his men while fending off the worms with his mace.

This is my chance.

With the rogues preoccupied, no one would see her escape, and by the time the battle was over she'd be long gone.

When Bronx's back was turned, she shuffled to the edge of the forest and ducked into a thicket of bush ferns. Out of sight, she went to work on the rope binding her wrists, pulling at the loose end with her teeth. Luckily the knotter was incompetent, and she was able to free it with ease. Then she went to work on her ankle bindings, the frantic sounds of battle ringing through the forest all around.

Free!

She wasted no time. On her belly, she started across a clearing towards the dense cover of forest. Glancing back to see if she was being followed, she caught a glimpse of the fighting through a break in the trees.

She could see the back of a worm. He was dragging something, or someone, along the ground. She felt pity for the unfortunate rogue.

Then worm moved to one side, and she saw his victim. *The straw-haired girl!* Her limp body trailed along the ground behind the worm.

She's dead!

Wakíŋyaŋ was about to start crawling again when the girl's arm clawed at the sky. She looked towards the dear trail, the open forest, freedom's warm embrace, then back at the girl's ragged, limp body...

Inhale

Hold

Exhale

With lightning speed she grabbed a cedar branch from the ground and ran at the worm.

She knew he sensed her approach, as he hastened his efforts to drag the girl to his tunnel. *If he manages to pull her underground, she's lost forever.*

Then she was upon them,

in the air,

club raised over head,

war cry cutting through the melee.

Both hands gripping the cedar branch she swung with all her might, catching the creature on the side of the head. His body crumpled to the ground. She dropped the branch, hoisted the girl over her shoulder, and turned to run into the woods.

She had only gone a short distance when a terrible pain tore through her calf. In her haste, she had failed to recognize the signs of a worm hole, had passed right over the hidden entrance, and one of the creatures had reached up and sunk his claws into her.

Her legs buckled, and she fell forward. The little girl's body flew off her shoulder and landed in the clear.

No no no, this is NOT good!

Worms could lock themselves into their holes with their lower legs, using the barbed claws that stuck out from the insides edges of their ankle and knee bones, making it virtually impossible to pull them out.

The creature's talons sunk deeper into her flesh, and the agonizing pain undermined her ability to resist as the worm drew her into the ground.

She kicked frantically at the worm's head with her free leg, but the blows were ineffective on his thick skull bones.

She thrashed side to side, her arms searching frantically for tree roots and rock to grab on to.

She had been close to worms before, but never a live one. She could see the blood moving through the veins on his neck—his thin, elongated nostrils opening and closing with each breath—his inner, second eyelids flicking closed from the top and sides each time she kicked at his face.

Death is like birth—Mother's words drifted through her mind—*a moment of transition from one state of being to another.*

Was this the moment of her death?

Her final battle?

As the worm dragged her towards oblivion, she let out a war cry. Ancestors would hear her and be there to welcome her home when she passed through the gateway to the next realm.

She let go of the pain that coursed through her leg.

She let go of seventeen winters of struggling to survive.

Adrenaline pumped through her flesh, coaxing euphoria along its chemical trail.

As consciousness faded, she looked up at the circle of light filling the opening of the tunnel. She blinked slowly, and when her eyes opened again the circle was filled with an image—snakes of matted black hair cutting through the yellow, like a tree's shadow at midday.

A mighty arm reached down through the darkness towards her.

Training Day

A mother cheetah and her cub sat on the weathered top of a red termite mound that crested the sea of elephant grass. The mother's head dropped low and forward, her gaze fixed on a small herd of gazelle in the distance.

The cub mimicked her every move, locking the gazelles' location into his internal compass. Once they descended into the grass, this compass would help guide them as they blindly stalked their prey.

The elephant grass here grew as tall as the elephants who roamed through it, providing prime forage for the herds of kudu, impala, oryx, and gazelle that, in turn, attracted the great cat hunters of the land. It was also a favorite snacking ground for cattle and rhinos, and it was these two herds that brought EnKare and EnKulupuoni here just after sunrise. As usual, Pilipili tagged along on his shoulder.

From the top of another termite mound a short distance away, EnKare could see the cub's eagerness and impatience. While the mother remained relaxed and completely motionless, the cub's shoulder blades kneaded up and down, small jolts of nervous energy rippling through the fur along his spine.

I feel you, little cub. My first hunt was no slice of passion fruit pie, believe me.

He wasn't here to sightsee. He had climbed the termite mound to keep an eye on the cattle that were grazing at the edge of the grass. But when he reached the top, he found he wasn't the first to think of it. Resting his weight on one leg and leaning against his spear, he remained completely motionless, an invisible witness to this young cheetah's training day. So long as the cats remained focused on the gazelle and not the cattle, he wouldn't intervene.

As he watched, his mind drifted to things he'd been ruminating on far too frequently as of late: his Lion Name; Olubi; worthiness; courage—things he'd rather not think about at all.

Olubi! His actions saved the lives of half the village. What is the likelihood of something dramatic like that happening again anytime soon? And even if it does, will I have the courage or the intelligence to respond the way Olubi did? He was named after the great Maasai warrior from the time before Iworo! What an honor. It wasn't that he was especially brave, or courageous. But he was smart. Really smart. Maybe that's it! Maybe I just have to be really smart, and then somehow my smartness will be enough. Who would I be named after? Dr. Wangari? That would be amazing.

He resented the pressure to be something he was not. He was surrounded by incredible people, strong, smart, connected, high functioning people. Surely their expectations of him were equally fantastic. When he thought about it, it seemed like an impossibility, living up to such standards.

"Pheeet pheeet!" A staccato bird whistle caught his attention, pulling him from his thoughts and causing Pilipili to stir from her spot under his braids. Baba emerged from the grass, just beside the cattle, and motioned for him to come.

The cheetahs were on the move, heading in the opposite direction. Satisfied that they posed no danger, he slid down the mound and followed a pathway through the grass to his father's side.

"It's all clear, Baba. The cheetahs are heading towards the gazelle, which are on the other side," he indicated with his hand.

His father responded, "Oh good. After lunch we'll check on the rhino herd. Two of the mothers are expecting any day now. When the babies come, one of us will stay with them until the little ones are strong enough to fend off predators."

As usual, EnKulupuoni's words revealed his authority. They came out sounding both gentle and firm, definitive yet flexible, wise but unpresumptuous. In many ways this reflected his character.

Baba was a towering figure. Not necessarily in physical stature, though he was tall, with a slender, muscular build. No. It was his presence. An energy that extended beyond the boundaries of flesh. You could see it as a glow in his eyes and hear it as a tone in his words. With just a touch he could sense one's mood, and alter it if he chose to.

He was a much older father than most of EnKare's friends'. Much of the population was younger than his father. *In fact, there are only a handful of people in all of Africa who are older than Baba, and Mama is one of them. They might be two of the oldest people on earth! No, wait. Jioba's grandparents are still alive, and they are even older. They were around before Iworo...*

"Son," Baba's words startled him. "Let's eat."

Heart Path

Picking up their cowhide shoulder bags and ingri water gourds, they walked to the shade of a baobab tree. He spread his shuka on a flat patch of buffalo grass at the base of the trunk, while Baba lay his spear to rest against the tree's smooth bark. The morning chill gave way to a sun-drenched blanket of air that warmed his skin as it moved slowly up the graduated escarpment.

Sitting cross-legged on the ground, EnKulupuoni pulled several waxed linen pouches and a small ingri from his bag, and laid them on the shuka. The pouches contained strips of jerked goat meat, nuts and dried fruit, and a stack of chapatis. The ingri was filled with a brew of dark, roasted coffee.

They sat in silence, savoring the food and listening to the sounds of the forest and savanna waking up. Pilipili, woken from her nap by the smell of food, joined them on the cloth and waited patiently for her share of the bounty.

"Baba," EnKare's voice broke the silence.

"Yes, son?"

He racked his brain for a moment, but couldn't put his question into adequate words.

"Mmm. Never mind."

After minute or two of silence, EnKulupuoni spoke. "Son, I have been waiting for the right moment to tell you the story of my Lion Name."

"You already told me about your Birth Name, ElKikau! First Born, right? You got that name because you were the first Maasai of your clan born on the surface."

"Yes. That is my Birth Name. I was referring to my Lion Name. EnKulupuoni is the name that my parents gave me when I was around fifteen. About your age. The name means Earth."

"I knew it meant Earth. But why did they name you that? I would have picked something like Fearless Warrior, or Lion Hearted, or Ancient Spirit. Earth just seems so… plain."

Baba smiled. "I thought the same thing when I was fifteen. In fact, I thought the whole business was nonsense. I was happy with my Birth Name and saw no reason to change it."

EnKare was having a hard time imagining his father as an impetuous teenager.

"My parents…your grandparents, who you never had the chance to meet, came from the time before Iworo. When the endless winter descended on Africa, they were living with a small clan of Maasai in Nandi tribal lands on the east side of the continent.

"In the distant past, the Nandi and the Maasai were enemies. They fought over land and had great battles. When the endless winter came, those that survived moved into a system of underground caverns known as Ngabunat. Your grandparents took refuge in this cave with a couple of others from our clan. Most of the survivors in the cave were Nandi. They could have exiled the Maasai, or worse, simply killed them. But they let them stay, and this one act of kindness bonded the two peoples and transformed them from enemies into friends.

"Your Aunt Naserian was only three years old when they descended into the darkness of the cave. She was nine when she saw the sky again. The world she returned to was not the one she had known.

"Shortly after returning to the surface, your grandmother gave birth to a little boy who they named ElKikau, First Born. I was malnourished and sickly. More than once, Mother rocked me to sleep, expecting me to never wake up again. It was so cold in those early days, and food was scarce. Your grandfather cut his own rations in half so that your grandmother could grow me inside of her. The cave, the cold, and the lack of food eventually took its toll on my father. I was three when he died. The only memory I have of him: I'm in his arms looking up into his tired eyes. He is looking at me. Smiling. His cheeks and eye sockets are sunken in and the lines on his face cut as deep as the Great Rift Valley. But the way he was looking at me… there was such love in that look. Such love."

Baba paused and took a sip of coffee from the gourd. He had never seen this side of his father before. He spoke very little of the early days, of his childhood. Now he understood why. So much sorrow and hardship. Who would want to relive that?

Silence.

A hornbill alighted on a leaf-barren branch somewhere in the baobab's canopy and noisily relayed his message of annoyance at their presence. As the bird flew off towards the east, Baba continued his story.

"I didn't know the world before Iworo. All I knew was the world around me. We grew up together, the world and me. What to most of the survivors was a harsh, foreign, and unpredictable land, to me was normal. More than half of the people who survived their time in the caves died when they came back up to the world above. Nothing was familiar to them. They were afraid, disoriented, heartbroken, and lacked the will to live.

"As any growing boy does, I spent all of my time running around, feeling the earth and understanding her more with each passing day. Others started to look to me for guidance. Which plants were poisoned? Where could we find clean water? How could we tell if an animal had been contaminated? You could say that I learned Earth's language and that I read new and fantastic adventures in her pages every day."

EnKare made another goat meat chapati wrap for himself and tore off a lion-sized bite. Glancing down, he noticed two perfectly round, moist eyes peering up at him.

"Don't worry, I'm gonna share it with you," he promised as he pulled off a piece of chapati and handed it to Pilipili.

He savored the image of Baba as a young man, living in the mouth of a cave, running wild in a fledgling world at the dawn of a new era. He was starting to understand the significance of his father's Lion Name. *Earth*!

"Is there more to the story, Baba?"

"One day I was exploring the caves, the very same ones that sustained us through the dark winter. I heard a noise coming from deep inside. When I reached the back of the tunnel, I discovered a juvenile white rhino cowering behind a boulder. Lured in by the salty rocks to lick, she'd become lost in the labyrinth and was starving to death.

"I tried to get her to follow me out, but she was too frightened to move. So, every day I brought fresh grasses and placed them close by. Then I sat down and waited for her to eat.

"One day she decided that I wasn't going to hurt her. There was no other food in the cave that day, other than the bunch of grass that I held in my hand. So as I walked away, she followed me all the way out, straining her lips to nibble on the food which I kept just out of her reach. When we made it back to the surface, she discovered the reward that I had left for her: a pile of fresh grasses a mountain high. At that moment we became the best of friends. We became family."

EnKulupuoni shot a high-pitched whistled through his tongue and lips. There was a crashing deep within the elephant grass, then Oldoinyo popped her head into the clearing and pranced up to them.

Pilipili greeted the monster by leaping onto her back, circling around to find just the right sit-spot, then plopping down on the base of her neck.

It was hard for EnKare to imagine that Oldoinyo was ever small. She lowered her head until her eyes were level with Baba's. He fed her a nut and tenderly stroked the side of her face. "We're about the same age, this one and me. A pair of old warthog farts."

EnKare laughed. Baba didn't usually use such language.

Pilipili jumped to the ground as Oldoinyo tootled off around the tree, nibbling on leaves and fresh shoots.

EnKulupuoni continued his tale. "She wasn't always the size of a mountain, you know. When I found her she only came up to my waist. We grew up together. I brought her to the best eating grounds, showed her where it was safe to bathe, and protected her at night by bringing her in to the boma with the goats and cattle.

"After a while it was I who was following her through the bush. We discovered new plants and animals at every turn, many of whom were injured or sick. In Oldoinyo's presence they were unafraid of me and would let me care for them, washing and wrapping wounds, bringing them food. One day, I realized that it was not by accident that we kept encountering the injured and sick. Oldoinyo was leading me to them intentionally.

"As I became familiar with, and befriended, more and more of our brothers and sisters, I came to understand that both human and animal people had brought with them certain memories of each other from the time before Iworo. They were afraid of each other. I did not live in that distant world, so I did not witness the imbalance. I couldn't imagine any being capable of bringing Iworo to an entire planet. Humans had betrayed the natural rhythms of life, had learned to fear and distrust each other, and so all beings feared and distrusted them. Oldoinyo helped me to understand this, and together we worked to mend the damage, to heal the wounds of the world. We have so much to thank Oldoinyo for."

"So, Baba, you were an ambassador between humans and the world, right?"

"That's not how I saw it back then, Son. I was just a boy, acting like boys do, interacting with the world around me. As the years passed I knew that I was supposed to be doing something significant in order to earn my Lion Name. But I was busy running around with Oldoinyo and getting into trouble. I couldn't have cared less about some ceremony, and I was happy with the name I had. So I pretty much ignored the whole thing.

"Until one day I couldn't ignore it any longer. On that day my mother and sister told me to gather my weapons, including that simi," he pointed at the short sword lying on the shuka beside EnKare, "and to follow them. They led me to a small clearing in the brush, and waiting there for us were the other six members of our small clan.

"We sat in a circle. Everyone was so serious. A tall, beautifully beaded ingri, one that had been brought into the caves from the time before Iworo, was filled with goat's milk and cow blood, and then passed around the circle.

"My mother was crying. She said that her son, the boy known as ElKikau, was dead, and that in his place was a man who would be known as EnKulupuoni, Earth. She said that I had become one with Earth. That Earth revealed herself to our people through me.

"I didn't understand what she meant. I cried that day, with my mother, for I knew that my time as a carefree boy was over, and I didn't feel ready to be a man. It was that same day, as we ate the roasted meat of a goat that was slaughtered for the ceremony, that mother told me about the Heart Path."

When his father said the words, a shiver ran down EnKare's spine. "What do you mean by Heart Path, Baba?"

"When all twenty one of her strings are perfectly tuned, the kora produces a sound so beautiful that new worlds are birthed in the hearts of those listening. Each kora is unique, its body parts coming from different woods in the forest, its strings from the intestines of different animals. Every kora resonates differently from the next. A person is like the kora— when perfectly in tune and resonating with the world around him, he is walking his Heart Path."

"So, is it basically a person's purpose? Their reason for being here?"

"In a way, yes. Perhaps. We'll come back to this conversation again." Rising to his feet, Baba gathered up the breakfast items and put them in his shoulder bag. "And don't worry so much about your Lion Name, son. It will find you when it is ready. Come. Let's go check on the herd. Make sure those cheetahs didn't decide to circle back."

He watched as his father walked off towards the elephant grass, then he dusted off his shuka and draped it over one shoulder, gathered up his weapons and called to Pilipili, who was napping in the lower branches overhead.

Heart Path? Seriously?

Seeing that his father had gone one way, EnKare took off in the opposite direction, figuring he'd meet up with them on the other side, and pick up any stray cattle along the way.

Following a game trail, he strolled for a while, ruminating on the mystery of the Heart Path. How could a person tune themselves? How would a person even know when they were in tune or if they were out of tune to begin with?

The trail led through a dense patch of jungle, twisting and turning its way through the maze of tangled tree trunks. The canopy overhead blocked out much of the light. The air was cool and the soft, moist soil under his feet was a welcome change. His father's words, *it will find you when it is ready*, played over and over in his mind. *But how can that be? And what if it doesn't find me until I'm an old man?*

A shaft of light illuminated the forest ahead, and he could see the path leading through a break in the tree line.

He stepped into the clearing and paused in the sunlight, thankful for the warmth. He was about to move on when his stomach dropped to the floor of his pelvis, and the hair on his forearms stood on end.

Turning his head, he found himself looking into the eyes of chui nyeusi, a black leopard.

He felt no fear, no urge to run away or to attack, though he knew this cat could snap his neck in an instant.

A calm energy came over him and he remained motionless, staring into the malachite eyes.

His peripheral vision dropped away, along with time, matter, thoughts, feelings—nothing remained of the world...

But the cat.

Coarse whiskers pulsed with her breath.

The faint shadow of spots hid beneath her shimmering, obsidian coat. Heavily muscled shoulder blades rested together on her back, rising gently with each breath.

Then she turned, walked across the clearing, and merged with the darkness.

EnKare traversed the open field to the spot where the cat had been, and discovered a smaller trail running parallel to the one he had been on.

He looked down the path, in the direction chui nyeusi had taken. Then, following in her footprints, he crossed the clearing and disappeared into the shadows of the forest.

Dominion

S he took a deep breath in through her nose, and beckoned her senses to return. The ground felt cold, hard, and damp.

Not my bearskin bed.

Wiping the sleep from her eyes, a wave of confusion washed over her as she focused on the surroundings. A moment ago she had been eager to tell Uŋčí about the horrible dream she had.

Bronx?

The straw-haired girl?

The worm attack!

This is no dream.

"OoooWeee, looky looky yer Royal Bossness. Lookn' like she done napin'. On yer feet, skeetvomit!"

That voice.

Her heart sank. A stabbing pain in her lower leg confirmed this was no dream. But how had she survived the worm? She remembered falling to the ground and the straw-haired girl flying out of her arms. She remembered getting pulled down into the worm hole and looking up and seeing a dark shadow over the entrance. Bronx! Had he saved her life? If so, why? And the straw-haired girl? What had happened to her?

Looking around, they appeared to be inside a cave or tunnel. Thick vegetation grew over the entrance, and the quality of light on the other side told her that night had come. The ground beneath her sloped off into the darkness at an awkward angle. Illuminated by the flickering flames of torch light, ribbons of red, orange, and yellow danced over the smooth, curving surface of the walls and ceiling.

She took a quick inventory of the captives. One of the older girls and the straw-haired girl were missing.

The worms must have got them.

Bronx's deep voice echoed through the tunnel."Hobbles come off. We make better time. Anyone who runs…dies."

Her wrists were tied behind her back again but her ankles were free. She rocked herself onto her knees and then to her feet. The pain in her calf was severe, but she could walk.

Fritz flailed around the group, rounding up the captives and corralling them into the center of the rogues. Once they were all clustered together, she noticed the straw-haired girl standing close by and sighed in relief. She reached up and tapped the girl on the shoulder.

"Do dat agin, an I'll eat dat finga." Fritz's raspy voice cackled from just behind her. Hot, foul smelling breath wafted across her neck and filled her nostrils.

She retracted her hand. The little girl glanced back and smiled weakly. Wakíŋyaŋ's eyes lit up, and she smiled back. This was a good omen.

"Let's move n' groove, wormbait!" Fritz screeched.

They trudged along, following Bronx as he guided them through the maze of tunnel splits and intersections with practiced skill. Clearly, this was his territory and he knew every inch of it, like she knew the woods around her village.

In places, the walls were fractured, forcing them to navigate through piles of boulders and rubble before reconnecting with the tunnel on the other side. In more than one instance, the floor simply wasn't there, and they had to maneuver over narrow bridges made from scraps of metal and wood lashed together. One missed step, and the abyss would swallow her forever.

In some sections, the tunnel floors were lined with iron logs that were spaced the same distance apart and parallel to each other. Uŋčí, who had lived in the time before the burn, called them *tracks*. This made no sense to Wakíŋyaŋ. They looked nothing like tracks, and she had studied the markings left by countless creatures. Her tribe had followed metal tracks like these as they migrated across Khéya Wíta, Turtle Island, but she had never seen them running underground before.

The air was cold and damp, and water trickled through fissures in the tunnel walls and ceiling. When they stopped to rest, a rogue filled a transparent gourd with this water and handed it around to the captives.

"Give my share to her. She needs it," Wakíŋyaŋ told the rogue, lifting her chin in the direction of the straw-haired girl. The child was slowly reanimating, but still looked lethargic and sickly.

After walking through an endless labyrinth of tunnels, they came out into a cavernous room. Torches lined the walls and there were side rooms and smaller passageways leading off of the main hall, some going up and others leading down, deeper into the earth. People moved about, carrying water, fire wood, and bundles of food. Guards were posted at each entrance and held weapons crafted out of metallic debris.

Someone called out, "They're back, they're back!" and in moments they were surrounded by tunnel people. They were dirty, with ratty hair and smoke stained faces, wearing bits and pieces of torn clothing made from salvaged city junk.

Everyone was reaching out, straining through the crowd to touch Bronx, which they did with bent heads and closed eyes. A curious show of prostration, she thought to herself.

Once they had touched their leader they turned to the captives, grabbing at their hair and touching their clothes. A woman inspected one of the little boys, prying his eyelids apart and yanking open his jaw to check his teeth. She gave Bronx a look of approval and then moved on to one of the older girls, inspecting her in the same manner.

Are we objects to them? To be scanned for defects? Appraised? Bought and sold, like people did before the burn?

"Nuf a dat lolli gagin'. Ya had yer fun, na git," Fritz screeched over the crowd, shooing them away with a flutter of his arms. "Hey Xanthan, mind doin' da honors a portin' dees heeps a skeetvomit to their new domisilioes?"

A tall, skinny man, with a permanent scowl smeared across his face, lumbered towards them. His beady eyes peered out through narrowly slatted lids nestled at the back of sunken sockets. The coarse, black wool of his eyebrows resembled hairy caterpillars crawling across a bulbous, slab of stone. His limbs were so long and thin, and his spine so curved, that his bony knuckles brushed against the ground with each pendulous swing of his arms.

Xanthan raised a knotted-oak-burl of a hand, pointed at an opening on the far side of the hall and said, "Move," in a monotone voice.

As they followed the tree-man out of the main hall, she glanced over at the twins. They appeared more alone and vulnerable than ever. She positioned herself close to their small, shaking bodies, and immediately their muscles relaxed and the tremors diminished.

Passing through the arched tunnel and along a bleak, smoke-blackened corridor, the five captives walked silently behind their arboreal guide. The passage opened up into another immense room, similar to the first. Tracks ran through the middle in recessed trenches with several wooden pole-bridges spanning the gap. Rustic trash and debris homes lined the walls and people came and went from low doorways.

How can they live down here with so little light? Without the sun, I think I'd go mad.

There were two places where the ceiling had caved in, one on either end of the great room. Iron rods had been placed crisscross over the openings, and narrow beams of dim light penetrated to the floor below. Early morning. It had taken them half the night to walk the tunnels.

They crossed a bridge, passed through an archway, and descended a metal stairway. At the bottom, the stairs joined another corridor, and at the end of that three guards stood before a heavy, wooden door.

"What goodies did ya bring fer us taday, oh bringer of the damned?" said one of the guards, chuckling as he punched one of the other guards in the arm.

"Hey! Quitit, Taco," the second guard whined in a high-pitched, nasal voice. "How many times I gotta tell ya, not ma right arm!"

"You're such a dimwit, Pills. That's not your right arm," said the third guard, with a hint of superiority in his voice.

"Shut it, Geiger! You wouldn't know yer right arm from yer… not-right arm if I chopped it off and handed it to you," said Pills defensively.

Geiger lifted an eyebrow. "I believe the word you are looking for is *left*, my friend. You would chop off my *left* arm and hand it to me." Arrogance dripped from his mouth.

"Don't ya mean you'd only have one arm left if Pills chopped off yer not-right arm and handed it to ya? And are we talking about chopping off your arm or your hand? I'm confused now," interjected Taco.

Pills snapped, "Stay out of it, Taco. I'm'a shut him down once-an-fer-all on this one."

"Excuse me!" A deep, monotone voice cut through the banter. "I hate to interrupt, but I've got wormbait to deliver."

"Now now there, big fella, calm down." Taco pulled back the series of bolts and pushed the door inward.

"Yer the one freakin' out, Taco," Pills whined.

"Am not," Taco sputtered. Then beckoning to Xanthan and the captives with a sweep of his outstretched arm, "Please, be our guests."

Wakíŋyaŋ followed the others through the doorway into a smaller version of the caverns they had already come through. A single torch, burning just inside the entrance, cast a low glow through the dingy darkness. Tracks ran through the middle of the room, and sitting on top of them was a series of interconnected cabins, the last of which was partially crushed under a mound of rubble. The dim flicker of torch light illuminated the inside of several of the railcars, from which shadows emerged and moved towards them.

As the figures drew closer she could make out their faces. There were four in all, two around her age and two elders. The elder woman motioned with her hand and said, "Come," in a hushed, raspy voice, and turned back towards the railcars.

"Not you."

She felt a cold, bony limb grip her shoulder.

Gesturing towards the doorway, the tree-man grunted, "You come with me."

"Looks like Bronx found himself a new toy. Good luck, sweet heart," one of the guards heckled as she passed by.

She gave him a nasty look, then followed Xanthan back the way they had come, up the metallic stairway, passed the residence cavern, and into the great hall where they had first arrived. She surveyed the surroundings carefully as they walked, looking for possible escape routes. They were somewhere deep underground. As far as she could tell, the only way in or out had a guard posted in front of it.

Anger, disgust, curiosity, and pity marked the faces that stared at her as she passed.

They exited the great hall into an arched passage. It was lined with burning torches, and there were closed doors spaced along the walls. At the end of the corridor were two guards who motioned for them to stop.

"What ya got there?"

"Bossman asked for this one to be delivered."

The guard looked at Wakíŋyaŋ, his eyes crawling all over her skin. She stood firm and indifferent. *Never let your enemy see you sweat.*

"I can see why," the guard said, wiping some spittle from the side of his mouth and making a low humming sound. Then he motioned them on with a wave of his hand.

Beyond the guards the corridor turned sharply, then revealed a metallic stairway stretching upward into the darkness.

The hair on the back of her neck stood on end as they ascended. Every muscle in her body stretched taut, and tiny beads of sweat clung to her upper lip. She could feel the adrenaline creeping into her bloodstream.

Three slow breaths.

They stopped at the top in front of a large door. Xanthan curled his fingers into a burl and hammered out a pattern on the old wooden panels. The sound ricocheted off the walls, echoing back from the bottom of the stairway, escalating into a cacophony of thunder, then trailing off to a distant rumble.

Deadbolts grated and the door swung open. A broad, bony hand shoved the middle of her back. She stumbled forward, then looked around apprehensively.

Two guards positioned at the door.

Curving walls. Round room.

Metal bars crossed over a gaping hole in the ceiling where diffused sunlight streamed in. Rubble from the hole above had been stacked into a circular wall on the floor beneath the hole, and a bonfire raged inside its circumference. The flames lapped at the opening, up through the metal bars, seeking oxygen from the open sky above.

For a moment she just stared. It had only been a few days since her abduction, but it felt like an eternity since she'd seen sister sky. At home she spent each day wandering under her, and said goodnight to the stars before drifting to sleep. To Wakíŋyaŋ, the sky was an old, familiar friend. She would read the sky, like the people of old would read books, and she would tell her everything she needed to know: the coming of a storm, the onset of an early winter, the location of a herd of deer.

Bronx's thunderous voice shattered her stream of thoughts. "Come. Let me see you."

The giant stepped out from the other side of the fire and stomped towards her. The two guards hastily exited the room through a side door.

"Don't be afraid," said the behemoth as he advanced.

She backed away until she was pressed up against a wall, never taking her eyes off the giant. *One of these doors has to lead out of here.* Adrenaline flooded her bloodstream, and her heart pounded against her rib cage.

As she moved, the wall behind her gave way, and she cautiously backed into the opening. With a quick glance she determined that this was just another room, not a way out. There were bearskins stretched over the floor with a torch burning on either side.

Bedroom!

The realization struck her with the force of a bear paw hitting her in the chest. The breath drained from her lungs and her hands turned cold and moist. Now she understood why she had been sent to him and what he intended to do with her.

She turned to make a quick exit from the room.

Too late.

Bronx's silhouette filled the doorway.

Her muscles activated and she dropped into a combat stance, legs straddled and bent at the knees, arms extended and ready to fight. She assessed the room for potential weapons, but besides using one of the torches as a staff, her search came up short.

Then she saw it.

The firelight streaming in through the doorway reflected off something shiny on the giant's outer thigh.

Knife!

With a hard swallow, she pushed the irony to the pit of her stomach, where it soured like spoiled milk. The only weapon around was strapped to the leg of the very reason she needed a weapon in the first place.

She would have to face her fear...by embracing it.

Bronx stepped through the opening, advancing with power and determination in his stride.

She held her ground.

In every situation there was the right moment to take action. A moment too soon or too late would determine her fate.

He reached his arms out to grab her by the shoulders.

She had been connected to her Spirit Animal for as long as she could remember. When she was an infant, Uŋčí had made her a black jaguar toy from a piece of bear fur cut to shape, sewn up, and stuffed with dried grass, two jade stones for eyes. Since that time the great cat had become her closest ally, teaching her to stalk her prey and to become invisible to the other creatures of the forest. They danced the story of life and death together on many hunts—though always with Wakíŋyaŋ as the hunter, not the hunted.

She felt the whiskers around her muzzle bristle and twitch, her razor sharp claws extending outward, shoulder blades drawing together and lifting off her back.

In the space between the wingbeats of a hummingbird, a calculation passed through her mind.

Then she moved

Fluid as water

Precise as lightning

Dropping below his swinging arms, she planted her hands on the floor beside his forward foot and cartwheeled along the side of his body.

Completing her rotation, she pushed off the ground, and as her torso rose passed the giant's leg, she drew the concealed blade from its sheath on his thigh.

The moment her feet hit the ground she turned towards the door to make a run for it, but the guards had already stepped through the opening, weapons drawn.

Trapped!

Wingbeat

Calculation

Moving—she bared her teeth and let out a roar. Then she dropped to one knee, gripped the leather handle of the knife with both hands, and pressed the blade's jagged edge against the skin of her neck.

She closed her eyes tight.

Not this, nor any other creature, will ever lay their hands on my living flesh.

Then she pushed the blade into her skin.

Mrs. Msoke

Her home was a modest, thatched-roof hut on the north side of town near the river. From her living room she taught social studies and the art of language. Mrs. Msoke's presence in the village could be compared to the invisible force that compels the ocean tides; subtle, unobtrusive, yet steadfast and undeniable. She represented a copula, a bridge between the past and present. Her knowledge of the languages, cultures, politics, and ways of humanity, in the time before Iworo, made her a living encyclopedia in EnKare's eyes.

"Today, class, we will be discussing the concept of slavery and reviewing how it is addressed in our African Charter. We must not let the history of our planet fade away in the ashes of Iworo. We can use the knowledge of what we have done in the past to guide us towards a sustainable, beneficial existence on earth."

EnKare was fascinated by stories of the days before Iworo, and her passion for the subject always made for an entertaining experience. She loved to dress up in the clothing and apparel of the time periods she taught, and made all her own costumes to match.

Today she was wearing off-white hemp fabric, fashioned into a long, plain dress with short sleeves, and a head wrap. The fabric was coarse and uncomfortable looking. She said it was an example of the clothing of the African slaves in what used to be the Americas. This posed a stark contrast to the bright colors and intricate patterns that people wore around the village.

"What is slavery?" she asked the class.

Jioba shot his hand up in the air and bounced up and down on his rear end until she called on him.

"How old are you again, Jimmy?" EnKare teased under his breath.

"Yes, Jioba, what can you tell us about slavery?"

As Jioba rose to his feet, EnKare put his hands over his face and shook his head. *Oh no. Here we go again.* They were taught that the sun was the center of their solar system, but in Jioba's world, Jioba occupied that position.

"My grandmother told me that a slave is a person who was stolen from Africa by the Portuguese, British, Dutch, Spanish, and Italians, and then sold to someone in the Americas to do labor for them by force, without remuneration. They were the property of their owners, like you and I might own a...shovel. Here's a little tune on the subject from a good friend of mine, Mr. Bob Marley. The song is Buffalo Soldier. If you know the words feel free to sing with me." He clapped his hands and did a little dance while the class clapped along.

When the verse was over he took a deep bow and plopped back down on the floor.

"Nice one," EnKare whispered. "I don't think I've heard it before."

"Chabalangus, bwana! It's a classic!"

Even though he acted embarrassed, he actually liked hearing his friend sing. Only Jioba could turn a lightning storm into a lighthearted game of chicken, a deadly flood into a casual rafting trip, the subject of slavery into a foot-stomping sing along. He might play around, but on the subject of slavery he spoke from a place of deep personal, ancestral knowledge. Jioba came from the Bube tribe, and in the time before Iworo many thousands of his people were sold into slavery in the Americas.

"Thank you for that delightful performance, Jioba. Yes, what you speak of is known as the Transatlantic Slave Trade. Slavery is the forced servitude of any individual by another. So, was slavery confined to just the TST? And did it only involve Africans and Europeans?"

A girl at the back of the group, named Rose, joined the conversation. "Actually, the Romans had slaves, didn't they?"

Then everyone in the class started chiming in.

"Ya, and the Greeks, they had slaves."

"And the Persians, don't forget about the Persians."

"The Moors..."

"And the Egyptian Pharaohs, they had lots of slaves. And they were Africans. Wait a minute, Africans owned slaves too?

Mrs. Msoke raised a hand to quiet the class. "OK, hold on a minute, we're all talking at once. First of all, yes. All of the major civilizations practiced slavery. All that you mentioned, and many, many more. But it wasn't just an empire thing. Smaller groups, like tribes, bands, and clans practiced it too. In the time before Iworo, slavery had existed among most groups and civilizations of people all over the planet, on every continent, north and south of the equator."

"But not us Africans, right? I mean, other than the Moors and the Pharaohs."

"That's a good question, Jomo. It might surprise you, class, that before Iworo, from the northern coasts to the very southern tip of our continent nation, we Africans bought, sold, and enslaved *each other*."

The class went silent.

EnKare looked at Jioba, who was staring at Mrs. Msoke in disbelief. She paused long enough to let her words sink in, then added, "The first people to profit from the Transatlantic Slave Trade were the African Chiefs and warlords who captured men, women, and children from rival tribes and sold them to the Europeans. It was a convenient way to get rid of the competition. Many African families became incredibly powerful, and astronomically wealthy, selling each other to the highest bidder. Supply and demand. Like a poisonous snake, eating it's own tail.

This was a sobering revelation, and the class remained silent.

Then EnKare raised his hand. "Mrs. Msoke, I thought...I mean I didn't know that we..." He was having a hard time accepting it.

"I know, EnKare. The horror of that distant time is almost impossible to comprehend. It's no wonder that age ended in Iworo."

Rose asked, "Mrs. Msoke, would it be reasonable to say that Iworo cleansed the world of slavery?"

"That remains to be seen, Rose. It is certainly fair to say that a global culture of slavery, greed, and racism, played a significant role in a series of historical events that culminated in an event that came very close to terminating human life on earth. As far as we know, only Africa has a radiation-free environment suitable for people to live in. The nuclear nations of the world blew each other to dust and ashes. Thanks to the Wenye Hekima, all forms of slavery and servitude have been banished from our lands. That includes physical, emotional, and financial slavery, and it's important that you understand the difference. We don't use money, have no banks, debt, or interest, and we practice a collective ownership of resources, because financial slavery is as destructive as emotional and physical slavery. It would appear that we have been given the opportunity to learn from the mistakes of our ancestors. The question is…will we?"

"Mrs. Msoke, as far as we know the European nations no longer exist, so why do we continue to learn and speak their languages?"

"That's a good question, Kimu. It's precisely because they may not exist as a people that we are compelled to preserve whatever parts of their culture we can, for humanity's sake. It is also why we learn and use both the metric and the imperial units of measurement, along with all of our own ancient systems. When there's only one way to describe something, we lose some of the spicy variety that makes life so magnificent. Just imagine, one day English, French, Portuguese, Castillano, and the other languages we learn in school, may once again be spoken around the world, and it would be thanks to our efforts to preserve them. Like I always say, class, humans and their cultures are like wild flowers; the more colors there are, the more beautiful the world is."

The Proposal

As they strolled along the shops, something Mrs. Msoke said in class that morning bothered EnKare.

"Hey, Jimmy, do you think it's true, what Mrs. Msoke said about Africa maybe being the only place left on earth with humans?"

"Don't know, bwana. There might be mutant humans out there!"

"Monsters!"

"Half-human-half-rock-people!"

"Hideous fish-human-plant creatures that eat radiation soup for breakfast!"

Jioba sighed. "Ya, bwana. If any humans survived Iworo out there, they aren't human any longer. Tu Sabes? Hey, you wanna go get an ice coco and look at girls down on the beach?"

EnKare looked at his friend suspiciously. "Sounds good, bwana. Who knows, maybe we'll run into Mandaha."

Jioba blew a puff of air through his pursed lips and shrugged his shoulders in an effort to look uninterested. "Mandaha is," he paused for a moment and his eyes glassed over as he stared out over the ocean. Then he snapped out of it and continued, "Mandaha is OK. But there are plenty of other fish for me, in the sea, I've got to be free, you see…" Then transitioning smoothly, he crooned the mushy lyrics to another pre-Iworo love song from his endless mental archive.

EnKare joined in on the chorus, and just like that, they danced and sang their way down the reed-matted sidewalk to Mama Sana's ice coco shop.

As they passed Concha's Café, Señora Concha spun out of the doorway, swinging her hips, arms over her head and beaded hair braids flying in her face. EnKare exchanged hip bumps with the robust, ocean appareled woman, which nearly sent him flying off the sidewalk, before continuing on their way.

Suddenly, Jioba tripped on some invisible obstacle and fell flat on his face.

This can only mean one thing.

Looking up, sure enough, there was Mandaha at the end of the block, walking towards them.

Jioba sprang to his feet and carried on walking as though nothing had happened.

"You OK, bwana?" EnKare yelled ahead to his friend.

Looking back over his shoulder, Jioba responded, "Yes. Of course. What makes you think I'm not OK?"

"Hey, Jimmy, watch out for that..."

Jioba walked straight into an old metal post.

"...Sign."

Stunned, he staggered backwards and fell onto his rear end. A moment later Mandaha walked up to them.

"Are you OK, Jimmy? I swear, bwana, you are one seriously accident prone boy." She grabbed on to Jioba's arms and helped him to his feet. "Did you not see the sign post? Right in front of you?"

The three of them looked at the sign, which read, "CAUTION! ELEPHANT CROSSING!" in bold red print.

Mandaha ogled, "Hey, didn't you put that sign up, Jimmy?"

They all burst into laughter. Jioba had painted the sign himself as part of an elephant awareness campaign.

Laughter contained, they sat down on the bench in front of Mr. Mtube's blacksmith shop, with Jioba in the middle.

"You where, so, going Mandaha, are?" Jioba's words creeper-vined out of his mouth in a tangled mess.

"I'm heading up to Ms. Rita's shop to help her arrange flowers for a wedding."

Staring straight ahead, little beads of sweat started to from on Jioba's upper lip. "Wedding. Good."

"What are you up to?"

"We're drinking Accra, then sailing to ice coco," Jioba attempted.

"How hard did you hit your head, bwana? Here, let me take a look." Mandaha ran her fingers gently over the growing lump on Jioba's forehead as he sat motionless, staring wide-eyed at the sea. "You need to be more careful with this pretty face of yours. Hey, EnKare, Mama said we're having dinner at sundown tonight, and she wants you to be there. Why don't you join us, Jioba?" Then Mandaha stood up, said her goodbyes and continued on her way.

As she walked away, Jioba looked on with a beatific smile plastered across his face, clearly drifting off on some cloud.

"Jimmy? Hey, Jimmy? JIOBA!"

"Hm?"

"So. Are you ready to get that ice coco and go look at girls down on the beach?"

Then, as though snapping out of a hypnotic trance, Jioba chortled, "Chabalangus, bwana, I was born ready."

They stood up, Jioba steadied himself for a moment, then arms slung around the other's shoulders, they trotted off down the sidewalk.

When they arrived at Mama Sana's place, two strangers were stepping out of the doorway. He instantly recognized the two men who had been looking for a ride to Accra. Jioba shot him a look that said, *told you they'd be back.*

"Gentlemen, we were hoping we might find you here. If you recall, my name is Tomobo, and this is my colleague, Jafra. We spoke the other day about employing your services to take us to Accra. Do you remember?"

Jioba got a puzzled look on his face, turned and winked at EnKare, then, in a confused voice, exclaimed, "Services? To Accra?" Then, as though struck by a returning memory, "Ah yes, of course, the gentlemen looking for passage to Accra before the next full moon. How could I forget. You'll have to excuse me, I get so many inquiries. Can't keep them all straight. You know how it is."

Tomobo extended a hand in greeting, and said, "We would like to make you a proposition."

They all exchanged greetings, ordered their ice cocos and walked out onto the beach. It was mid afternoon, and the sun peeked intermittently through the moisture laden clouds that lingered overhead. The air smelled of hyacinth and sweet seaweed. EnKare wore his shuka around his waist and went without shoes or a shirt, while Jioba wore nothing more than his hemp shorts. In contrast, Tomobo and Jafra wore slacks, off-white tunics, and nice leather sandals.

Jioba started, "Don't be afraid to get your feet wet, gentlemen. Until the rain comes, it's gonna stay as hot as a Swedish sauna out here."

And how on earth would you know what a Swedish sauna feels like?

The boys were already calf deep in the clear turquoise water when Tomobo and Jafra rolled up their pant legs to join them. They meandered slowly down the beach discussing the business at hand.

There was a hint of eagerness in Jioba's voice. "So what is this proposal of yours?"

"You provide safe passage to Accra, getting us there before the next full moon, all of the provisions, food, and water for the duration of the journey."

"And what do we get in return?"

There he goes saying "we" again, as though there is more than just him involved here. He better not be talking about me.

"What you get is a place to stay at my Auntie Beeke's house, in the center of Accra, with all the good food and drink you need for two days…" Jioba scrunched up his nose in disapproval, "ah, three days, while you prepare for the return journey. And then all the provisions of food and water for your return trip. Plus your pick of new materials for your boat, sails, oil stains, wood conditioners, you name it."

Jioba's nose began to scrunch again.

"And I was thinking that if you succeed in getting us there with time to spare, I'll personally show you around Aye Market."

Jioba stopped on the spot, extended his hand, and, with a serious expression on his face, blurted, "Gentlemen, we accept your proposal." Then, gesturing towards EnKare, he added, "My shipmate and I would be honored to take you to Accra. We leave the day after tomorrow!"

Before EnKare could get a word in edgewise, Jioba and the two men waded off down the beach, busily discussing trip details and logistics. He plopped down in the shallow water, looked out past the waves, and sipped on his not-so-ice coco.

Chabalangus!

This time my friend, you're on your own. I'd rather fall into a tangled mass of sleeping green mambas, then spend even one night at sea on that floating bathtub of yours.

Wit'é

She was so frail. Barely more than skin stretched over a light frame of bones and muscle. Dotted freckles splashed across her nose like the first stars peeking through the sky at dusk. She lay snuggled up beside Wakíŋyaŋ, head resting on her chest and arms wrapped tightly around her ribcage. They had found an empty space in one of the railcars and cleared out a spot to bed down. As they lay there looking up at the faint torchlight dancing on the ceiling, Wakíŋyaŋ recounted the story of what had happened in the monster's lair.

"Were you afraid I wouldn't come back?" she asked, looking at the little girl's frightened face. She waited a moment for a response. The child hadn't uttered a single word since their meeting on the beach, right before the worm attack. But her eyes said *yes.*

"Would you like me to tell you the rest of the story of what happened in there?"

The little girl gave her a squeeze and another affirmative look.

"I snatched a knife that Bronx had strapped to his leg and turned to run out the door, when I saw that two guards were blocking my escape. Bronx came at me." She clenched her jaw and dropped the tone of her voice. "I knew I was outnumbered, but I wasn't going to let that man lay one finger on me. So I closed my eyes and pressed the knife to my neck, ready to take my own life, if it came to it."

The little girl looked up with fear and concern in her eyes.

"Don't worry, I'm still here, little one," she consoled. "And then the strangest thing happened. He said..." She paused and took a deep breath in, recalling the intensity of the moment. Then, in her best Bronx impersonation, "please... don't!"

The straw-haired girl giggled and beamed at her with a sparkle of delight.

Wakíŋyaŋ recalled the urgency in his tone when he said the word *please.*

"I opened my eyes to see what was happening and found the doorway unguarded. Bronx was slowly backing away from me. Come here, little one. We have to do something about this hair." She sat up and leaned her back against the wall of the cabin. The little girl sat cross-legged in Wakíŋyaŋ's lap. As she ran her fingers through the golden locks, pulling apart one ratty knot at a time, she could feel Uŋčí combing out her own hair, sitting by the fire in the center of her small house, in her village by the sea.

"You must be wondering if I stabbed him with his own knife, or if I ran out the door and made a miraculous escape? Neither. He said," again in her Bronx voice, "please put down the knife." This made the little girl giggle again. "Then he promised me that if I spared my own life he would never try to...lay a hand on me again. Then they brought me back down here, back to you."

She was still perplexed by the whole affair. *Why hadn't he let me kill myself? And why did he let me go? Does Bronx have...feelings for me?* This was even more frightening than the thought of being violated by the giant. She pushed the thought from her mind.

The little girl turned around and hugged her tightly.

"What do I call you, little one? Do you have a name?"

No response.

"Well, until you tell me what your name is, would you like me to give you one?"

Freckles stretched across the girl's face, eyes twinkling their approval.

She paused for a moment, allowing her mind to go blank, searching for a feeling in her gut. "You will be called... Wit'é. In my language it means New Moon. We can call you Wí for short. Do you like it?"

The child looked up at her, face glowing, tears welling. She nodded and then buried her face in Wakíŋyaŋ's chest and fell asleep.

Yuška

She didn't know exactly what fate awaited Wit'é and the rest of the slaves, but what she did know is that they had to escape before something terrible happened.

Carefully and quietly, she moved the child's sleeping body onto the floor and stepped out of the railcar. With everyone asleep, this was a good time to explore. If this dungeon was to be her new home, she wanted to know everything about it: every fallen rock, every hiding place.

Every possible escape route.

She walked into the center of the room and stood motionless for a few moments, allowing her eyes to scan her surrounds in the dim lighting. She looked up at the ceiling, which towered overhead and well beyond reach. It was relatively nondescript, except for a faint glow coming from a spot off in one corner.

She walked over to the source of light and discovered that part of the ceiling had fallen in. The hole had been barred with iron rods, so escaping that way was out of the question.

All our air comes in through that hole.

Positioned directly below the hole was a large metal pot, which was catching water that percolated down from the outside world. The rhythmic dripping into the metallic pool echoed faintly off the cavern walls.

If this is how we collect all our drinking water, we'll have to ration it carefully, now there are so many more of us.

She walked over to the only apparent door, the one with the three heyókȟa guarding it. From there she made her way round to one side, following the wall. Aside from the occasional rusting metal frame or broken tile, the wall stretched on with no doorways or side rooms.

At the far end of the cavern, behind the last connected railcar, a narrow footbridge spanned the gap that the tracks ran through. She crossed the bridge and headed towards the far corner. As she approached, the stench of human feces and urine became overwhelming. The floor dropped away into the darkness, and judging from the smell rising from the hole, she had just found the communal pit toilet. The stench was not something she was accustomed to. Back home, they composted all their waste and used it in the vegetable gardens and orchards as fertilizer. It never smelled like this!

Even if there was a way out at the bottom of that hole, who knows how many arm lengths of human waste one would have to swim through to reach it? She tried to imagine how bad things would need to get before she'd wade through that filth in order to find freedom. To her surprise, it wasn't hard to do.

Hopefully it won't come to that!

She backed away and kept moving along the wall. Here she found a few more signs of life. There was a fire pit made out of stones and pieces of rubble with a few coals still glowing in it. Around the pit, a kitchen and dining area had been set up, with a few pots and pans, a metal grill made from scraps of iron rod, a few wooden spoons, and a stack of plates and bowls molded from clay and sand. Nothing that resembled a knife, of course.

She left the kitchen area and continued along the back wall until she arrived at the place where the railcars disappeared into the rubble of the collapsed ceiling. It was an eerie sight, like the earth was devouring a large, metallic worm. No torchlight came from inside the enclosure, so she approached and peered in through the half open doorway. No one had chosen to bed down here, and she quickly understood why. A rank odor of bat guano permeated the air.

That's odd. The bats must be coming in through the hole in the ceiling at the other end of the dungeon. Or is there another entrance?

She stepped into the cabin and looked around. One half looked like all the others, a door at the end, seats against the walls. The opposite end was crushed flat under a pile of boulders—the railcar bent and twisted as it transitioned into a constricted mass of rust and rock.

Turning towards the rubble end, she advanced along the center isle. The ceiling height slopped lower and lower, until she dropped onto all fours and wriggled her way across the floor. Movement was slow, methodical— avoiding jagged edges of torn metal and shards of crystal.

Crawling through the debris reminded her of days spent stalking deer in the woods around her village. She'd creep along the forest floor or slither under pȟahíŋ brush, setting her bow in front of her, body lifting off the ground on the tips of her toes and forearms and floating forward a thumb's length at a time. Every dry leaf and dead branch had to be set aside without making a sound. Concentration had to be total and sustained.

Her mind drifted back. She'd been out hunting. It was a hot, muggy, summer afternoon. That day she saw a tȟáȟča, a mighty stag with antlers that pierced the sky. It walked across a clearing and lay down against the trunk of a white oak. She noted the air currents through the forest canopy, then dropped low to the ground and fox-walked her way towards the majestic creature.

In order to remain down wind, she had to travel right across the middle of the clearing where dry oak leaves littered the ground. The slightest crunching of leaf or snapping of twig would give away her position.

Whenever she hunted, she would call upon Igmútȟaŋka Sápa, her black jaguar ally, to come dance with her in the physical world. Uŋčí had taught her that once a person obtained such a gift, she had to maintain the relationship in order to not lose the ally. The best way to do this was by calling to it and allowing it to enter the person's body. Uŋčí called this dancing your Spirit Animal. In this way the spirit could experience the physical world, a realm that was otherwise unknown to it, and in return it would guide or help the person, enabling her to do things she could never have done on her own, to embody the gifts and knowledge of that entity.

She recalled how Igmútȟaŋka Sápa had come to her that day, on the next breath of warm summer air, and with the stealth and skill of the black jaguar dancing within her, she had started out across the clearing—three points of contact with the ground at all times, one hand carefully relocating leaves and twigs. When the wind hissed through the branches overhead, her fourth limb touched down—body weight slowly shifting onto three points, waiting for the sky to sigh once again.

Little mounds of dirt had been turned up by the pispíza. She had made her way through the leaves, from one mound to the next, until all that stood between her and the deer was the broad trunk of the white oak. Under the tangle of lower branches she had crept, until she could reach out and touch the bark of the tree. Then she squatted down and observed.

She remembered how the loamy soil felt on the soles of her feet, the smell of tannins in the oak leaves, the musk of the stag. She remembered the water that had collected in the shady places between the leaves, a gift from the rainstorm the night before.

The deer's body was stretched across the width of the trunk, its back half visible on one side and its armory of antlers stabbing out on the other. Flies that landed on his amber coat were quickly whisked away by muscle vibrations just beneath his skin.

On that day she did not kill the ťháȟča. She had felt she was in the presence of an Elder, a teacher, a keeper of the forest. As she admired the animal's grace and power, a pispíza had popped its head up from a hole in front of her and scanned the area for danger. Then, deciding that there was none, it scampered out of its hole and ran past, just in front of her knees.

She had done it! Igmútȟaŋka Sápa had shown her how to be invisible! It was one thing to remain undetected by the mighty ťháȟča, but the humble pispíza was another matter all together. They were the forest lookouts—an alarm system of high-pitched barks that alerted all the creatures of the land at the slightest presence of danger. And here was one of them, right at her feet, gnawing on an acorn, oblivious to her presence.

When the pispíza had ducked back down its hole, she had leaned forward and smacked the stag squarely on its behind. The deer sprang to his feet, cleared a small ravine in three great leaps, and then ducked behind a tree. Then he popped his head out from behind the oak and gave her a look of surprise and annoyance.

"That was just to keep you on your toes, old man," she had said to the beast. "Being careless will get you killed around here. But I'm sorry I interrupted your nap."

She smiled at the memory.

But this wasn't a forest floor. What she smelled now was not the rich soil of her hunting grounds, but the rank ammonia of bat guano.

Her thoughts shifted to her loved ones. She thought of Uŋčí. *Who would be bringing Grandmother meat to cook or gather wood to keep the fire burning?* She thought of Níškola's wet nose pressed against her cheek, the smokey walls of her home, the placental whoosh of waves caressing the sandy shoreline below the village.

For the first time since she was taken, the full weight of her dilemma pressed against her, limp, and heavy.

She began to weep, the feelings of helplessness and sorrow washing over her like a lunar tide rising.

She wept in silence. There was no need to burden the unfortunate souls in that dungeon with more sorrow than they already carried in their hearts. Her tears ran down her cheeks and fell onto the cold, indifferent, steel floor.

She wept until all the sadness and fear drained from her body, until there was nothing left of the world but cool acceptance, and the beating of her heart.

A shiver ran down her back. Had she imagined it or had she just felt the slightest current of air moving over the wetness of her cheeks and neck?

Could it be…?

She crawled forward, holding her face just above the floor, pausing to see if she could feel the current.

Nothing.

And then it came.

Unmistakable.

A puff of cold air caressed her damp skin, causing involuntary spasms to ripple through her body.

It was coming from a crack between two pieces of metal flooring.

If fresh air is coming from somewhere under me, that could mean…

Mother's words...*assume nothing, follow the evidence as it presents itself.* Perhaps it was just hope speaking to her now—desire masquerading as reality.

Then it came again, gentle as a sleeping baby's breath.

Touching the crown of her forehead to the floor, a single word slipped from her lips as she emptied the contents of her lungs.

"Yuŝká."

Chabalangus!

With the first glow of morning smiling off the water below, a yellow tailed swallow emerged from his mud nest and sailed out over the sea. Moments later, the colony of earthen nests that covered the seaside cliff, came to life. A cacophony of sound spilled out into the still morning air—babies squawking in hunger, mothers humming and consoling, fathers announcing their departure to find food. Then, as though summoned by the gonging of a bell in a distant town square, a hundred thousand swallows departed all at once in a flurry of beating wings—diving down, down to the water, then rolling, drifting, and gliding out to greet the world.

A swallow passed in front of EnKare's face, inches away, momentarily distracting him. He watched as the little bird banked and whirled in pursuit of a terrified dragonfly. He was sitting on the bow of Jioba's boat, looking back at the shore and waving to the lineup of friends and relatives who had gathered on the sand to see them off. He wore a pair of canvas shorts that Jioba made for him, and his shuka was draped over his shoulders. The morning smelled of sweet lavender and coconuts.

This was a big deal. A big deal indeed! This was a *chabalangus* moment, if ever there was one. They were sailing to the legendary city of Accra. The Garden City!

Just getting to this point had been a wild adventure, starting with how fast the news of their journey had spread throughout the village. As he walked home that fateful afternoon, fuming at Jioba and ruminating on reasons not to go along on this half-brained adventure, children had already started approaching him, tugging on his shuka, squealing, "EnKare, no fair, you get to go to Accra. Take us with you. Take us with you!"

After their meeting on the beach, no sooner had the men departed then Jioba stumbled into Mandaha, literally, and told her the news. That same afternoon she called the town together for a meeting in central market.

In a matter of hours the entire affair had become a communal event. In the two days since Jioba had sealed the deal, with spit and a handshake, everyone in Mbini had come to know about the adventure, and everyone had chipped in to help make it happen.

Mrs. Tulu baked them fresh bread. Strapping and equipment tie-downs came from Mr. Bioko's leather shop. Mama Sana helped stock the coolers with block ice, and gave them twelve coconuts. Señora Concha, who loved to weave in her spare time, supplied them with a stack of freshly woven reed mats to use as bedding. EnKulupuoni provided strips of dried meat and Okuruwo sent them off with three ingri filled with fresh cream and yogurt.

It was said that Mbini's was a town that moved to the rhythm of one heartbeat. Now, he understood why.

That night he had expressed to his mother his hesitation and his reservations about going.

"I'm not a water person, Mama. I don't swim that well. I don't know the first thing about catching fish, sailing, the wind. I don't know how to read charts. How could I possibly be of any help to Jioba? He'll just have to babysit me. I'll create more work for him, I know it. He'd be better off going without me."

Okuruwo had sat quietly, listening, giving him time to express himself. Then, holding his hands in hers, "Do you remember what your Birth Name means, son?—"

—His thoughts were whisked away on the swallow's tail feathers as Jioba came along the side of the boat from the cockpit, sat down beside him and threw an arm over his shoulder. They waved towards the shore and the town waved back.

"Ya ready for this, bwana?"

He didn't respond right away. Was he ready? Somehow he hadn't fully embraced the reality that in order to adventure around the world he'd have to travel over water…eventually. He was nervous. Afraid. He had never been farther than a few kilometers from home, never away from family for more than a couple days. It had all just happened so quickly.

But hadn't he been dreaming about being a world traveler for years? About exploring all of Africa and beyond, into Nchi Mbaya? Why had he been so against the idea of going in the first place?

He looked into Jioba's joyful eyes, and now, believing it for the first time, "I'm ready."

Jioba sprang to his feet and clapped his hands loudly, as if calling a class of rowdy children to attention. Jafra and Tomobo came up onto the deck, and the four young men stood and faced each other.

"Gentlemen, welcome aboard the fastest boat in ALL of Mbini. Welcome aboard… the *Mandaha*!"

EnKare choked on his saliva.

"I know what you're thinking, bwana, but you're just plain wrong. Mandaha means Moon in Himba, and I think it's the perfect name for my boat. Yes, that happens to be your sista's name as well, but I assure you, there's no connection. I chose the name because here, on her maiden voyage, it is the moon that dictates our arrival time. And it was by the light of a full moon that I put the finishing touches on her. It just works, OK?"

He didn't utter a word, but looked on in amusement as his Jioba continued boasting about the boat's qualities.

"She is seven meters long. Her ribs are made from whale bone and her mast from the strongest coconut trunk. Her hull is made from resin hemp-fiber boards, thin, light, and super strong. And her rudder comes from the wood of the baobab tree. She is strong, light, and fast."

EnKare sneaked a word in under his breath."I'm sorry, are you describing the boat, or my sista?"

Jafra chuckled. Tomobo glanced furtively at the ground. Perhaps a little embarrassed.

"Ha ha. Very funny, Toots," Jioba scolded. Then brushing the joke aside, "We will be in Accra well before the next full moon! Our first stop will be on Ëtulá a Ëri, my island, for more supplies and to say hi to my family. With a steady wind, we will arrive there tomorrow afternoon. Then from there, it's open seas to Accra."

He was excited to meet Jioba's family. His Grandparents, Auntie and Uncle, and two Cousins all lived together under one roof. Jioba was born there and grew up in the house next door. When he was six, his parents decided to sail to the mainland to be part of the growing community of Mbini. He didn't know when the last time his friend had been back.

"First mate, prepare to hoist mainsail," Jioba declared, like the admiral of a fleet.

EnKare took one last look at his family on the shore. Mandaha's cheeks glistened in the morning sun. Mother's face calm and reassuring, an arm wrapped around sister's shoulder. Father standing tall and stoic.

The tendons of his neck strained as he swallowed, pushing down the fear, the anxiety, the apprehension. He waved at the beach one last time and yelled out, "We'll be back by the new moon." Then he jumped up onto the deck and grabbed hold of the main halyard and shouted, "Ready, Capitán!"

Jioba called out, "Hoist the main sail!" then ran to the bow and hauled in the anchor as fast as he could, and sprinted back to the cockpit. The boat glided forward, parting the placid morning water.

EnKare lifted the door to the anchor hatch and carefully coiled the chain and lowered the anchor into the box. Then he sat down, straddling the prow of the boat with one leg dangling on either side of the hull. He didn't want to look back. He knew he'd only be gone for a short time, but two or three weeks at sea was beginning to feel like forever. He looked down at the water rushing past.

If this is what it takes to be a world traveler, then I better get used to it.

Bimi & Bapu

The first leg of the trip, the crossing to Ëtulá a Ëri, was a breeze. He busied himself tackling little jobs; pulling lines, sweeping the deck, lounging around day dreaming about exploring wild and exciting new lands. Tomobo and Jafra spent most of the day playing board games like tavla, the Turkish name for backgammon, and bao, a version of mancala from the east side of the continent.

As evening rolled around he took the helm from Jioba, who disappeared below deck to cook their first meal. The smell of red chili, oregano, bay, rosemary, thyme, and fennel rose up from the cabin, carried on the sweet notes of Jioba's singing. The aroma reminded him of his little bushbaby friend, Pilipili, who he had named after the spicy mixture of chili and herbs. He would miss the company of his little friend. In protest to his leaving, the little bugger hadn't even shown up to say goodbye.

It was a simple dinner of rice pilaf, spiced with Jioba's own blend of pilipili and bits of meat, kale, onion, and garlic, with fried plantain, and yogurt fruit salad for dessert. Being their first meal at sea, they could have been eating a bowl of mushed oats and found it just as good, such was their excitement and cheerful mood.

After dinner, the two men thanked Jioba then retired below deck. Wired with excitement, the boys sat in the cockpit talking late into the evening.

"I'm still not sure this is really happening. Do you think I'm a good enough swimmer to be so far from shore?"

"Toots, did you know that most people drown in less than four feet of water? Distance from shore has nothing to do with it. Besides, we're talking about the *Mandaha* here. She is virtually unsinkable, like the Titanic." Then, with a grin stretching from ear to ear, "Oh, and what do you really think of the name, *Mandaha*? Has a nice ring, no?"

"OK, first of all, the Titanic SUNK, so that's not a very encouraging comparison. And secondly, I don't think *Mandaha* is gonna be too happy about having a boat named after her. But I won't tell her if you don't."

Without hesitation they danced out a handshake.

"But I'm serious, Jimmy. What are we doing?" Lowering his voice, "Are you even sure you know how to get us to Accra?"

Jioba whispered back, "Just between you and me...no." Then, before EnKare could protest, he added, "I've never been there before, so I can't say with certainty that we'll make it. Storms sink boats all the time, or I might misread a chart and we end up missing our mark by a few hundred kilometers. You never know."

"You never know? A few hundred kilometers? So you mean this floating bathtub might become our no-longer-floating tomb?" A moment of despair washed over him, then dissipated. He was toying with Jioba...sort of. Even if it was in the back of his mind, he knew that *world explorer* was synonymous with *risk taker.*

Steering away from the topic of disaster, Jioba reassured, "I'll start teaching you how to read charts tomorrow, and how to use the sextant. That way you'll be able to help me plot courses, and you'll have a better idea of what we are up against."

This did make EnKare feel a little better.

The ocean slipped smoothly along the boat's hull.

Jioba asked, "What do you imagine Accra is like, Toots?"

EnKare had spent much time contemplating this topic and was more than happy to elucidate. Evening hours drifted by as the young explorers rapped on about the mysteries and wonders of a world that had only existed in their imaginations.

It wasn't until a soft glow to the east faintly illuminated the distant silhouette of their homeland, that they realized they had talked through the night.

The next day was spent, much like the last, preparing and eating meals, playing board games, and tending to the boat's needs. Other than a few mild arguments, like who was responsible for the mysterious disappearance of some raisins that had been left out after breakfast, the journey thus far was a relatively smooth affair.

The boys went over the charts time and again, until EnKare slowly began to grasp the art. It wasn't the mystical and illusive craft of reading tossed bones that his mind had made it out to be. It was, in essence, another form of map reading, and once he understood the purpose and use of the compass, parallel ruler, dividers, protractor, and sextant, it all made sense.

Sometime around midday the island came into view to the north. By afternoon they swung around the southern shore and pulled into the irenic Bahía De Luba. They then set a course to Luba, the small seafront village where Jioba was born. An hour later they dropped sails and glided smoothly up to the wooden dock in the center of town.

EnKare jumped out with a bow line in his hand and proceeded to tie off the front of the boat, then ran down the dock and caught an aft line as Jioba tossed it to him. Once the boat was secured, Jioba and the two men jumped down and joined him.

"Well everyone, welcome to my hometown," Jioba said smiling with his whole face. "Wait here a moment." He walked to end of the rickety dock where it met a dirt road and stopped a little boy who was passing by.

He bent down and said something to the boy, who took off running, then walked back to the others.

"Does anyone know we're coming?" examined EnKare, swaying a little bit on his feet.

"I don't see how they could," responded Jioba. "Hopefully they still remember who I am." Then changing topics, "Don't worry, bwana, you'll get your sea legs soon enough."

"I hope so. Because right now it feels like the whole world is rocking! How about you two," EnKare asked, turning to their passengers, "how are your legs holding up?"

Jafra sighed, "A little wobbly, actually."

Tomobo responded, "Jafra, here, is a land animal. But me, I spend more time on the water, like my Uncle Kodo. My sea legs are doing just fine. Thanks for asking."

It hadn't been more than a minute or two when the little boy came around the corner, pulling a woman by the hand.

"Auntie Nelly!" Jioba cried out. "It's me." He ran towards the woman, who promptly dropped the little boy's hand and ran to meet him, arms outstretched, shrieking with excitement. She wore an earthen-red dress made from a single piece of cloth that wrapped around her waist and chest and then tied behind her neck. On her head was a white sash that coiled up from her forehead and held her hair back. Her neck and wrists were adorned with silver, amber, red coral, and turquoise beads.

Jioba led the women over to the group. "Auntie Nelly, this is my best friend, EnKare," he said, putting an arm over EnKare's shoulder. "And we are taking these two gentlemen to Accra. This is Tomobo and Jafra."

With tears in her eyes, Auntie Nelly grabbed Jioba by both cheeks and said, "Not another word, my boy. You lot come with me. There are some people who are going to be very happy to see you." She took Jioba by the hand and led them down the road, shouting, "Our Jimmy's home! OUR JIMMY'S HOME!" to everyone they passed.

When they arrived at Auntie Nelly's house she was still yelling out the news of Jioba's return as she opened the door and burst inside. The entire family sat on the floor around the dinner table, which was covered in scrumptious foods.

"Move over, Bapu! We've got four more coming to dinner, and you'll never guess who one of them is," Auntie Nelly shrieked with excitement.

Two of the oldest people EnKare had ever seen rose to their feet and approached Jioba. With tears in her eyes, the elder reached out and placed her hands on Jioba's cheeks, just as Auntie Nelly had done.

"Is that you Jimmy? Is that really you?" The wrinkled skin of her hands was thin and frail, but her voice was smooth as shea butter. "I told Bapu you'd come see us one of these days. He said; 'Bimi, we'll be long dead by the time he makes it home again.' *He he he*," she giggled like a little kid, then added, "Told you so Bapu."

Once all the hugging, kissing wet cheeks, and crying died down, Auntie Nelly announced, "Now. Why don't you introduce your friends, and tell us everything. E-very-thing!"

Tomobo stepped forward and greeted the family. "My name is Tomobo, and this is my friend Jafra."

"We are honored to be here, in your beautiful home." Jafra bowed his head slightly.

Jioba bragged, "We are taking these men to Accra, and you know, Ëtulá a Ëri just happened to be on the way, so..."

"And who's this, then?" Bapu had his head cocked to one side, eyebrow lifted, and was staring at EnKare.

"This," Jioba plopped an arm over EnKare's shoulder, "oh, no one really... just my best friend and first mate, EnKare. But I call him Toots."

EnKare smiled. "And don't you forget it, Jimmy." Then he shook the elders' hands. "It is truly an honor to meet you both. I've been hearing about you for so long. I feel like you are already family."

"Come, come all of you. Sit with us and eat. If you are with Jioba, you are with us." Bapu had that same smiling face that Jioba was famous for, and the twinkling eyes of one who had seen another world, a world before Iworo.

They all found a place on the floor around the table, and Jioba told the family about their adventure. Auntie Nelly sat quietly and listened. Being a woman of the sea, she understood what was needed to make a trip such as this. Then she blurted out, "OK OK OK. So! You will all be our guests. Tonight we eat, celebrate, and sleep. Tomorrow at dawn, we find you all the provisions you need and then send you on your way." Everyone nodded in approval. Then with a softer tone she certified, "But on your return trip you two boys will stop off and see us again. And this time you'll stay for a little longer, right?"

The evening was filled with singing, drumming, laughter, and stories. There was so much catching up to be done. The family wanted to know all about Jioba's life in Mbini, and about his mother's life too…in detail! And there was food. A lot of food. EnKare was awestruck by the number and variety of seafood dishes, and Auntie Nelly kept bringing them out, one after another. He must have eaten at least six new types of seafood that he never even knew existed. And the spices! Each steaming, sizzling dish brought a new and tantalizing aroma that left him searching for just a little more room in his belly, for just one—more—bite.

"*Ahhhhhhi!*," Auntie Nelly shrieked. "I see you like to eat, EnKare! Good. But save a little room for desert." His eyes grew wide. "It's passion fruit mousse with Bimi's special meringue topping." His eyes grew wider! How on earth was he going to fit it all in?

Later that evening, Bapu approached Jioba. "Jimmy, I want to show you something. Follow me."

Jioba grabbed EnKare by the arm and they followed Bapu out of the kitchen, down a hallway, and into a medium sized room. Tomobo and Jafra stayed behind, engrossed in a story Bimi was telling about the time she visited the old world city of London. As they entered the room, Jioba looked like he was about to pass out with excitement.

"What is it, bwana?"

Jioba was actually speechless, an occurrence that happened only once in a mango moon. Then he found his vocal cords again. "This is the world famous music collection that I'm always telling you about. Bapu, this is incredible! It's...it's even bigger than I remember!"

Bapu just smiled.

EnKare walked over to a wall which had floor to ceiling shelves that were filled with really large, really thin books. Three of the four walls of the room were exactly the same.

"Those are records, Toots. Each one is filled with the most incredible music. Hey Bapu, can we listen to some?"

"That's why we're here, my boy. That's why we're here."

Jioba started to rummage through the stacks, flipping from one record to the next.

"Look here." He pulled one and held it up. The words Toots And The Maytals were written in bold above a picture of the musicians. "This is one of my favorites, bwana! I can't wait for you to hear it."

"Wait a minute, are you telling me that you named me Toots after this musical group? And this whole time I thought it was because I could fart louder than you." This sent all three of them into a fit of laughter, followed by finger whip-snaps and a three way handshake. *Bapu may look like a petrified banana, but he's actually just another one of the boys!*

Jioba flipped through a few stacks and then pulled out another record. This one had the words Jimmy Cliff across the top with a picture of a man below it. "And this right here," Jioba said, cradling the record in his arms, gently caressing the cardboard sheath, "is Jimmy Cliff."

Bapu, who had been standing quietly and watching, finally spoke up. "When Jioba was three I played him that record for the first time. After that it was all he ever wanted to listen too. So I used to hide it on these shelves in a different, random place every time, and no matter where it was, Jioba would find it. He'd just go right to it, as though he knew it was there all along. After a while we started calling him Jimmy, and the name stuck."

"Can we play this one, Bapu?"

EnKare watched as his friend pulled a thin, shiny, black disc out from the square paper casing. The disk had little grooves and ridges on each of its flat sides that spiraled round and round, and there was a hole dead centered that passed all the way through it. Jioba handed the record to Bapu who took it over to an odd looking device in one corner of the room.

"This record player was an antique even in the time before Iworo," Bapu hummed, running his hand over the polished metal surface of the long, curving bell that protruded from its side. "But I always enjoyed the sound of vinyl more than any of the other fancy music devices they came up with after that."

He grabbed a handle that was sticking out of the back of the box and wound it in a circle several times. Then he placed the disc on top of a circular platform, allowing a small metal pin to fit snugly through the center hole on the record. He lifted a small arm at the side of the machine and placed it near the outer edge of the record, and then flipped a small lever. The circular platform began to spin and a sweet melody floated from the metal bell.

EnKare recognized the tune.

The lyrics used the metaphor of crossing many rivers to depict the hardships that one faces over a lifetime. He had heard his friend sing this song more times than he could count, though he had never heard it accompanied by so many different instruments. The sound was full and rich.

They played record after record, singing along, drumming on whatever they could find in the room, discussing differences and similarities between the musical styles. They only took one short break, and that was to run to the kitchen for a second helping of dessert, which, against Auntie Nelly's protests, they brought back into the music room with them, giggling like a pack of naughty school boys.

For EnKare, this was an awakening, a musical journey into the past. And listening to Bapu's stories of the time before Iworo was like discovering the Rosetta Stone. This wondrous old man had actually traveled to Europe and the Americas, had been to the ancient cities while there were still millions of people coursing through their streets. He had looked down upon the world from thirty thousand feet up, while floating through the heavens in an air-ship. Bapu was a treasure, in every sense of the word—a man who had lived in two worlds, survived six years of pitch black and bitter cold—who still laughed and played with the spirit of a child.

Stowaway

The last bag of provisions was loaded as the sun peeked over the volcano that watched over the little town of Luba. The whole village had come to the docks to see them off. After all, it wasn't every day that Jioba came home. Bapu had tears in his eyes, and Bimi was doing her best to keep her composure.

EnKare was focused on the journey that lay ahead—six days and six nights, miles from land, in a floating bathtub! Ready or not, he had come too far to turn back now, and he sensed that Jioba actually needed his help to get them there safely.

With *Mandaha* loaded, Jafra and Tomobo on board, and Jioba at the rudder, he pushed the fattened craft down the length of the dock and hopped on. Like a child pulled from his mother, the soles of his feet strained for the wooden planks of the dock as they parted land once again.

While Jioba spun the boat round to catch the wind, he hoisted the sails. In moments, they were slicing through the Bahía De Luba, heading straight out into the endless.

About an hour off shore, EnKare went aft and plopped down on the bench opposite Jioba. "I finished organizing all the stuff your family gave us. If we happen to find an island with ten or twenty shipwrecked sailors on it, we should have no problem feeding them," he joked.

"Eh, bwana, better to be safe than sorry! Tu sabes," Jioba responded.

"Jimmy, let me know when…" He stopped mid-sentence, and his jaw dropped open. Not three hundred feet off the stern of the boat a whale punched through the undulant surface. Such was her mass that, at first, he thought he was witnessing the birth of an island erupting from the sea floor.

She rose up from the depths, driving all but the tip of her tail straight out of the water. Long, whitish blue grooves ran down the neck and belly of the creature. A couple sucker fish attached to her back were holding on for dear life as the whale's body rose higher and higher, twisting and arching, belly towards the sky.

She towered a hundred feet over their little boat, and hung there for a moment, as if suspended in time.

Then, with the calamity of a tall tree tumbling into a tranquil forest meadow, she plummeted towards the unsuspecting surface and landed broadside on her back.

The resulting *SMACK* cracked the heavens open, and the sea turned into an angered beast. Seconds later the waves reached the boat and she pitched violently.

Wild-eyed, EnKare looked at Jioba and managed to squeak out, "Bwana!" in a raspy, high pitched voice.

"That, my friend, was Mama Bulu! Guardian of the sea," Jioba shouted reverently.

Tomobo and Jafra, who were just coming up from the cabin when the whale breached, gripped each other tightly.

Jafra shrieked, "Quick, everyone overboard! That thing could eat this whole boat!"

Tomobo warned, "No, better to stay on board. It might not come back."

"You have nothing to fear, gentlemen. She eats krill," Jioba pacified.

Jafra shrieked again and gripped Tomobo tighter. "It eats to kill. You heard him. It eats to kill! Quick, overboard."

"No. I said she eats krill. KRRRILL! Little, microscopic shrimpy things. She doesn't even have teeth. We probably stirred them up with the boat as we passed over. That, my friends, was a good omen. Despite being ten times bigger than *Mandaha*, she is as gentle as a giant tortoise. Have you never seen a blue whale?"

Heads shook vigorously. Aside from Jioba, no one else had seen a whale like that before, let alone one leaping into the air a stone's throw away!

It took a moment for EnKare's heart to calm.

The crew sat quietly for some time, allowing the awesome event to fully sink in.

The mood on board was light and cheerful as a steady wind blew them onward across a blue and white canvas of sky and sea.

EnKare was just drifting off to sleep, splayed out on the bow in the shade of the sail, when a sharp scream from below deck jolted him. He shot a questioning look at Jioba, who was stuck tending the tiller, then sprang up and ran over to the hatch.

"What's going on down there," he called into the darkness.

No answer.

He dropped down through the hatch, ready to confront the worst, then relaxed and chuckled. Tomobo was pressed up against one side of the hull, an outstretched arm with trembling finger pointed at Jafra's head. Jafra sat motionless, unblinking.

Perched on the top of his head, gripping tufts of his hair with her front hands, and the man's ears with her back hands, sat a small, equally perplexed galago.

"Pilipili?" EnKare's voice was incredulous, scolding, and joyful at the same time.

The little ball of fur leapt from Jafra's head, sailed across the cabin, and landed on EnKare's shoulder. He turned his head to the side and she pressed her tiny, wet nose against his.

"You know this...creature?" Jafra gasped.

EnKare sighed. "Yes. This little piece of work is Pilipili. She's my galago friend. She went missing the day before we left Mbini. I thought she was just pouting because she couldn't come along. Now I know what you were really up to, you sneaky little..."

Jioba shouted down, "Pilipili! Are you serious, bwana? Well, that would explain the missing raisins, and the chunks of coconut I've been finding all over the kitchen. Ha! This whole time I thought one of you bugas was sneaking food in the middle of the night."

Pilipili bedded down under EnKare's braids as he climbed back up through the hatch.

"What are we gonna do, bwana? We can't take her to Accra, can we? I can't believe she got herself onto the boat, and managed to stay hidden this whole time! I should be vexed, but I just can't stay angry at her. I mean, look at her, bwana."

"Well, Toots, we can't exactly turn around ya know. We've got a deadline to make." Jioba paused. Then, with a straight face, said, "Well, I guess we can always use her for bait. See if we can catch another whale, or something."

"Ha ha. That's not funny. it's a good thing we have all this extra food. She's small as an ant, but eats like a lion, tu sabes."

Dorado

At some point in the lazy day, Jioba asked him to take over the helm while he baited a whalebone fishhook, tied the line to the aft cleat and cast it off the stern of the boat.

"What if it hooks the whale by accident?" Jafra shuddered. There was real concern in his voice.

"Don't worry about my friend," Tomobo said, putting an arm over Jafra's shoulder. "What he lacks in experience he make up for with naivete."

"Oh, is that so? I'll show you naivete. Come here, bwana." Tomobo tried to make a quick escape, but Jafra grabbed one of his arms and the pair tumbled across the deck and landed in a mutual headlock.

"OK, OK, bwana. Udo. Udo!. You win." Jafra let go of Tomobo's neck and the two lay on the deck, panting and laughing.

Jioba giggled. "Well, that's one way to settle it. Don't worry, Mama Bulu is long gone. She only eats tiny little things anyway, like galagos, for example."

EnKare looked at Jioba with a raised eyebrow. "And more galago jokes? OK. Looks like someone else could use a headlock."

Handing the fishing line to EnKare, "Cálmate, bwana. Here, hold it gently between your fingers, and tell me when you either feel a vibration or some change in the tension."

EnKare put his fingers on the string as he was instructed. At first, every vibration, every tug and bump had him thinking there was a fish on the line. After a while, however, he discovered a recurring pattern—he got used to what the line felt like without a fish on it. He left his fingers resting gently on the cord and preoccupied himself petting the sleeping fur ball on his shoulder and studying the interplay between the wind and the surface of the water. Something about being on the ocean, looking at the sea drift passed. It coaxed the mind into wandering. Hours could pass unnoticed.

Then something hit the line hard!

It happened again, this time jolting him back to the present moment, and he turned to Jioba yelling, "Fish. Fish, fish, fish!"

"Tomobo, take the tiller," Jioba babbled. He disappeared into the cabin and returned with a carved wood hand-reel that he placed on the line. Pulling on the cordage, he created a length of slack, which he quickly wrapped around the reel. He repeated this process again and again, each time waiting for the fish to let up just long enough for him to wrap the cord again.

"I forgot to grab the net. It's in the cabin. Can someone bring it? quick!"

"Got it!" Jafra appeared at the hatch with the net. "Is this the one you mean?" Then he positioned himself beside Jioba with his upper torso dangling over the stern railing.

When the fish was only a few feet from the boat, Jafra dipped the net into the water, and, with EnKare's help, they carefully hauled the sequined bounty over the railing and onto the cockpit floor.

The strangely beautiful creature was at least four and a half feet long with a raised dorsal fin running down the length of its back. Little dots and stripes of color ranging from dark blue to yellow and aquamarine traversed the length of its body, which graduated from its tall, flat forehead, to the narrowest point just before the sharp 'V' of its tail.

Jioba immediately dropped the reel and pulled a knife from a small equipment hammock on the side of the cockpit. He put one knee over the body of the fish to prevent it from thrashing, thanked it for its sacrifice, and then, with speed and accuracy, ran the blade up through a gill and into the fish's brain.

The thrashing stopped instantly. He then removed his knee and put a hand on its side until its heart stopped beating.

"This, my friends, is Dorado!" He introduced the fish like it was a brother.

This dorado, this magnificent gift from the sea, fed four hungry sailors, and a galago, for the next five days. They took turns creating new recipes with the firm, sumptuous meat. EnKare spiced and grilled the fillets, using his antelope and kudu steak recipes. Jioba prepared fish tacos with mango salsa, a gumbo soup, and an assortment of stews. Tomobo and Jafra created a type of curry. Said it was lacking a few key ingredients to make it authentic, but as far as EnKare was concerned, it was magic in a mouthful.

Hooked

The days drifted by effortlessly. EnKare enjoyed the work around the boat and the long stretches of lounging on the deck. In the evenings Jimmy gave him lessons on using the sextant, and he slowly increased his skill at star and chart reading.

He also improved at the game of tavla and even managed to defeat Tomobo a couple times. The four of them were becoming friends, which was a good thing. He shuddered at the idea of them *not* getting along. Four young men—on a small boat—in the middle of the ocean—for a week! Not a pretty picture.

Thus far, one of his favorite things about Jafra and Tomobo was that they helped with the washing up after meals. This made him especially happy. Frankly, he'd rather sleep on a bed of elephant dung, than have to do the washing up.

Even though *Mandaha* was outfitted with Jioba's own version of an autopilot, really nothing more than a rope tied to the tiller, someone had to take the night watch just in case anything went wrong. The boys had worked out a schedule where one of them would take the first part of the night while the other slept, and then they'd trade off.

According to Jioba's charts, they would be arriving in Accra sometime in the afternoon of the following day. That night, EnKare drifted off to sleep to the soothing sounds of water lapping against the hull, and Jafra snoring. He was in the middle of a dream where he was riding on the back of a rhino-sized dorado when he was woken by a finger tickling his nostril.

"Stop it, Pilipili," he moaned, half asleep.

"Yer it," Jioba giggled and then tumbled onto the mat beside him and fell asleep instantly.

"Guess it's my turn to keep watch," he said under his breath as he draped his shuka over his shoulders and climbed through the hatch into the cockpit. Pilipili, creature of the night that she was, was already waiting for him as he took up his post by the tiller. "I'm glad you're here, Pilipili. I never would have thought a galago could make it as a sailor, but you seem to be getting the hang of it just fine. Capitán Pilipili. It's got a nice ring to it, hey?" The little fur ball was sitting on the tiller handle, gazing forward into the darkness. If one didn't know better, it would appear she was steering the boat.

The wind held steady at around seven knots, which was perfect for sailing through the night. There wasn't a cloud in the sky, and the moon, about three or four days from full, reflected off every riffle and white cap, casting the ocean in a surreal metallic shimmer.

He felt small.

Really small.

The charts showed land one hundred and fifty nautical miles away, but drifting out in the endless expanse his mind had a hard time believing it. He missed his family. And that big, giant Oldoinyo. They had only been five days on the water, but it felt like a hundred. He sorely missed land, solid ground, the feel of dirt between his toes. On land, he knew where he stood with water, he had some control over his relationship with it. But out here there was only water, and she was the master.

He listened to the gurgles and splashes lapping against the hull, the gentle breeze snapping the sail tight, the boat's wooden parts moaning and creaking quietly under the strain. There was a rhythm to the sound, soft and soothing, and his eyelids grew heavy.

Not wanting to doze off, he lashed the autopilot cord to the tiller, got up and made his way along the port side and onto the foredeck. He wasn't tethered to the boat in any way, so with everyone asleep, if he fell overboard, they'd sail on without him and he'd be lost and alone and left for dead.

Something about being up on the nose of the boat felt comforting. Staying low to the deck, he crawled his way out to the foremost point and laid down with his chest resting on the bowsprit and his arms dangling towards the water on either side. He quickly became mesmerized by the movement of the water whisking past, just out of reach. Below him, the prow parted the dark liquid, which curled over into little wakes like the rolling waves that washed up onto the beach back home.

Just as he felt himself start to drift off, the surface of the sea was broken by a shiny, grey dorsal fin. He retracted his arms instantly.

Shark!

The fin disappeared into the darkness. Then two fins surfaced, one on either side of the prow, and vanished again. When the fins surfaced again there were three. For a moment he felt compelled to go wake Jioba to let him know that their boat was under attack. Then the thought dawned on him that sharks' fins don't go up and down, in and out of the water. These were dolphins!

Seriously EnKare, sharks?

Feeling a little silly, and glad no one was around to witness it, he dropped his arms down again and felt the tension leave his body. He'd never been this close to dolphins before. They were swimming in the bow wake, catching a ride, coming to say jambo. He watched as their bodies cut effortlessly and silently through the water. They were so quiet that, had he not been lying there in the first place, they would have come and gone without him ever knowing.

As the first glimmer of light bent around the curvature of the earth, smudging out the most distant stars from the night's sky, one by one his new friends dipped below the surface and disappeared. Hours had passed in the company of the dolphins, though it felt like only minutes.

He returned to the cockpit and pulled a banana from his bag of snacks. The lonely, homesick feeling in the pit of his stomach had dissolved, and he felt content. Happy. Even out here, lifetimes away from home, there were new friends to be made—on, and off the boat.

An hour later Jioba popped his head up from below deck. "Jambo, bwana. Everything go smooth last night?" He stepped into the cockpit, yawned and stretched.

"Smooth as dolphin skin," EnKare replied.

That morning, Jafra made a hearty breakfast of fruit with yogurt, scrambled eggs a la smoked dorado, toast, and coffee. Tomobo did all the washing up.

"This wasn't in the agreement, was it?" EnKare teased. "Not that I'm complaining. Those were the best eggs, bwana."

Jioba added, "And thank you for washing up, Tomobo. But seriously, you didn't have to."

"Nonsense!" Tomobo said with a smile. "You got us to Accra on time. More than on time. This is the least we could do."

"Well, we haven't arrived yet. But we should be close. Toots, if you climb up to the stork's nest, you might get lucky and see land," Jioba suggested.

"What stork's nest? Oh, you mean the cross bar? Are you sure my weight up there won't capsize us?"

"There's only one way to find out, bwana!"

He had climbed the mast before, but never while the boat was at sail.

It can't be much harder than climbing a coconut tree in a windstorm.

And it wasn't. Getting up the mast was easy. Getting seated on the crossbeam, however, took some careful maneuvering. Now this, surely, was the best seat in town. The wind in his face! Unbeatable views in all directions!

After the better part of an hour, still no land in sight, butt falling asleep, he decided to come down from his perch. He called out to let Jioba know he was descending, when something on the horizon caught his attention.

At first he couldn't tell if he was seeing land or just the dark mass of a cloud formation.

Then there was no mistaking it. There it was, the Accra coastline stretching out before his eyes.

"LAND! LAND!" he yelled excitedly. "Straight ahead, Capitán." His spirit soared. He felt like a bona fide world explorer seeing the coast of an undiscovered continent for the first time. This one moment made the entire voyage worthwhile. Was this the feeling that they sought, all the adventurous souls over the millennia, who had left the comfort of home and the company of friends and loved ones to travel the seas? Now he understood what it was they were seeking.

This...moment!

This...feeling!

Just how far would he go in pursuit of other moments like this? What would he be willing to sacrifice? One thing he knew for certain...

He was hooked.

The Veil

As if waking from a deep sleep, a dreamless state of sensory absence, consciousness returned slowly and incrementally. From non-existence, her sense of self returned, followed by an awareness of place. She figured she was lying on her back with her eyes open, because she could see a faint glow reflecting off of the low ceiling where she had bedded down beside Wit'é.

She reached for the straw-haired girl, just to make sure she was sleeping safely beside her, but couldn't move her arm. She tried lifting her head. Nothing. Then she tried to sit up, but again nothing.

Something was wrong. It was as though her body was unable to receive the commands that her mind was sending it. She couldn't hear anything, like her ears were plugged with tree gum. She couldn't scream, though her desire to do so was growing.

Panic began to well inside her. The feeling escalated, and as it grew she became aware of a new sensation, a high pitched screeching within the bones of her own spine.

The tone rose up her back, increasing in intensity, until it filled her head, reverberating off of the inside of her skull.

Just as the intensity of sound was about to overwhelm her, there was a pop and a flood of energy exploded out of the top of her head.

She sat up. All sense of panic had vanished and the blaring tone was gone. She rose to her feet, walked to the door of the cabin and looked out into the darkness of the dungeon.

She turned to look back at Wit'é. What she saw was so outside the scope of her expectation, so beyond her experience, that all she could do was stare.

Wit'é slept soundly on the hard metal floor, and lying beside her, on her back, eyes wide open and staring up at the ceiling was… herself.

Her field of vision pulsed, and the ceiling of the cabin came into focus again.

Pulse—she was looking at herself lying in bed.

The image shifted between these two scenes several times, as though her consciousness was alternating between two states of awareness; one, of the person lying down, the other, of the person at the doorway.

"Don't look at yourself," a voice commanded from behind her. It was Uŋčí's voice! How was this possible? She turned to face the voice, and there was Grandmother, standing a short distance away in her bearskin robe, long white hair unbound and flowing down over her shoulders. There was a faint luminous quality to her body, and Wakíŋyaŋ could see the far side of the dungeon right through her, as though she was looking at a ghost.

"What are you?" Apprehension tightened her throat. "Are you Šuŋgmánitu, coyote trickster? What have you done with my Uŋčí?"

Pulse—ceiling

Pulse—apparition

"Little Thunder, listen closely to my voice and don't stare at my image." The voice was that of a younger version of Grandmother. "I am no Šuŋgmánitu. I am Wakȟáŋ Kiktá. What you are looking at is my energy body. This world is new to you. Staring at any one image for too long will deplete you of your energy, and you won't be able to sustain my image. In this world, you are like a newborn. Each phase of your learning will be slow and methodical, and it will take time, as did your learnings in the physical world. Try to sustain your journey long enough for me to explain to you what is happening.

"You have stepped through the veil once again. On your first journey, you came to see me at our house in the village, two days after you were taken. You spoke to me from the doorway. Right now your physical body is there behind you, lying in the spot where you went to sleep, and standing before me is your spirit, your energy body, that has emerged. Don't look back at your physical self until you are ready to rejoin your body.

"The sensation you felt was your spirit detaching itself from the physical. Don't worry, you'll get used to it. When this happens you are able to pull back the veil that keeps you from seeing during your ordinary waking state. When you travel on this side of the veil the rules and restrictions of the physical world no longer apply. Take the memory of this lesson back with you to the physical world. You must train yourself to pass through the veil at will."

"I don't understand, Uŋčí. I want to come home, I…"

Wakȟáŋ Kiktá interrupted her words. "It will take some time before your mind is able to recall the experiences of your energy body. It is not essential that this happens, but it will help you set your intent, and find your way forward in the world of the spirit. In order to help you with this, you must assign yourself a trigger from the physical world, a person or a place, or it could even be a color or a smell, that triggers your memory of your spirit walks."

The image of the hand-sign for friend, used by the people of her village, popped into her mind. It was a hand, held upright in a fist, with the first and middle fingers extended towards the sky, like a pair of rabbit ears.

"Once you have this awareness," the apparition continued, "you can use your intent to further your explorations on this side of the veil."

Wakíŋyaŋ felt a fatigue come over her. She turned around and looked at herself lying on the floor next to Wit'é, then walked over to her bed, dropped to the floor and laid back down into herself. The moment her energy body reunited with her physical, she slipped into a deep sleep that lasted the remainder of the night.

Bearings

Rise n' shine, worm bait!" Fritz's screeching voice yanked her awake. "Mustn't let da day go ta waste, so make haste, or we'll mush yer bits'n pieces into paste."

She had hoped to never hear that voice again. Turning to wake Wit'é, "Quick, little one, we have to get up now," she hummed in a soft voice.

Something about last night, something happened. A dream? She wanted to take a moment to focus on it and to work through it in her mind. But the scarecrow's incessant ranting wouldn't permit it.

When all the slaves had gathered in front of their cabins, Fritz split them into three groups. Wakíŋyaŋ quickly stepped in front of Wit'é and pulled the child's small frame close to her, obscuring her from Fritz's view. She wanted to keep her close, to keep an eye on her.

When they were all split up, Fritz bobbled and spasmed his way to the front of the group, where he proceeded to bark the day's work schedule at them.

"OK, worm bait, mosta y'already know da drill, but for soma ya fresh meats, dis'll be yer first time! Today we chopp'n woooo...oooood," the wiry man howled, throwing his head back like a deranged wolf. It looked like even more of his scalp had been taken over by whatever mange had left it looking like a diseased pine forest. He stared at the group out of his bulging, goo-crusted eye, and continued with his speech. "Cuz it ain't gonna chop itself. We gots ta keep da home fires burnin', da meat on da spits turnin', an da little minds yernin' for some good learnin'. OoooooooWee! Now dat were a good one!"

When he was done complimenting his own primitive rhyming skills, he crepitated his way over to the large door and banged on it repeatedly. Rusty hinges screeched and groaned as the heavy aperture swung open.

"Oh goodie." Pills was the first to speak, and the sarcasm dripped from his lips. "I can't wait to be out in the woods babysitting you lot."

"Just remember," added Taco, "if any of our mutant cousins happen to attack us while we're out there, you'll find out real quick why we call you *worm bait*. Once we get to the surface, each of the groups that French Fry here split you up into," Fritz grunted and glared at Taco through his gooey eye, "will break off with one of us," gesturing to himself and his two companions.

"Don't let my friend Taco here scare you," Geiger added. "Your chances of becoming worm bait are pretty slim. Say, one in thirty. But if any of you try to escape, we'll track you down with the hounds, drag you back, and then feed you piece by piece to the BigBossMan. When it comes to fresh meat for dinner he's not picky. Now let's move out!"

They traveled back through the network of tunnels and into the great hall. Some children stopped the game they were playing to shout obscenities as they passed by. From there they took a side tunnel and climbed a stairway. At the top they stopped at a guarded check station. The way out was blocked by a massive double door made of whole tree rounds lashed and bolted together. The colossal gateway was as wide as Uŋčí's hut, and even taller, and filled up most of the tunnel.

"Morning, Friday," Taco greeted one of the guards.

"Mornin', Taco. Whatcha got cookin' today?"

"Today's wood day. We got three groups a worm bait goin' out. We'll need a stack of straps," Taco replied.

The guard disappeared into a side room and returned with a large bag that he handed to Taco.

"Have fun today, boys," the second guard chided as he pulled back the heavy bolts. Then the five guards leaned in with all their weight and slowly heaved the gate outward.

The group stepped out into a clearing of rubble. A thick vegetation of bushes and vining trees grew overhead and surrounded the clearing, obscuring the gateway from the outside world.

They passed through the green curtain and out into the open air. It was the first sunlight Wakíŋyaŋ had seen in many days. She closed her eyes and turned her face up to the sky. Others in the group did the same.

If work means getting to be outside then it's not so bad. Anything is better than staying locked up in that dark hole.

"OK, worm bait," Taco's voice interrupted her thoughts, "Group one goes with Pills, group two with Geiger, and group three with me."

There was Wit'é and two other slaves in Wakíŋyaŋ's group, and she kept the straw-haired girl close as they followed Taco over the rough terrain. He rambled on and on about how dangerous it was, how there were sink holes everywhere that dropped straight into worm nests, and that if anyone fell in one they'd be left for dead.

The trees and underbrush grew dense from the ground, which was a chaotic tangle of eroding ashen rock and rusting iron, making travel slow and tedious. She had the impression that they were traveling over the remains of a once mighty city. Uŋčí had told her stories of the great cities in the time before the burn. But why anyone would want to live in a village with houses stacked on houses, with few plants and animals around, was beyond her comprehension.

Her suspicions were confirmed when they came into a clearing in the trees on top of a small rise that looked out over the canopy. For as far as she could see in all directions, piles of greystone and iron heaped into mounds grew up from the green blanket of forest. They varied in size from small hills, like the one she was standing on, barely cresting the tops of the trees, to towering mountains of rubble; the ghostly remains of buildings that must have kissed the sky.

The work was hard enough, but nothing she wasn't accustomed to doing back home. They weren't allowed to carry any tool or device that could be used as a weapon, so they spent the day picking up smaller pieces of dead wood, snapping off low lying branches, and breaking larger logs into smaller pieces by smashing them over the sharp edge of a boulder.

At the end of the day the slaves stacked their wood into organized piles and then lashed them tightly with the leather straps that Taco handed out. She noticed that the technique the slaves were using was inefficient and cumbersome, so she demonstrated her own way to Taco, who was so impressed that he instructed her to show the others.

She helped everyone reorganize their wood piles and then showed them how to lash the bundles in such a way that the extra strap came up and over the top of their foreheads. In this way the load was supported on the carrier's back and held in place by their forehead, leaving the arms free for balancing over the rocky terrain.

Throughout the long day of work, Wakíŋyaŋ had been taking in her surroundings, getting her bearings on the layout of the land. She took note of the tallest mountains of rubble and was able to see the shoreline in the distance wrapping from the west side, around to the south, and all the way up to the east. *We're either on an island or a very large peninsula.*

As the day came to an end, Taco's group met up with the other two groups outside the entrance to Bronx's domain.

"What's with the fancy strap work?" Geiger asked, clearly admiring the size and tidiness of the wood stacks in Taco's group.

"Just a little idea I came up with this morning," Taco replied. Wakíŋyaŋ shot him a sideways glance, but said nothing.

"Well, you'll have to show us how to do it, oh master strapper," Pills chortled.

"Next time we're out for wood I'll have that one over there teach it to everyone. She seemed to pick it up the fastest," Taco croaked, gesturing towards Wakíŋyaŋ.

Walking up to her, Geiger speculated, "Hey, isn't this the worm bait that we sent up to BigBossMan the other day?" Then moving uncomfortably close, he added, "I can see why. I wouldn't mind taking this one for a little private wood collecting myself."

I'd like to see you try it.

Geiger reached out to stroke her hair but Taco cut him off, "Uh, hey buddy. Better not. Don't you remember? BossMan gave orders that no one was to lay a finger on that one. Punishable by death!"

"I know," Geiger snapped, reluctantly pulling his hand away, "but that means there must be something really special about her." Then turning towards Wit'é, "she's too old now anyway, but this one here is just right..."

Wakíŋyaŋ stepped in front of Wit'é, looked directly into the guard's eyes. "We are one flesh. Anything you do to her, you do to me." Her words were calm and controlled, so imbued with power and resolve that Geiger giggled involuntarily and looked away.

"Relax, worm bait. She's not my type anyway." Geiger attempted to brush it off as though he was just messing around the whole time.

"OK, 'nough fun n' games. Let's load em up and get this wood down into storage," Taco yelled.

Maggot

The darkness of the dungeon was a stark contrast to the brilliant light of the world above; however, her eyes had no trouble making the adjustment. Uŋčí had tried to explain it to her once. Something about a layer of reflective tissue in her eye that other humans didn't have, made it so she could see things in the darkness that others could not—gave her the night vision of Igmúthaŋka.

She sat on the floor of their bedroom, and Wit'é kneeled behind her, combing out and braiding her long, dark hair. As the girl's nimble fingers whisked about, gathering up loose strands, they chanced upon the lump under the skin at the base of Wakíŋyaŋ's neck. Though she only touched it gently, Wakíŋyaŋ grimaced and grabbed hold of the little girl's hand.

Wit'é jerked her arm away and recoiled into the corner of the cabin.

"I'm so sorry, Wí, I didn't mean to startle you. I forgot all about the skeet bite."

She reached up and felt the welt on the back of her neck. Since her abduction she had completely forgotten about the bot fly larva growing under her flesh. Now that she was aware of it again, she realized that the whole area was achy and tender. It had been over half a moon since the bite, so the bot would be nearly grown by now.

The second stage of its gestation is when bot larvae really become active, eating more and more of their host's flesh to sustain their rapid growth, and becoming more mobile. This maggot could eat its way towards her spinal cord or carotid artery. It could eat its way into her brain!

"Wí, I'm so glad you discovered my bite. I had forgotten all about it. Do you think, if I show you what to do, you could help me get it out?"

Wit'é's eyes lit up and she scurried back over to Wakíŋyaŋ, nodding her head up and down vigorously. She reached back to show Wit'é how she wanted her to proceed, but the little girl swatted her hand away and immediately went to work massaging the sides of the lump between her thumb and first finger.

"Oh, you've done this before!" she exclaimed in surprise. "I should have known."

The larva's body is covered in little barbed spikes. When it feels threatened in any way it raises the spikes, making it impossible to tear it out of its host without ripping flesh and causing irreparable damage. By gently massaging the larva through the layer of skin, Wit'é was able to coax the maggot into a relaxed state while edging it closer and closer to the original skeet bite hole that it used as an air vent.

"Hey Wí, we have to find a way to open up the air hole, because the larva's body is way too big to fit through it as it is."

Looking around the cabin, she found a scrap of sheet metal that had rusted off one of the walls, and cleaned it off with saliva and a piece of clothing.

"It's not the cleanest knife, but it will have to do," handing the blade to Wit'é and then bracing herself. "OK, see if you can widen the air hole, then we'll try again."

Once again Wit'é knew exactly what to do. She held the tip of the scrap metal over the small flame of their torch until it was red hot. Then without hesitation she inserted the pointy edge into the small opening, and with a swift jerk of her wrist, tore the hole open.

Blood oozed from the wound and trickled down Wakíŋyaŋ's back. With the hole now widened, Wit'é returned to massaging the larva. She must have known what to feel for because, at just the right moment, she moved her fingers to the end of the maggot, furthest away from the enlarged air hole, pinched, and forced her fingers sharply towards the opening in one abrupt move.

The relaxed larva popped out with such momentum that it bounced off the ceiling and landed on the far side of the cabin.

I'm sorry little friend. Your journey ends here.

The tension drained from Wakíŋyaŋ's body, and she sat back onto the cool floor, relieved. Wit'é then took the poultice of herbs that Wakíŋyaŋ had secretly gathered while working above ground, and dressed the wound.

"Thank you, Wí," she sighed, turning towards the little girl. Wit'é smiled up at her then raised her right hand and formed a fist, with her first and middle fingers pointing upwards.

"Friends?! Yes! Of course we are. Wí?" Wakíŋyaŋ's mind reeled.

How does she know that sign? Is it used by other tribes in the area?

Then her stomach shifted. She scrunched up her face, looked at her little friend, and in a very soft voice acknowledged, "The veil." Then her mind conjured up an image of Uŋčí, and she remembered her dream. *Was it a dream?* There was something odd about it, but before she could give it her full attention, Wit'é jumped to her feet and tugged on her shirt.

"What is it Wí, where are you taking me?"

The little girl dragged Wakíŋyaŋ out of their cabin, across the tracks, and all the way over to the kitchen. As they approached the fire pit she could see that everyone had gathered. The elderly man and woman were at a table rolling out balls of acorn dough. Now she understood why Wit'é had been so pushy. Her stomach was calling the shots.

Wit'é found a spot between the twins by the fire and wedged herself in, while Wakíŋyaŋ stepped over to the table and offered a hand with the dough. Once the dough was all rolled out the group gathered around the fire, taking turns flipping and passing around the warm bread.

This feels like home.

Through the evening the fire popped and sizzled to the low hum of story telling. She learned a little about each of her new neighbors. There had been four slaves in the dungeon when she arrived. The kind, older gentlemen called himself Clifton. His skin was dark and rough and scored with deep lines, but he keep the tight curls of white hair on his head and face short and neat.

The Dungeon Mother, as they called her, was an olive-skinned, elderly woman named Bay. She had been there longer than any of them, and the sparkle of life in her eyes was beginning to fade. She kept her silver, wavy hair pulled up under a drab piece of cloth wrapped tightly around her head. She had Grandmother's same maternal energy, and it was easy to be around her.

Then there was the buttermilk skinned fellow named Jack, who didn't talk much and was sullen most of the time. On the occasion he lifted his head up high enough, soft green eyes would peek out from behind a mop of sandy hair.

A young lady named Hiva, who had a fiery personality that hadn't been beaten out of her yet, had dark, piercing eyes which peered out of the golden skin of her round cheeks, and long black hair that cascaded over her stout shoulders. She had the distinct impression that this girl was a warrior, like herself. Perhaps even a hunter.

Hiva came from a village, not much different from her own, on the west side of the bay. They hunted and fished and grew their veggies within the protection of village walls. Their social structure, however, was completely different, and Wakíŋyaŋ listened intently as Hiva told them about being raised by two mothers.

Such was their custom for the women and the men to live in separate homes with two separate long-houses for their respective gatherings and ceremonies. A person had a biological mother and father, but parenting was a community affair.

Not a bad idea. I only had the one set of parents, and they're both gone.

Then there were the new arrivals who had come in at the same time as her. Brooklyn, who had features similar to her own, though her eyelids were cast low and stretched tightly over her eyes, obscuring the jet black irises that hid beneath. And there was Clair, who's skin was the color of tanned rabbit, with a wild tangle of dried sage hair on her head, who shared Wakíŋyaŋ's love of medicinal herbs.

And then other than Wit'é, there were the twins. When she discovered that they were called Bark and Bite, she couldn't help but laugh, and it didn't take long for them to live up to their names. With a bit of nurturing, the two little coyotes were feeling much better, and in no time got into all sorts of mischief around the dungeon. They finished each other's sentences constantly, or one would simply look at the other and respond as though words had been spoken. Sometimes whole conversations took place with nothing but strange sounds, grunts, and giggles. It was odd at first, but she soon realized they could read each other's minds.

Uŋčí had always told her that where you lay your head, that is your home, and who you break bread with, that is your family. She wasn't so sure. Home was the village, and family was Uŋčí, Níškola, her friends. But the bread in her belly did feel really good, and the friendly faces were comforting, even if she was deep underground, in a cold, wet prison.

The Garden City

After securing the *Mandaha* to the dock, alongside dozens of other vessels, he leapt down and followed Jioba along the wooden planks towards the beach, Pilipili clinging tightly to his shoulder. When they reached the sand, EnKare dropped onto his knees and kissed the ground while Pilipili did little somersaults. He rolled onto his back, his face now covered in fine white silica. "Chabalangus, bwana! It feels good to be on solid ground again. Look at Pilipili. She feels the same way."

Jioba was sprawled face down on the beach, arms spread wide trying to hug the whole planet.

Tomobo and Jafra approached, and Tomobo beamed, "Rafiki zangu, shall we make our way to my Aunt and Uncle's house? They live in one of the garden towers near the center of town."

"What about the boat?" inquired Jioba. "Will it be OK?"

"We may not be in small town Mbini any more, but I assure you, there's no crime here. Everyone has what they need, and if someone needs help we all come together to bring them up. The boat will be fine right where it is. This, gentlemen, is The Garden City!" Tomobo declared triumphantly, with a broad sweep of his hand.

As they made their way through the hustle and bustle of the beachfront shops, EnKare was struck by the sheer number of people. All he had ever known was his small village of perhaps sixty inhabitants, and there were more people than that here in this one market.

And the stalls were filled with fruits, vegetables, and breads the likes of which he had never seen. He wanted to sample each and every one of them that very instant. He could tell that Pilipili was having the same thoughts by the way small beads of saliva gathered around her lips, and her eyes bulged wider than normal.

"You stay close to me, Pilipili, at least until we learn our way around. This isn't Mbini anymore." Then he pursed his lips and made a gentle sucking sound. The fur ball held his ear in one tiny hand, his nose in the other, and pressed her little face against his cheek.

They wandered through the market rows until they merged onto a wide, grass-covered road that led away from the beach. There were shops and houses lining the sides of the field-like street. Ahead, the buildings got taller; some with four, five, and six stories, taller than any building he had seen before.

EnKare pointed at the rising towers in the distance. "Hey, Tomobo, what are those?"

"Those are the Garden Towers, though what you can see from here is just the first few rows." Tomobo flashed a proud smile. "My uncle lives in one of them, right in the middle. We're heading there now."

EnKare and Jioba simultaneously whip-snapped the air, then danced out a handshake.

Jafra added, "And just wait till you taste Auntie Beeke's cooking!" Then he sucked his lips into his mouth and made a loud *pop*.

For a while EnKare walked in silence, mouth open and head tilted back, taking it all in. The Garden Towers were not individual buildings but one continuous, interconnected structure—a giant, verdant, termite mound. Constructed of mud, sticks, and round timber, the builders had utilized every available surface for growing things. There were vegetables sprouting from pockets sculpted onto the sides of vertical and sloping walls, fruit trees leaning from terraces, balconies, and rooftops, and flowers, succulents, edibles, and ornamentals everywhere. There wasn't a right angle on the buildings. Instead, walls curved and twisted, doorways and windows arched, and roof lines sloped gently. Strings of passion flowers cascaded down past potato patches, cabbages, and kale, colorful bougainvillea vines grew over windows and doorways, and terraces and balconies brimmed with stalks of corn, beans, and zucchini gourds.

The streets through the Garden Towers were spectacular, winding and weaving through and among the homes. There was no concrete or asphalt to be found, only grassy paths through orchards and garden patches and clusters of banana and palm trees. It was impossible to tell where the streets ended and the buildings began.

"This way, gentlemen," Tomobo called out. He led them through the labyrinth, touching plants affectionately and waving to friends along the way. "If you are hungry and you see something that is ripe, you just pick it and you eat it," he declared with a smile. EnKare could tell that Tomobo was in his element here, he was home.

Jafra gave a live demonstration, picking a custard apple from a low hanging branch and biting into the sumptuous, creamy white flesh.

Meanwhile, Pilipili leapt from EnKare's shoulder and bounced along the banana fronds and swung from the vines that lined the path.

Jioba, who had been singing softly as he wandered along, suddenly stopped in his tracks and blurted out, "Toots! You smell that, bwana?" He closed his eyes, tilted his head back and dramatically sucked in a long breath of air through his flared nostrils.

Using his diaphragm, EnKare pulled and pushed air in and out through his nose in a series of short, rapid puffs. He opened his eyes really wide and smiled. It felt as though his face had been pressed into a bouquet of flowers, or a bowl of fruit salad. The fragrances were so intense.

"Papaya, passion flower, loquat," he exclaimed between bursts of breath. Then looking over, he noticed Tomobo and Jafra staring at him, and Jioba giggling. "What? Hey, don't knock it till you try it. Every other mammal on earth does it, and for good reason. You increase the volume of air over your olfactory nerves. If you want to smell like a hyena, you have to *smell* like a hyena."

Jioba leaned towards EnKare and sniffed. "Well, mission accomplished, bwana."

The laughter died down, then all four of them were snorting air.

"Hey, this does work," exclaimed Jioba. "Pineapple and custard apple."

"Kaffir lime and mangoes," Tomobo sang.

"Salak and longan fruit," added Jafra.

"Salak and what'an fruit? I've never heard of those," EnKare mused.

"Gentlemen, we have fruit here in the Garden City from the far corners of the world," Tomobo boasted. "Lychees and rambutan from China and Eastern Asia; caimito, carambolo, and lulo from South America. You could try a different fruit every day, and in half a year you wouldn't have tried all of them. You'll go to Aye Market later, but now let's go meet my family."

He led them through a grove of red banana trees and into the mouth of an arched doorway. There was no door, just a passage that sloped gradually upwards in a sweeping spiral. The dirt floor felt cool on EnKare's bare feet. Smooth, curving walls of the hallway were lit from one side by round openings that looked out over the town, and lined on the other with doors. It felt like he was walking through the inside of an ant colony. The dirt used to build the towers was a rich, red ochre, similar to the clay back home.

Tomobo rapped his knuckles against the wooden planks of one of the doors. Before he could strike a third time the door was thrown open by a vibrant, middle aged woman dressed from head to toe in colorful kente cloth.

"Tomobo!" she practically screamed with delight, "I knew that was you, my boy. Your uncle thought you might be arriving today. Come here and give your Auntie Beeke a kiss."

Tomobo's whole body went limp as she pulled the young man into her colorful sea of fabric and planted loud, wet kisses all over his head.

When he surfaced for air, the exuberant woman bubbled, "Akwaaba adamfo! Welcome friends! Come inside, all of you. You must be tired and hungry after such a long journey. And who is this that you have with you? Jafra, my boy!" she squawked with delight.

She's not looking directly at anyone. Wait a minute. She's without eyesight? For a moment EnKare was confused.

Jafra made no protest. His body went limp with submission to the fate awaiting him as Auntie Beeke rushed in and gave him the same treatment Tomobo had received.

"Now, come out onto the veranda, introduce me to your three new friends, and tell me all about your voyage from Mbini. Your Uncle Kodo is at the shipyard working on the *Buganvilla*, but you'll get to meet him later." She was looking towards EnKare and Jioba with a big smile on her face.

How can she possibly know we are here? And Pilipili too? She did say the three of us.

The rounded walls and floors were covered with cow and goat skin carpets, woven tapestries, hanging baskets, and painted plates and bowls. Potted flowers and fruit trees lined the room partitions, branches and vines reaching up to where the walls cambered into ceiling. At one end of the living room was a double doorway leading out onto a balcony. Brilliant orange, radiant red, and dazzling sky blue bougainvillea vines were interwoven and growing all the way around the opening.

Niiice!

EnKare smiled. Bougainvillea was his favorite plant. The variety and intensity of colors were unmatched in the world of flowers. A tree, a house, a fence, a street, were all naked in his eyes, if not graced with the meandering vine of the bougainvillea.

They followed Auntie Beeke out on to the veranda where she had a feast of fruits, breads, and juices spread across a mahogany table that was low to the floor and surrounded by a colorful assortment of ornate cushions. She shrugged and said, "Like I said, your uncle thought you might be arriving today, so I took the liberty of preparing a few things."

A few things?

He took a seat and listened as Tomobo recounted the highlights of their journey. On the table were fruits that his eager taste buds had never had the pleasure of experiencing, and as the group chit-chatted back and forth he satisfied their curiosity with a nibble here—and a nibble there.

Looking out through the banana fronds and papaya leaves, he could see a large swath of the city. Accra was even more magnificent than he had imagined it to be. He saw at least three parks, several football fields, and a stadium, like something out of ancient roman times, with its amphitheater of sloping seats surrounding a green field at its center. Every roadway had been converted into an orchard, a garden, a butterfly sanctuary, or a playground.

"Isn't she beautiful?"

"Oh! Ya. Sorry, Tomobo. I was just admiring the view. I've never seen anything like it."

"Tomobo, my boy, why don't you take your guests to see Aye Market? They can meet your Uncle Kodo later, no? You do want to see the market, don't you, boys?" Auntie Beeke declared.

EnKare looked over at Jioba, who was grinning madly and nodding vigorously.

Then, simultaneously, "We'd love to!"

Bag o Bones

Jafra and Tomobo gave a parting handshake and agreed to meet later that evening. EnKare and Jioba walked beside Tomobo as he led them through the greenways of the city. On more than one occasion he had to smack Jioba on the back of the head to get him to stop staring at the colorfully dressed young ladies promenading the streets.

"Toots!" Jioba protested loudly. "What ya do that for, bwana? I can't help it. I've never seen so many beautiful women!"

Jioba made a good point. He, too, had been admiring all of the beautiful people of the town from the moment they stepped off the boat, only he was a little more discrete about it.

"I don't blame you for looking, just try to make it a little less obvious, bwana. At least try not to drool all over yourself."

They came to the end of a narrow alley, shaded by tall adobe houses on either side, and stepped out into the sunlight.

Tomobo turned and announced, "Gentlemen, this is Aye Market, the heart of Accra and the center of life itself. This is where I'll leave you for the afternoon. Treat yourselves to anything you like. Just tell the vendor you are with Kodo. And don't worry about finding your way around or getting lost. We're a big town, but not that big. Everyone still knows everyone, so you'll be easy for me to find. I'll come get you later this evening. O dabọ, awọn ọrẹ." Tomobo bade his friends goodbye, turned and disappeared amidst the throng of market goers.

EnKare was overwhelmed. He stood on the spot, slack-jawed, staring at the entrance to the market. It was more than beautiful. More than he could comprehend. Tapestries of every print and pattern were strung up and suspended above the rows, providing shade and bathing the market in a kaleidoscope of color.

"Well," EnKare spoke up first, "shall we…"

"Yes, bwana! We shall," Jioba shouted as he grabbed EnKare by the wrist and plunged headlong down one of the market's main arteries.

Booths brimming with exotic fruits and fresh veggies lined the pathway.

"What is that," EnKare asked one of the vendors, pointing at a small red fruit with a shiny skin and soft spines.

"That is a rambutan," the vendor responded. "It originated in Asia. A place called Indonesia. Would you like to try it?"

Dozens of samples later and deep within Mami Wata's Underwater Garden, Jioba's nickname for the market, EnKare stopped to rest.

Mami Wata's Underwater Garden! Ha. Jimmy's a genius. From the outside it looks like an ordinary market, but once entered, and its magical fruit eaten, its victims are condemned to wander its streets till the end of time. Not a bad way to go!

In the Bakers' Quarter they feasted on warm and doughy oven fired breads, and jelly and cream filled pastries. The savory and sweet crepe were a hands-down favorite for both of them. Jioba described them as thin, French chapatis filled with love.

The leather section in the Artisans' Quarter was incredible, and EnKare tried on hats, belts, and jackets. But the backpacks impressed him the most. He even found one that had a place for his ingri, rungu, and extra room for a lunch and whatever else he might need while out herding.

Paintings, sculptures, pots, plates, bowls of fired clay! His senses were ablaze, skin tingling, mind dancing.

"Hey, Jimmy," he called out. Jioba was busy trying on a sheep's wool Sherpa hat, complete with ear flaps that dangled down over his round, smiling cheeks. "Not sure how, but I'm getting hungry again. What do you say we find some food carts?"

Jioba responded enthusiastically. "Chabalangus, bwana! Now you're speaking my language."

Being the independent creature that she was, Pilipili had long since bounded off to explore on her own. EnKare was used to this, however, and wasn't too worried about it.

They wandered down alleys lined with hand-hammered copper pots and corridors of flowers. As they passed through an area of carpets hanging from wooden dowels, a young girl stepped out from behind a curtained stall squashed between two shops and beckoned to them with a wave of her hand.

He was struck by how out of place this little girl was. She had hazelnut chocolate skin, a narrow, high-bridged nose, and straight, chestnut hair that sat on her head like a mop. Her eyes—pools of color that graduated from brilliant yellow sunbursts around the pupil, through forest green and ochre, to a smoky dark-grey band around the outer edge of the iris. They were the most mesmerizing eyes he had ever seen. And her clothing! Paisley patterned pants, baggy, blue and gold, pulled tight at the ankles, a crop-topped shirt of the same fabric, with long flowing sleeves that bunched together with drawstrings at the wrists. Draped lightly over her head, cascading around her hips, and thrown back over her shoulder was a sheer, turquoise and magenta scarf with hummingbirds embroidered on it. She wore large golden hoops on her ears, nose pierced on one side, and several rows of colorful beaded necklaces draped around her neck.

"Come," she said to EnKare, pulling on his hand and gesturing towards the curtained door. "My grandfather has been expecting you. Come." Even her accent was mysterious and out of place.

He looked at Jioba with raised eyebrows, and queried, "What do you say, bwana? Should we check it out? I mean her grandfather has been expecting us, after all."

"Sure, Toots," picking at the corner of one nostril, "It's not like we have someplace else to be."

The girl pulled back the curtain, and they followed her through the opening. They barely fit inside the narrow corridor, which was cast in cool blues and greens from the tapestried walls and ceiling. The girl parted a second curtain and motioned for them to step through. EnKare's olfactories were greeted by the scent of sweet incense, as he ducked his head and stepped into the darkness.

There, in shadows, was a man sitting cross-legged on the carpeted floor behind a low wooden table. On the table rested a small leather bag and a single candle that cast a faint glow over the man's drawn face—a face more ancient than the weathered stone of Elephant Rock—with cavernous eye sockets receding into corniced cheekbones, and the narrow jawline of a jackal. His umber skin shone, smooth and faintly glowing. Long, straight white hair twisted up into a bun on the top of his head, and a wispy, silver beard sprouted from his chin and brushed the table, evoking the faqirs of ancient India.

And this head, which hailed from the dawn of time itself, sat squarely on the lean, muscular body of man in his thirties. The juxtaposition was unsettling.

"Sit, young travelers, and let the bones tell you of what was, what is, and what is to come." He spoke with the same accent as the little girl, and at such a deep frequency that EnKare could feel it vibrating in the pit of his stomach. He glanced at Jioba, who shot a look of mild concern back at him.

As they sat down on the cushions, the old man pulled open the bag and spilled the bones out onto the table, all the while keeping his gaze fixed on a point in space between them.

"Mmmmmmm," His voice rumbled quietly. Then he remained silent and perfectly still, never once looking down at the bones.

After a couple of minutes, which felt like hours, EnKare looked over at Jioba, tilted his head, squinted one eye, and shrugged his shoulders as if to say, *what's going on?* Jioba drew the corner of his lips down and shrugged back.

The old man's voice hummed again in a soothing tone, and then at last he spoke;

"From freedom to slavery you ride the waves

Once you stop looking, the heart finds what it craves

There is no hope till all hope is gone

So you follow the water, you follow the song

On Tendua's path you have chosen to be

Follow her through the darkness, and you will be free

The Saptarishis point the way home

When little Prince Dhruva sits high on his throne"

EnKare, who had been engrossed in the bones on the table, was confused by what he heard.

He looked up at the soothsayer to ask for clarity and almost leapt out of his skin. For a fleeting moment, the image of a black leopard was superimposed over the old man's face, or had the man's face contorted to resemble a chui nyeusi? Either way, the effect only lasted a moment.

EnKare blinked several times. *Was it just the darkness of the room, and candle light playing off incense smoke that created the illusion?*

Shaken, he rose to his feet. "Meda wo ase, Opanin." He respectfully thanked the old man in a local dialect.

"Aapaka svaagat hai," the old man responded in a language he had never heard before.

"We have nothing to barter with you," EnKare continued, "but we are with…"

"Kodo, theek hai," the old man finished EnKare's sentence, bobbling his head in a gesture that was neither a nod nor a shake, but a combination of both.

Once they were out of the dark tent and back in the bright, colorful hustle and bustle of the market, the boys turned to each other and burst out in laughter.

"Bwana, what just happened?" Jioba sputtered.

"No lo sé amigo, but, but, but did you see the leopard? The chui nyeusi? It was there in his face, or it was his face, or…" he struggled to find an appropriate description of what he had seen.

"Chui nyeusi? Na, bwana, but did you see the sea turtle? The old man's whole head turned into the head of a leather back. It scared me so bad that, for a minute, I thought I soiled my shorts!" Jioba contorted his face, lifted a leg and pretended to check his britches. This caused them to laugh even harder, which then morphed into clapping and singing as they turned the old man's words into a song.

Then, following their noses, at the request of their grumbling stomachs, they danced their way to the food carts at the center of the market.

"Jimmy, Jimmy, Jimmy, come here." He dragged Jioba by the arm, pulling him out into the middle of the food carts. "Smell THAT!" They stood back to back and closed their eyes, breathing in the magic.

Jioba broke the silence. "I'm so hungry, Toots, I could seriously eat a whole kudu right now!" They finger whip-snapped the air then slapped out a handshake.

"And so we shall, my friend, so we shall. Twendeni!"

The Rounds

I thought we'd find you here," a voice called from the edge of the food court. It was Tomobo, and he was standing with another man. "Come, gentlemen, I want you to meet my uncle Kodo."

Uncle Kodo looked as though he had been forged by the sea herself. Every muscle in his body flexed and drew tightly under his skin, which was sun-darkened and calloused by the chafing wind and salt water. The hair on his forearms had been bleached white by the elements. His bald head glistened with sweat and sat squarely on his latitudinous shoulders.

There was something in the man's eyes—eyes that were circumscribed by deep, cutting smile lines, which ran contrary to the rest of his appearance. They were kind eyes, friendly even.

After brief introductions, Tomobo said, "You two look as though you could use a bite to eat. Let's do the rounds, shall we?"

EnKare look at Jioba, who was grinning and nodding his head so enthusiastically that it was a wonder it hadn't popped right off.

They started at a small booth serving a fermented cabbage dish, called kimchi. The vendor's family had immigrated to Africa from Korea three generations ago, and she had kept the family recipes alive. He liked the tangy, spicy flavor and the contrast of the cold cabbage on the bed of steaming rice.

Next, they moved to a cart where a man was making empanadas. They were similar to roti, but thicker and filled with savory stews or sweet creams and fruit. The vendor was a descendant of Argentinian immigrants who had moved from the harsh living conditions in Buenos Aires, to a small coastal village in Tunisia. Of all his family, he alone had survived Iworo, then made his way south to Accra.

After devouring three or four empanadas each, they pulled up some small wooden stools and sat down next to a vendor roasting cassava root over a charcoal pit. The root was sliced down the middle, doused in lime juice and pilipili, and served on clay plates. Exotic foods from around the word were amazing, but nothing beat a local classic like cassava and pilipili.

EnKare thought of his little galago friend and smiled. *Where on earth is she? Well, at least she won't go hungry around here.*

"Gentlemen," Kodo spoke with a mouthful of cassava, "thank you for getting my nephew and his friend here so quickly. I didn't think it was possible. You must be quite the sailors."

Jioba beamed with pride.

Kodo continued, "I'm sure Tomobo told you all about my ship, the *Buganvilla*, and about our venture to set up new trading routes to the north, along our Mediterranean coast?"

EnKare remained quiet. *Buganvilla! Great name for a ship.*

"Yes," responded Jioba. "You are leaving in a day or two, on the next full moon, right?"

"That's right." Kodo paused. "Listen, I'll get straight to the point. Two of my crew have jumped ship and I'm looking for replacements. From what Tomobo says about your skill and experience, I'd like to offer you the positions. I'd like you to crew my ship, along with Tomobo and Jafra. What do you say?"

EnKare started to say, "Well, actually, this was my first…"

Jioba cut him off and blurted out, "This is our first major job offer, other than bringing Tomobo and Jafra here to Accra."

Then the questions started.

"How will we notify our families?"

"There is the matter of my boat."

"How long will we be gone?"

"Where exactly is the voyage headed again?"

"How much experience should one have for a voyage like that?"

Kodo raised a hand. "These are all great questions. Important questions. There is much for you to think about. I don't need your answer till tomorrow morning, so for tonight we eat, we dance, and we celebrate you bringing my nephew home safely."

The sun had dipped low on the horizon, and thousands of colorful solar lights illuminated the market. A group of performers gathered in the space at the center of the food carts and started their show. Drummers pounded on goat and cow skin drums while the troupe used music and dance to tell the story of the Wenye Hekima, the founders of United Africa.

He was impressed with the dancers' costumes. Each was dressed in the traditional clothing and adorned in the cultural accessories of the Elder they represented. Seeing the Himba dancer playing the role of his mother made him homesick. He thought of her and smiled. If she could only see how, even here in Accra, she was celebrated with such love and joy.

Everyone back home knew that he was the son of Okuruwo, the Sacred Fire of the Himba people, but here he was unknown. There was something refreshing about the anonymity, and he intended to keep it that way.

His thoughts returned to the more immediate question at hand; would they join the crew of the *Buganvilla*? Would he realize his dream of exploring the world? Or was that biting off more chapati than he was ready to chew?

New Salt

Nausea. The rougher the seas, the more his stomach acids churned and boiled. Not the sort of night one writes home to mom about.

"Rise n' shine, ye old sea dog." He opened his eyes to the sight of Jioba's upside down face looking at him. On account of EnKare not feeling well when they went to bed the previous evening, Jioba had taken the top bunk, from which he was now dangling, goofy smile and all. The blood had rushed to his head causing his cheeks and eyes to puff up. He looked like a happy blowfish. Jimmy had a way of cheering him up, no matter what state his body was in.

"Have you seen how fast we are going?"

EnKare looked out of the porthole window beside his bed. The sea was racing past in a blur of foam and spray. Like a small picture frame with an ever changing image projected on it, one moment he was looking at wave crests and the next a dark and murky underwater scene. He looked at Jioba and grimaced. The room rocked side to side and he felt he might be sick again.

"C'mon, lazy bones, it's time to go topside. We need to learn how to run this beauty! Capitán Kodo and the others are waiting." Jioba flipped himself over the edge of the bunk and landed in a squat.

Things were moving so fast. Just yesterday they were running wild in the streets of Accra, and now they were at sea, members of an elite group of world explorers. Furthermore, they were crewing the most advanced ship in the world! What a ride.

"Cálmate, bwana! I only found out that I didn't vomit myself to death about five minutes ago. Some of us weren't born on a boat, ya know," he muttered while pulling himself up and slipping on his canvas shorts.

A knock came at the door. Tomobo wedged into the opening to stabilize himself. "Training day, gentlemen!" he cheerfully yelled into the room. "Jioba, you'll be shadowing me today, and EnKare, you'll go with Jafra. The wind has picked up out of the south, and we'll be raising the sails in five. Let's go, gentlemen!" His voice trailed behind as he vanished from the doorway as quickly as he had appeared.

EnKare glanced at his weapons, which were propped at the head of his bed.

Don't imagine I'll be needing those today. Although Jimmy might need a little herding. You never know.

Jioba had already disappeared out the door. EnKare followed him into the hallway. Everything was lustrous, polished metal. The walls, floor, ceiling, and even the stairway glimmered in the natural light that flooded in through the portholes.

As he stepped onto the aft deck, the dazzling morning light bathed him in the full realization of where he was, and what he was doing there. Sun-warmed, salty Atlantic air filled his nostrils, bursts of spray billowed past as the boat sliced through the sea—and Africa, his beloved continent, rose up out of the ocean in the distance, like a giant sleeping elephant. He paused at the top of the steps, senses coming to life, and breathed in the moment.

They were on the lowest of three decks, on the stern of a ship that was as wide as a blue whale and half the length of a football pitch. Two masts sprouted from her midsection and tickled the sky. He craned his neck to see the stork's nest perched at the top of one of the masts. *Now that is a proper stork's nest. One day I'll climb up to you,* his stomach turned and complained loudly, *but today is not that day.*

Something wasn't right, but he couldn't figure out what. Then it struck him like a rhino sneeze, and he realized the sails weren't up. How could they be sailing without sails?

"Gentlemen!" Capitán Kodo's voice came from behind. "Welcome aboard *Buganvilla,* the most advanced ship in the world. We are currently cruising at fifteen knots, propelled entirely by electric impeller jets that run off hydrogen generators and salt water batteries. EnKare, you and Jafra will master and maintain electrical systems, hydro generators, batteries, impeller jets, lighting, plumbing, refrigeration systems, deck and hallway illumination, and the sonic anti-fouling system. Jioba, my nephew will help you master running systems, foil operation, solar sails, rigging, propulsion, anchors, charts, maps, and piloting. We are a skeleton crew on a ship designed to run with twice our number, so you will all master your departments, as well as train in and have a working knowledge of all aspects of running the ship. We'll discuss a meal prep schedule and other mundane tasks later. Now, we take advantage of this wind and hoist the solar sails. With a little luck you'll get to see what this ship was built to do. Let's get to it!"

The one-way conversation ended, and Capitán Kodo ran up the steps to the middeck and disappeared through a doorway. EnKare glanced at Jioba and was relieved to see his friend looking just as bewildered as he was feeling. *Jet-propulsion? Solar sails? Sonic anti-fouling? What language was he speaking?*

He waved a quick goodbye to Jioba as they split into two groups and raced off in different directions. Following Jafra up the steps, they made their way to the first mast on the middeck. With Jafra barking instructions over the wind chatter, they walked the length of the boom unbuttoning the white canvas sail covering. Folding the cover meticulously and placing it in a gear chest at the base of the mast, they then released the halyard clamps and checked to see that nothing would interfere in the raising of the sail. Then he followed Jafra to the second mast, on the foredeck, and repeated the procedure. From there they went to the front of the boat where a narrow walkway led out onto the bowsprit.

"The jib sail is rolled up inside that tube," Jafra yelled, pointing at the long, narrow cylinder that extended at an angle from about a foot above the top of the side rail, to the top of the mast. "There's a pin there at the bottom of the cylinder, connected to a short safety wire. We don't want you dropping the pin overboard," Jafra teased. "All you have to do is head out there, pull out the pin and let it dangle from the wire, then come back."

"I don't suppose there's a little safety wire for me too, is there?"

EnKare had been out on the bowsprit of the *Mandaha* too many times to count, but this was different. Maybe it was just the increased speed, but the seas appeared much rougher than he had experienced before? Everything was bigger, faster, louder.

Scarier!

But before the fear could really set in, he remembered his encounter with the dolphins on the crossing to Accra. With a calm confidence he took a deep breath, stepped onto the bowsprit, and shuffled his way out to the forestay. Wind-whipped spray blasted his eyes as the ship surged forward, pitching and heaving like a bull rhino in rut.

It took all his concentration to locate the pin and pull it out without getting swept overboard. The moment the pin was loose he stood up, and, without warning, his stomach surged and he vomited…directly into the wind.

As he stepped back onto the deck, it didn't matter that his face was covered in his own nauseant, or that Jafra was bent double in laughter. He was alive! That alone was a fact worth celebrating.

Composure regained, Jafra pulled a green flag from his back pocket, raised it over his head, and traced three large circles in the air. "I'm letting Capitán Kodo know that the sails are ready for hoisting. Quick, follow me! You've got to see this. You're about to find out why we call her *Buganvilla*!"

They retraced their way to the stern of the boat where Jioba and Tomobo were already waiting.

"Look!" Tomobo shouted, pointing at the masts.

EnKare watched as the hard, metallic ship transformed before his eyes. Like a forest butterfly emerging from its pupa, all four sails unfurled simultaneously and rose into the sky, outstretched wings billowing and rolling in the wind. The sails were not made of canvas, like those on Jioba's boat. They glistened in the sun and reflected a shimmering rainbow of color that danced over the face of the sails as they undulated. Then the ship made a slight turn to port, sails snapped tight, and she charged forward.

EnKare yelled, "*Buganvilla*! I get it!"

"Those, my friends," Tomobo strained over the howling wind, "are the solar sails." There was such pride in his voice. "Now quick, back to the front!"

In all the excitement and frenzy, EnKare had forgotten about the vomit on his face. He ran behind the others, back up the steps, past the masts, to the front of the boat where he had just come from. Tomobo and Jafra grabbed onto the bulwark railing on either side of the bowsprit, leaned their weight forward, and motioned for EnKare and Jioba to do the same.

He obliged, though reluctantly. Then the strangest thing happened. It felt as though Mama Bulu had surfaced below the ship, lifting the entire vessel out of the water in one steady movement. How was this possible? He looked over the side, and sure enough the hull was rising, steadily, up out of the churning, tumultuous waves. As their speed increased, the vessel lifted higher and higher until the hull was floating just above the surface of the sea.

He stepped back in disbelief and looked at Jioba, who was still dangling over the railing, hooting and howling into the wind and laughing hysterically.

Jioba yelled, "Can you see this, bwana? We're flying! We're flying, bwana. Tomobo, you never told me our ship could fly!"

EnKare felt a wave of nausea wash over him again, and then he lost his equilibrium and stumbled backwards. A firm hand gripped his upper arm and helped stabilize him.

"Wewe ni mzungu, bwana," Jioba chided. "You should see your face, Toots, it's like the sails on the *Mandaha*."

"Mimi si mzungu, Jimmy, but I do feel a little kizunguzungu. Everything is spinning." EnKare twirled his finger in a circle beside his head.

"Just don't vomit on me. We'll get you below deck. The boat rocks less down there, so that should help." Jioba threw EnKare's arm around his neck and helped him back to their cabin.

Old Salt

Within the first week of sailing many things improved in EnKare's world. His stomach-churning trips to the head decreased, while his understanding and appreciation for the ship grew.

He felt great pride to be African, such honor to be crewing on the only ship on earth that could fly. Capitán Kodo had explained how it worked. Adjustable metal blades fixed to the belly of the ship, called foils, caused the craft to rise out of the water. The faster they went, the higher up she would rise, gliding along on the foils and effectively cutting hull drag and stabilizing the pitch of the boat. They weren't *actually* flying, since the foils never left the water.

But to EnKare, when the ship was foiling, it may as well have been flying. Instead of plowing through the chop, tossing and pitching like an elephant with a leech lodged up its nose, the ship would glide smoothly, as if skimming over a thin layer of flamingo poop coating a great salt lake. Though his mind couldn't fully comprehend how the foil system worked, his stomach understood it perfectly well.

This morning it was his turn to wake Jioba. He had been lying there for at least an hour, watching the sky outside his window turn from obsidian, to gold-dusted indigo, and listening to the low rumble of Jioba's snoring. Rolling onto his back, he kicked the wooden slats of the upper bunk.

"Rise n' shine, Oldoinyo! What's the point of super quiet propulsion jets when you've got an old fashioned internal combustion engine roaring right above you?" He kicked the bed again.

Jioba let out an extra loud snort then dangled his head over the edge and, in a groggy voice, said, "I don't snore, bwana." Then in a matter-of-factual tone he added, "C'mon, lazy bones, let's get to work," as if he was the one who woke up first all along.

Munching on a banana and a chunk of coconut meat, EnKare stepped into the hallway, waved a comical salute in Jioba's direction, then headed off to perform his morning work. He descended a flight of polished aluminum steps, opened a heavy metal door by spinning a hand wheel, and stepped into the engine and systems room.

Grabbing a clipboard from its hook beside the door, he ambled past various monitors and banks of blinking lights that flanked the walls of the room, checking off little boxes as he went. Every system on the ship amazed him, but one in particular stood above the rest: the antifouling system. Jioba had to swim under his boat every few days to scrape off crustaceans and barnacles that fixed themselves to the hull. If he didn't, the build up would take over the boat and it would become a floating reef in no time. The simple system on the *Buganvilla* worked by pulsing a specific sound wave through the aluminum hull of the ship. Scientists in Accra had figured out the precise frequency to deter crustaceans. The system used a trifle of electricity, didn't pollute the water, and was harmless to sea life and crew.

A perfect system.

When he was done in the systems room he passed through another door labeled engine room and proceeded to inspect the salt water batteries, the hydrogen generators, and the propulsion jet engines. The jet engines were impossibly complex machines that took up most of the room. When he was done he hung up the clipboard, closed up the rooms, and went on deck. It was his and Jioba's turn to make breakfast.

On the way to the galley he almost tripped over a chicken. The hen let out a belligerent *BA-GAWK*, pecked at one of his toenails, then turned and waddled off in search of some unfortunate stowaway grasshopper.

He traced the hen's path back to the chicken coop that had been added to the outside wall of the main cabin and lifted the lid to one of the layer boxes. *Perfect!* Three beautiful eggs were clustered in the middle of the grass nest. A quick search through a few more boxes yielded enough eggs to whip up an omelet for the crew. With his calciferous bounty nestled carefully in his shuka, he entered the main cabin and made his way through the mess hall to the galley.

As the sun's rays bounced off the ocean and beamed through the windows, Jioba danced into the room, clapping his hands and singing another tune from his Grandfather's record collection. EnKare joined in the singing and started banging a wooden spoon on the counter. Jioba picked up a cheese grater and a knife and rounded out the percussion with a syncopated scratching. By the time the chorus came around, they were dancing, beating on pots, and striking any surface that made an interesting sound.

The only one not amused by their playing was Pilipili, who had been sleeping soundly in a dark corner of one of the cupboards. When the pans started clanging she headed for the door and disappeared, off to find a quiet corner where she could sleep away the day.

Must be nice, Pilipili. No morning chores, no cooking and cleaning. Wouldn't mind changing places with you for a day!

When the song had run its course, they slapped out a *Buganvilla*-influenced handshake—lots of new wavy motions, some staged stumbles, and a mock vomit to round it off.

"So, what are we making for breakfast, Toots?" Jioba asked.

"Ha, that's right. I'd kind of forgotten why we were in the kitchen in the first place." EnKare shrugged, walked over to the fridge and opened the two enormous cooler doors. Without verbalizing any conclusions, he pulled out an onion, some carrots, a bunch of spinach, a handful of basil leaves, three tomatoes, three yams and a piece of ginger root. They spread the ingredients out across the counter.

"I think I'll do a sweet potato stew with some left over snapper from yesterday's catch," Jioba declared.

"Sounds good, Jimmy. I'll scramble these eggs and make some chapatis."

By now they had adjusted to cooking for five hungry men. On the first few attempts, portions were a little light, and moods were a little heavy. The correlation between caloric satiation and the crew's performance had quickly become clear.

He diced up the spinach, a basil leaf, a tomato, and half the onion, then cracked the eggs into a bowl and stirred in all the choppings. Then he pulled out a gourd containing wheat flour and went to work making the chapati dough. In the meantime, Jioba stepped out of the kitchen to grab a coconut from one of the many rope baskets that were hanging in random places around the ship. The baskets of fruit, piles of sugar cane, sacks filled with coffee beans, legumes, and grains, the chickens meandering about the decks—all this brought a sense of familiarity, of home, a breath of life into an otherwise sterile metal landscape.

Jioba husked the coconut on a metal spike attached to a small wooden stool just outside the kitchen door. Then he cracked the nut with a machete, catching the water in a large bowl. He set the bowl under the serrated edge of a wedge-shaped piece of metal that was attached to the other side of the stool, took a seat, and proceeded to scrape the coconut against the blade, catching the shredded meat in the bowl.

"Hey, bwana, what can I do to help?" asked EnKare.

"Just dice the sweet potatoes and the rest of the onions," Jioba replied over his shoulder

Over the next half hour they worked together to bring the dishes to life, dancing and chanting the names of each ingredient—a playful homage to the lives taken in order to sustain their own.

The onions, basil, and yams went into a large pan to simmer in the coconut milk. Next, Jioba tossed in a handful of peanuts, thinly sliced red snapper meat, three whole red chilies, two handfuls of raisins, and a sprinkle of salt. While the yam dish simmered, EnKare poured the scrambled egg mixture into another pan and stirred continuously as the dish cooked. Once the eggs and chapatis were done, EnKare turned to his friend. "Would you like to do the honors, bwana," he asked, pointing to the long, gently spiraling cow horn hanging on a hook beside the kitchen door.

"Na, Toots, I still haven't got the hang of it. When I blow that horn it sounds like one of the chickens dying a slow, painful death, tu sabes. You do it."

EnKare stepped out onto the middeck, put the horn to his lips, and let out a series of sharp blasts followed by a sustained note. It had become his signature call to mealtime. As he lowered the horn his gaze stretched out over the horizon to the north and something odd caught his attention.

"Hey, Jimmy, come out here."

Jioba stepped into the doorway, a sheepish grin on his face and a folded piece of chapati disappearing between his lips. "Whuth up, bwana," he managed through a full mouth.

"Have we turned directions or something? I thought Africa was in that direction. That is north isn't it?" He pointed off the starboard beam of the ship.

Jioba glanced at the sky, then swept the horizon all the way around the boat. He swallowed his mouthful of chapati, then said, "Ndio, bwana, that is north. I don't see Africa anywhere. Strange. I thought we would have turned by now to head up along the north western coastline and through the Straits."

"Hmm. Maybe we just can't see it. I don't know. C'mon, let's go eat!"

Blindsided

Dead calm. There wasn't a breath of wind across the ocean for as far as he could see. Pushed up by some distant storm system hundreds of miles away, low, gently rolling waves kissed the prow as the ship sliced through the water at a steady clip.

Amazing. The sails aren't even up, and we are still going fast.

Jioba lazily cautioned, "Eh, Toots, don't drink all of that. Save some for me."

The boys looked like a pair of beach bums, stretched out on hammocks strung up on the lower deck. EnKare was sipping on the sweet nectar of a coconut while looking out at the rolling ocean speeding by.

"Cálmate, bwana. It's still almost full." He tossed the husked nut over to his friend.

Three days had passed since they noticed that the continent was no longer visible, but he had been too busy with work to have given it much thought. Now that they had a little down time they returned to the conversation.

"Hey, Jimmy, have you noticed Jafra and Tomobo acting a little strange lately?"

"No, Toots, why?"

"I don't know, exactly. They just seem a little on edge."

"I suppose so. But we've all been working really hard. I know I've not been Mr. Happy Hyena at all times, that's for sure," Jioba joked.

EnKare thought for a moment, then added, "Does it bother you that we haven't been able to see Africa for days now?"

"Na. I'm sure Capitán Kodo is just taking a wide birth around the outside of Cape Verde and the Canary Islands, before bringing us in through the Straits of Gibraltar. Maybe there's some dangerous shorelines he's trying to avoid."

"Ya, I suppose you're right." EnKare sighed.

Tomobo descended the steps from the middeck and walked up to them. "Uncle Kodo has called a meeting, gentlemen," he said in his usual polite, cheerful voice. "We'll meet in the stateroom in ten minutes."

"What's the meeting about?"

"I have no idea. Sounded important, though. I'm gonna go find Jafra. I think he's fishing off the prow."

As Tomobo disappeared up the steps, Jioba looked at EnKare with a glint in his eyes. "The *stateroom*," he said in a regal tone.

"I know, bwana, I've never even been in the *stateroom*. Have you?" Jioba shook his head. "Should we at least go and put a shirt on or something?"

A couple minutes later the relatively dressed boys emerged from their cabin and met up with Jafra and Tomobo on the middeck. EnKare couldn't help but notice that the young men had a different take on getting 'dressed up' than he and Jioba.

To get to the stateroom they had to go through the wheelhouse, the brain center of the whole operation. One wall was completely devoted to charts and maps, while another was filled with devices, such as a sextant, a telescoping monocular, and electronic contraptions with dials, nobs, and switches. There were two piloting wheels, one beside the other, each with a full set of system controls and readouts.

They passed through a doorway to the left of the wheels and descended a wooden staircase that opened into the stateroom. It was unlike any room he had seen on the ship, or anywhere for that matter. The walls and floor where covered in richly toned mahogany boards, and ebony beams arched overhead, holding up a sandalwood ceiling. Cabinets and lamps were made from exquisitely carved acacia wood. Everything was sanded and oiled. Soffited lights, where the ceiling and walls met, cast a warm and welcoming glow over the room.

Unlike the rest of the ship, which was made out of rustproof aluminum, all the metalwork here was oil-rubbed brass. Off to one side, Capitán Kodo was sitting on a dark stained leather sofa. On the wall above his head hung a mighty shield made from a cross sectional slab of baobab root. There were nine chevron shaped notches carved into the outer edges of the shield and evenly spaced around its circumference. From each of the nine notches a straight line was chiseled to a carved circle at the center, creating the image of a sun emanating its rays. He recognized the emblem. It was the Shield of Africa. *From many we are one*. He wondered which of the notches was meant to represent his mother.

"Gentlemen, please, come join me," the Capitán said, motioning for the four young men to take a seat on an adjacent sofa. Kodo sat quietly for a moment, as if trying to choose the right words. The silence cast an uneasy mood among the crew, and EnKare shot an awkward, questioning look at Jioba, who replied with a baffled expression of his own.

"Well," the Capitán's voice startled. Jioba nearly fell off the couch from the jolt. "There really is no easy way to say this, so I'm gonna just lay it out straight for you. I'm sure you've all noticed by now that we aren't hugging the head of Africa. We aren't anywhere near the Straits of Gibraltar. In fact, we aren't going to the Mediterranean at all. We *are* on a mission to establish a new trade route, though not along the northern coast of Africa. Gentlemen," he paused again to clear his throat. "We are traveling to Nchi Mbaya."

This sparked a barrage of comments and questions from the crew:

"Impossible!"

"It's forbidden!"

"It's contaminated!"

"But how can we go there? No one has ever gone there before."

"Why did you lie to us and tell us we were going to North Africa?"

"Yes, and…"

"Gentlemen, please calm yourselves for a moment. I know you will have many questions and many concerns. I will answer them all as best I can. But first, I'll leave you for a few minutes to talk it out. We'll reconvene here in half an hour." The Capitán rose to his feet and left the room.

The four young men look at each other, each with some variation of shock or horror on his face. Then the debate began.

"There's nothing there but wasteland and clouds of toxic gas. The water boils in the lakes, and nothing can live there. NOTHING!" EnKare was shouting.

"I've heard rumors of monsters," Jafra added.

"Has my uncle lost his mind? I mean, what would be the point of setting up a trade route with a land that is uninhabitable and has been utterly destroyed? There's nothing and no one there to trade with!"

EnKare looked at Jioba, who was sitting quietly, deep in thought. "Hey, Jimmy, what do you think? You haven't said much."

Jioba looked at the others. "I, too, was raised with the stories of Nchi Mbaya—acid rain, man-eating monsters, toxic fumes instead of air, a barren wasteland where nothing lives, an expanse of destruction a thousand times more harsh and forbidding than the Sahara Desert." He stood up. "I know the stories, but are they true? No one has been, so how do we really know?"

The others voiced their protests, but Jioba continued. "I mean, the same toxic clouds rained acid down on Africa for six years. Six cold, endless winters brought most life on our continent to an end.

The water was poison. The air was foul. But look at us now. A mere half century after Iworo, life has returned to Africa in spectacular ways. We are discovering new species all the time, our waters are pure. Plant and animal life is flourishing. Mother Earth has shown us how she can heal. Perhaps Nchi Mbaya is no different."

The room was silent for a moment as Jioba's words sank in. "But, Jimmy," EnKare spoke up, "have you forgotten that Nchi Mbaya, unlike Africa, received hundreds, if not thousands of direct hits. We're talking hundreds of thousands of megatons of nuclear bombs scattered across the continent. It was literally blown to pieces. The radiation levels at the impact zones, all the major cities, would be thousands of times greater than the radiation we got in Africa."

"This might be true," Jafra butted in, "but the Americas are vast continents of land, and in many areas there are hundreds of miles between these target zones. The long term radiation from the blasts would have climbed into the stratosphere and blown around the planet. The areas farthest away from the impact zones might have had a similar healing and recovery time to what we experienced in Africa. No?"

"OK. OK, Jafra," Tomobo interjected, "so let's say you are right. Let's say that there is life in Nchi Mbaya. I still don't see the point of us going there. If everything was blown to pieces then what could there possibly be for us to bring home?"

"Resources," Jioba said. "Resources. Think of the sheer volume of resources, metals, electronics, building materials, fabrics. I don't know, anything that didn't get blown up. The west was infamous for plundering and hording the world's resources. From Africa they took precious metals, minerals and gems, fruits, nuts, grains, coffee and cacao. They also took our petroleum oil out of the ground and used it to expand their wealth and power and to build their weapons. Much would have been lost in Iworo, I'm sure, but anything that remains? We could be the first to set up this trade route. The first to prove that there is, or is not, life in Nchi Mbaya." Jioba was jumping up and down with excitement.

"OK, calm down, bwana. I don't know." Then turning his question towards Tomobo and Jafra, "What do you think of all this? Clearly Jimmy here thinks it's a good idea."

After a moment of silence, Tomobo spoke. "I don't know either. I have so many questions for my uncle. Perhaps once I have those answers I'll be able to make up my mind."

The half hour seemed to fly by, and the crew was still deep in debate when the Capitán entered the room again. He took his place on the opposite sofa and opened the conversation.

"Well, now that you've had a little time to talk it over, I'm sure you have some questions for me."

The first to speak was Tomobo. "Why did you lie to us? Why did you lie to *me*?" There was a touch of hurt and betrayal in his voice.

"If the Council of Accra had known of my intent they would not have granted me use of the ship," Kodo confessed. "And if I had mentioned even a word of it to any of you then the whole town would have known in a matter of days. You know how word gets around? A people of secrets, we are not."

Jioba's hand was raised as though he was back in Mrs. Msoke's class.

"You don't have to raise your hand, Jioba," the Capitán said with a smile.

"What if any one of us decides we don't want to go? Do we even have a choice in the matter?"

This was the very question that EnKare had on his mind, but he had felt awkward about asking it. Thank goodness for his fearless friend.

"Gentlemen," the Capitán responded, "I deceived you, because without this ship there would be no voyage into the unknown. But there can also be no voyage without a willing crew. I vow that if even one of us is not fully invested, we'll turn north and carry on with the plan as you originally knew it."

This response surprised EnKare, but it did relieve some of the tension in his neck and stomach. He took advantage of the silence to ask a question of his own. "Why Nchi Mbaya? Why is it so important to go there?"

After a moment's pause the Capitán answered. "I'm friends with a couple of scientists in Accra. They believe it is possible that enough time has gone by for the American continents to have recovered from Iworo, for there to be life there, for the environment to no longer be toxic. If this is true and it is safe again, then what an adventure and what an honor to be the first humans to set foot in the old world. If we succeed in proving that Nchi Mbaya has healed herself, we could bring this information back to Africa and use it to convince the Wenye Hekima to lift the travel ban. And there is also the possibility that we might discover vast quantities of valuable resources that will help Africa into the future. We may be the first to discover new species of plants and animals. To set foot where no one from our time has before. This is why I'm a sailor, an adventurer, instead of a farmer or a shop keeper. The mysteries and magic hiding beyond the waves speak to me, and I can only heed the call and follow my heart. So each of you must ask yourself: why are you here? Does the unknown just over the horizon beckon to you as it does me? If not, we turn north. But if we are indeed cut from the same cloth, then gentlemen, our destiny awaits us at the mouth of the Hudson River, in what they used to call New York City."

The Deal

The dungeon door swung open with a grinding scream, and Fritz convulsed his way through the opening. "OoooooWeeee, wormbait! Ain't it yer lucky day, this ain't no roll in da hay, I've come here ta say dat his Highest Lord Highness is payin' y'all a visit."

Back-lit by the torchlight in the hall, Fritz looked more like a disfigured dust broom than a human being, and Wakíŋyaŋ couldn't help but giggle.

"Look Wí, he looks like something my friend Níškola dug up in the forest and dropped at my door," she whispered. The two of them giggled quietly as the talking scarecrow continued his speech.

"Na come out yer rat infested hidin' places, don't be shy ta show yer faces, line up out here in da open spaces, n' get down on yer knees."

Wit'é looked at Wakíŋyaŋ, unable to mask the fear hiding behind the glassy surface of her eyes.

"Come on, Wí. Don't worry, just stay by my side, and you'll be fine," she consoled in a soft, reassuring voice, pulling the straw-haired girl to her feet. They made their way out of the railcar, lined up in front of Fritz with the others, and got down on their knees.

Why is Bronx coming all the way down here? He hasn't come down once since I've been here.

A shadow obscured the light in the hallway, and Fritz scurried to one side as the leviathan stooped his head and stepped through the doorway. Wakíŋyaŋ hadn't seen the giant since the incident in his living quarters, and his presence struck a nerve in the pit of her stomach. The hairs on the back of her neck stood on end, and, without thinking, her fingers curled into fists.

Bronx muttered something to the scarecrow, who responded promptly with, "Yes yer Highest Up Bossness Masta." Then Fritz laboriously worked his way down the row of slaves, and came to a halt in front of Wakíŋyaŋ. "Come with me, wormbait. His Lordness wants ta talk wit ya."

Wit'é grabbed Wakíŋyaŋ's hand.

"Don't worry, little one, I'll be back before you know it. Stay here and help look after the others until I get back," she whispered in the little girl's ear. "You know, even in this dim light I can see the freckles on your nose."

Wit'é slowly let go of her hand and looked on with moist eyes as Wakíŋyaŋ rose to her feet and followed Fritz and the giant out of the dungeon.

They walked through the passageways in silence. Occasionally they'd pass a rogue who would stop whatever it was he was doing to bow to his leader, and to toss her a dirty look.

Eventually they came to a broad, wooden door in the side of the tunnel. Bronx pulled a key from under his fur and unlocked it. He took the torch from Fritz, disappeared into the room, and a moment later returned with an object in his hand.

Wakíŋyaŋ's eyes widened, her lips parted, but she didn't make a sound. The giant was holding her bow and quiver. She followed in silence as they moved down the hallway, out into the great hall, and over to a cluster of tables and chairs. Bronx sat down and motioned for her to do the same, then sent Fritz away with a grunt. Without taking her eyes off the bow she slowly sank onto the wooden stool.

They sat in silence until Wakíŋyaŋ's words shattered it. "What do you want?" she asked dryly.

"You hunt." She could feel the giant's voice vibrating the table. "You make this weapon." He wasn't asking a question. "You teach rogues how to hunt. To make weapon."

She looked directly into his eyes. "Why should I? Why should I help you?" She made no effort to mask the loathing and disdain in her voice.

"You get own room. No more dungeon. No more slave. You Bronx rogue." Then, setting the bow on the table, "You use this again."

She looked at the piece of wood in front of her. For a moment her face softened as she gazed fondly at the bow. It connected her to her people, her village, to Uŋčí and Níškola—to the hickory tree she had fashioned it from. She recalled the smooth, cold surface of the sandstone rasp she used to shape the wood. The sinew that backed the bow and corded the bowstring, the skin used to make the rawhide glue that bound all the parts into one, had come from a tȟáȟča she hunted three summers ago. The bow connected her to the birch tree which blew over in a winter storm, the bark of which she used to make the varnish that sealed and protected it from the elements. This was her favorite bow, a labor of love. She reached out to touch it, but the giant pulled it away.

She looked up at Bronx, the fire returning to her.

"You teach rogues to hunt. To make weapons from forest." There was little emotion in the man's expression or voice, but somewhere beneath his hardened exterior she detected something human. Something vulnerable. He needed her.

"OK. I'll teach you. But I'll continue to sleep in the dungeon with the others so long as I can come and go as I please, to bring food and medicine."

Bronx nodded his head in approval, and she reached for her bow.

He held it firmly. "You only have arrows when we hunt."

She nodded an agreement, and the giant relaxed his grip. She pulled the bow into her arms, turning it over several times, scanning it from top to bottom. Even the slightest crack could cause the bow to snap under tension. Her friend, Avani, had lost an eye that way.

Fritz's loud, twangy voice startled her from behind. "Ya made a deal wit da Masta, na it's time to make good. Git yer stuff ready, an meet back here lickety split. It's hunt'n time. And, sunshine," he moved in close enough that she could feel his foul breath on the back of her neck, "don't even think 'bout runnin' off, less ya feels like being da one we a hunt'n."

Don't worry, I'm not running off just yet. I'm not going anywhere without Wit'é.

Back in the dungeon she showed everyone her bow and let them know what had happened. Hiva was particularly excited about the bow but looked a little disappointed when she heard about the arrows.

"Why didn't you take the room, honey?" Bay asked. "Just think, you could sleep in a *real* bed again." As enthusiastic as her words were, the tone and delivery betrayed the fact that the old woman no longer knew what sleeping in a *real* bed felt like.

Wakíŋyaŋ responded bluntly. "The rogues are not my people. I make my bed where I make my home—here, with you."

Her words were well received. Even Jack managed to crack a smile.

Hiva came in close, and touched the bridge of her nose and forehead to Wakíŋyaŋ's. "Be careful out there. Don't do anything I wouldn't do."

Wakíŋyaŋ smiled. Then, turning to Wit'é, "I'm going out on a hunt now, but don't worry. Stay close to Dungeon Mother, and I'll be back before you know it. And you two," she looked down at the twins, "are going to have to let go of my legs now so I can leave."

Bark and Bite looked up at her with mischievous little eyes, then took off running, squealing and giggling.

Sea Creature

The hunting party consisted of herself, Bronx, and seven of his most able-bodied warriors. She led them onto a bluff that looked out over the expanse of patchy rubble-and-forest to look for signs of game. Almost immediately she spotted a herd of tȟáȟča grazing in an open field in the direction of the bay and pointed them out to Bronx.

They were a comical looking bunch. Bronx wore his customary bear furs and carried his iron mace in one hand and a spear in the other. The spear was made from three iron rods twisted together in a spiral and ground to a jagged point.

Lethal, but short range and likely to damage the meat.

The other hunters wore trash they had scavenged off the ground. It was on the soles of their feet, tied around their arms and heads, and fashioned into clothing. One wore armor that covered his shoulders, chest, and upper back, like he was going into battle. Another had crafted an elaborate headdress out of ferns and tufts of grass that stuck out in all directions and hung down over his shoulders. One hunter was naked, but for a thin loin cloth tied around his waist. He had painted lines and circles over most of his body with clay. His outfit made more sense than the others, but collectively the group looked silly, and there was no way they were adept at stalking. Killing, on the other hand, was almost certainly second nature to them.

There was one important thing they had overlooked. They had done nothing to mask their own eye-watering stench.

We'll never catch anything at this rate! A tȟáȟča could smell these heyókȟa from across the bay.

She led them down from the rubble mound and into a thicket of trees where she had seen the remains of a raccoon. "You must mask your own smell, or the deer will smell you before you can get in close enough to make a kill. Take this," she said, carefully lifting the putrid carcass up by the fur side and handing it to Bronx. "Now rub it all over your skin."

The large man took hold of the rotting carcass then paused for a moment and looked at her as if to ask, *are you sure about this?* She motioned for him to proceed.

The giant's emotions, which normally remained cloaked behind his stone-chiseled features, peeked through as he rubbed the rotting raccoon flesh over his own. For a moment she thought she saw the big man heave a little and grimace.

When the last of the hunters had reluctantly performed the smelly task, Bronx handed the carcass to her and said, "Your turn."

"There are many ways to mask your scent. I'll teach you another," she said, motioning for them to follow her into an adjacent clearing. She pointed out a low growing plant that was teeming with little bell-shaped, white flowers, then stooped to the little bush and caressed it with her hand. She whispered an apology and a thank you, then pulled off a handful of flowers and leaves from lower branches that were not exposed to the sun.

"We call this plant maštíŋska tobacco," she informed as she rubbed the poultice under her arms and around her neck. "It works as well, if not better than rotting animal flesh. Come, the herd of tȟáȟča are this way." She took off walking towards the bay, trying her best to keep a strait face. But on the inside she was dying with laughter.

The hunters were looking slightly displeased with their new scent and rather annoyed at their teacher for not showing them the maštíŋska tobacco first.

As they navigated the rough terrain, she spoke about the prey they were stalking. "Tȟáȟča, what my people call them, are one of the most difficult animals to hunt. They use their sense of smell and their hearing to detect danger. They don't use their eyes as much, so if you mask your scent and move silently you have a chance of getting in close. But the tȟáȟča has an even more powerful tool for detecting predators." She paused for a moment to think about how best to explain this concept. "They can... read your mind." She paused again, then judging from the confused looks on the rogues' faces she tried to explain. "Whatever is going on inside of you, your thoughts, your feelings, they make a vibration, like the rings that spread out over the water when you throw a stone into it. They can detect these vibrations from a great distance. So, to hunt the tȟáȟča, you must learn to turn off your thoughts and feelings, to be silent on the outside and on the inside, right up to the moment you make the kill."

Her words were met with blank stares.

OK, perhaps a little beyond their comprehension.

Shifting tactics, she attempted to explain the importance of killing the deer in the proper manner. This meant taking the deer's life swiftly so as to minimize pain and suffering, and in such a way as to limit the damage to the meat and skin. Though a direct hit to the heart led to a swift kill, she preferred to target the more difficult neck or head. This way her prey would feel no pain, the meat and the heart and organs would not be damaged, and there would be no hole in the skin to sew up later.

As they drew closer to the grazing animals she signaled for everyone to travel silently. She observed the leaves in the trees and turned her face from side to side to detect the direction of the wind. They were down wind from the tȟáȟča. As soon as the deer came into view the hunters dropped low into the tall grass and inched their way forward.

Much to her surprise, and despite their silly attire, these men could move in silence. This was one lesson she would not have to teach them.

They stepped when the wind rustled the leaves overhead and whistled through the branches. When the deer stooped their heads to nibble on the fresh grass shoots, they crept forward in unison.

The stalking process was slow and methodical, and the rogues observed her keenly throughout. At last they found themselves in a dense patch of shrubs looking down on the herd which grazed a stone's throw away. Behind the deer, the water of the bay stretched towards the horizon.

Beyond the bay Wakíŋyaŋ could see the faint outline of a distant shore and, for a moment, she was distracted by thoughts of home. Then, catching herself, she cleared her mind and tightened the muscles in her legs, pulling herself up into a low straddle-squat. Through the bushes she could see the deer. One in particular stood out. It was a young male with a wounded back leg that caused it to limp as it moved.

Never take the healthiest or the strongest, she could hear her father's words. *Seek out the wounded and the disadvantaged. By removing them, you make the herd stronger.*

With an empty mind, she nocked an arrow, brought the black obsidian tip just above the level of the bushes and drew the birchbark fletching to her chin. The young deer lifted his head and looked over his shoulder towards his companions, exposing the full flank of his golden brown neck. As the muscles of her fingers softened to release the string, the weight of a heavy hand gripped her shoulder.

The hand belonged to Bronx. He looked intently at her for a moment then turned his brow toward the bay and made a slight gesture with his chin. Relaxing the bowstring, she followed the giant's gaze out into the bay until she spotted what he was looking at.

The...thing, whatever it was, refused to register in her mind, and left her staring, dumbfounded, blank.

The hunters watched in silence until Bronx gave a signal for them to follow. He took off running through the forest with all but one of the hunters close behind. The remaining hunter, clearly there to keep an eye on her, gestured with his head for her to follow the group.

As she ran she contemplated her options. She could kill this one guard now and slip into the forest undetected. She'd have her freedom, yes, but what about Wit'é and the others? No, she couldn't leave them behind. A shudder ran through her as she thought of her young friend in that lifeless place. Besides, there was something compelling about what she had seen in the bay, and she felt a vague pressure in the pit of her stomach.

Wakíŋyaŋ and her watchdog caught up to the others as they were clearing branches from a patch of ground, revealing a crevice in the mound of rubble below their feet. One by one they followed Bronx through the opening and into the darkness. Just inside the entrance she paused and looked back at the light, then proceeded down through the maze of boulders and debris.

They descended for a while until the route opened up into one of the railcar tunnels. The hunter who had been left to guard her pulled a small torch bundle from his hunting bag and lit it with several swift strikes of his flint stone against a piece of iron rod.

They took off running again, following the tracks. Bronx kept up a vicious pace; quite remarkable, she thought, for a person that large. She also realized that all that time spent cooped up in the dungeon had taken its toll on her stamina. Normally she could run beside Níškola all day long without getting winded. But here she was now, sucking in oxygen as though her life depended on it!

Water seeped through cracks and dripped down between the tracks, forming a rivulet. The rivulet grew into a stream, and then into a swift river, and the hunters were forced onto a raised platform against the tunnel wall, just wide enough to shimmy along sideways.

They traveled on until the tunnel abruptly ended at the edge of a cliff. The ground had been scooped away, as by the mouth of a celestial monster that had descended from the stars to feast upon the earth. Even the metal tracks had been sliced clean off. The river of water shot straight out of the tunnel and plummeted through the air until it crashed down as a torrential rain on the canopy below. Just beyond the thin strip of trees the bay stretched out into the distance.

They scampered down the boulder field to the right of the tunnel and then along a narrow deer trail that led through the forest. As they approached the treeline and the edge of the pebble beach, the giant signaled for them to stop and stay low.

At first she couldn't see anything out of the ordinary.

Then it appeared.

An object, unlike anything she had seen before, drifted into view. The entire vessel was made from shiny metal that reflected the sun's rays, casting rainbows of light across the water. Two metal trees rose up from the center of the thing, piercing the sky. Round holes along its side looked like the dark, shiny eyes of a fearsome sea creature.

There was not a breath of wind over the bay, and yet the creature drifted silently across the water as if pulled from below by a tethered whale. This was some magical apparition, some creation of her own mind.

She closed her eyes for a moment, wondering if the vision would still be there when she opened them again.

It was.

Soup

Soup! That's what he called it. Not the warm, salty broth filled with veggies and chunks of tender meat that Mother made for dinner. Not that type of soup. Soup was what he called the dense, wet fog that stretched out before them now, reaching to port and starboard for as far as the eye could see. The sky above and behind was blue and the water calm, but just ahead the soup absorbed everything: light, air, sound!

Pilipili appeared to sense the danger and tucked herself further into the safety of his ochre red braids. The boys, who were stationed on the prow as lookouts, exchanged glances. EnKare was relieved to see his own concerns echoed in Jioba's expression.

The star readings and the charts indicated that land was less than a kilometer away, and yet a whole continent was presumably hiding in the mist.

Unwilling to show her true self.

Or blown away, bombed beyond existence.

The Capitán called a meeting in the wheelhouse, and they all gathered to hear what Kodo had to say. "Listen, men." A slight strain in the man's voice betrayed his fear. "We don't know what lies ahead. Radiation. That fog might be filled with deadly gases. We don't know what lifeforms exist or whether or not they are dangerous. So all of us need to be on high alert, and the minute someone detects anything unusual, report it, and we'll do what we need to do to protect ourselves and get back to a safe environment."

Sails down and auxiliary motors humming, the tension on aboard was palpable as they slipped silently into the soup.

All was quiet.

The sun barely penetrated to the surface of the sea.

They sailed into an instant twilight.

EnKare held his breath, too afraid of what might be lingering in the murky atmosphere. When his lungs began to burn and his diaphragm contracted involuntarily, he wrapped his shuka cloth over his mouth and nose and cautiously allowed the cool, moist air to filter in. When that didn't kill him instantly, he raced over to Jioba, to make sure he was still alive, and to give him the good news.

Emboldened by the discovery of clean air, they forged on through the stillness.

When at least three eternities had passed, in boy time that is, like a curtain, the soup parted and they burst out into the dazzling light of day just as abruptly as they had left it.

As though it had stopped somewhere back in the brine, EnKare's heart contracted in one monumental beat—*tha-BUMP*—and his eye's widened to the size of breadfruits. In the distance, the verdant, vibrant green shoreline of a bay wrapped around them on three sides.

"Chabalangus! I don't know about you, Jimmy, but I feel like, like…"

"Like Abubakari, eight hundred years ago when he came to these same shores, bwana!" Jioba blurted.

"Exactly! Look at the water, and the trees, the TREES, there are trees here, which means there is LIFE in Nchi Mbaya! Life, bwana, do you know what this means?" He was yelling with excitement.

"OK, relax, Toots. Life, yes, but we don't know what kind, so keep your eyes peeled like the Capitán told us to, just in case we see something moving on shore."

"You're right, Jimmy. But I thought we were going to die back there when we entered the soup. Instead we didn't, and now," he swept his hands out before him," look where we are. The first Africans in the old world since Iworo."

A handful of fins broke the smooth surface as a pod of dolphins passed by. In front of them the water riffled as a school of herring fed on a phytoplankton bloom. All across the bay creatures big and small leaped into the air and dappled the tranquil lagoon with splashes. On shore was a similar display. A thick blanket of trees and vegetation covered the land, and in the distant sky winged creatures hovered and drifted. So many questions were answered all at once. Yes! Life had returned to Nchi Mbaya.

EnKare was beside himself. For the first time in his life he felt a sense of purpose, like he was doing something meaningful. But would his parents be proud of him? Or would they think him selfish and reckless for leaving and breaking the rules?

"Toots, LOOK!" Jioba was pointing at a clearing in the forest.

EnKare could see a small herd of gazelle or impala grazing in a field of tall grass. They were different than the gazelle back home. These had no stripes or ribs of varying color, just a solid light brown coat, and some had horns while others did not. And what strange horns they were, starting at two spots on their skulls and branching, again and again, until they crested like ornate headdresses. He'd never seen horns displayed like that.

"They're so beautiful, Jimmy."

"I feel like I'm looking at something impossible, that just can't be," Jioba said in a soft voice. "We have been taught to believe this place was toxic, uninhabitable. But look at it. Look how much life there is!"

"You see all those mounds, there, rising up out of the forest?" EnKare gawked, pointing at the landmass off the starboard of the ship. "Do you think that's what's left of the city? Piles of rubble where there used to be buildings? They say those buildings used to reach into the clouds for more than a kilometer. I can't even imagine..."

As he inspected the landscape more closely, it dawned on him that they might be witnessing the remains of what had been one of the greatest cities on earth, in the time before Iworo. And now, nothing. Piles of rubble. Giant, eroding termite mounds sticking up out of the forest canopy. Jioba must have had the same realization because the two young men stood in silence, taking it in, as whisper-quiet jets sent the *Buganvilla* gliding silently into a cove carved into the shoreline.

"Prepare anchors!" The Capitán's order rang through the stillness and echoed off the nearby cliffs. The crew snapped to attention and ran about the decks preparing the ship for anchorage in the protected shoal. Anchors dropped and the ship secure, the Capitán called for another meeting in the wheelhouse.

"We're here, men, and we're alive. We made it!" The Capitán's words were met by a cheerful whooping and hollering from the crew. EnKare was dying to tell the Capitán about the animals they had seen grazing on shore, and the schools of fish and the dolphins—but he held his tongue until he was asked for the report. Tomobo and Jafra had similar accounts, and for a time the men talked excitedly about what they had seen.

"This is a good sign, gentlemen," Kodo reported. "But it doesn't mean we can be complacent. It is possible that life here has adapted to an environment that is still toxic to us. So monitor how you feel physically, your skin, breathing, heart rate, and look out for fevers or nausea."

"If nausea is an indicator, then EnKare is done for," teased Tomobo.

Jioba snarffled into one hand and whip-snapped the air with the other. "What about frequent vomiting, pale, greenish skin, and a general whiny disposition? Are those signs of a toxic environment too?"

EnKare bit his lower lip and reached out to grab Jioba by the neck. "Actually, I'm feeling a little nauseous right now, come here, bwana."

Jioba slapped his hand away, and they started scrapping with each other in mock battle, oblivious to the others standing there.

The Capitán tolerated the behavior for a moment then regained order and laid out the plan. "You don't know what we're going to encounter out there, but at the very least we'll need these for hacking our way through the undergrowth," Kodo cautioned as he handed out machetes. Within minutes the crew was rowing one of the ship's lifeboats towards shore.

EnKare was ready. Ready for anything and everything. He had all three of his weapons on him—rungu and simi on his belt.

Spear at his side.

Mutants

One final pull on the oars and the lifeboat ground to a halt on the pebble shore. The boys hopped out into the shallows, grabbed the side rails and pulled the craft as far up onto the beach as they could. The others followed suit and, collectively, they lifted the boat and ran it up to the forest line. When it was safely tucked into the bushes and covered with branches they gathered together at the water's edge.

EnKare tried to pay attention as they discussed what to do next, but all he could think about was the fact that he was here, standing on another continent. Never in all his most creative fantasies had he imagined something as magnificent as this. Everything around him was new, different. The trees and shrubs looked nothing like the ones back home, and their leaves grew in shapes he had never seen before. The air was cool and dry and filled with a million fragrances that he had never smelled. He stooped down and picked up a handful of pebbles and rolled them in the palm of his hand. Even the stones were different, though he knew they they were just stones—probably made from the same minerals found back home.

"Gentlemen, we'll head up the coast till we find a break in the forest. I'd like to get to the top of one of those mounds that we saw from the ship so we can look around."

Flinging the pebbles out into the water, EnKare lifted his hand to his face and breathed in deeply through his nose. Even the earth smelled different here. Then he turned and followed his compadres up the beach.

After a short distance they turned into the woods and followed Kodo along an animal track. The boys stayed to the back of the group, chatting excitedly, pointing at insects, rodents, bushes, trees, snakes—any and everything that crossed their path.

"Look at this one, Jimmy," he said, pointing to a small bush covered with little, white flowers. "They're like little bells."

The path ahead opened up into a clearing in the forest where they paused to check their bearings. Kodo turned to face them. EnKare happened to be looking up, watching a large, winged creature flying over the clearing, when something leaped from an overhead branch.

"Capitán! Look out!" he shouted.

Kodo jumped forward and whipped around just as the thing landed on the ground in front of them. It carried a wooden spear that it raised over its head, opened its mouth and let out a high pitched scream.

Then the forest came alive. Creatures fell from the sky, and the very ground around them began to move. They materialized from...everywhere—appearing from under stones, rising up out of the forest debris, soil, rocks, and foliage clinging to their bodies.

Human! Only...disfigured.

One eye.

Three eyes.

Three arms! Grossly disproportionate body parts—bulges on the sides of heads, backbones that arched up over skulls—no lower jaw; tongues flapping unconstrained.

Mutants!

Pilipili leaped from his back to a low hanging branch, then quickly disappeared into the safety of the forest. Then the mutants closed in all at once, screaming and slashing with weapons, and before he could make sense of what was happening, the chaos of a life and death struggle exploded all around him.

EnKare's brain shut down.

Completely.

His spear slipped from his fingers, making a soft *thwunk* as the forest litter welcomed it into its foliar embrace. His rungu and simi hung apathetically at his hips; forgotten, forlorn.

Nothing...

Deafening screams of terror, roaring, rushing wings swooping overhead; everywhere, everything all at once thrown into pandemonium...

Still nothing. He just stood there.

Paralyzed.

Then

Something

Took over.

Something in his core. His nostrils flared, the fine hairs on the back of his neck bristled on end, and his senses caught fire.

Dropping to the ground, he ripped a handful of moist soil from the forest floor, erupted from all fours straight up, and hurled the dirt into the face of an attacking mutant. While the creature struggled to clear its eyes, he dropped low again and turned towards Jioba, who was hacking frantically at the air while mutants came at him from all directions.

His back legs discharged again, like two springs set free at last from their tormented bind, and he catapulted towards Jioba just as a creature leaped onto his friend's chest, knocking the boy to the ground. The mutant held a weapon, a large stone lashed to the 'y' of a stick. It lifted the club over its head, screaming, and brought it down towards Jioba's face.

Every muscle activated, EnKare focused his energy on the singular task of reaching Jioba before the club did.

A calculation sped through his subconscious mind at the speed of light, followed by a conclusion, and then a dreadful realization; he wouldn't make it in time!

Jioba is lost…

In the same instant, something whizzed over his head and struck the creature in the chest. Its body fell limp, but the club, moving slower now, continued its descent towards Jioba's skull.

He dove through the air, outstretched hand making contact with the stone just inches above his friend's head. The impact was enough to deflect the club to one side, and he came crashing down in a heap on top of Jioba and the lifeless mutant.

"Thanks, bwana," Jioba grunted as he pushed the dead weight of the mutant off of him.

"C'mon," EnKare said, hopping to his feet. He pulled Jioba up, drew his simi from its sheath, and wheeled around to face the next attack.

That's when he noticed that a second group of fighters had joined the battle, only these combatants were armed with iron weapons and appeared to be more human looking than mutant. To his relief the newcomers were defending his group against the attack. One, clearly the leader, was twice the size of an average man and the body of any creature unfortunate enough to be in his path was torn apart and sent flying. He growled and roared with the intensity of a lion, and it could be heard over the calamity of the battle.

While the giant man and his soldiers were able to fend off the attack from the edges of the clearing, more were dropping down out of the trees with every passing moment. EnKare grabbed Jioba's arm and rushed headlong into the throng of clashing bodies.

A swift blow to the back of the head caught him off guard.

His vision went black.

Then stars danced before him as he staggered on his feet.

Something fleshy landed on top of him, and he collapsed to the ground.

When his vision returned he saw that a mutant with no lower jaw was sitting on his chest. It lifted a rusty blade and slashed viciously at his throat. But before the knife could make contact he grabbed the creature by the wrist.

With the jagged shank hovering inches from the flesh of his neck, the creature placed both hands on the knife and leaned its weight forward. The jawless face hovered just above his, saliva dripping freely from its dangling tongue. He arched his back in an effort to push the creature away, but could not. The muscles in his arms burned and slowly began to fatigue. He would only last a few moments longer.

As his adrenal glands emptied their contents into his bloodstream, his mind drifted on the chemical cocktail; warm, sandy beaches of his hometown; mother's kind eyes; father's leathery hands; Mandaha's mischievous smile.

His arms began to relax.

Then, as if watching a play, he observed as a body sailed overhead. This soaring siren, this airborne ally caught hold of the teeth of his attacker's upper jaw and ripped the creature from his chest, head first. In mid air the mutant's blade found the flesh of the newcomer's arm and tore into it eagerly. As the pair of bodies hit the ground, the warrior produced an arrow from nowhere, and plunged it into the creature's chest. Then without hesitation, she extracted the arrow, sprang to his side and extended a hand.

"Get up, quick!"

EnKare looked up through the tears and dirt in his eyes. For an instant he thought he saw the body of a chui nyeusi standing over him. He rubbed his eyes and looked again.

This time he saw a young woman, a warrior, dressed in animal skins and adorned with colorful stone beads and shells. Her long, black hair was braided and held back with strips of tanned leather. Her skin was the light brown of a mucuna seed and her eyes were a piercing ebony. And he could understand her language, though her accent was foreign.

"You saved my life, and my friend's life, too…"

"Move!" The warrior yelled. Then, as though riding a bolt of lightning, she drew an arrow and sent it flying past his head—before he could turn to see what was happening, she fired two more arrows.

By the time he made it to his feet again the battle was dying down. With the help of the giant man and his warriors the mutants were being forced to retreat. As the creatures fled they carried or dragged the dead and wounded away with them. Then just as abruptly as it had started, the battle was over—nothing but blood-stained rocks and leaves left behind to memorialize the event.

As soon as the last of the creatures vanished into the woods he ran to Jioba's side. "You OK, Jimmy?"

"I've been better, bwana," Jioba responded, rubbing a bloody spot on the side of his head. "How 'bout you, Toots?"

"I can't believe we're still alive. What about the others?"

Jafra and Tomobo were lightly wounded with scrapes, cuts, and bruises. Tomobo was standing close to Kodo, who had fared the worst of them all. He was bleeding from a wound on his head and a large, open gash ran down the side of his neck. He was still standing, and though the wounds looked bad, EnKare felt that his Capitán would be fine, once they were aboard the ship where they had medical supplies.

The giant warrior, who had disappeared into the woods after the creatures, stepped back into the clearing. He approached the group and spoke. "Your leader." His voice rustled the leaves in the trees.

Kodo stepped forward and grimaced. "I am the Capitán of these men, and of the ship the *Buganvilla*. We are here…"

Before Kodo could finish his sentence the giant let out a blood chilling roar and swung his mace at Kodo's head.

EnKare watched in horror as his Capitán's body sailed through the air and landed a few meters away in a heap.

"NO!" Tomobo screamed, and turned to run to his uncle's side. But the giant grunted and his men surrounded the Africans before any of them could move. The warriors, who had saved their lives only minutes ago, stripped them of their weapons and pushed them face down into the dirt, lashing their hands behind their backs. Once they were securely tied, the men hoisted them back to their feet.

"Run, and you die," the large man bellowed, pointing towards Kodo's lifeless body. "You Bronx slaves now. Move out!"

As they left the clearing, moving slowly along an animal trail, his mind reeled. *What just happened? Is Kodo…dead? Who are these people? What were the creatures that attacked us? Why did they attack? Nothing makes sense.* As they walked silently along the forest trail he looked up and caught sight of the warrior who had saved his life. A feeling crept up from the depths of his abdomen and quickly overwhelmed him. He had never known such a feeling before. A potent combination of grief, anger, disgust, and loathing caused his bound hands to shake.

The warrior looked back at him, and for the second time their eyes met. The first time, he had felt an electric shock that had bewildered and confused him. This time the hatred that now filled his heart flowed freely from his eyes and pierced hers.

The look that she returned, however, caught him off guard. It was not filled with anger or hatred or fear. It was a look of…sorrow. But why? Why had she saved his life only to take him prisoner? And had the giant said the word *slave*?

Bronx slave?

Familiar

The immense wooden doors swung inward, and Bronx stepped through the entrance to his domain, followed by the hunting party, Wakíŋyaŋ, and the four new captives. She dreaded returning to the dark, cold, wetness of the underground tunnels that, for now, had become her home. She could see that, for the rogues, it offered shelter and protection from a hostile world. But to her the world was not hostile, it was nurturing, vibrant, alive. These caves, on the other hand, pressed in on her, stifling her spirit.

"Dungeon," Bronx grunted, and with a wave of his hand several guards appeared, carrying spears and lanterns, and escorted the new captives away.

She watched as they departed, heads bowed, beaten and limping, disappearing into the darkness. Her heart sank at the thought of more young lives lost to the misery of the caves. She turned towards the giant, trying her best to match his stoic indifference, but unable to prevent the anger and disappointment seeping from her eyes. "I need supplies to doctor their wounds."

"Fix own arm, leave slaves to fix selves," Bronx growled.

"The dungeon has no air circulation. Infection is likely. If their wounds become infected they might die. If you want to loose your new slaves, then fine." She shrugged and turned to walk away.

"OK," the giant's voice echoed off the tunnel walls. "You fix them."

A few minutes later she stepped past the harassing remarks of Taco, Pills, and Geiger into the outstretched arms of Wit'é, who came running straight at her the moment she stepped through the door.

"OK, Wí, OK. I'm back. I'm back. *Shh shh*, there there, it's OK. I'm back now." She consoled her little friend who clung tightly to her neck, scrawny legs wrapped snugly around her waist. Clifton, Bay, and the others had come to the doorway to meet her as well.

"Who are the new ones? Where are they from?" Clifton asked.

"Ya, and what happened out there?" Brooklyn added.

"It was…horrible," Wakíŋyaŋ groaned, her brow tense. "I'll explain everything soon, but first I'm going to go see if they need help dressing their wounds."

Hiva stated, "That's a good idea. They looked pretty beat up. But who are they, anyway? Where do they come from?"

Wakíŋyaŋ shrugged. "I have no idea."

She carried Wit'é and the medical supplies back to their bedroom. As she walked, Wit'é lightly touched the open gash on her arm, and her eyes grew wide. She gripped the leather folds of Wakíŋyaŋ's clothing and looked up at her, tears welling in her anxious blue eyes.

"It's OK, Wí, it's not as bad as it looks," she soothed, setting down the wóphiye of medical supplies and pulling out the contents.

The gash was every bit as bad as it looked, if not worse. She hadn't really thought of it until now and with the sight of the damaged flesh came an explosion of pain. The blood around the edges had dried, but the inner layers were still moist. The rusty blade had sliced clean through the skin and partway into the meat of her forearm and she could see the cutaneous layers and strands of muscle.

"Perhaps we should take care of that." Bay's voice came from the entrance to the railcar. Wakíŋyaŋ turned around to find the whole group peering in at her from the doorway. She had intended to find the new captives and offer to clean and bandage their wounds first. But Bay was right, she'd best tend her own wound now to prevent it getting infected.

Wit'é darted out of the railcar and returned a moment later with a container of water. With Bay and Wit'é's help they cleaned around the wound and then flushed open the gash.

"Thank you, Water," Wakíŋyaŋ said in a soft voice. Uŋčí had taught her to take nothing for granted and to respect and be thankful for the whole of creation and for each of its individual parts. How Bronx fit into that equation she wasn't sure. At this moment she didn't know if he qualified as a part of creation at all. And was he really worthy of her respect and thankfulness?

"Thank you, Wí. Thank you, Bay," she exclaimed awkwardly. She wasn't used to receiving help from anyone. It felt...good.

While the two worked patiently on the wound, she related the events of the afternoon to her curious friends, who had crowded around. Every now and then Bark and Bite would gasp and cover their faces, or look fearfully at Wakíŋyaŋ with tears in their eyes. Speaking the sequence of events out loud made it seem less like a dream, and more frighteningly real. There were many unanswered questions that she was itching to ask the captives; like where they were from, why they were here, and what the large, metal, floating village sitting out in the bay was.

Once clean, Hiva used the fresh yarrow that Wakíŋyaŋ had picked on the trek back to the tunnels, and made it into a poultice to disinfect the wound and stop the bleeding. After a few applications of yarrow, Wit'é held the two sides of of the cut together while Hiva applied a poultice of fresh plantain and then wrapped the wound tightly with a softened leather strap.

"That should do it," Hiva announced, smiling broadly.

She thanked everyone again, then turned to Wit'é. "Well, should we go see if those young men need patching up?"

Wit'é nodded, but her face betrayed concern.

"I know. After what happened out there they might not be too happy to see me. Well, there's only one way to find out. Come on, let's go."

She pulled her little friend to her feet, put the medical supplies back into the wóphiye, grabbed the small torch that hung on the wall, and stepped out into the darkness. After checking in several railcars and walking the periphery of the hall, she concluded they must be in the half-crushed railcar at the end of the line. As they drew nearer, low voices coming from inside confirmed her suspicions. She motioned for Wit'é to stand behind her, then pried open the door.

"GET OUT! Leave us ALONE!" a voice yelled.

She stood her ground. The four men were huddled on the floor with their knees pulled up to their chests. All were cradling their heads in their hands except for the one who was yelling at her, the one she had pulled the mutant off of. The one with the long, red braids. She looked at him for a moment, then looked away.

"You have wounds. We must dress them. If they become infected—"

"You killed our Capitán, now you want to dress our wounds?" the voice dripped with incredulity. Now all the young men's heads were raised, anger and fear in their eyes.

"I am one of you. I'm a captive here..." Wakíŋyaŋ spoke gently, but again she was cut short.

"Liar! I saw you with those men. You did nothing when that giant killed Kodo, and you weren't tied up like the rest of us."

She slowly lowered herself to a squatting position and set the medical supplies and the lantern down in front of her. Wit'é's slight frame appeared in the doorway, and she stepped over and sat cross legged beside

Wakíŋyaŋ. The little girl's presence seemed to calm the men a little, though the tension in the room was still palpable.

She tried to explain. "One moon ago I was taken from my village by the same men that have now taken you. They took this little one," she motioned, wrapping an arm over Wit'é's shoulder, "on the same raiding hunt. Everyone in this dungeon is a slave, just as you are."

"Then why were you fighting alongside those men, and why were you not tied up as we were?" one of the men probed.

"I made a deal with Bronx, the big man, that I'd teach him and his men how to hunt and how to make hunting weapons in exchange for use of my bow and the freedom to come and go from the dungeon as I please," she explained, feeling a twinge of regret for having made the deal. It sounded self-serving when she explained it that way.

"Then why..."

"Please. There will be plenty of time to talk, but now we must see to your wounds." Then, with gentle determination in her movement, she brought the lantern and the wóphiye and squatted beside the young man closest to her. "Wí, will you run and fetch us some water," turning to look. But Wit'é was already gone. A moment later the pitter-patter of bare feet announced the little girl's swift return. Wí handed the container to Wakíŋyaŋ and smiled.

Smiling back, "You did it again, Wí, you read my mind. I don't know how you do that."

Wit'é's smile got wider.

Her years of studying the different herbs of the forest with the apothecary, and following Uŋčí around the meadows, had made her quite adept in the healing arts. It was a marvel that Grandmother never tired of her endless questions—What's that used for? Why are you picking those? Are you sure that's the right one? Anyone but Uŋčí would have been driven to the brink of madness.

With Wit'é at her side, she turned her attention to dressing the men's wounds. When she got to her third patient, a boy with a round face and short, curly hair, she found he had a nasty, swollen gash on his forehead, various scrapes and cuts on his knees and elbows, and one of his fingernails was ripped off. When she was done cleaning and bandaging him, she turned towards the last one in line, the one with red braids. He, too, was bleeding from his head.

"I'll dress my own wounds. Leave the supplies and get out."

She could hear anger, frustration, and despair in his voice. "OK, but make sure you clean well. The dampness of the dungeon causes infection to spread easily. We will go and prepare some food and water for you. You have to keep your strength. On the other side of the cabins, at the other end of the hall, you'll find a small fire burning. When you are done here come meet us there." She pointed in the rough direction of the kitchen.

With nothing more to say, she reached out for Wit'é's hand and they two turned and left.

"Well, that didn't go *too* badly, did it, Wí?"

The straw-haired girl squeezed her hand.

But there were still more questions than answers. *Who are they and where are they from?* They didn't look or dress like any people she had seen before. They spoke with strange accents and used words she had never heard. And the one with red braids—there was something beyond her understanding with that one. She could feel it each time she looked into his eyes. Something different, but…

Familiar.

Mother Less Child

The dungeon smelled of mildew and smoke. EnKare pulled his shuka over his shoulders and hugged his knees close to his chest for warmth.

Dreary.

Cold.

Moldy.

A heavy despair closed in, compressing his temples and nagging at the pit of his stomach. His body shook as his mind raced from one thought to the next, trying to make sense of what had happened, looking for a glimmer of hope at the end of a path that appeared hopeless. The gruesome image of Capitán Kodo's limp body lying in a heap of leaves on the forest floor plagued him.

He thought of his mother and father, of Mandaha and Jioba's mother.

They will never see their sons again. Mandaha will be without a brother.

They would never know what had happened. He felt his parents' anguish as though it was his own, and tears flowed down his cheeks. Perhaps it was better for them not to know what had happened. That way they'd be spared the knowledge that their son had died on a distant, diseased continent, slowly rotting in a cold, wet, cave. That their son had died a slave!

"Hey, bwana." Jioba's voice caused his morbid thoughts to slink away into the recesses of his mind. "Should we go?"

EnKare swallowed back his silent weeping and responded, "Go where?"

"Go find the fire, like she said. For some food and water," Jioba answered.

It was just like Jimmy to be thinking about his stomach at a time like this. It almost brought a smile to EnKare's lips

"I agree," Tomobo's voice came from the end of the railcar. "We should go."

A wave of anger capsized EnKare unexpectedly, and he shouted, "How can we trust her? How? You saw what they did to your uncle. And now you want to go and eat her food and drink her water, like nothing ever happened?" He shook as the words spewed from his lips, not thinking about what he was saying. "I don't trust her eyes. Have you seen the way they reflect the light from the torches? It's not natural."

Jioba responded in a somber tone. "What other choice do we have, Toots? Her eyes are definitely the least strange thing I've seen since we landed here. Look, we'll need to eat eventually. Besides, I think she's telling the truth. Before we go we should clean you up. You should have let the lady do it, bwana. She seemed to know what she's doing."

Tomobo and Jafra murmured an agreement. EnKare was no less banged and scraped than the others. He had a gash on the top of his head and cuts and bruises on his arms and legs.

"Hand me that container, would you," he said to Jafra. "If there's any water left in it I'll just wash up a little with that." He dipped the corner of his shuka in the water and dabbed at the worst of his cuts on his knees and elbows. When he was done he looked up at the others, and murmured with resignation, "OK. Let's go."

As he spoke the words he noticed two little faces peering in at them from the doorway. As soon as he saw them they let out a little *screech* and disappeared.

Tomobo picked up the lantern, the others gathered the supplies that the lady had left, and they stepped cautiously out of the railcar. Another shiver ran through EnKare's body and he quickly realized that all his heat was being pulled down through the bottom of his feet, into the cold, hard, floor. He had left his sandals on the ship. He'd have to find something else to wrap his feet in.

As they moved along the back wall of the dungeon he contemplated their predicament.

Slaves. Are we to become slaves? The warrior lady said she was a slave, like the rest of us! How can this be happening? Why did I ever agree to come to this place?

All he had wanted was the life of an adventurer, an explorer, to know the freedom of traveling the world without restrictions, without barriers. Was he a fool to think that the world would just open its arms and welcome him in?

Following the faint orange and yellow glow flickering off the dungeon wall, the boys crossed a makeshift bridge that spanned the tracks. The wood creaked and groaned sympathetically under the weight of their tired, beaten bodies.

Once on the other side, he could see the source of the dancing light. A low fire crackled in the rim of a burnt out truck wheel, illuminating a kitchen and gathering area that had been built up around the fire pit. The kitchen was made of scrap wood tables with various containers on top and underneath, presumably holding food supplies and water. Next to the fire was a tall, spindly looking rack lashed together at the corners with cordage, pieces of meat dangling from its dowels. The warrior lady and the young girl were accompanied by several others, including the two little faces he had seen at the doorway. They were all sitting on logs positioned around the fire, talking in low voices.

As they approached the circle the warrior lady beckoned them with a hand gesture and said, "Come, get warm and meet everyone. There is food and water for you."

EnKare waved back, hand in the air with his first and middle fingers sticking straight up. Earlier, he'd been quite hostile towards the young lady, and even though he doubted she'd recognize the archaic hand sign for peace, he was at least proud of himself for remembering it. The warrior lady stared at him for a moment with a look of shock and bewilderment. He quickly lowered his hand and looked away. He was only trying to make amends. He hadn't even considered that maybe that sign was offensive to these people.

Way to go, EnKare. Smooth.

The Africans stepped into the circle and took seats on the logs around the fire. The little girl tugged on the warrior lady's leather skin garment and looked up at her. Even though the little girl didn't utter a word, the warrior lady responded as though she understood her perfectly.

"You're right, Wí, we should do that," the warrior lady confirmed. Then, looking over at EnKare and the others, "This is Bay, and Clifton, the elders of our group. My name is Wakíŋyaŋ, this is Wit'é, and those two little ones are Bark and Bite." Then the others introduced themselves, making their way around the fire.

After Jioba, Tomobo, and Jafra had done the same, EnKare looked up at Wakíŋyaŋ and, with a hint of residual distrust in his voice, said, "My name is EnKare." As he spoke the words, his mind drifted to something the old soothsayer had said to them that day in Aye Market: *From freedom to slavery we ride the waves...* Could the old man's words be coming true?

The warrior lady named Wakíŋyaŋ pulled some pieces of meat from the drying rack and handed them around while the little girl, Wit'é, passed around fired clay cups filled with fresh, cool water. The dried meat was tough at first, but as his saliva softened it the subtle flavors flooded his mouth.

"Thish meat ish sho good," Jioba gushed with a full mouth. "What ish it?"

"That is the flesh of the tȟáȟča."

"Thaa...thaacha?" Jioba questioned, pausing for a moment in his chewing and looking fearfully at the piece of meat in his hand. "What'sh that? Not shum short of monshter or anything ish it?" He asked apprehensively.

The young lady smiled, and the firelight danced off the surface of her eyes. A moment that didn't go unnoticed by EnKare. It somehow lifted the blanket of doom that lay heavy over everything. For a moment there was beauty in the dungeon.

"Eh, bwana, are these eyes yours?" Jioba whispered in his ear. "I found them just now after they popped out of your head!"

"*Shhh,*" he whispered back, with an accompanying scowl. OK, whatever. I'm not—I wasn't looking at anything. She's probably one of them, sent here to spy on us.

"No, it's not a monster. Tȟáȟča is my tribe's word for the type of deer that we hunt for meat. Do you like it?"

Jafra responded, "The more I chew it the more flavors there are. Is that just in the meat?"

"No," answered the young lady with the beautiful smile. "When the meat is still fresh and warm, I wrap it in various pȟežúta," she paused, seeing the puzzled look on their faces, "uh, herbs...from the forest. The flavors soak into the meat as it dries."

Tomobo remarked, "I guess it's kind of similar to our impala or gazelle."

"What are gazel and impala?" the young lady named Hiva asked, with a puzzled brow.

"Gazelle," Tomobo corrected her pronunciation. "They are types of African deer, I suppose."

Wakíŋyaŋ got a strange look on her face. "Where is your tribe from?"

"We are from many different tribes that have united," EnKare answered. When he saw that she was still puzzled, he added, "We are from Africa."

"Afrika?"

Bay spoke up. "That's a land far across the sea, honey. The place where some of Clifton and my ancestors came from a long time before the burn. Some of Bronx's ancestors too. They were brought here as slaves. *Humph.* An look at us now."

EnKare thought of Bronx, and then of Mrs. Msoke's words, *we Africans bought, sold, and enslaved each other.* His heart bled.

There was an uncomfortable silence in the group, then Wakíŋyaŋ asked, "And you came all the way here from...Africa, in that shiny boat?"

Letting his gaze drift aimlessly down past his bloodied knees to his cold, bare feet, another wave of helplessness washed over him. With a quiet voice he answered, "Yes."

Gradually the voices and the sounds of chewing and gulping died away until all that remained was the *drip, drip, dripping,* of water seeping through the cavern walls, and the low crackling of the fire. The group sat in silence, mourning their common misfortune—mourning the loss of Kodo; Capitán, uncle, father, husband, friend.

EnKare withdrew into himself

Into the silence

Into the cold.

From the stillness, a low, sorrowful song rose up from the floor of the dungeon.

"Sometimes……………...I feel………...like a motherless child…"

He recognized the voice, though he had never heard his friend sing with such melancholy. The heavyhearted words resonated off the cavern walls and lodged themselves in his chest.

"Sometimes……………...I feel………….like a motherless child…"

Another wave of anguish moved painfully through him, only this time he no longer had the energy to weep.

"Sometimes……………...I feel………….like a motherless child…

A long……….. way………………...from home…

A long……….. way………………...from my home."

The blue melody echoed in the chambers of EnKare's heart, turning his thoughts to family, friends, and loved ones—turning his thoughts to home.

To freedom.

The twins buried their little faces in Bay's skirt.

The cavern walls wept for those it held hostage, while salty tears dripped from wet cheeks, *sizzling* and *popping* in the smoldering flames of grief.

With his eyes closed, tension stretching the skin of his forehead, Jioba sang his verse again.

"A long………..way…………..from my home."

Hardened

The Sun rose from the east. Iworo hadn't changed that at least. At first the thin ocean mist that blanketed the land glowed with a hint of rose. The water vapor warmed and began to move, circling and spiraling, forming pink eddies and currents that danced around hill and tree tops. When at last the sun peaked over the horizon from its distant resting place over his beloved Africa, its fiery rays blazed through the trees and kissed the ground. Like a waning tide, the mists retreated down through the valleys and out to sea.

The moment the light hit him he understood why they had come up from the tunnels before dawn. This way their eyes could adjust incrementally to the intense light. As it was, he found himself squinting through the rays so as not to miss a moment of the sunrise. They were standing on a massive mound of rubble, the remains of what must have been a truly monumental building. Similar mounds rose up out of the forest, dotting the landscape in all directions.

It was an eerie sight that sent a shiver down his spine. He had never seen such total destruction before. Back home he had witnessed the intentional demolition of buildings so that the materials could be repurposed. But this, this was something else. For all the time he and Jioba had spent fantasizing about what it might look like in Nchi Mbaya, the reality was more sobering and horrific.

They had been put to work almost every day since being captured. Half a moon had passed, and the relentless grind was wearing on everyone. The goal today day was to collect firewood. The slaves had been taken up out of the tunnels and split into three groups. Separated from his friends, he was relieved to find himself in the company of Wakíŋyaŋ and the little girl, Wit'é.

"And remember," the ornery looking guard named Geiger began to say.

Wakíŋyaŋ interrupted. "If any of us tries to run away we'll be wormbait. Yes, we know."

Geiger sneered back, "Be careful, princess, you won't be Bronx's favorite forever. Just show these wormbait what to do."

As they moved over the terrain, breaking off dead branches and picking up bits of scrap wood, he was struck by the contrast between the bleak ruins of the city and the raw beauty of the forest.

There were once millions of people, all living on top of each other, right here. And only a few hundred years before that it probably looked more like it does now, minus the giant piles of rubble.

Every now and then he looked up and saw Wakíŋyaŋ working nearby. She was clearly adept with her hands and made the work look easy.

Everyone in this place looks so…hardened, or calloused. I hope that doesn't happen to me.

He wasn't sure what to make of it. Were there other creatures out there, like the mutants that had attacked them? Everyone kept talking about worms. What could be so dangerous about worms?

Looking over at Wakíŋyaŋ, he tried to strike up a conversation. "You said you were taken from your tribe. Is your village somewhere around here?"

Without looking up, Wakíŋyaŋ illuminated, "I come from just across the bay." Then she motioned with her chin to the south.

"What are your people called?" He didn't fully trust her yet and was trying to find out a little more information without sounding too nosy.

Wakíŋyaŋ responded, again not looking up from her task. "We call ourselves Wašúŋ Wóniya. Our name comes from the Spirit Cave that my grandparents lived in for seven winters at the time of the burn. We are a mixture of people, customs, and languages, like you, though much of our culture and identity comes to us from my grandmother, Wakȟáŋ Kiktá. She likes to say that we are shaped by the spirit of the land, that our culture is given to us by Mother Earth and Father Sun. She, like my grandfather and my father, is descended from the Oglala Lakota, a people who existed before the burn. My mother was descended from the great Sámi tribes of the far north. She always told me that long ago, her people lived with the land, with the earth and the sun."

"If you go back far enough, I imagine everyone did. Live with the earth and sun, that is." EnKare made small talk. "I've heard of the Lakota. We learned about them in one of my classes. Weren't they from a place on the west side of the United States?"

Glancing over at him with a puzzled look on her face, Wakíŋyaŋ asked, "What is united states?"

This confused him. "United States. You know, what this land was called before Iworo."

"Iworo? Look," Wakíŋyaŋ was starting to sound a little annoyed, "my people call this land Khéya Wíta. Turtle Island."

He liked that for some reason. There were no states left to be united anyhow, and reflecting on the maps he had studied in government class he could see how the land could resemble a turtle, or perhaps a manta ray, or some other large, wide-bodied animal.

"I like that name, Khéya Wíta," he offered. "Iworo is the word we use back home. You know, for the war."

"Here we just call it the burn."

Not wanting to overdo the questions, he busied himself collecting wood for a while. Something she said struck a cord in him. Her village was just across the bay. Then why hadn't she tried to escape yet? Surely she could survive the journey home, being as skilled in, well, everything, as she was.

He moved closer to her again, trying his best to make his movement as inconspicuous as possible. When he was close enough, in a hushed voice he asked, "Hey, why haven't you tried to escape yet? You said your village was close by, right?"

Wakíŋyaŋ turned her head swiftly and shot him a look that said, *shut up!*

Redbraids & Acorns

The fire popped and hissed as Wit'é fanned the base with a stiff piece of rawhide. Working alongside Brooklyn, Jack, Hiva, and Clair, Wakíŋyaŋ busied herself on one of the kitchen tables, rubbing herbs into slices of fresh meat, peeling the hard skins off roots and tubers, and soaking acorns in a tub of water. As she worked, the four Africans entered the kitchen, and the friendly one with the beautiful voice asked if they could help. In no time she had the young men elbow deep in acorns.

As they worked together she thought about the four newcomers. There was the one who lost his uncle on the day they arrived. Tomobo. He seemed withdrawn and sad, and understandably so. Then there was the one named Jimmy, or Jioba, she wasn't sure which it was. The angry suspicious one called him both names. She appreciated his singing. It was a simple act that had brought them all together. The one they called Jafra was perhaps the most handsome of the lot. He reminded her of a boy she had been interested in back in the village.

And of course there was Redbraids, the one they called EnKare. There wasn't much to say about him other than that he was angry, and suspicious.

And his hair was so different from the others'.

And he had kind eyes. And his high cheekbones and full lips complimented his strong shoulders. And red did look good on him. And she loved his beadwork jewelry. And she was fascinated by his plug earrings.

But really, there wasn't much to say about him.

She was generally curious about the Africans, about their lives at home. They seemed so knowledgeable about some things and then so ignorant about others. They didn't know how to fight or defend themselves, that much was clear, but they were not strangers to hard work. And then there was the metal ship, something beyond her understanding of the world.

"So, do you not have mutants in Africa?" she asked as they worked the acorns back and forth through the water. She was trying her best to not sound overly interested.

"No way, bibi," Jioba answered casually.

Redbraids clarified, "Well, actually we do. No, think about it, Jimmy. They say that some trees and animals in Africa grow much bigger now than they used to before Iwaro, uh, the burn. Like the giant toads in Sobaco? Or EnKishón? Apparently it's caused by mutations. I guess they didn't use to be that big."

Jafra entered the conversation. "What I think she is asking is if we have any human mutations in Africa."

Jioba pointed at Redbraids and said, "The closest thing to a mutant that I've ever seen back home is this guy right here."

Redbraids swatted Jioba's shoulder. "I see your sense of humor is returning, bwana."

Then, to Wakíŋyaŋ's horror, Redbraids picked an acorn out of the tub and bounced it off of Jioba's head.

"Oh, that's it, Toots. Ya dead, bwana," Jioba yelled while pulling two fistfuls of acorns out of the water.

"NO!" Wakíŋyaŋ shouted.

Jioba dropped the acorns, which landed in the pot, splashing water into his own face. Redbraids whipped his hand in the air, producing a loud snap and then gripped his mouth to stop himself from laughing.

In a sharp, commanding tone, Wakíŋyaŋ said, "Those acorns have to feed everyone in this cave." *What's the matter with these boys? They act like children sometimes.*

She turned back to her task of peeling roots.

Phop! An acorn bounced off her head.

She rotated slowly towards the young men, who all appeared deeply engrossed in their task of washing acorns. No one had ever thrown an acorn at her before. No one had ever thrown anything at her. *They wouldn't dare.*

In a slow, serious voice she asked, "Who threw the acorn?"

The group of boys kept their heads bowed low, but she could see their bodies bouncing and convulsing in the fire light, suppressing their childish giggles. This was no laughing matter. This was food. This was serious! She glared at them for a few moments then turned back to her task.

Phop! A second acorn bounced off her head, accompanied by a cacophonous explosion of *snarfles* and *giggles*. She could feel her blood rising and the skin on her forehead wrinkle with tension. Who did these Africans think they were, throwing acorns at her, wasting food? Before thinking it all the way through, she picked up the hodoimo potato that she was working on, whipped around and hurled the heavy tuber into the pot of water at their center. The resulting splash jetted up into their unsuspecting faces, and for a moment they sat wide-eyed, staring at her in disbelief.

"Oops. Sorry about that. My hand slipped," she said casually, trying her best to keep a straight face as she returned to her task. *Perhaps that will quiet them down a bit.* Brooklyn and Hiva were already laughing under their breath, but Jack remained straight faced, as usual.

The truce, however, only last a moment. But this time, to her surprise, it was Wit'é who started it. She had been too busy dealing with the miscreant Africans to notice that Wit'é had pulled a spare bag of acorns out from under the table. Before she could stop it, a barrage of acorn-shot whizzed past her head, striking all four of the young men at once.

This time, Jack laughed.

Wakíŋyaŋ turned to Wit'é and started to say, "Not you too…, "when all at once the kitchen came alive in a frenzy of splashing water, flying acorns, giggles, screams, grunts, and exclamations.

Wakíŋyaŋ wasn't going to partake in this childish, wasteful game—that is until Redbraids hurled a full mug of water that hit her directly in the face. After that, she was in it to the bitter end.

The torches burned slowly through their fuel as outright pandemonium ensued. Bark and Bite were particularly adept at sneaking in under feet and tables to launch acorns scavenged off the floor, before disappearing again into the dark. Even Jack came alive, hollering and letting out war cries. Clifton and Bay were the only ones with sense enough to stay out of the kitchen during the battle.

After the food fight Bark and Bite curled up by the fire and fell asleep, Clair sang softly to herself, and Brooklyn whistled a cheerful tune. Besides a little water and some acorns that needed to be washed off and tossed back in the pot, not much had really been wasted, after all. For the first time since she had been taken captive, the dungeon felt less like a prison and more like a home. She was beginning to have a better understanding of who these Africans were. *Perhaps they're not all that bad.* Though she still hadn't figured out how Redbraids had known the hand sign from her village.

The hand sign. The veil.

She recalled having a conversation with Uŋčí. Something about learning to walk in her spirit body, passing through a veil between worlds.

Had that conversation been prior to her abduction? Somehow the hand sign had caused her to remember bits and pieces of a conversation that she was unaware had ever taken place. For a moment she saw the sign, superimposed in front of her, then the image of Grandmother standing in her bearskin robe with her hair down and flowing. Maybe someday it would all make sense.

Broken

The work today was collecting scrap metal. EnKare and Jioba ended up in Pill's group, and Wakíŋyaŋ and the others were off in some other part of the ruined city. Metal work was harder than wood collecting, and more dangerous too. Rusted jagged points were a constant threat, and without the cover of the forest the midday sun dehydrated and exhausted the body.

EnKare had started the day already feeling a little off. He had a splitting headache and muscle aches, so stumbling around a rubble graveyard was the last thing he wanted to do with his day.

And he missed Pilipili. He hadn't seen her since their abduction. She'd most likely be fine, but the threats here were different than the ones she was used to back home. Any number of things could catch her off guard. Was she scared and alone, lost in some distant part of the forest? He wished she'd never sneaked onto the *Mandaha*.

Hiva, who was also in his group that day, had wandered out of sight, so Pills stepped over a rise to check on her whereabouts. Taking advantage of the situation, he tugged on Jioba's arm, and the two sat down on an eroding slab of concrete for a breather.

"We can't do this forever, Jimmy," he sighed. "We've got to find a way out of this. We've got to escape."

Jioba slowly nodded his head in agreement.

"What are you two wormbait doing?" Pills screamed. "This ain't break time yet, you know?"

They were caught off guard. "Take it easy, bwana, we only just sat down…" Before Jioba could finish his sentence Pills drew a wooden club from his belt and smashed it across Jioba's temple.

"Don't talk back, wormbait, it's not good for yer health," Pills cautioned, then turned and wandered off.

Jioba's body was knocked clean off the slab, and he curled up on the ground, clutching his head in his hands and moaning softly. EnKare immediately dropped down beside him.

"Jimmy, Jimmy? Are you OK, bwana?"

"Ya. Ya, Toots, I'll be alright," Jioba grimaced and wiped the blood from his face. "Chabalangus, Bwana! He got me pretty good."

"Come on, we gotta get up before that maniac comes back." He pulled Jioba's free arm over his shoulder and hoisted him to his feet. Anger was such a foreign emotion. He had felt it for the first time when Bronx killed Capitán Kodo. And now he felt it again, as though something with a hot, iron grip was reaching up into his gut and clamping down on his insides. The muscles in his shoulders and arms trembled involuntarily and his fingers curled until his knuckles popped.

We've got to escape! A spasm of pain split his skull from the crown to his cheekbones.

They'll kill us all. His skin flushed, the breath from his nostrils burned his lip.

One by one…they'll kill...us... His thoughts blurred. His mind went blank. Then his legs gave out and his body dropped away.

* W *

Wit'é ran to get the wóphiye with the medical supplies while Wakíŋyaŋ cleared a place by the fire. They laid Redbraids' body down gently then instructed Jioba to do the same.

"I'll be fine, bibi, it's just a bump," Jioba protested.

"If you don't want an infection, like your friend here, then lie down and let us take care of the wound." Wakíŋyaŋ spoke firmly and with confidence. It seemed to reap good results with these boys. In reality, she wasn't that confident at all about Redbraids' condition. He hadn't cleaned his head wound, as she had told him to do, and now the infection had taken hold.

If infection has spread to his blood, then death will take him quickly.

Redbraids lifted his head and with a week voice asked, "Jimmy, you OK, bwana?" then passed out again.

The young man's braids had covered the injury on his head, and a cluster of them was matted in dry blood and crusted over the gash. Bay heated some water in a small clay pot and Wakíŋyaŋ used the water to loosen up and untangle the matted hair. She carefully pulled aside the braids to expose the wound.

What she saw caused her heart to sink. The infection had spread under his scalp, causing his skin to swell and pull away from his skull bones. The gash had remained closed, and dirty, for too long.

She turned to Wit'é to ask for a favor, but her freckled friend wasn't there. A moment later she heard *pitter-patter* as Wit'é returned, holding an object in her outstretched hand.

How does she do it? It's like she can read my thoughts.

It was the same piece of sheet metal they had used to remove the bot larva from her neck.

Handing Hiva the piece of metal, "Will you pass this over the flames?" Jioba sat up with a concerned look on his face. "We have to open the wound to drain the fluids and clean the infected flesh," Wakíŋyaŋ told him. "Hiva is just making sure the blade is clean."

"Yes, I get all that," Jioba answered in a flustered voice. "But is he going to be alright?"

"Of course he is. And when we're done with him we'll take a look at your head, too."

There was no point in upsetting him further. She didn't actually know if Redbraids was going to be alright. A few winters ago a friend of hers back in the village, Čhaŋšká, had been too stubborn to clean out a scratch from a zitkála attack. He developed a fever and, despite a valiant effort by the village Wíŋyaŋ Wakȟáŋ, the medicine woman was unable to save his life. Uŋčí had told her that it is the spirit that decides when it is time to leave one body and seek another.

She didn't really know this African boy well, but she hoped it wasn't his time yet.

There was work to do. She cleared her mind and focused on the unpleasant task at hand. Hiva handed her the blade while Bay and Brooklyn prepared a poultice of mashed yarrow leaves and warm water. With a steady hand, she hooked the point of the sheet metal into the corner of the wound and, with a slight sawing motion, made an insertion.

Immediately the built up fluid oozed out. With her fingertips she felt around the edges of the engorged flesh and then, with steady pressure, pushed in against his skull and slid her fingers towards the opening. The fluid, a creamy, foul smelling mixture of blood and pus, bubbled to the surface and ran down the boy's neck. Wit'é used a damp piece of buckskin to sponge up the purulence as Wakíŋyaŋ continued to milk the wound.

After all the fluid was extracted, she held the cut open with a small stick and poured warm water into the opening until the cavity was filled, then flushed the effluent out again. She repeated this until the ichor ran clear, then stepped out of the way so Bay could apply the poultice and wrap his head.

Still holding the piece of sheet metal, Wakíŋyaŋ turned toward Jioba and said, "OK, now it's your turn."

Pointing a trembling finger at the metal in Wakíŋyaŋ's hand, Jioba stammered, "Not with that...thing, bibi, no way. You stay away from me."

Wakíŋyaŋ smiled and handed the piece of metal to Wit'é. "Look, no knife. I promise. We do, however, need to clean out that cut on your head so you don't end up like him." She motioned towards Redbraids.

* E *

He noticed the pressure in his head and something wrapped tightly around his chin. He also noticed a slight weight on his chest and a familiar smell. When the mucilaginous goo cementing his lids gave way and he managed to open his eyes, his vision was blurry.

He smiled weakly.

"I knew you'd find me."

A tiny pink tongue licked him on the tip of his nose.

"But how? How did you manage to get in here?"

The little pink tongue licked his nose again.

"I missed you too. I thought I might never see you again."

A soft voice just above his head said, "So you know this little creature?" It was Wakíŋyaŋ's voice. Then he felt a hand on his forehead, which moved to his cheek.

"This is Pilipili. She's my bushbaby friend. She wasn't supposed to come here, but she stowed away on Jioba's boat. You've probably never seen one before, have you?"

"Stowed away? Bush baby? No. I've never seen anything like her." Wakíŋyaŋ sounded confused.

"How did she get into the dungeon?"

"She climbed down through the crack in the ceiling where we collect water. She dropped straight into it. I don't think I've seen such a small creature make so much noise before."

He smiled and stroked the soft fur along the top of Pilipili's head. "No, she never has liked getting wet."

"Speaking of water, I think your fever might be breaking. If you can sit up a little, I'd like you to drink some...if you can."

With great effort he pulled himself up to where he could lean against one of the logs near the fire. Pilipili looked a little lost at first, lacking her customary hiding place beneath the forest of braids. As he sat up, she leapt to Wakíŋyaŋ's shoulder and ducked under the long, flowing, black curtain.

"She likes you." His head pounded.

Wakíŋyaŋ handed him a clay mug, and he drank the cool liquid. The water had a refreshing, fruity flavor.

"I infused it with blackberries," Wakíŋyaŋ informed. "Try to drink as much as you can. It will help wash the fever out."

"What happened? Where is everyone? Why is my head all wrapped up?"

He listened to the young warrior's soothing voice. She told him that he had passed out earlier that day, above ground, while collecting scrap metal. Pills had wanted to leave him as wormbait, but Jioba and Hiva had refused. Pills allowed them to carry him all the way back to the dungeon as long as they carried their load of metal as well.

Is that even possible? They...saved my life!

Then she related how she had discovered the infection on his head and had lanced and irrigated the wound, and then how Bay and Brooklyn had prepared and applied the poultice.

Hearing her story, the memory of parts of the day slowly returned.

"But what about Jioba? Is he OK? Pills nearly killed him..."

"He's fine," she reassured. "We took care of his wound...right away," she added, with a hint of antagonism in her voice.

Could he blame her? He'd been too angry, and stubborn to accept her care, and it had nearly cost him his life.

After that, everyone had gone to bed except for Wakíŋyaŋ, who had stayed behind to watch over him and to change out the poultice on his head as needed.

They saved my life. All of them. Jimmy. How could you have carried me and all of your scrap metal? I saw your head. I saw Pills hit you. He could have killed you, Jimmy.

As he thought about Pill's senseless attack on Jioba, he found himself getting angry again. He stewed for a while in silence then looked up at Wakíŋyaŋ. "We have to escape." She looked back at him but didn't say a word. "Did you hear me? If we stay here, we're going to die, one way or another, we're all going to die."

Wakíŋyaŋ sat quietly, staring at the fire. She seemed to be deep in contemplation. The flames crackled, wheezed, and popped as she stirred the ashes and added another log.

Just when he felt he could bear the silence no longer, she looked at him, and in a hushed voice, "I have a plan."

Hip's Good

Cold polished rock pressed in from all sides as they maneuvered silently through the labyrinth of schist boulders and greystone. One moment they were crawling on their bellies through impossibly narrow tunnels, and the next shimmying between behemoth blackstone slabs that stretched upward beyond the torchlight's reach. Following Wakíŋyaŋ's lead, they descended deeper and deeper into the earth.

They were traveling light, carrying only what they needed to make the journey. Wakíŋyaŋ had her bow, a quiver of arrows, a torch, and her wóphiye containing dried meat, acorn flatbread, and some medical supplies.

For three days they had prepared. They worked as slaves during the day, and spent nights turning scrap wood into fire hardened spears, clubs, and arrows. Even Bark and Bite made their own little clubs. The weapons were rudimentary, but considering the time and material restrictions, they had come out better than she had hoped for.

This stretch of the journey was taking longer than she anticipated. She had not factored in so many of them making the escape at the same time. Her original plan included only her, Wit'é, and perhaps Hiva. But then Bronx captured the Africans, and Redbraids had insisted that not one of them be left behind to live as a slave. And so here they all were, fourteen people and one bushbaby, crammed into a space barely large enough for three, with no guarantees on a way forward and no option of turning back. They were committed to one of two paths.

Freedom, or death.

After a short break to let everyone catch their breath, Wakíŋyaŋ used hand gestures to point out the way forward. She took off her wóphiye and quiver, and, along with her bow and torch, handed them to Redbraids and Jioba. Then she stepped behind a small boulder and disappeared through a narrow hole in the ground. Once her feet came to rest on solid ground, she looked up to see Redbraids' illuminated face looking down through the hole at her. She motioned for him to pass down the weapons and supplies first, then for the rest of them to follow.

Once they were all safely through the opening Wit'é moved in close, looked up at her with shiny, blue eyes, and smiled weakly. Wakíŋyaŋ hoisted Wit'é up into her arms to comfort her. Then, speaking for the first time since they began their escape, she address the group. In a whisper she said, "We are in one of the train tunnels now. If we are to speak it must be done quietly. The sound can travel great distances down here. This is as far as I have been. Going forward we'll have to choose our path wisely."

Then, looking at the little ones in the group, she asked if anyone was hungry or tired. Bark and Bite nodded their heads in perfect unison, and she smiled. "And how about you, Clifton? Bay? How are you holding up?"

"Oh, honey, my knees have been aching me for the past ten winters. Ain't nothn' different 'bout today." Bay responded in her usual positive tone. "In a moment or two I'll be good as new."

Clifton smiled but remained silent.

When the twins finished gnawing on their small pieces of dried meat, the group gathered everything up and prepared to move out. Bark and Bite, however, remained sitting. It was clear that they felt they had walked far enough, and that was that.

Redbraids approached the twins and squatted down. "You two ready to go for a ride?" Bite looked up with sad, tired eyes, his lower lip popped way out, and he nodded his head dramatically. "Come on then," Redbraids encouraged, as he lifted Bite onto his back. He wrapped his shuka under the little boy's behind, then brought the ends up under his armpits and tied them together behind his neck. Then he looked over at Jioba and said, "You get the heavier one, bwana."

To Wakíŋyaŋ, the kind gesture didn't go unnoticed. With Wit'é still clinging to her neck, she looked at Redbraids. "Thank you."

He smiled back.

How had she not noticed it before? When she realized she was staring at him she quickly looked away, but his smile remained etched in her mind. "We should keep moving," she muttered, trying not to sound too awkward.

One direction was blocked by a cave-in, which took the guesswork out of which way to go next. The group headed off down the tunnel, the twins, Wit'é, and Pilipili hitching rides while the others hauled the supplies. They arrived at an intersection and came to a halt. There was some discussion over which way to go, but there was no compelling reason to pick one way or the other.

Redbraids offered an observation. "What if we just follow the water?"

Hiva asked, "Why? What's so special about the water?"

"It's not the water itself, but where it is going that is important."

"He's right," Jafra chimed in. "Water flows downhill until it reaches a common level."

"The sea!" Jioba whisper-shouted. "So all we have to do is follow that little stream," pointing at the rivulet running down the center of the track, "and it'll take us right to the ocean! Right?"

"Okay, don't get too excited. That water could be flowing anywhere," Wakíŋyaŋ reasoned. Then looking over at Redbraids, she added, "But that is the best option I've heard so far. I say we follow the water." With that, they headed off down the tunnel, following the growing trickle while Bark and Bite napped blissfully on their human steeds. Each time they came to an intersection they followed the path with the greatest volume of water.

The escape was going smoothly so far, and the mood in the group reflected it.

"So what's the plan again," Clifton asked, "you know, once we make it to the sea?"

She had never seen the old man in such high spirits. He had lived out his youthful years working as a slave for one warlord after another, and like Bay, he was fast approaching the age of *retirement*, as the rogues called it. Retirement meant being used as wormbait or being set free. However, to be set free really meant being left in the forest with no weapon, too old and tired to defend one's self, with no place to go home to. In other words, wormbait.

"When we get to the ship," Jioba explained, "if the rogues haven't completely stripped it yet, we'll sail it over to Wakíŋyaŋ's village. That's the plan, right?"

Redbraids nodded, then queried, "Hey Wakíŋyaŋ, how did you discover that there was a way out of the dungeon, right under our own heads?"

"And how long have you known about it?" Hiva added.

"Ha. That's a funny way to put it. It was actually right under your own head, wasn't it?" Wakíŋyaŋ told them about her first night in the dungeon. How she had explored it from top to bottom, eventually ending up on her belly at the back of the crushed railcar, the same car that the African's had been sleeping in for the past half moon. She had detected an air current against her face, which had prompted her to pull back the rusty sheet metal flooring where she discovered a narrow opening in the greystone below the car, just wide enough to squeeze through. While the other's slept, she had explored the caves several times, eventually finding the point at which it connected to the tunnel system that they were now in. But that was as far as she had gotten.

"Now, honey," Bay exclaimed, "if you knew 'bout that hole in the dungeon all this time, why didn't you up 'n git out a long time ago?"

She looked down at Wit'é, who was now walking beside her and holding her hand. Wit'é looked up and smiled knowingly. "It was just never the right time. Then the Africans showed up, and Redbraids here insisted that it was either all of us, or none of us."

"Hold up! Look at this, everyone." It was Jioba, who had been walking a little ways in front of the others.

As they approached, she could see what the fuss was about. The tunnel ended abruptly and the cool evening air from the outside world brushed against her cheeks. The rails at her feet were sheared off, and the tunnel floor gave way, dropping into the darkness that swallowed their torchlight like a hungry shadow creature. Her eyes adjusted, and she saw an escarpment of boulders off to one side.

"That's the way down," pointing towards the rockfall.

Climbing over and exploring boulder fields was one of the twins' favorite things to do. Well rested now, they dismounted their rides and eagerly led the descent. Pilipili jumped down from her perch on Tomobo's shoulder and sprang into the darkness after them.

It wasn't until they reached the bottom that the full scope of their surroundings became apparent. They were standing on the floor of a vast, gaping void in the surface of the earth. Whatever had caused it had torn a hole in the ground so deep that several tall pine trees could be stacked on end within the caldera. High above the crater's rim, heavy thunder clouds whipped passed, parting on occasion to let the light of the full moon illuminate the cavern. They stared, spellbound, at the scene before them. Ribbons of water shot out from the chopped off openings of several train tunnels scattered across the up hill edge of the cavern, sending at least a dozen silvery falls cascading down through the pale light.

When the clouds parted again, Wakíŋyaŋ froze. A chill ran through her blood and danced up the center of her spine. A frightening silhouette was etched into the sky above the rim of the crater—a head of snakes attached to a giant's body, the dreaded mace that had taken Kodo's life pointing down at them.

Bronx must have figured out that we escaped. But how? Someone must have come to check on us this evening and found us gone.

The details weren't important. Getting out of there was. They couldn't go back the way they came, in case they had been followed, and they certainly couldn't climb out of the cavern with the rogue hunters waiting on the rim. She looked at Redbraids and motioned with her head towards the silhouette of the giant.

The moment he spotted Bronx his eyes widened, and he whispered, "We've got to get out of here, NOW! Quick, follow the water. If it's flowing down hill and not forming a lake, then it's got to lead to a way out."

No one else had noticed the rogues, which was a good thing. The last thing they needed was for everyone to panic and start making irrational decisions. Redbraids was right. All the water entering the cavern ran together to form a stream. Without wasting another moment she set out following the water to the far edge of the crater, where it burped and bubbled down through the rocks and into the ground.

"Spread out and look for an opening big enough for us to climb through," she instructed the party. Things were suddenly not looking so good. The rogues were aware of their location, and from her reading of the sky, a storm was developing overhead.

"Over here!" someone yelled out. Jack and Tomobo were pointing down at an opening in the ground just a short distance from the terminus of the stream.

There was no time to explore the opening. She lifted the torch, looked around the group, and then with Wit'é following close behind, climbed in. Then they were back underground, sliding over moist boulders and squeezing between slabs. The rocks at this end of the crater were large and angular, creating a chaotic maze of passageways and openings.

Keeping an eye on the little ones, the group stayed close to the sound of the rushing water, following it down through the layers of rock and eroding greystone. The surface was slick with condensation and moss, and they moved slowly to avoid slipping. If anyone were to fall into that creek the earth would swallow them forever. The wet, black rocks devoured what little light the torches produced, making it hard to predict which way to go. They stopped periodically to let Bay and Clifton rest and to give the children a nibble of flatbread. Most of them were accustomed to darkness and moisture, living in the dungeon for so long, but with the narrow space between the rocks and the lack of headroom, claustrophobia was inevitable.

When they found themselves in a small clearing with an earthen floor and enough room for everyone to sit down, Wakíŋyaŋ suggested they rest and discuss the path forward. This was the first patch of soil they had encountered since dropping back down into the earth, and it felt good on her skin. She dug up a handful of the loamy soil and let it sift through her fingers.

We must be getting close to a low point. What else would explain a soil deposit like this?

The thought hadn't sunk all the way in when she became aware of an odd sensation in the pit of her stomach. It felt like when she would jump off the cliffs into the lagoon near her village. She looked over at the others just as a soppy, vacuous gurgling erupted all around. Then the ground beneath them gave way.

As if the world suddenly fell into a thick brine, everything around her moved slowly—bodies suspended, swimming through invisible quicksand.

Terror frozen on Wit'é's face—

Arms reaching upward—

Torches—

Spears—

Clubs flying through the air.

Screams barely uttered…

Then cut off, as if caught in the throat by the icy hand of fear.

Impact racked her body as she slammed into a solid surface.

Then all was silent.

From the silence came muffled crying, then moaning, and gasping.

Wit'é, where is Wit'é?

She had felt the young girl's hand firmly grasping her own just moments ago. At a light touch on her shoulder, she turned around. Wit'é sat right behind her, dirty, a little scraped up, but smiling. She breathed a sigh of relief, wiped the moist dirt from her face and then assessed the situation.

Jioba was buried waste deep in the earth with his arms raised over his head, spear in one hand and extinguished torch in the other. Pilipili, looking a little dazed and confused, was sitting right on top of his head, her long tail wrapped for dear life around his chin.

She did a warm body count; Hiva, Clifton, Bay... Everyone but the twins. Where were the twins? The sound of muffled sobbing led her to a small mound. With Wit'é's help she pulled back the layers of soil, working carefully in case either of them was injured. A hand's depth down she unearthed a small, shaking leg. They cleared away the dirt and, to

Wakíŋyaŋ's relief, found the twins, sobbing, shaking, covered in mud from head to toe, but unharmed.

With a little help from Redbraids and Jafra, Jioba was pulled from the mud, shaken up but still smiling.

"Bay, Clifton, are you injured?" Wakíŋyaŋ explored.

"Honey, it'd take more than a little fall to shut this 'ol gal up. Clifton, how's the hip?" Bay inquired.

"Hip's good."

Worms

Is anyone hurt?" Wakíŋyaŋ looked over the bodies heaped in a pile of mud all around her. "Brooklyn, Clair? You doing OK?"

Clair heralded, "I'm fine. Brooklyn landed on top of me, so I'm guessing she's fine too. Brooklyn?"

"Ya. I'm good. What about you Jack? Anything broken?"

"Yes. My behind. But I'll live."

"What happened?" Hiva wiped the mud away from her face and looked around.

Tomobo declared, "The whole floor just caved in. What is this place anyway? Where are we?"

Jafra sounded confused and alarmed. "Ah, my torch is out. Jioba, yours is too. Does anyone have a torch that's still lit?" No one responded. "No? Ah, then how come I can still see? Is anyone else seeing this? There's some sort of light."

Satisfied that no one was injured, Wakíŋyaŋ turned her attention to their surroundings. They had fallen into a room, or a cave. Not like the railcar tunnels. Smooth clay walls arched overhead and radiated a faint blue glow. It was as though something, or someone, had taken firesand and plastered it onto the walls intentionally. *An effective way to illuminate the underground, but who would want to have light down here? Could this be...* Her breath caught in her throat.

"Shhh. Quiet everyone. I think we've fallen into a worm nest." For a moment there was total silence, except for the hum of lungs pulling air and the erratic percussion of water trickling.

Redbraids whispered, "What do you mean you think we've fallen into a worm nest? What does that even mean? What is a worm nest? What is a worm?"

Ignoring the questions, she contemplated their situation. She, and two of the other young ladies in the group, had started their išnáthi with the waxing of the full moon. From a great distance worms could sense a single drop of blood dissolved in water or exposed to air. Under these circumstances, their chances of being detected were greatly increased.

Jioba cleared his throat. "You're joking, right? These would have to be some giant worms to make a tunnel this big." There was a note of disbelief and sarcasm in his voice. Then, reacting to the serious expression on her face, "Oh. You're not joking, are you?"

She put her finger to her lips to signal everyone to remain silent. She thought for a moment. It was impossible to climb back up through the ceiling. The opening was too high for them to reach. "We have to get the torches lit, now!"

"Bay whispered, "What for, honey? I can see just fine as it is."

"The only thing that I know of that worms fear, is fire. I think it's too bright for them. It blinds them. Here," taking a piece of flint from her wóphiye. "The sooner we have fire the safer we'll be." Only one of the torches was dry enough to receive the spark and ignite. *It'll have to do until the other bundles dry out.*

She handed the torch to Redbraids. "Let's make a circle around the little ones. They'll be safer that way. That fire might be the only thing that gets us out of here. So please, don't let that flame go out."

Redbraids nodded his understanding.

Things had gone from bad, to much, much worse. Bronx and the rogues were predictable in battle. She new their weapons and their skill levels. They had a good chance above ground because it was her domain. But this! What if they *had* fallen into a worm nest? She had never been below ground, into the kingdom of the worms, and the very thought chilled her blood.

"Well," she broke the silence, "we can't sit here waiting for them to find us. Keep the circle tight and pass the torch to whatever side a threat is coming from." She pulled her bow from her back, nocked an arrow, and with a slight gesture of her head, motioned for the group to follow her down the tunnel.

Movement was a little awkward a first as they adjusted to their formation. Redbraids headed the group, holding up the torch, while Wakíŋyaŋ positioned herself at the back, bow at the ready.

The walls were rounded and smooth. The makers had coated every surface with a slick, wet mud that was rich in firesand. She felt as though she had shrunk in size and was walking along the inside of some creature's intestines.

After a short distance the small passage opened out into a larger channel. There were smaller shafts leading off of the main tunnel in all directions, some going straight down into the floor, others veering off at odd angles from the walls and ceiling. A small stream ran along one side of the main passage, and she immediately recognized it for what it was; an aqueduct. The earthen floor had been molded into a semi-cylindrical tube that carried the main flow of water. Openings in the aqueduct allowed for controlled flows along smaller channels molded into the floor of side tunnels. This was a sophisticated underground water system.

The moment they entered the larger cavern her senses were overwhelmed by a pungent odor; fresh compost mixed with a tangy musk of rotting citrus; unlike anything she'd smelled before.

"Holy hippopotamus, look at this!" Jioba had left the circle and was standing at the entrance to a side tunnel, pointing his spear.

She looked down at Wit'é, who was tugging on her arm and shaking her head with an urgent look on her face.

The group moved over to where Jioba was standing. Wakíŋyaŋ could see a small circular room. Something shiny, and fleshy, hunched over near the far wall, rose up off the ground the moment the faint torchlight passed over it, revealing two smaller creatures huddled below.

Jioba screamed and stumbled backwards into the group. As they retreated the creature came to the entrance, sunk her claws into the walls on either side, tilted her head back, and let out a sustained, screeching ululation that rang through the caverns.

No, no, no, this is not good.

Redbraids shouted over the deafening scream, "What is that thing?"

"That's a worm!" Wakíŋyaŋ shouted back. "We have to go. Grab the little ones and run! Wit'é," she said looking at her small, trembling friend, "stay close to me and you'll be OK." Bark, Bite, and the little bushbaby hopped onto the Africans' backs, and the group took off running.

"Follow the water! Follow the water!" Redbraids kept shouting.

As they ran through the main passage more worms appeared at side openings and screamed the same alarm.

Some of them had little worms clinging to their legs, looking on at the spectacle or screaming with the others. These worms were significantly smaller than any Wakíŋyaŋ had seen above ground.

Mothers with their children!

It dawned on her that they weren't just in a worm nest, but in an entire worm village! So where were all the males?

That question was answered all too soon. The alarm, which now vibrated throughout the tunnel system, had been effective. A worm appeared in an opening on the ceiling just in front of them, dropped onto the floor and stood up. She had never seen one that large, or that heavily muscled. He was nearly twice the size of the mother worms.

He curled his clawed fingers inwards, raised his arms out to the sides, lifted his chest and roared directly at them. Through his translucent skin she could see ribs heaving, muscle fibers pulling and drawing, like the strings of a mannequin working to animate a ghostly corpse.

She drew back her bow string, but before she could let the arrow fly the worm leapt straight up and disappeared through the hole he had dropped down from. As they took off down the tunnel again, more worms appeared. For the moment they seemed to be observing. Were they too afraid of the torch flames?

A series of three staccato screeches blasted from behind. She glanced back and saw the oversized worm standing in the middle of the tunnel. He clearly stood out from the rest. A layer of skin stretched from ear holes on the side of his head to the top edges of his shoulders, and as he breathed the skin drew taut. A similar web of skin grew from his elbows and attached along his ribcage and looked like a pair of diaphanous wings when his arms stretched to the sides.

They might be afraid of the flame, but that's not why they aren't attacking. They're waiting for orders!

The giant worm barked a second round of staccato screams. A soldier worm lifted a wooden gate on the aqueduct and water flowed onto the tunnel floor.

Then the leader dropped onto all fours and charged straight towards them. He gained speed then dove through the air, landing flat on his stomach, sliding along the slick tunnel floor, faster and faster, carried by the flow of water. The other soldier worms did the same, each clinging to the legs of the ones in front of them, and in moments the tunnel was transformed into one long worm, sliding towards them, claws bared, teeth snapping. All the while, more worms tumbled out of holes in the ceiling and joined the attack.

A worm dropped right into the middle of their circle landing on top of Hiva. She threw herself backwards and knocked him off. Redbraids tossed the torch to her and she turned and waved it wildly in the creature's face. The worm screamed and staggered away, clutching his eyes.

Wakíŋyaŋ shouted, "Keep your spears pointed towards the openings above and to the sides. I'll try to clear the path ahead."

Each time a worm dropped to the floor in front of them she sent an arrow flying, either wounding or killing it. The rest of the group swung clubs and jabbed spears at anything that came within striking distance. They were able to keep up their pace, but the snake of worms was gaining on them.

The tunnel ahead ended abruptly, ceiling curving down to meet the floor.

This is it! This is where we make our stand.

Wakíŋyaŋ held out her arms, and the group ground to a halt behind her. A quick look down brought her a renewed sense of hope. The floor of the tunnel dropped away into the darkness at a steep angle and was scooped out like a trough. A portion of the water from the aqueduct had been diverted down the hole and the clay was slick and wet. This was their only chance of escape, but the worms would be upon them before they could all make it into the opening. She had to slow the snake's progress.

One good shot.

She yelled, "Everyone duck, NOW!" as she whipped around, arrow nocked and bow at the ready. She pulled back the string, and sighted down the arrow at the worm leader. Only the top of his head and his shoulders were visible.

It makes sense now. They attack in this formation because it keeps their vulnerable parts protected behind a wall of thick skull bones. There's no way in!

Then, to her horror, her breathing suddenly stopped and she was paralyzed.

An intense ringing vibration started at the base of her spine, then tore its way up her back and exploded straight out the top of her head.

She looked down in wide eyed terror at her own body standing there with the others, arrow drawn back, but barely moving, as though they were all trapped in thick honey.

She looked towards the worms, and the next thing she knew she was head to head with the leader, hovering in front of him, almost touching the skin of his forehead with her nose. She could see through the flesh on his skull, the veins carrying blood.

Her gaze drifted down the side of his head, past his lobe-less ear—a small opening covered by a flexible flap of skin—and then down the web to the creature's neck.

There, in a slight depression where his neck met his shoulder, she could see six narrow slits.

Gills!

Then she was struck with a knowing. This was the worm's one vulnerable spot, through the gills, between the collar bone and shoulder blade, into the middle of the ribcage to the worm's heart.

This was the path her arrow must seek.

An instant later she felt herself smash backwards into her own body, and at the same moment the loud ringing stopped and her muscles came back to life.

Still sighting down the arrow, she adjusted her aim, made a random calculation to account for the misshapen arrow shaft, then let it fly.

Having had so little time to make them, and none of the right materials, her arrows had been flying unpredictably, and this one was no exception. It sped directly for the worm's soft spot, but at the last moment curved outward and struck the creature in the fleshy muscle of his shoulder. Instantly a curtain of worms closed in, protecting him from the next two arrows that she had already released.

She turned to Redbraids. "Follow the water, right?"

He nodded, "Always."

"I think this is some sort of slide," she gasped, pointing into the darkness ahead. "Maybe a way out of here? I don't know, but we don't really have a lot of options right now." She motioned towards the fast-approaching worm mass with her chin. The arrows had slowed them a bit. But would it be enough?

Redbraids shouted, "Everyone follow Wakíŋyaŋ. It's our only chance!"

She took hold of Wit'é's hand. "Do you trust me?"

Wit'é looked up at her with a mix of hope and fear, and nodded her head. Moving together, they stepped off the edge and disappeared into the darkness.

Then they were gliding through the deepest reaches of the underworld, flying down the slick, earthen tube, liquid sparks bursting all around as fireclay reacted to the friction of their bodies. The sounds of screaming echoed all around, as the tunnel serpentined through bedrock, twisting and turning, rising up over small humps and plummeting down, down into the unknown.

She had no idea where the passage led, or if they were falling to their deaths. At any moment they could meet a wall of stone or drop into the abyss. She was terrified. Didn't know if she was even breathing.

But she was also more filled with life then she had ever been before, flying through the fire-speckled oblivion. It was pointless to imagine the worst, so she held tightly to Wit'é's hand and gave herself over to the feeling—

To the not-knowing—

To the moment.

Then Mother Earth shuddered and gave birth to the newborns, who flew from the tunnel and skidded across the flat, clay-slicked floor to a stop.

Moments later, in groups of two or three, the others came shooting out and landed in a heap beside them, hooting and hollering in fear or delight. With a quick check, she confirmed that no one had been injured.

Somehow, the torch had survived the journey. It rested firmly in Jioba's hand, which was still raised up over his head. He was covered with a thick coat of mud and had a big grin on his face. He looked up at the flames and in a casual voice declared, "Saved it, bwana."

"They'll be coming right behind us. We need to find the way out, and quickly," Wakíŋyaŋ urged, taking the torch from Jioba and looking around.

They were in a cave with low ceilings and a sandy floor. At one end was the tunnel they had come through. The water cascading from the opening washed out onto the sand and disappeared. On the opposite side of the cave, the sand dipped down into a pool of water. There appeared to be no way in or out of the cave, other than the tunnel they had come down, and that was not an option.

Redbraids walked over to the edge of the pool and waded in, as Pilipili climbed up onto the top of his head. Like the rest of them, she was covered in a layer of mud. He dipped a hand below the surface then brought it up to his mouth. Spitting it out he turned to the others and said, "It's salty. Jimmy…"

Before he could finish his sentence, Jioba ran towards him. "Ya, Toots, I'm with you, bwana. I'll see if it connects." He waded straight into the pool and vanished under the surface.

Wakíŋyaŋ looked at the spot where Jioba had disappeared, and began to worry when he didn't come right back up. Redbraids remained in the pool, not taking his eyes off of the glassy surface.

Finally, the water stirred and Jioba popped up, grinning from ear to ear. "It connects! It connects! The bay is just on the other side. It's a short swim, and then it's ice cocos on me!" he announced, not even trying to contain his excitement.

"OK. But we have to go, now," Wakíŋyaŋ implored. "I can hear the worms coming. Everyone, move into the pool. If you can carry your weapon, then bring it. If not, then give it to someone who can, or just leave it here. Jioba, you lead the way."

"You ready, little one?" Jioba asked Bite. "Big breath…" and the two disappeared below the surface, the little boy clinging to Jioba's neck.

"Hold on tight, Pilipili. You're not gonna like it, but it's the only way out. Just don't let go." Then Redbraids dipped below the surface with the little bushbaby clinging to his braids.

Hiva was next to go under, Bark clinging to her back, cheeks puffed in a big-boy effort to hold his breath.

As the others moved into the pool and prepared to dive, Wakíŋyaŋ looked back and saw Bay standing on the sandy shore, holding the torch in one hand and a spear in the other. "What are you doing, Bay? We've got to get out of here!"

Resolve and acceptance was chiseled into the old woman's face. "I can't swim, honey. Never lived down by the water, ya know?"

Wakíŋyaŋ left the pool and rushed towards her friend. "You can just hold your breath and I'll…" her words were cut short.

"Them worms'll be down here any moment now. I'm a give 'em a piece of my mind. Buy y'all some time, if you know what I mean."

"Bay, NO!" Wakíŋyaŋ protested. "Please."

"My road ends here, honey." Bays words were firm. Final. Then she looked directly into Wakíŋyaŋ's eyes. "Thank you for the best night of my life. Now git." And with that, the strong elder turned and headed straight for the mouth of the tunnel.

Wakíŋyaŋ waded into the pool, tears flowing down her cheeks. She looked back once, just in time to see Bay ferociously swinging the flame at the first worms to come through the opening. Then she turned away, took in a deep breath, and slipped beneath the glassy surface.

At Any Cost

The moment his head surfaced he was hit in the face by the foaming white crest of a wave, followed by the stinging spray of salt water whipped over the surface of the sea by a gale force wind. He reached up, then breathed a sigh of relief when he felt Pilipili's wet frame clinging to the top of his head. Then, like glass fishing buoys bobbing to the surface, the others popped up into the churning surf, floundering and gasping.

The underwater cave let out in a small, rocky cove. The shore was only a short swim away and the wind blew them there with little effort.

When they were all on the beach he made a quick body count. The twins, Clifton, Wit'é, everyone seemed to be there, except… He turned to Wakíŋyaŋ to ask if she had seen Bay, but when he saw the pained look on her face he understood. He wanted to reach out, put a hand on her shoulder, tell her he was sorry, but the urgency the storm created left no time for comforting.

Clifton noticed Bay's absence as well. He looked over at them with a mixture of hope and fear across his brow. Wakíŋyaŋ shook her head slowly and cast her eyes down at the sand. The old man grimaced. Then he lifted his head. "We've got to push on. She'd want us to push on."

Rain fell in torrential sheets, caught by the wind and hurled sideways. The group scurried up the beach and ducked into the thick treeline to take cover.

"I think I saw the ship," Jioba cried over the cacophony of wind-torn leaves. "Lifeboat is just up the beach, if it's still there."

"Let's stay off of the sand and travel in the trees," Wakíŋyaŋ shouted. "We'll have better protection from the storm."

He glanced at her with a knowing look. The others still had no idea that Bronx and the rogues were after them, and they could be attacked at any moment. The rogues would have figured they were headed for the ship, which meant they could be anywhere in the vicinity, waiting to ambush.

Wakíŋyaŋ had managed to swim through the cave with her weapon and supplies, as had Jioba, Tomobo, and Jafra. EnKare had lost his wooden spear somewhere in the sea right after surfacing. Spear-less and without torchlight, he felt particularly vulnerable.

Traveling through the darkness over rotting logs, wet debris, and moss covered rocks, they crept along the coastline as the storm raged on. Moving through a clearing between two giant trees he caught a glance out into the boiling waters of the bay. There it was! Their ship was moored, right were they had left it, and though it was being tossed like a rag in a puppy's mouth, it was in one piece.

"The ship!" Tomobo pointed a quivering hand. "We can still make it, right?" Hope, fear, sorrow, all smashed together in the crease between his eyebrows. EnKare placed a reassuring hand on Tomobo's shoulder and nodded his head; though a kernel of doubt, somewhere deep within the folds of his gut, questioned if that was true.

A holler from the front told him they had found the lifeboat—then they were scrambling, pulling back forest detritus, tearing at choker-vines, ivy, and roots. Once uncovered, they turned the lifeboat upright and dragged it to the sand. The oars and rudder were in good condition. It would be a tight fit, but somehow they'd get everyone on board.

"OK, here's the plan," Jioba belted over the storm. "The little ones will get in the boat now. The rest of us will drag it down the beach and into the water. The waves have picked up, so we'll have one shot to get it right. EnKare, you, Wakíŋyaŋ, Tomobo, and Hiva work the oars. I'll be on rudder."

Everyone acknowledged the plan, and then Bite, Bark, and Wit'é climbed into the boat and huddled together on the floor, their slight, drenched bodies shaking. EnKare positioned himself at the front, opposite Hiva, and the others lined up along the sides behind them. Following Jioba's lead, they walked the boat out into the full force of the storm, then, staggering against the wind, crossed the beach to the water's edge.

"Not yet!" Jioba yelled.

EnKare knew what his friend was doing; watching the wave pattern, waiting for a lull. There was an art in launching a boat from the shore without getting capsized. And Jioba was a master of that art!

A large wave broke and the whitewater roller in, picking the boat up off the rocks.

"Now!" Jioba screamed. "Push, PUSH, **PUSH!** Give it everything you've got!" The retreating wave whisked the boat off the beach as everyone, except Clifton, piled in.

"Grab hold!" EnKare urged. Already chest deep in water, Clifton managed to grab on. Firmly in his grasp, EnKare threw his weight backwards, dragging the elder's body over the side rail and into the relative safety of the boat. The other's had already started rowing. EnKare reached for his oar, dropped it into the lock, and fell into rhythm.

"Pull…" Jioba chanted.

The muscles of his back strained as he heaved on the wood.

"Pull…"

Back to the waves, into the driving wind.

"Pull…"

Eyes fixed on Jioba. Eyes trained on his Capitán. Watching for the signal; *hold up, pull harder, pull double time.*

They cleared the beach breakers, the most treacherous part of the launch, and were making good headway out into the deeps. The little boat, adrift on an immense sea of black, rose up to the crest of a wave, wind and rain battering it relentlessly, the storm's deafening violence all around— then dropped down the other side into the trough where all was quiet, an eerie pause before climbing once again into the madness.

Jioba glanced to the right, his body became tense, and he rose halfway off of his seat on the stern of the boat. "Look out!" he boomed, waving his free arm frantically, motioning for them to move away from the side of the boat.

Before anyone had time to react, there was a crunching clatter of metal striking metal, and EnKare looked down to see the front half of a spear protruding through the boat's aluminum sidewall, missing his leg and stopping just shy of Bark's chest.

Reaching over the side, he yanked the spear loose, held it up in the air and shouted at Jioba, "My spear, bwana, look, it's my spear. Haaa!" He couldn't believe it. He had given up hope of ever seeing his trusty lance again, moons ago.

He looked in the direction that the spear had come.

Darkness.

The damaged lifeboat began taking on water. As they rose to the crest of the next wave, the moon peeked through a gap in the clouds, and for a moment the world was bathed in light. A football field away, two rogue boats crashed over the crest of a wave and headed straight for them. The *Buganvilla*, straining on her anchor chain, was roughly the same distance away.

We've got to make it to the ship before they do.

The moment it became clear that they were being pursued the crew leapt into action. Wakíŋyaŋ left her place at the oar so she could position herself on the prow of the boat, bow drawn and ready. There was a quick shuffling around as Jack, Clifton, and Brooklyn jumped on the oars with the others. EnKare was surprised to see Wit'é pop up beside him and grab on to his oar. She looked at him with wild, determined eyes, and then the two fell into rhythm with the others, pulling with all their might.

Pilipili, who had previously been holed up under one of the seats, fled the incoming water and retreated to her spot under her blanket of braids.

Clair grabbed a container that was floating around in the bottom of the boat and started bailing it out at a frantic pace.

As they crested the next wave Wakíŋyaŋ let three arrows fly in rapid succession. It was impossible to see if any hit their mark as they disappeared into the night, but a glimpse of light from the moon revealed who was pursuing them. One boat carried Bronx, Fritz, and a couple of hunters, while Geiger, Pills, and Taco worked the oars in the other boat alongside several more hunters.

The rogues turned course and were now heading directly for the ship as well, though they were still fifty oar strokes behind.

It was now a race for freedom.

A race for survival!

Between the anchor chain and the mooring line that held the *Buganvilla* perpendicular to the storm surge, she strained under the steady assault of wind and waves.

Reaching the rope ladder that was still dangling over the starboard bulwark of the ship, Jioba bellowed, "Oars in!" Then he pulled the rudder hard to one side, bringing EnKare right up to the wooden steps.

Climbing aboard would be a difficult task for all but Pilipili, who leapt from his shoulder, scampered up the ladder, and disappeared over the side like it was a stroll through Sobaco.

One moment the lifeboat was halfway up the side of the ship and the next, the bottom step of the ladder was almost out of reach as the two vessels bucked and pitched independently in the storm swells.

Clair yelled, "Hurry up! I can't keep up with the water coming in. We're gonna sink!"

EnKare stood on the rim of the boat, gripped the rope ladder with one hand, and helped Wakíŋyaŋ and Hiva guide the others up with his other hand.

The Twins darted up the steps effortlessly, followed by Wit'é and Clifton.

Just as the elder cleared the bulwark, the two boats rocked apart, leaving EnKare dangling in mid air. Wakíŋyaŋ extended a hand and grabbed him by the ankle while Hiva grabbed Wakíŋyaŋ's other hand and anchored herself to one of the seats.

The the boats rocked together again, and this time Tomobo, Jafra, Jack, Brooklyn, and Clair managed to make it up to safety.

Then Hiva jumped onto the steps. When she was part way up she extended an arm towards Wakíŋyaŋ. "Quick, hand me your things."

Wakíŋyaŋ passed her bow, quiver, wóphiye, and EnKare's spear to Hiva, who tossed them up onto the ship's deck, then slid over the bulwark and out of sight.

With just the three of them left to go, he held tight to the rope, and howled, "Wakíŋyaŋ, you go up next…" But as she stepped onto the edge of the lifeboat and reached for the ladder, he heard the ship groan and the sound of fibers tearing—

Then a loud *SNAP!*

The hemp mooring line broke, and the tail end of the ship swung around and smashed into the lifeboat.

Jioba and Wakíŋyaŋ were thrown into the water as the dinghy's frame buckled under the bulk of the ship's hull.

He hung in the air, suspended from the one hand that still gripped the ladder tightly. Then the ship picked up speed on its pendulous path and slammed broadside into another wave.

Instantly he was ripped from the steps and cast into the icy darkness.

When he surfaced, he looked around for Wakíŋyaŋ and Jioba, but all he could see was the churning surf and windswept spray. He knew it was too soon to presume the worst, but a feeling of panic and dread coursed through his body.

The ship swung onward, towards Bronx's boats, and either crushed them, or at least slowed their progress.

He swam towards the prow of the ship, his insignificant frame rising and falling with the passing waves like a piece of flotsam.

As he rose to the top of the next wave, he thought he saw a head bobbing in the distance. He tried to scream their names but ended up with a mouthful of sea foam. On the next rise he kicked his legs frantically to bring his body a little higher above the surface.

Sure enough, there they were, a dozen strokes in front of him. This time his scream found air through which to travel.

Jioba heard the call and turned and waved wildly back at him.

As he swam up, Jioba sputtered, "Toots! I thought you were...kwisha kabisa...bwana!"

EnKare didn't have the energy to respond.

"Swim...for the anchor chain...It's our only...chance of getting on board." The wind howled around them. "The anchor chain," Jioba repeated.

EnKare nodded his head.

Finding his friends alive, a new vigor surged through him, and he swam for the ship with everything he had. They had climbed up chains countless times back home, but never in seas like this, and to such a height. This would be tantamount to scaling a coconut tree in an earthquake.

Amygdala

They slipped, clung, gripped, and floundered their way up the thick metal chain, until at last all three were standing safely on the foredeck. They locked arms and brought their foreheads together in a circle, and for a moment, the storm ceased to exist.

EnKare gasped, "I'm so happy to see you two."

Wakíŋyaŋ confessed, "I was happy to see you too."

Jioba declared, "It takes more than that to keep us under!"

The celebration was short lived. There was still so much to do if they were to have any chance of sailing out of the storm.

EnKare probed, "What's the plan, my Capitán?"

Jioba smiled. "Capitán? I like the sound of that, bwana. I'll head for the bridge, you go for the engine room. Wakíŋyaŋ, can you check on the others? Get them all to safety. At the back of the boat, the stairs go down to cabins. The little ones will be safe there."

"Háŋ, Capitán," she confirmed.

"Follow me," EnKare advised. They ran along the ship, heading for the stern where the others had come up the rope ladder.

As they approached the group, Hiva cried, "You're alive! We thought you were shark food. Here, take these." She handed Wakíŋyaŋ and EnKare their weapons. "Where's Jioba?" A wave struck the side of the ship and sent a sheet of water over the top of the deck.

"Jioba's on the bridge," EnKare sputtered, then realizing that no one knew what the bridge was, he clarified, "...uh, the Capitán's room, where you steer the ship. Up there." He pointed to the wheelhouse.

"Where are the little ones?" Wakíŋyaŋ inquired.

Clifton responded. "Brooklyn and Clair took them down those steps over there to get them out of the storm."

EnKare thought for a moment. "Jafra, can you come with me to the engine room? We've got to get this boat running. Tomobo, take a couple of people with you to the bridge. Everyone else, this way. Come on!"

Lights came on automatically as they descended into the belly of the ship.

Lights still working. That's a good sign. Let's hope there's enough juice to power up the jets.

The wheel-lock to the system's room door spun as effortlessly as ever. Once inside, Jafra picked up the check list while EnKare opened the door to the engine room. Before leaving the ship they had shut down all but one of the salt water batteries in order to maintain a few of the more sensitive instruments on the bridge. A quick glance at the screen confirmed that the photovoltaic cells embedded into the ship's decking had done their job. The batteries were all fully charged.

He opened the electrical panel, flipped the breaker, then ran to the intercom next to the door. He pushed in the button labeled *bridge* and said, "OK, Jimmy, we have power. Please confirm. Over."

He released the button. A moment later Jioba's voice *crackled* through the loud speaker, "That's Capitán Jimmy to you, bwana."

He chuckled to himself. Jioba's boundless optimism never failed to amaze. He pressed the button again and advised, "Standby for a system's report," counted to three, very...slowly, then added, "Capitán!" in a sassy tone. He giggled under his breath, then he popped his head back into the systems room. "Jafra, we have power, bwana! Can you confirm when everything's alive?"

Jets powered up, they closed the rooms and headed towards the bridge. Most of the help would be needed on deck. Jafra continued on as EnKare stopped in at his room to check on Wakíŋyaŋ and the little ones.

He opened the door and peered inside. Sure enough, Bark and Bite were up on Jioba's bunk playing under the covers. Clair and Brooklyn were siting on the floor wrapped in blankets, and Wit'é was sitting on his bed. She looked up at him with a big smile.

"Everyone doing okay?" he inquired.

Clair responded, "Better now. Hey, this place is incredible."

"Where's Wakíŋyaŋ?"

"She went to help on deck. You just missed her."

"Just wait till we get out of here. I'll take you on the grand tour," he beamed with pride.

That same instant a scream rang out from topside. Bark and Bite stopped rough-housing and poked their heads out from under the covers.

"What was that?" Brooklyn implored.

"I don't know. Stay here and guard the little ones. I'll go check it out." He grabbed his spear and turned to leave. Wit'é jumped up from the bed and followed him to the doorway.

"No, Wit'é, you stay down here with the others. It might not be safe." He closed the door hastily and ran out of the room.

When he reached the top step he looked out across the deck to determine where the scream had come from. The rain had subsided but the wind was blowing fiercely, and the sea still rampaged on all sides.

There was no one there.

"*Yaaeeeeeeeeeee!*"

This time the cry came from the front of the boat. He bounded up the steps to the middeck and was following the pathway to the bridge when Hiva approached, waving her arms frantically and shouting.

"Calm down, Hiva, calm down! What's going on?"

"Bronx……...on board………..he's gonna kill……Wakíŋyaŋ," she spluttered between gasps of air as she dragged him towards the front of the ship.

He had never seen Hiva so worked up before.

Wakíŋyaŋ's in real danger!

They ran past the wheelhouse and up the steps to the foredeck. As they rounded the corner he saw Jafra lying down, propped up against the front wall of the bridge. Blood dripped from the side of his head, and he wasn't moving.

EnKare stooped to check on his friend. *Still breathing.*

Hiva pulled on his arm again and motioned towards the front of the boat with her eyes.

He crept along the pathway leading past the foremast and out towards the prow of the ship. Moving silently forward, his foot struck an object, and he looked down to see a splintered section of bow. The other half lay a few feet away.

Not good.

They stepped past the mast and onto the anchor deck. Then he froze.

His mind raced as a mixture of fear, self doubt, adrenaline, and panic ran through him at once. The last time he had faced danger such had been when they were attacked by the mutants. Had it not been for Wakíŋyaŋ's arrow, Jioba would have died.

What if my spear misses?

What he kills Wakíŋyaŋ?

Why is Hiva not attacking? No. She has no spear. No weapon.

I have the spear. But…

What if my spear misses?

He stood motionless.

Staring.

Fear was his master now, and it had taken control of his mind and body. He couldn't could run, or attack, and his thoughts were caught in a loop, repeating themselves over and over.

Wakíŋyaŋ was on the ground with her back against the bulwark. She looked small and frail in comparison to the giant man that loomed over her. Her mouth was bleeding, and she looked scared. Not once had he seen her show fear; not in the worm nest, not when fighting off the mutants, and never in the presence of Bronx or any of the rogues.

The leviathan reached down and grabbed her by the neck with one hand, lifting her body up into the air.

Her feet thrashed at the void.

She tore at his fingers and kicked wildly at his body—a stick-figure waging battle with a baobab tree.

Then, something shifted inside him. Like a switch being flipped on, he snapped out of his paralysis.

Remembering the spear gripped tightly in his hand, he nodded at Hiva, then stepped forward and was about to charge when a small figure darted past.

Wit'é!

He reached out to stop her, but she was long gone, sprinting towards the giant. When she reached him, she leapt at his back and ran straight up his body, fingers grabbing flesh, clothing, ropes of hair, like she was climbing a matapalo vine up a giant eucalyptus tree.

She tore and bit and ripped with the ferocity of a cornered warthog— fingers searching for tender eye meat—feet kicking and clawing. Every part of her body weaponized, activated.

EnKare spun the spear around, the way Olubi had shown him, so that the narrow tip at the bottom was pointing at Bronx. This way the leaf-shaped spearhead trailed behind, stabilizing the spear's path through the air, like the fletching on an arrow.

He drew back his arm...but Wit'é's frame blocked the target.

She must have found a sensitive spot on the giant's face, because he suddenly let go of Wakíŋyaŋ, who fell to the deck, gripping her neck and gasping for air.

With both hands free, the man reached back and grabbed the fearless girl by the scruff of her neck, pulled her thrashing body from his shoulder, and held her up for a moment at arm's length, as if to acknowledge the bravery and courage of his little opponent.

Then he tossed her body into the sea, like he was flicking an annoying bug from his hand.

"NOOO!" EnKare bellowed at the top of his lungs, and as the giant spun around to face him, Wakíŋyaŋ staggered to her feet, climbed onto the bulwark and dove out into the darkness.

While Bronx turned to watch Wakíŋyaŋ vanish overboard, EnKare ran forward and hurled his spear with all his might—

"*YEEEAAAH!*"

Driven by the force of his scream, the weapon ripped through the air and struck the man in the chest, right of center and just below his shoulder. It hit with such force that the tip went clear through his body and half way out the other side.

Bronx looked down at the metal protrusion growing from his body. He let out a roar and gripped the spear with both hands.

In the same instant, someone sprinted past.

It was Jioba!

He was holding onto a halyard line and running towards the giant. Then his feet left the ground, and he sailed through the air, the line carrying him in a climbing arc. His bare feet struck Bronx in the side of the head with a muffled *crunch*.

The giant stumbled, caught his leg on the bulwark, and flipped over the side of the ship.

Then EnKare was running—

Diving over the railing—

Drifting out into the void.

Gone

Lying asleep with the blankets pulled up to her chin, she looked...different. The hard edges of her face had softened, and all the tension in her body was gone. She looked peaceful. Maybe a little too peaceful. From the chair beside her bed, he leaned forward and stared intently at the smooth skin at the sides of her throat. A barely perceptible pulse throbbed just under surface. He leaned back again and breathed a sigh of relief.

He cared.

It was strange really, just how much he cared.

He had scarcely left her bedside in three days, monitoring her fever and giving her coconut water whenever she was conscious.

There was a light tapping on the door. Jioba popped his head inside. "How's she doing, bwana?"

He stood up and stretched his arms. Another night of sleeping in the chair, and his body felt like it was crystallizing in a Z-shape. He put his index finger to his lips, grabbed his shuka and motioned for them to step out into the hallway.

"She's sleeping. Her fever broke early this morning, and she's been out ever since. She's alive." He looked at Jioba with a tired smile on his face.

"Good." Jioba sounded relieved. "Now let's get you some food, Toots, and maybe a little sunlight too."

Topside, they made their way straight to the galley. A wind was blowing steady from the south, solar sails fully deployed and stretched tight, and the *Buganvilla* was flying across the surface of the ocean on its foils.

His skin welcomed the sun's warm rays, soaking up the radiant energy like a sponge. The salty smell of the sea filled his nostrils as he took in a deep breath. It felt good to be back on the water. Working together, they whipped up a pot of coconut rice topped with fillets of steaming dorado seared in pilipili and lime juice, then plopped down on a couple of wooden seats just outside the kitchen door. As far as EnKare was concerned, food and fresh air were kind of like...he and Jioba. Inseparable.

"I can't believe there was food left on board," EnKare mused, scarfing down the rice like he hadn't eaten in three days. Apparently most of the perishable foods in the storeroom had either, well, perished, or been looted. But the dry staples, which had been locked in a cabinet, like rice, beans, coconuts, and spices, were right where they had been left. The dorado had gotten itself hooked on Jioba's line earlier that morning.

EnKare smiled to himself. It would be impossible for anyone to starve to death. *The ocean will always provide.*

Between mouthfuls, Jioba bantered, "The rogues, or someone, must have come aboard. They took all of the maps and navigational charts. They left the sextant though. Probably didn't know what it was. We'll be sailing by the stars from now on, bwana."

Just then Bite whizzed past with Bark hot on his tail, screaming their heads off.

"Well, we don't have chickens anymore, but at least we have those two," Jioba chortled.

"What do you think took all the chickens?" EnKare pondered. "If they had all starved to death then we would have found carcasses lying around. No?"

"I bet you it was the rogues, or those big bat things. What did Wakíŋyaŋ call them, zitca's or something like that?"

Changing the subject, "Hey, Jimmy, I'm sorry I haven't been around much to help out." He lowered his head and stared at the reflective surface of the deck.

"Toots, we got it covered up here, bwana. We actually have a bigger crew now than when we came across."

EnKare looked up at Jioba with concern. He remembered the night of their escape, seeing Jafra lying on the ground bleeding from his head. He had been so focused on Wakíŋyaŋ that he had forgotten all about it.

"How is Jafra? Is he OK? How is his head?"

"Cálmate, bwana. Ask him yourself."

He turned in his chair to see Clair, Brooklyn, and Jafra coming around the corner from the foredeck.

"He lives!" Jafra exclaimed.

"I was just about to say that. How's your head, bwana? I thought you were kwisha kabisa." He was relieved to see his friend alive and well.

The young man's head was wrapped in a bandage, and some dried blood marked the location of his injury. "I think I had a bit of a concussion, but that's about it."

Jioba teased, "I think the concussion might have helped a bit." Which brought about a swift slap to his shoulder from Clair, who didn't find the joke funny at all.

"How's Wakíŋyaŋ?" Brooklyn asked cautiously.

He shared what he could about her condition. "Her fever comes and goes. She's still unconscious at the moment, but drinking plenty of coco water when she's awake." Reflecting on his own words, the report didn't sound all that positive. So with a smile he added, "But all in all she is doing better. She'll be up and running in no time." *It's better to be positive, rather than accurate about things like this, isn't it?*

Shortly, Jack, Hiva, and Clifton came by on their way to do some deck chores, and they too exchanged battle stories and checked in on everyone's well being. Since loosing Bay, Clifton had been a little more reserved, a little less talkative. He and Bay had lived together in that dungeon for years. Loosing her had to be hard.

The mood on the *Buganvilla* was a juxtaposition of joy and melancholy. On the one hand there was a lightness. With the heavy weight of slavery lifted from their shoulders, everyone walked a little taller with a spring in their step. But the cost of freedom had been high, and he could see it reflected in their eyes—a sadness and an uncertainty of what was to come.

He was relieved to see that everyone was adjusting as well as could be expected to life on board the ship, not the least of whom Bark and Bite, who had tried to sneak past them to steal food from the kitchen at least three times since they sat down to eat. They appeared to be unfazed by...anything! He tried to imagine the pain they had endured at such a young age. They lost their parents, their tribe, everything they knew, were worked as slaves, and now had lost some of their new family as well. They had no home, no security, and yet here they were, laughing, running, and playing with reckless abandon.

Maybe hardship and uncertainty are all they've ever known. Or maybe it's because they are so young. To them, this is just another day, no different from the last. Is that what my childhood was like? He tried to recall how life felt when he was their age.

He took his plate into the kitchen and helped Jioba with clean-up, then thanked his friend for the food and headed back to the cabins to check on Wakíŋyaŋ. As he took the last step down onto the aft deck, a wave of nostalgia swept over him. He walked to the edge of the ship and leaned against the bulwark, looking over into the dark water rushing below.

His mind drifted to home, to Mbini, to Señora Concha with her bone crushing hugs and mouth watering food, to Mr. Bioko, Mrs. Rita, and Mama Sana with her ice cocos. Oh, what he would give for one of Mama Sana's ice cocos right now.

Then his mind seized control of his thoughts all together, and took off running—Mandaha and his parents flooded in. Mandaha! Not knowing if he was dead or alive, she would be sick with worry! He felt a pain in his chest just imagining her suffering. And what would his parents think? Here he was supposed to be doing something good in the world, who knows, maybe even earning his Lion Name. Instead he was off sailing aimlessly around in a stolen boat, causing his loved ones to worry, and coming home with nothing to show for it. He would remain a boy in his father's eyes, forever! And what would his mother think? By the age of six she led her people out of the caves and into the new world. He was fifteen, and what had he accomplished, other than breaking the rules and breaking his parents' hearts?

Wiping the tears from his cheeks, he descended the stairs and walked down the hall to Wakíŋyaŋ's room. Pausing at the entrance, he composed himself and then opened the door quietly to peer inside.

The bed was empty.

"Wakíŋyaŋ," he called out softly. There was no reply. He looked around the room, but she was nowhere to be found. He knocked on the bathroom door. No answer. He repeated her name even louder, then opened the bathroom door and looked inside. Nothing.

Strange. She must have slipped passed me somehow.

He retraced his steps to the middeck, passing Clifton and Hiva who hadn't seen her either. Then, as he was approaching the bridge, Bark and Bite came running up, waving their arms wildly and screaming and screeching about how they had just seen Wakíŋyaŋ making her way towards the front of the boat.

"Did she look OK?" he asked once the twins had calmed down a bit. They shook their heads.

"And you're sure she went this way?" he questioned, then took off running before the twins could do more than nod their heads up and down in unison.

Rounding the corner of the wheelhouse, he sprinted past the foremast and out onto the deck. Then he saw her. She was standing at the spot where it all had happened, gripping the railing with both hands and looking out at the ocean, her body trembling.

"Wakíŋyaŋ!" he shouted, running towards her. She let go of the bulwark and slowly turned. Her face was pale and moist, and her eyes were bloodshot.

"Wit'é!," she called out in a feeble voice. "Where is Wit'é?"

He reached out and caught her by the shoulders just as her legs buckled under her quivering frame. He could feel the heat radiating from her clammy skin.

"It's your fever, Wakíŋyaŋ. We have to get you…" He didn't finish his sentence.

She looked directly into his eyes and in a soft, searching voice, "Wit'é. Where is she?"

His throat became dry, and he swallowed hard. His breath caught in his chest. His lower jaw began to shake. His mouth opened to speak but a wave of grief rose from his abdomen, the tension drawing his eyebrows tightly together.

It's my fault.

Guilt drenched him.

I could have done more. I could have gone back in again.

Guilt turned to regret.

If I hadn't hesitated, and just thrown my spear before Wit'é got there, I could have prevented…

Regret lost its bravado and sizzled into a cool shame.

I don't deserve a Lion Name. I don't deserve any name at all!

Shame fell apart under its own unbearable weight, leaving him standing there with the only emotion that could shoulder the burden of all that he was feeling in that moment—

Sorrow.

Then he broke the silence. "She's..."

"Gone." The word came from Wakíŋyaŋ's lips, a barely audible breath. Her mouth opened, as if she were about to say something more, but instead her body went limp and she melted into his outstretched arms.

Incantation

Plumes of shimmering vapor rose up from the hardened red clay to form great, ethereal clouds, as the sun's radiance beat down on the rain-drenched village courtyard. Typical of the day after a midsummer storm, the world was buzzing with life. Fishers chattered excitedly in the underbrush. A wolverine screeched in the distance. Raccoon, ring-tailed coati, mongoose, weasels, and mink darted about hunting and collecting food, while zičá scurried along the top of the village boundary wall, sounding their high pitched whistle-barks and flicking their bushy red tails this way and that. Children played in mud puddles as the villagers picked up broken branches and debris scattered by the storm.

A few of her friends walked by at a short distance but didn't notice her when she called out to them. *That's a little odd. Maybe they didn't hear me.* She crossed the courtyard and approached the entrance to Uŋčí's house. It felt like she hadn't seen Grandmother in at least half a moon. And Níškola, where was that great beast hiding? She longed to run her fingers through his soft wooly fur and press her check against his warm, wet nose.

She stepped into the open doorway and paused for a moment to let her eyes adjust.

"Come in, Little Thunder, and sit with me by the fire," Grandmother greeted. She had her back to the door and was busy tending to something on the flames. The smoke drifted up through the vent in the thatched roof.

She closed her eyes and breathed in deeply through her nose, savoring the aroma of spicy grilled tȟáȟča steaks and crispy acorn flatbread. From the corner of her eye she glimpsed the formidable mound of fur that was her four legged friend, sprawled across the floor to one side of the doorway.

"Níškola!" she called out, and was about to rush over and throw herself on him.

"Wakíŋyaŋ," Grandmother's voice stopped her in her tracks. "Leave Níška for now and come sit with me."

Níškola lifted his head off the floor and whined softly, then let out a throaty grunt and lay his head back down. Uŋčí was using her 'no nonsense' voice, so she made her way over to the fire and sat down on the floor.

"Is there something wrong with Níška? Why won't he come say hi to me?"

Wakȟáŋ Kiktá set the food she was cooking on a warming stone, then took a seat on the floor in front of Wakíŋyaŋ. Though she couldn't bring her grandmother's body completely into focus, the elder's eyes shone with the brilliance of river polished crystal.

"Níška can sense that you are here, but he cannot see you. He misses you terribly, you know." A smile stretched across the weathered skin of her face. "He circles the village at least once every day looking for you, then comes back in here and lies down to wait for you to come home."

"To come home? I don't understand. I'm home now. What do you mean he can't see me? Has something happened to his eyes, Uŋčí?" Her voice rose in pitch.

"Little Thunder, you are not here in body. You have traveled through the veil to come home. You know this place better than anywhere in the world, so it is natural that your energy body brought you here when your life is in danger." Grandmother spoke her words directly.

"What are you talking about, Uŋčí? What do you mean, 'when my life is in danger?' I was just out…" Her words were interrupted. Something was odd about the way Grandmother looked at her, an unblinking stare. And she was holding her left hand up in the air in a fist, making the sign for friend.

Then it struck her like a hot summer wind blowing in from the south; *the hand sign, the veil, my abduction, Bronx, the Africans, Redbraids, Wit'é… Wit'é!* She felt a pull at the center of her gut, as though a rope had been tied to her spine and someone, or something, was pulling on it from behind. Grandmother's image pulsed and began to fade.

A moment later she opened her eyes. The underside of the top bunk came into focus. She turned her head and looked out of the round, polished crystal window at the sea as it sped past. She was lying in bed with the blankets pulled up to her chin, covered in sweat. Being home again, talking with Uŋčí, seeing Níška, had all been a dream. Then she remembered what had woken her up so abruptly. Wit'é! She was about to throw back the blankets and jump out of bed when a voice startled her.

"You must rest, Little Thunder. You'll need all your strength if you wish to remain in this body."

That voice. Wakíŋyaŋ lifted her head to see who had spoken and was even more confused when she saw Grandmother sitting at the foot of the bed.

"Uŋčí! I…" Her voice caught in her throat. How was this possible? Overwhelmed with confusion, she felt like she was going to be sick to her stomach.

"Breath in deeply, Wakíŋyaŋ. You are wondering how this can be. How am I sitting here on this boat with you in the middle of the ocean? You came home to see me, but you did not travel of your own intent. The veil. You have been learning to move through it with your energy body. One part of you came to me just now, without the other part of you knowing, and now I understand why."

Wakíŋyaŋ noticed a look of deep concern on Grandmother's face.

"As your energy body left my house just now, I followed you back, through the veil, and here we are." Then she made the sign for friend again. "I like your choice of memory triggers, Little Thunder. It is a powerful sign, and it has worked well in bridging the two worlds in which you exist. It's no coincidence that Redbraids and your little Wit'é are both familiar with it."

Redbraids? How could she know about him? And Wit'é? Wit'é!

A terrible pain gripped her chest, and she strained to lift her shaking body up from the bed. What had become of Wí? She struggled to remember, but as she tried to retrace the events a part of her mind felt numb, and the pain in her chest increased.

"Lie back down, Little Thunder. Oh my my, you'll be the death of this old lady." She took in a deep breath. "Now, allow what you know to be true, to blow through your branches. To resist the winds of change you risk having your roots torn from the earth."

Wakíŋyaŋ closed her eyes tightly and gripped the damp blanket. She could feel her airway closing off and lightning bolts of pain shooting through her neck—the weightlessness of her body hovering over the decking as Bronx squeezed her throat tighter and tighter.

Then she was on the ground, back against the railing, fighting to pull in air, lungs burning.

And there was Wit'é, a fearless, ferocious wolverine, clinging to the giant's neck, ripping and tearing at his flesh with every part of her body.

With an effortless flick of his arm, Wit'é's little frame went over the edge of the ship, still kicking and clawing at nothing, her straw-blond hair trailing behind as her body plunged into the churning sea.

The steel railing felt cold and lifeless to the bottom of her feet as she leapt from the ship, aiming for the spot Wit'é's body entered the brine. The icy water chilled her skin as she pulled and kicked,

down,

down,

reaching with o u t s t r e t c h e d fingertips—

searching the darkness like a blind child lost in the woods,

desperate to find the familiar, to find Wit'é's warm flesh.

nothing.

down

down

down

Nothing.

Then it all came back, the gift of recollection—not with her mind, as in a memory returning, but with her whole body, reliving the event in the flesh and blood.

She understood.

Wit'é was gone.

She felt a deep surrender wash through every cell in her body. She stopped pulling, stopped kicking, stopped searching the emptiness with her fingertips.

Calm—her body suspended in an infinite graphite pool, untouched by gravity, beyond the reach of any world.

Goodbye Wí. Thank you.

She opened her mouth, and the sea rushed in. It was quiet. Her body curled into a fetal position.

Suspended there for an eternity, she felt...loved, unconditionally, cradled in Mother Earth's arms. In this place she knew she could stay forever.

Then the stillness broke, and she tilted her head back and opened her eyes. There was a distant, dim circle of light filtering down through the depths. A darkened face appeared silhouetted in the circle, wild ropes of hair undulating in the currents, an outstretched arm reaching down through the murk.

She did nothing. Unwilling to leave the embrace that held her without judgment or expectation.

But to say would mean leaving the world behind.

Not yet. There is more for me to do.

Slowly, she reached up through the tenebrosity—towards the light—towards life.

She opened her eyes. Uŋčí was still sitting at the edge of the bed, looking at her with kindness and understanding. She opened her mouth to say something, but as she did so, a weight lifted from her chest, and with it a flood of emotions rose to the surface, and she started to cry. She cried with an open heart, for her friend Wit'é, for Bay, for Kodo.

As she wept, Grandmother stood by her side, hands held out over her body, softly singing the words of a healing incantation.

After a while her sobbing died down, and she lay quietly, listening to Grandmother's voice.

A knock came at the door, and she looked up at Uŋčí, who's eyes were squinted nearly shut from the grin on her face.

"Redbraids is here to see you," she teased, with a knowing rise and fall of her eyebrows. "Remember, Little Thunder, he fought to save your life...but in the end, it was your choice to remain among the living."

Grandmother faded away just as the cabin door opened.

Redbraids popped his head through the doorway.

Ready To Fly

"Hello? Is someone in there?" There was no answer so he turned the handle and peeked inside the bathroom.

"What are you looking for?" Wakíŋyaŋ's voice sounded week and depleted.

He walked over to the bed and squatted down beside her. "Oh, nothing really. I just thought maybe you had a visitor or something. Before I came in I thought I heard...oh, never mind."

She must have been talking to herself again. Fever.

"So how are you feeling this morning?" he questioned, placing the back of his hand on her forehead. "Feels like your fever has broken. I'll leave you to rest. You want any coconut water before I go?"

Slowly sitting up and looking out through the round porthole window, she drew in a deep breath, "I'd like to go up into the sun."

"Oh. If you're sure you're feeling up to it, some fresh air might be a good idea." Then, standing and walking towards the door, he continued, "I'll just be waiting for you outside, whenever you're ready." *her lips smile, but a sadness lingers in her eyes.*

Pacing back and forth in the hallway, he thought about the recent, tragic events.

How will she take it when she finds out that we are already half way to Africa? She probably already knows. And what about Wit'é? She was a sister to that little girl. Maybe she'll hate me for it. Maybe she'll blame the whole thing on me. If I hadn't gone down to turn the engines on I would have been up on deck to help fight Bronx. His thoughts crashed abruptly into his skull bones as the door opened and Wakíŋyaŋ stepped out to meet him.

"Ready?" As soon as the question left his lips, he realized that he was asking so much more than she was ready for.

"Ya. I'm ready."

On deck, an endless expanse of ocean stretched out before them. The surface absorbed the late morning rays so completely that the only light strong enough to fight its way back to the surface radiated a deep, cerulean blue. High overhead a pair of albatross drifted lazily in long, protracted circles, gliding effortlessly on thermal currents. They were standing at the stern of the ship, leaning over and watching little whirlpools in the narrow strip of turbulence trailing behind the *Buganvilla*.

Lifting her head and gazing towards the distant horizon, Wakíŋyaŋ's words broke the silence. "Where are we?"

He cleared his throat. "Somewhere in the middle of the ocean."

She cocked her head sideways and glared at him. "Obviously. What I mean is, where are we going?" There was a hint of annoyance in her voice.

EnKare remained silent. Then he grimaced, and muttered, "Africa."

After a short pause, she sighed, "I don't understand. Why didn't we just cross the bay and go over to my village? It was not far away."

He thought back to the night of their escape. Nothing seemed to go right. He cringed at the thought of Bay facing the worms on her own. *She sacrificed herself to save all of us.* And Wit'é! Wakíŋyaŋ would be dead if not for the little girl who showed more courage than nine lions put together. He tried his best to explain that the storm was too strong, that the winds were threatening to push the ship into the rocks. That another boat filled with rogue warriors was trailing them. He explained that the storm lasted for two full days and it was all they could do to navigate away from the treacherous shorelines of the bay and head for open seas. He reasoned that Wakíŋyaŋ was the only one who knew the way to her village and that she was unconscious for several days and unable to guide them. He explained as best he could, but even as the words left his lips he knew they'd offer little comfort.

She remained quiet as he spoke. And when he was done she looked at him, and with a slight smile of resignation on her lips, she acknowledged, "So, I guess we're going to Africa."

"I'm sorry. It seemed like our only option at the time."

She turned her gaze back to the horizon and stared at it intently, as if by doing so she could summon her beloved continent, pull it back into view from beyond the curvature of the earth. For a moment he followed her gaze with his own, then he dropped his head to watch the ship's turbulence again. As he did so, he noticed something that caused his heart to jump. Where they were holding the railing, the little finger of one of his hands and the little finger of one of her hands were touching, ever so slightly.

His throat suddenly felt drier than the Sahara at midday. Trying to draw as little attention to himself as possible, he glanced at their hands then looked away just as quickly.

Does she know that our fingers are touching? She probably doesn't care anyway. I'm making too big a deal out of nothing. It's just a coincidence. Our hands happen to be up on the railing at the same time, and...or did she move her hand closer to mine intentionally? Wait a minute. What do I even care anyway? She's is not my type. She's way too bossy, and way too serious. But she is strong. And really, really skilled with her bow. And I guess she's pretty courageous. And she's kind, the way she looked after Wí...

"*Ehhem,*" the sound of Wakíŋyaŋ clearing her throat caused his last thought to get stuck in his own, and he slowly looked up to see her staring at him. Moving only her eyes, she looked down at their hands and then back at him.

In a cold, dry tone, "Don't get any ideas. The last boy who touched my little finger? Let's just say it was the last little finger he'll ever touch."

EnKare quickly retracted his hand from the railing and held it close to his chest. "I'm sorry. I didn't mean...I think it was just an accident," he explained, brushing it off as though he had no idea their fingers were touching in the first place. He cautiously glanced over to see if she accepted his reasoning.

"Relax, Redbraids, I'm just messing with you." A sly grin spread across her lips.

He stared at her for a moment. Then, trying to mask his own smile, critiqued, "That's not funny, you know. For a moment, I thought you were serious. And, Redbraids? What? Who's that?"

"Oh. Right. That's what I call you. Apparently not out loud, though. Redbraids, cause, you know, you have..."

Pointing at his own head, "Ya. I get it."

Wakíŋyaŋ smiled. "Exactly. And you thought I didn't have a sense of humor."

Hey, she's smiling again. This is a good sign.

Just then he felt a stiff breeze across his face, and he looked out at the ocean. A short ways off, the surface of the water was dark and rough with white caps starting to form. As the wall of wind whipped over the surface it reminded him of the view atop Elephant Rock, watching hundreds of thousands of wildebeest stampeding across the sea of grasses to the northeast of town.

Then it occurred to him. "If we can get to the front of the boat before that wind reaches us," pointing towards the wildebeest stampede, "there's something I want to show you." Forgetting that she had been on the brink of death just a day earlier, he grabbed her by the hand and took off towards the foredeck without giving her a chance to respond.

When they reached the prow everyone was there waiting to greet Wakíŋyaŋ. After all, they hadn't seen her awake since the night of the escape. Bark and Bite latched on to her legs and wouldn't let go as the others showered her with hugs and kisses.

Hiva was the last to approach. The two warriors clasped hands and pressed the bridge of their nose and the flat of their foreheads together. Words were unnecessary.

Then the wind blasted across the side of the ship, and everyone reached for the top-rail of the bulwark.

"Are you sure it's a good idea for us to be up here in the front in all this wind?" Wakíŋyaŋ shouted.

Clifton yelled back, "You get the best view from here. Oh, you're gonna love this, honey."

"View? Of what?"

"Just hold on tight, it'll be a bit rough at first." Jack hollered over the hissing and howling of the wind. Even sullen Jack had come alive since their escape. Freedom looked good on the young man.

For a moment, the sails flailed as the two air currents collided. Then they snapped tight, and the vessel surged like a pouncing cat. The water beat against the hull of the ship as she sliced through the chop, faster and faster.

Wakíŋyaŋ looked at EnKare, the fear beginning to show in her eyes. He returned a steady, reassuring gaze, then shouted, "Get ready to fly!"

Burial At Sea

A light breeze insisted Wakíŋyaŋ's hair pester her eyes and tickle her nose. Any other day, she'd tie it back. But not today.

They sat in a loosely formed circle on the lower deck, at the back of the ship.

Each of them held an object. Something small. Something of their own, or found around the ship. Something that reminded them of Bay. Of Wit'é. Of Kodo.

"I chose this, because Wit'é could eat. I could never understand where she put it all." In Wakíŋyaŋ's hand was a small piece of bread. The little girl had left nothing behind. Not a scrap of clothing or piece of jewelry. The sea had taken all that there was of the straw-haired girl.

Tomobo extended his hand. Dangling from his fingers was a thin leather strap with a fishhook pendant carved from bone. "My uncle gave me this when I turned twelve. It's been around my neck ever since." He rubbed his thumb over the smooth surface, gazing into its curving depths.

Clifton held up a dingy piece of cloth. "Might just look like a dirty 'ol rag. And...that's exactly what it is. When Bay gave it to me, it was fresh and clean. Ha! Look at it now."

They sat together as the sun dropped down to kiss the earth. They sat together and told stories about the departed.

Jafra chuckled. "Remember that time we were out camping, and we were playing a game of hide and seek? Remember? It was night time. A moonless night. We all got scared because we thought a hyena was lurking in the darkness at the edge of camp."

"Ha. Turns out it was Uncle Kodo, hiding in the bushes, farting.

"Farting?"

"Ya. Farting. What that man could do with a fart. Unbelievable. And it wasn't just warthogs. He could mimic elephants at the watering hole..."

"A serval cat's growl..."

"Dolphin chatter! *Hahaha.* Seriously! What that man could do with a fart."

Jafra let out a long sigh, and the circle sat quietly.

"I didn't know Bay like you did, Clifton."

Wakíŋyaŋ was surprised when Jack spoke up.

"But I remember one time. This was years ago. Long before you all showed up," motioning towards all the recent arrivals in the group." We were out collecting firewood. Back when Bronx ran the work crews. I dropped my woodpile. I just wasn't strong enough to carry it. Bronx smashed me good. But Bay. She walked right up Bronx and smacked him. She had to climb a small boulder just to reach his face. She smacked him and said, 'That's ma boy. Don't you beat ma boy, now. You hear me?' We didn't see her for a week. Thought she was dead. I've never seen bravery like that. Not like that."

Clair reminisced. "I remember the first time Wit'é told me she loved me."

What? I never heard her speak a word?

"Not with words, of course," Clair continued. "But with her eyes. And it's not like it was difficult to learn her language. She'd speak to you, and teach you how to understand her, all at the same time. There was never any doubt about what she was saying. You just...knew."

The stories died down as the sun melted into the water, dispersing its molten wax across the sea in puddles of crimson and gold.

The crew stood and walked to the railing at the back of the ship.

One by one, they tossed the item they were holding out into the ocean.

Wakíŋyaŋ looked at the piece of bread in her hand. *So that you never go hungry, my friend.*

Then she let bread fall from her fingers, and watched as the churning waves devoured it.

Feeding Frenzy

Day after day the ship sailed on, a lone traveler on the endless blue. The crew worked together through fair and foul weather, mastering the craft, navigating by star and sextant. Bonds of friendship grew as strong as the hemp fibers of the ship's mainsheet. They became family, a rag-tag clan of fugitives bound together in their struggle for survival, running on skill and determination, running on hopes and dreams.

On this morning, the water jets hummed as they cruised over a dead-calm sea. The calm shattered as Bark and Bike burst into the wheelhouse. "Capitán Jimmy, Capitán Jimmy," they shrieked. "Jafra said jellies ahead. Jellies ahead!"

Jioba cut power to the jets as the sleek craft glided silently into the middle of the gelatinous colony. The ship bobbed motionless on the glassy surface as they waited for the drifting mass of jellyfish to pass by. With no end in sight and not wanting to plow through or risk sucking one up into the water-jet intakes, they had no choice but to wait patiently until the currents moved them along.

Presently, a bale of giant leatherback turtles arrived at the scene, lured by the promise of an easy meal. The crew looked on as the hippo-sized giants plied through the jellies, rolling on their bellies, gracefully corkscrewing, effortlessly scarfing up mouthfuls and chomping in delight.

The bits and pieces that fell from their beaks soon attracted a school of herring, who materialized from the depths in vast numbers. The water all around the ship began to pop and bubble, as though the ocean had fermented. Then seabirds materialized from above, circling, swooping, diving into the chaos, then taking flight again with mouths full of wriggling silver.

In no time, the placid sea transformed, erupting into a feeding frenzy. Every living thing out there had received an invitation and was showing up to the party. Sharks came for up for a nibble, bottle nosed dolphins darted around turtles snatching up herring, and a school of giant tuna plied through the center in rigid formation, like a platoon of warrior fish sailing into battle.

At one point a majestic blue marlin made a spectacular entrance, racing at full speed and in a straight line. All creatures big and small darted to one side or the other as it parted the sea, its serrated dorsal slicing the surface, creating a tearing, deafening ruckus as it sped past.

EnKare had never seen anything like this. He, and the others, stared in disbelief as the scene played out before their eyes. A tragic opera. Marlin and dolphins leapt, sharks and turtles circled and spun, big fish chased small fish chased smaller fish. Gulls, albatross, boobies, petrels, frigates, and terns patrolled the skies, diving into the melee in choreographed synchronicity, peppering the briny stew.

Fashionably late, a pod of humpback whales crashed the fiesta. It was to be expected. Jioba always said that where there are herring, there are humpbacks. They lumbered into the center of the action and then added their own spice to the chaos soup with a round of tail slapping and full-body-breaching acrobatics.

EnKare looked over at Wakíŋyaŋ and noticed that she was staring, wide eyed, at the birds.

"What are those?" she implored, pointing a finger at the sky.

"Those are...birds," he responded slowly. *How can she not know what birds are?*

Then it struck him, like a wasp dive-bombing his head, and he slapped himself on the cheek. Try as he might he couldn't remember seeing a single bird the entire time he was captive in Nchi Mbaya. There were giant flying fox zitkála things, bats, and a few other strange looking creatures in the air, but never a bird. Not once. Had Iworo destroyed bird life in Nchi Mbaya?

"They're amazing," she remarked.

He agreed, though he wasn't thinking about birds. He had become mesmerized watching her watch the avians, and for a moment he was whisked away on the wings of a mythical creature. The commotion of the moment faded into the background, and all that remained was a smile; bright, curious, determined eyes that burned in the darkness, like glowing embers peeking out from the ashes of last night's fire; hair that cascaded in a mercurial obsidian flow down over smooth neck and strong shoulders.

Time slowed to the pace of an elephant's heartbeat, and he found himself lost between the measured palpitations.

"Eh, bwana," Jioba sounded distant and metallic.

He turned toward the voice and was surprised to see his friend standing right beside him. The smiling boy whip-snapped the air and then placed the center knuckle of his index finger between his ivory teeth, and bit down. Then he pointed directly at EnKare's face, his eyes growing wider and rounder each moment. "I know that look. Chabalangus, bwana! I know that look!" Then he broke into a love song, dancing around EnKare, flapping his arms like a goofy, smitten bird.

And all the while EnKare was swatting at his friend in a frantic effort to get him to be quiet. The last thing he wanted was for Wakíŋyaŋ to see them chasing each other around, like a pair of drunken ostriches. Never mind the incrimination of what Jioba was saying.

When they calmed down a bit, Jioba looked over at him and let out a big sigh. "I miss Mandaha."

"It's only a boat, Jimmy."

"I'm serious, Toots. When we get back, I'm gonna tell her how I feel about her. I thought about her every day that we were locked up. The idea of never seeing her again hurt worse than being a slave." He looked longingly toward the distant horizon, out past the tide of jellyfish and the feeding frenzy. Then he turned to EnKare. "So what about you, bwana? I see the way you look at her."

"What? How do I look at her? I mean, it's complicated. She...takes everything so seriously, and she's...kind of scary!"

"She drives you crazy? Ya, I know. Mandaha drives me crazy too."

"Ya, I suppose she does drive me a little crazy. But what I can't figure out is why I can't get her out of my mind."

Whip-snapping, "That, my friend, is the mystery of *love*."

EnKare screwed up his face and looked sideways at Jioba through one eye.

"Love?!?"

Tapetum Lucidum

As the days grew warmer the twins grew bolder. In the beginning they had only climbed the rigging a few feet off the deck, goading each other to go higher, craning their necks to get a peek at the stork's nest perched high atop the foremast. Each day they climbed the rope ladder until their fear outpaced their burning desire to be there, on that high platform where, legend had it, they could see past the edge of the world.

Jioba had told them that from the stork's nest one could see all the way to Africa! The twins had been hearing stories of the African homeland ever since their journey began, and they wanted to be the first to see it. They *had* to be the first to see it.

This time it was Bite's turn to test his mettle, and he might have made it all the way to the top had the seas not kicked up and rocked the boat beyond his liking.

The crew took turns being on night-watch. The ship was fully automated so, technically, everyone could go to sleep and the ship would run effortlessly through the night on autopilot. What the ship couldn't do, on account of the rogues destroying the depth finder, was detect large objects floating just below the surface, or change course abruptly when needed. It was precisely for the things the ship couldn't do on its own that a night-watch was necessary.

Tonight was EnKare's turn. Jioba stayed up with him for a while to keep him company, and the two lounged in the hammocks, staring up at the stars and tracing the constellations with their fingers.

"Do you think we are headed in the right direction, Jimmy? I mean, I know we have the sextant and all, but in the end it's just us floating around out here. At least that's how it feels sometimes."

Looking up at the sky and pointing, Jioba elucidated, "Well, you remember Ursa Major, the Great Bear? You follow the seven stars of the Big Dipper there, line up the outer two stars of the kettle, and they point…"

"At Polaris. Ya, I know, bwana. But how can the North Star help us when we are trying to go southeast?"

"Well, the further south we go, the lower on the norther horizon Polaris will be, until we cross the equator. Then she'll disappear from the sky all together. And look. See how she's hovering there, just above the surface of the ocean? I'd say we are right on the equator at this point, so all we have to do is keep the ship pointing east, and sail on. That should get us home."

"Should?"

"Well, we had another clue the other day. Remember, about a week ago, the colony of jellyfish? All those birds? Most of them don't travel more than a couple hundred miles from shore. But we're supposed to be in the middle of the Atlantic, right? The only way that could have happened was if we were close enough to land. From my memory of the charts, we must have passed slightly north of the island of Ascensión. It lies just south of the equator and right in the middle of the Atlantic. It's the only thing that makes sense. If I'm right, bwana, then we're on the right path! We head east and *BANG*! We run right into Mbini.

They bantered for a while longer, then Jioba surrendered to the rocking and hypnotic whooshing, mumbled goodnight, and went off to his cabin to sleep.

EnKare lay in the hammock for a while longer, counting the stars in Orion's bow. Then he made his rounds, checking the system and engine rooms, walking the decks, peeking into the wheel house.

Satisfied, he meandered until he found himself on the foredeck. He walked out to the bowsprit, then lay down on his belly, letting his arms dangle freely on either side of the narrow walkway.

He quite enjoyed the evening shifts. Something about being alone, the night, on an infinite ocean of blackness. The winds tended to die down with the setting sun, leaving the surface of the sea a glassy mirror reflecting a universe of starlight.

As the ship sailed on, gently rising and falling over rollers born in a windstorm half an ocean away, he imagined that he was flying through the galaxy, riding on the nose of an airship that was parting the very fabric of space as it sailed across the cosmos.

As he lay there, caressed by the cool evening air, the soothsayer's words drifted into his mind. *From freedom to slavery we ride on the waves... Well ya, that happened. Once we stop looking the heart finds what it craves... Mmm, not quite sure what that has to do with anything. There is no hope until all hope is gone, but we follow the water and we follow the song... OK, this one makes no sense at all. And Tendua's path? The Saptarishis and Little Prince Dhruva? What are they all about?*

A noise from behind brought him back down to earth, and he looked over his shoulder to see where it had come from. The faint glow of two eyes appeared to be floating above the deck. He blinked, and the rest of Wakíŋyaŋ came into focus.

"Hi there," she whispered as she walked up. "I didn't mean to startle you."

"No, no, that's alright," He responded. "Your eyes. I mean, surprise. I mean, you took me by surprise, that's all. What are you doing up?"

"I don't know. I couldn't sleep, and I didn't feel like lying in bed any longer, so I came up to look at the stars and listen to the night. That looks like a nice spot. Do you mind if I…"

"No, of course not. Here," scooting his body over to one side. "There should be enough room for both of us on here."

She lay out on the narrow walkway beside him. After a moment of silence, she questioned, "My eyes, do they...bother you?"

He recoiled slightly, and gave her an incredulous look. "Bother me? How could…? No! I think it's amazing! I mean, you are amazing. I mean, they are amazing. I wish I could see in the dark." He paused for a moment to regain composure. "When did you find out about your...gift?"

"Well, I had an unfair advantage when we played hide and seek around the village. I could see just fine while everyone else stumbled around in the dark. Although, if there were any torches lit, the reflection in my eyes would give me away." She smiled." Grandmother told me that it was a gift from Wakȟáŋ Tȟáŋka, Great Spirit. I guess that before the burn, things were different. We had, what did you call them? Birds. Like the ones we saw the other day. And we didn't have worms or monks, and people didn't get big, like Bronx, or have strange eyes, like me."

Strange? No. Amazing. Beautiful.

"Well, I like your eyes." The moment the words left his mouth he felt his heart rate increase and his throat go dry. *Oh no! That wasn't supposed to come out! I wonder if her night vision let's her see color changes, cause my face must be dark red right now.*

She smiled and looked up at him. Her eyes absorbed the collective light from a trillion stars, then her tapetum lucidum reflected it back at him. For a moment he froze, unable to look away. Then, remembering himself, he turned and looked down into the star speckled blackness below.

They lay quietly, observing the sounds of the night and gentle caress of the cool air as it passed over their skin, until EnKare's words shattered the crystal veneer of the universe. "You must really miss Uŋčí, and your home. I'm sorry you got dragged out here. I'm sorry for Wí and Bay. I'm sorry for everything."

She smiled at him inquisitively. "Hey, did I ever tell you about Níškola, my friend back home?"

He shook his head.

"He's really tall. And big and strong."

He cocked his head to one side and raised an eyebrow involuntarily.

"He has kind, gentle eyes, and he's the best friend I've ever had. I've known him since I was a little girl. We were bonded when I was seven winters," she added with a hint of maleficence in her smile.

He cleared his throat, then, trying not to let his voice give away his mounting anxiety, he calmly stated, "Oh, I didn't know you had a boyfriend back home. Nishkola. I'm sure I'm not pronouncing that right. That's a nice name. What does it mean?"

"His name means tiny, though he's anything but small."

Anxiety mounting...

"He also has enormous teeth. These ones," she reached into her mouth and gripped her two canines, "are longer than my thumbs!"

His scrunched up his face, astonished and a little confused.

"He's also covered from head to toe with a long coat of thick, colorful hair. He told me his name at our bonding ceremony."

He didn't know what to think, and he stumbled to find the words that came next. "Well," cautiously, "I think he sounds like quite an interesting fellow. You must really miss him." He was more than confused at this point. He had never heard of a person like that, but he had seen some pretty extreme mutations back in Nchi Mbaya and figured anything was possible. *What do I say? I don't want to be rude. This guy sounds...well...hairy! And really? She's just telling me about her boyfriend now? I mean...*

"Redbraids!" Wakíŋyaŋ's voice melted his thought. "My friend, Níškola, is the largest malamute in the village."

"What? What's *malamute*?" He was even more confused.

She answered casually, "A malamute is a wolf-dog." Then she burst into laughter. "You should see the look on your face, bwana," she giggled, gripping the bowsprit so she wouldn't fall off.

He narrowed his eyes and glared at her. "Oh, I see how it is. You think that's funny do you? Well, I too have a friend, not sure if you've met her. She's really, REALLY cute. She has a precious little pink nose, two big auburn eyes that, by the way, can also see really, really well in the dark. She has a dainty little mouth and small, but strong, hands. She also has a tail, is covered with delightfully soft fur, has oversized ears, and sometimes poops on people she doesn't know. Her name is..."

"Pilipili?" Wakíŋyaŋ finished his sentence.

Playing along, "What! How did you know that?"

"Mmm, don't know. Lucky guess, I suppose."

So no boyfriend. That's good. I mean...whatever. It just is...and there's that smile again. Oh boy, I'm done for.

As they looked out into the night sky, one star demanded attention more than its unnumbered siblings. It winked and flirted from behind its sable shroud.

The star appeared to be growing larger.

And larger.

Then, as if set on fire by some cosmic torchbearer hiding among the stars, the object burst into flames. More than a momentary scratch on the sky's face, the celestial bolide slowly arced through the firmament, its flames trailing behind like the tail of a planet-eating dragon. Tumbling over itself in a leaden, incandescent fury, the asteroid lit up the night and danced golden and blood red upon the onyx sea.

It was close.

So close.

With unblinking eyes he saw burning bits, loose scales peeling away as it spun—popping, bursting, and sparking down, knifing into the innocent sea to be extinguished in a flash. And then, far enough away to elicit the illusion of safety, the firebeast smashed into the world, the midnight sun extinguished, the impact slap reaching their ears with disjointed delay.

Turning to look at her, EnKare started to say, "What was..." but the words trailed away.

"I...have...no...idea." Her words came out painfully slow.

He had grown up with the legends and folktales that spoke of millions of unmanned spacecraft, satellites that had been orbiting the earth since the time before Iworo. People had put them up there for communication, as weapons, and to gather data about the solar system. They say that they put them up there with no way of bringing them down again, and that one day they would all come crashing back to earth. Even though their destructive civilization was gone, the earth would have to endure the beatings for hundreds of years to come.

Even if this was just another piece of space trash, he preferred the image of a planet-eating firedragon.

They talked into the night, speculating about firebeasts, chatting about malamutes, galagos, and birds. He tried his best to describe as many birds from around Mbini as he could while she hung on his every word.

She told him Uŋčí had spoken of the feathered beasts, relating their significance to the lives of their ancestors, and how now, after witnessing them for herself, Grandmother's tales took on new meaning. They shared stories of their homes and families, comparing, laughing, and teasing.

He began to feel something. Being a novel sensation, he didn't know what to make of it. It was different than the physical attraction he had for her, and very different to the annoyance he had previously felt. This was comfortable, relaxed, like he could be himself.

Sometime in the early hours of the morning, their talking died down to mumbles, the mumbles cooled to a whisper or two, then by the time the stars pulled the sun's chariot to the surface of the obsidian sea, all was quiet aboard the *Buganvilla*.

Wóniya

I want to know more about the veil. What is it? Where is it? How do I travel around in it? Can anyone do it?" She was asking questions as quickly as they were popping into her mind. "And I guess I want to know, what's the point of it all?"

She was sitting with Grandmother, cross legged on the ground in the shade of an unfamiliar tree. In fact, nothing about the place was familiar, except for Uŋčí.

"OK, sweetheart, I can only answer one question at a time." She could hear the patience straining in her grandmother's voice. "I'll do my best to explain, but you must understand, Little Thunder, that you can only really know these things by experiencing them for yourself. My words can only serve to guide."

She was intrigued, particularly by the way Grandmother said the word *know*. "Please continue," she urged.

The Elder sat quietly for a moment, the wrinkles on her brow betraying her careful contemplation. Then she began to speak, and Wakíŋyaŋ listened with all her senses.

"The veil is the space that exists between matter, between particles, between planets, solar systems, constellations, universes, and even dimensions." Her words soothed, like hearing a familiar song.

"OK, I understand that, I think. But Uŋčí..."

"I'll get to all that, my impatient one. It is all around us. It is what exists where there is no matter. It is the void through which energy travels. For example, the energy from Father Sun travels through the veil."

"So how do you and I travel through it? We aren't the sun. We're flesh and blood." Then realizing she'd interrupted again, she humbly offered, "Sorry. Please continue."

"Matter contains energy. You contain energy. We exist in both forms. Our matter is animated, brought to life, by our energy. We are both, though some are only conscious of their physical form. And then there are beings who only exist in energetic form, such as spirits, orbs, sprites, shades, shadows, and allies. These beings have no bodies, no physical presence, at least not in this dimension, and yet they exist. Like your Igmúthaŋka Sápa. When you dance him you are giving him a body through which to experience our world, to exist on a physical plane. And in return, he teaches your body directly. Like how he taught you the ways of stalking and the hunt.

"We possess the ability to focus on either of our forms. We can even be conscious of both at once."

Grandmother paused at this point in her teaching. "Don't stop, Uŋčí. I'm paying attention, I promise."

Grandmother scanned her with a careful gaze, then continued. "How does one move in the veil? Your attention is where you focus your consciousness. First you must fix your attention on your energy body. Then you use your will to move your energy. Since your consciousness is now focused on your energy body, you are now aware of, conscious of, everything that your energy body experiences as it travels."

Wakíŋyaŋ was a little confused. "So what happens to your physical body while your energy body is out playing around?"

"Well, my love, not all your energy leaves your physical body when you enter the veil. If it did, your physical body would die. A portion remains behind—in the same way you don't have to be conscious of your heart beating for it to continue doing so. What is important to understand is that it is all a matter of where you focus your attention."

Eager to understand more, Wakíŋyaŋ quizzed, "So you said that one uses her will to move her energy around through the veil. What is my will?"

Wakȟáŋ Kiktá smiled, the skin around her eyes forming deep lines that spoke of hardship and joy. "Your will, my love, your will is the focusing of your power. When you take your energy, your power, and you focus it on a specific task or goal, that is called using your will. When you were little and you wanted to learn something, like hunting or trapping, or running across a thin log high above the forest floor, you used your will to do so."

"How, Uŋčí? Please explain it to me," she implored.

"Your intent is what you choose to focus your will on. You set your intent and focused your will on completing the task. You focused all of your energy on it and you persisted, over and over, till you succeeded. You happen to have a very strong will, Little Thunder. It is how you got your name. So to travel in the veil, you must first train your awareness on your energy body, then you must focus your intent and use your will to move around. In the same manner that you taught yourself to crawl, then to walk, then to run, you teach yourself to move through the veil. Baby steps."

Wakíŋyaŋ smiled. "OK, I think I understand at least some of that. Especially 'baby steps.' But you haven't explained one thing. What's the point of it? Why learn to do it in the first place?"

"That, my dear," Grandmother smiled broadly, "is for you to determine for yourself. When one has learned to walk, they might ask, why should I learn to run? Can you imagine being born a seabird, like the one's you saw from the ship, but never bothering to learn to fly? We are born of Mother

Earth, our physical parent, and of Father Sun, our energetic parent. And as such we have two birthrights: the physical and the spiritual. The veil is the realm of the spiritual.

"In the veil we are free from the restrictions of the physical world, such as linear time and single dimensions. We can pass through solid matter, travel great distances in the blink of an eye, visit the past, and even witness different possible futures. We can commune with the energy bodies of plants and trees, and they can teach us things we couldn't possible learn on our own."

Wakíŋyaŋ looked at Grandmother in disbelief. Then a series of connections intersected in her mind all at once. "Wait, so when I dance my Igmútȟaŋka Sápa, he experiences this world through my body. But that means that I can also travel in the veil and visit him there in his energy form, right?

"Yes."

"And back in the worm tunnel, when I became paralyzed, and popped out of my head and floated above my body, and then suddenly appeared right in front of the worm leader without experiencing anything in between, I was moving through the veil, right?

"Exactly. You are taking your first steps. But before you learn to walk in this new world, you must learn to crawl. So let us do an exercise. I want you to find your physical body, without returning to it, and tell me what you see." She spoke in a calm but powerful voice. "Yes, Little Thunder, we are in the veil right now. But you already guessed as much. This," she waved her hand and it passed right through Wakíŋyaŋ, "is not your physical body."

There was a surge, then she was floating in the air over the bow of the ship. She could hear Uŋčí's voice saying, *resist the urge to return to your physical. Just observe and then come back to me.* Below, she could see herself lying on the narrow nose of the ship. She appeared to be asleep.

Beside her was Redbraids. The two bodies lay close together, their chests rising and falling as if one breath filled their lungs. She felt homesick, but not for any particular place. It was more of an overwhelming desire to return to her body, to the world she knew and understood.

Then she heard Uŋčí's voice calling her back, instructing her to resist the feeling, to will herself back to the place where Grandmother's voice was coming from. She looked away from the bodies lying on the deck below, and in an instant she was sitting under the unusual tree again, looking at Uŋčí.

"So, here we are. Are you OK? You look a little shaken." Grandmother was sitting cross legged on the same spot.

"I'm fine. I think it's going to take a little getting used to, all of...this." She waved her hands around, passing her fingers through the faded borders of her own body.

Wakȟáŋ Kiktá changed the subject abruptly. "Tell me about Redbraids." A broad smile stretched across her face.

Wakíŋyaŋ smiled back apprehensively. "I don't know. He's just a silly boy. He's always joking around and playing games."

"Oh, that sounds terrible." Grandmother had that mischievous tone in her voice again. "After all the hardship and loss that you all have been through, he should be acting more serious, and somber, yes?"

"Yes," Wakíŋyaŋ sputtered, incredulously. She wanted to feel angry at him, but instead she just felt...admiration! Which confused her even more. She looked out across the grasslands, and her eye caught site of a slight movement at the edge of a low, dense, thicket of bushes. When she focused on it she realized it was an Igmútȟaŋka Sápa, like her own ally, but shaped a little differently. It's purple-black coat glistened in the warm sunlight that radiated across the valley. The cat turned its head and looked directly at her with brilliant, verdigris eyes.

As their gaze met, a series of images flashed into her mind in rapid succession: Igmúthaŋka, standing on a rocky bluff; Redbraids walking in a meadow of tall grass beside an off-white, giant beast that had two horns jutting from the bridge of its nose; Wit'é smiling at her; an infinite burst of stars rushing past; a beautiful orb pulsing through vibrant colors then transforming into a giant woman. The images kept coming, faster and faster, beyond her mind's ability to compartmentalize and store.

Then it stopped as the cat turned away, slipping silently into a grove of thorn-covered trees.

She turned to ask Grandmother if she had seen the black cat when a small seed, or pebble struck her. She looked up into the heavy, leafless branches overhead and saw a grey galago that looked a lot like Pilipili. It grinned, cooed and chattered a little, then threw another seed at her. She watched as the seed sailed through the air and struck her right in the head.

Wait a moment. How can I feel that? I thought I was in the...

Ah Free Kah

With moderate effort she peeled one sleep-stuck eye open just in time to see a pebble bounce off Redbraids' face. He groaned and slowly lifted his eyebrows up until his eyelids had no choice but to follow. Then all at once his eyes sprung open. He seemed shocked and surprised to be looking right into Wakíŋyaŋ's face.

"We fell asleep!" he said in a groggy panic, wiping the saliva from the side of his mouth.

Looking around, she quickly realized that the two of them had indeed fallen asleep on the ship's bowsprit. Her physical senses returned, accompanied by a horrifying awareness: she and Redbraids were holding hands! All five fingers were interlaced and locked together! She lay there for a moment contemplating how best to extract herself from the incriminating predicament, relieved that no one had witnessed it.

"Good morning, lovebirds."

They both sat up in a hurry. Jioba squatted on a short, wooden stool with Pilipili propped on his knee, a small handful of pebbles in one hand and a victorious grin plastered across his face. He started to sing a care-free tune about two little birds perched on his bowsprit.

She looked at Redbraids, whose face was turning all sorts of interesting colors. *He's blushing. Oh no, am I blushing too?* For a moment she felt trapped. They were discovered, and there was no getting out of it.

But then something about the way Redbraids' face was all screwed up with embarrassment struck her as funny. The whole thing suddenly seemed hilarious, and she erupted with laughter. At first Redbraids looked horrified, but then his face relaxed and he too started to laugh.

"Well, it's a good thing there were no emergencies last night, eh, bwana?" Jioba teased.

As the boys bantered, her mind drifted off. It had been a fun night. She had never really talked with someone like that before. She couldn't remember everything she had told him, but there were some things that she had never shared with anyone, not even Uŋčí. And at what point had they started to hold hands? It just...happened. She smiled. He was just a silly boy, yes, but his eyes were so kind...and the way his lips reflected the sunlight when he smiled...and he listened, he actually listened, not just with his ears but with his whole body. She felt like she could tell him anything.

A cacophony of exited, high pitched screeches rang out from high overhead, rudely interrupting her pleasant thoughts and stopping the boys' conversation on the spot. The ruckus was coming from the stork's nest high atop the foremast. She didn't have to look up to know who was making it. Bark and Bite had made it to the top at last! The screaming could have been heard on the other side of the world, and before long the entire crew was gathered to see what was going on.

"Whoa whoa whoa! Slow down now," Jioba shouted. "I can't understand a word you two are saying!"

The twins calmed themselves just enough for Bark to yell down, "We can see land!" followed by Bite screaming, "We can see Afrika!"

Jioba turned to look at the others, his eyes shining. "Did you hear that?"

Everyone started talking at once and the air buzzed with excited chatter.

"Well," Jioba piped, "someone needs to go up there to see what all the fuss is about. For all we know they just saw a little island, or a whale or something."

"I'm out," Clifton's scratchy voice was the first to speak up. "As much as I'd love to see what their little eyes are seein', my 'ol legs ain't what they used to be. I'd get half way up and then get stuck. Then we'd have a real mess on our hands, now wouldn't we."

Wakíŋyaŋ looked around the group. She couldn't believe that no one was scrambling to climb up the mast. "Well," she challenged, looking straight at Redbraids, "if no one else is going to go up there, I guess I will. Hiva," turning toward her friend, "are you coming?" With that the two young ladies began the ascent, followed by Jioba and Redbraids, while the rest of the crew gathered round the base of the mast to watch.

Of course Pilipili was the first to reach the top and was already sitting on Bite's shoulder. As Wakíŋyaŋ neared the platform, three small faces peered over the edge to greet her.

"We made it to the top, Waki, we made it to the top," Bite squealed.

"And we saw Afrika! Come here, we'll show you," Bark added with pride.

She pulled herself onto the platform and turned to give Hiva and the boys a hand up. There was barely enough room for all of them, crammed into the circular perch, with nothing more than a waist high railing between them and a nasty fall.

She gripped the rail and looked out across the ocean. As the ship pitched and lurched in the surf, the mast followed suit, swaying like a giant sequoia. It was a little unsettling, but she had climbed to the top of some of the tallest trees in Khéya Wíta, hugging the trunk as the howling wind set the entire forest oscillating like a field of buckgrass. This, she could handle.

"OK, you two," Jioba said to the twins, "where exactly did you see Africa?"

Struggling to contain their excitement, their little bodies strained dangerously over the railing as they pointed out past the front of the ship. A dark mass of cloud cover stretched across the horizon, blurring the lines of water and sky. Land could be hiding there in the obscurity, but it was impossible to distinguish. The six of them stood in silence, all eyes fixed on the horizon.

A gust of humid, warm air blew through the stork's nest and as it did, she noticed Redbraids and Jioba looking at each other and smiling.

Breathing in deeply through his nose, "Smells like..." Jioba started.

"Home!" Redbraids finished.

Excitement and anticipation silently spread through the stork's nest as they stared into the empyrean. After some time Jioba let out a big sigh. "OK, you two, was this whole thing just a trick to get us up here?" Bark and Bite shook their heads vigorously. "Well then, maybe what you saw was just a cloud. They can look a lot like islands or whole continents. We can't be that far off, though. You smell that sweetness in the air?" He took another deep breath in through his nose. "I should get back down and check the instruments and take a bearing."

"Wait," Wakíŋyaŋ uttered softly. "There." She pointed towards the clouds. "There."

At first, nothing. Then Bite screamed, "There, there, see, I told you so, told you so."

Then Hiva exclaimed, "Oh ya, I do see it. That's...incredible."

The clouds rearranged themselves and the outline of a continent materialized.

The stork's nest came alive with shrieks, whoops and hollering. Bark and Bite jumped up and down chanting, "Ah Free Ka, Ah Free Ka, Ah Free Ka."

Redbraids and Jioba looked at each other in surprise. "They're already African, and we haven't even arrived yet," Redbraids mused.

"We going home, Toots!" The boys engaged in one of their cryptic handshakes, then started leaping into the air and chanting along with the twins. Then the four young adults clasped arms over shoulders and formed a circle, still leaping up and down and chanting while the twins bounced around in the center.

Far below, the dance had caught on like wild fire. Even Clifton, with his weary old legs and bad hip, was jumping up and down and singing at the top of his lungs.

AH FREE KAH!
AH FREE KAH!
AH FREE KAH!

Home

"L ook!" His hand trembled with excitement as he pointed at the small town nestled along the shoreline where the mouth of the mighty Benito met the sea. "That's Mbini, that's my town," he proclaimed, tugging on Wakíŋyaŋ's arm. His face hurt from smiling. He felt such pride, seeing his little town from afar, and for the first time in moons he realized how much he missed it.

It was nothing like approaching Accra, where one could see the city lights from a great distance, with its bustling streets, famous markets, and a football pitch on every corner. No, Mbini was little more than a thin strip of shops along the seaboard with a handful of houses spread out into the countryside. But he knew everyone who lived there and considered them family. He knew every rock and stream, every pathway through the grasslands and forest, every living creature for a hundred miles in all directions. Oh, it felt good to be home.

He also knew the disappointed look on his mother's face when he messed up. Considering that he stole a ship, then completely obliterated the African Charter by sailing it to the forbidden lands, well, the very thought of facing her now brought on a dull ache in the pit of his stomach.

As they sailed onward, everyone was up on the prow, except for Jioba, who was in the wheelhouse piloting the craft safely through the inland waters. Then the first people came into view. They appeared as little specks scattered along the thin, golden strip of sand that separated the emerald green of the African continent from the endless blue of the great Atlantic Ocean.

Within a half hour he could distinguish the shapes of children playing on the beach. As soon as they saw the ship their casual play turned into a frenzy. They sprinted wildly along the sand, racing one direction then the other, waving their hands and pointing, jumping up and down, cartwheeling, hand-springing, and falling on top of each other. Soon, others came out of their shops and houses to see what the commotion was all about.

He turned to Wakíŋyaŋ. "Well, we made it. It's not much, but it's my home." He withheld his enthusiasm a little. After all, her beach, her home and family, were a long, long ways away.

She smiled back. "It looks so beautiful. I can't wait to meet your family. I've heard so much about Mandaha from Jioba."

"Ah yes, my family." He made little effort to mask the panic in his voice. "Well, at least they'll be happy to see *you*. Me, not so much."

She nudged his shoulder with her own. "It'll be okay, bwana, you'll see."

"Hey! You're picking up my lingo, bibi. You're gonna fit right in."

Sails down and running on jets alone they plied through the Bight of Biafra. As the *Buganvilla* approached, the throng of children swarmed to the river's mouth then veered off running for the docks. EnKare barked a few instructions to the others to facilitate a smooth landing, and in moments Jioba had the sleek vessel kissing the papyrus bumpers of the berth.

At first, the street at the end of the marina was empty and quiet. As they dropped the gangway the first wave of children spilled around the corner and charged the boat head on. Then, right behind them, the entire town flooded into the street and descended upon the ship, singing, and dancing in celebration.

Jioba, who had emerged from the wheelhouse, shouted to EnKare, "Hey, bwana, take everyone off the ship. I'll do a quick systems shutdown and then catch up to you in a minute."

He nodded then looked at the group, who seemed less than eager to disembark into the crowd. "OK everyone, don't be afraid," he teased. "This is how we show our love in Mbini." Before he finished his sentence, Bark and Bite slipped under his legs and charged down the gangway into the mess of children. He looked at the others, shrugged, and declared, "Ya. Like that! OK, here we go."

Pilipili leapt from shoulder to shoulder, Clifton to Hiva, to Clair, to Jack, to EnKare where she tucked herself neatly under his braids. "I bet you're excited to be home, and off this tiny, floating island." He felt her approval in the form of a single, wet lick on the back of his neck.

As they descended into the crowd the children formed a circle around them, calling out to EnKare, asking him where they had been and why they were gone so long, what kind of ship was that, where was Jioba's boat, who were these strange looking people? They reached out with their little fingers to touch the newcomers' skin and clothing. Beyond the ring of children the townsfolk danced, clapping their hands and chanting a song that had endured since the time before Iworo;

"Oke osimiri na-eduzi gị
Oké osimiri na-echebe gị
Daalụ nwanne nwanyị maka ịkpọtara ụmụ anyị n'ụlọ.
Nabata ụmụaka n'ụlọ. Nnọọ n'ụlọ"

"What are they saying?" Hiva shouted.

"They are thanking the sea for bringing us back safely," he shouted back. "And they're welcoming us home!"

Then Jioba came down the ramp clapping his hands and singing with the others. Seeing their local hero, the mob of halflings immediately sucker-fished onto his legs, freeing the rest of the group to move further into the crowd.

EnKare had the realization that, other than in school books, many of the townsfolk had never seen a mix of humans such as this. It wasn't until his recent trip to Accra that he himself had encountered so many variations of skin tone and bone structure. It had been both exciting and somehow comforting, seeing that such beautiful variety still existed among people.

All the familiar faces were there to welcome them home. Señora Concha was there in full color, shaking the peer with every sway of her hips. Mrs. Msoke waved from the back of the crowd. Mr. Bioko, the leather shop owner, Ms. Rita from the flower shop, Mrs. Buika the baker, and even Mama Sana from the ice shop were all there to welcome them home.

On the outside of the crowd, he spotted his family: Mother and Father, Mandaha, Auntie Naserian and Uncle Wafula along with Cousin Olubi. Beside them was Jioba's mother, Bötébbá, and then to his great surprise, Jioba's entire family from Ëtulá a Ëri, including Auntie Nelly and Uncle Balafu, his two cousins, even Bapu and Bimi! And, most surprising of all, beside them was Capitán Kodo's wife, Auntie Beeke!

How could they have known we were coming back? The ship's radio system was taken out by the storm the day we left Nchi Mbaya. There was no way to make radio contact even once we were close enough to African receivers. The thought only lasted a moment and was quickly replaced by a more urgent matter; would his family disown him right there on the spot?

The dancing and singing quieted as Okuruwo and EnKulupuoni descended the steps and moved slowly through the crowd towards him and the others. The look on his mother's face was serious and reserved. He gulped, then gently tugged on Wakíŋyaŋ's hand and whispered, "Those are my parents."

Wakíŋyaŋ's eyes grew wide, a hint of nervousness flashed in her expression.

When Okuruwo began to speak, the throng of singing children became silent, turning their innocuous faces up to look at her.

"Welcome to Mbini. Welcome to Africa. There will be time for stories. There will be time for celebration. For those of you returning home, now is the time to reunite with your loved ones. For those of you whose fate has delivered you far from home and family," she paused and then smiled warmly, "though we cannot possibly replace what you have lost, or understand the hardship you endure, I hope you will let us try. And for those of you who have not returned to us in the flesh, your loved ones are here to welcome your spirit home."

As soon as the last words escaped her lips the crowd began to stir. Two younger children approached Bark and Bite, grabbed them by the hands and led them to where their parents stood, greeting them with open arms. Soon after, each of the newcomers were approached and asked to come live in the home of one of the townsfolk.

Señora Concha, dressed from head to toe in a vibrant, impossibly colorful batik featuring a sea turtle, blue whale, and giant squid having in a tea party on the ocean floor, parted the crowd and thundered up to them. Wagging her finger, she scolded, "Jioba, ma boy. Na look what ya gone and done. I'll deal with you layta." Then she took one look at Clifton and belted out, "Honey, you commin' home with me."

Clifton's lips were smiling, but his eyes registered both fear and excitement as he trailed after his host.

EnKare felt a wave of pride wash over him as he watched his people extend their friendship, their love, and their homes to the rag-tag bunch of strangers that had washed up on their sleepy little dock. *This is what it means to be from Mbini, to be African!*

His smile fizzled a moment later as his mother approached them. "Mother…." he began to say, thinking that he needed to begin his explanation as soon as possible.

But Okuruwo extended her arms and clasped his hands in her own. She looked into his eyes with a stern, unwavering gaze. Then softening, the muscles in her face relaxed, and a current, maternal and nurturing as an onshore breeze, flowed from her lips. "Welcome home, son." She pulled him into her arms and hugged him.

For a moment, as can only happen in the presence of an unconditional love, the world faded away and he stood there, cradled in a state of perfect harmony and total surrender.

In the next moment he was facing his father, who held his shoulders with straight arms, gave him a stoic stare, then grunted and pulled him in. By the time it was Mandaha's turn, the whole family was wiping back joy, concern, relief, frustration, worry, and jubilation, expressed as tears.

When Mandaha was done scolding him for making her worry, she turned to Wakíŋyaŋ, who had been standing there watching the family reunion. "Hi. My name is Mandaha. I'm this bonehead's sista."

Wakíŋyaŋ smiled shyly. "My name is Wakíŋyaŋ."

"Walk…ing…young," Mandaha pronounced, sounding out the unfamiliar syllables. "Did I say that correctly?"

"Yes! You said it perfectly."

"Would you like to come stay with us in our home, at least until you settle in?" Mandaha inquired, much to EnKare's surprise.

"I couldn't…" Wakíŋyaŋ started to say.

"There are no guests in Mbini." Okuruwo set her hand on Wakíŋyaŋ's shoulder. "Only family. And today, ours has grown." She smiled, and Wakíŋyaŋ smiled back, and EnKare gulped and looked on in shock.

"Now if you'll excuse me, there's one pirate left that I need to speak to," Mandaha chuckled, winking at EnKare. Then she turned her gaze toward the far end of the dock where Jioba was telling stories to an ever growing pack of children. "Hey, bwana!" she shouted.

Hearing her voice, Jioba looked up and then pointed at himself and shrugged, as if to say, *who me?*

"Ya! I'm talking to you, bwana."

He waved at her coyly, a nervous smile on his lips.

She took off across the dock.

EnKare looked at Wakíŋyaŋ and hissed, "Oh no. Now he's in for it."

As Mandaha approached, Jioba began to slip into his usual, Mandaha-struck, bumbling self. "Hi Damhada, I mean Mandaha," he stammered. "I tried to call, but the phone lines were down..."

Before he could utter another ridiculous word, Mandaha leaned in and planted a kiss, right on his lips.

That certainly shut him up quick. He stood for a moment, motionless and wide eyed, his little spectators looking up at him in curious silence. Then, as though paralyzed by the kiss of a giant tsetse fly, he tilted back on his heels and fell like a dead tree blown over in a wind storm. His pack of half-lings swarmed in an effort to catch him before he hit the ground. It was a valiant effort, but his weight collapsed the pile, and they ended up in a heap, giggling and wriggling.

Extending her hand, Mandaha soothed, "Come on, silly, let's go." Hand in hand they made their way through the crowd to Jioba's family.

As they approached, Bötébbá swatted Jioba ceremoniously across the side of his head, then burst into tears and pulled her son into her arms. "I thought you had gone to be with Itòhí," she sobbed. "I thought the sea had taken you as well."

"No, Mama," Jioba consoled. "It wasn't my time. I'm sorry, Mama. I'm so sorry to have made you worry."

Mother and son held each other, shaking as one body.

For a moment, some part of EnKare's awareness expanded, and he was able to take in the whole scene at once. He watched mother and son reunite. He watched Tomobo holding up Auntie Beeke as she collapsed in his arms, grief flowing from her in shrieks and sobs. He witnessed families opening their hearts to strangers, and strangers being welcomed as family. There was joy and sorrow, in equal measure—and his people, strong enough to hold space for all of it.

When all the grief and worry had been wrung from Bötébbá by her son's steady arms, Jioba wiped the snot from his nose and looked up.

EnKare looked at his best friend in the whole world.

Their eyes met and instantly exchanged a silent knowing.

A knowing that only the best of friends can have. A knowing that said; *Can you believe it, bwana? We went to Nchi Mbaya! We made it back, and we're alive to tell the tale.*

He put his arm over Jioba's free shoulder. "Come on, Jimmy, let's go home."

As the last child rounded the bend towards town, still singing and dancing, all that remained was the silver ship, bobbing gently in the brackish water at the mouth of the mighty Benito River.

Sista

Light shining through a small, rectangular opening in the thick mud and straw wall beamed across her face, waking her from a deep sleep. For a moment she was disoriented, wondering where she was and why Níškola wasn't lying beside her. Then she opened her eyes and it all came flooding back. She was lying on a mattress of woven cattail reeds covered by a deer skin fur. Mandaha, who was lying on a bed just across from her, rolled over and opened her eyes.

"How did you sleep?"

Wakínyan smiled. There was something comforting about, well, everything around her. The house felt grounded and safe, the warm, moist air caressed her skin, and Mandaha felt like a sister and a friend. "I slept so well," she responded, sitting up and looking around the room. The ceiling was covered in thick, woven mats from reeds she didn't recognize, and the walls were artfully adorned with bird feather arrangements, woven baskets, skins, and colorfully beaded drinking gourds. Between their two beds was a low table with an oiled tree branch sculpture covered in beaded necklaces and bracelets. There was a wooden door on one side of the room and beside it, part way up the wall, was a small lever. She looked at the lever, then up at the ornate fixture in the middle of the ceiling made of interlaced antlers.

"Can I...?" She started to ask, pointing at the fixture on the ceiling.

"Turn on the light? Of course!"

Wakíŋyaŋ walked over to the lever and flipped it upward. Instantly the antlers burst into light and illuminated the whole room. She stared at it in wonder. She had been too ill, and too tired while aboard the silver ship, to think about the strange illuminations coming from the ceiling in all the rooms. But now, after a good night's sleep, there were a million questions bouncing around her head. Unable to restrain her excitement, she abandoned her usual reserve and calm demeanor and allowed her curiosity to spill over the floodgates.

"What is that? How does it light up? Is it like the firesand back home? The ship had the same thing. And in your kitchen, where did those flames come from that you cooked the food on? How does it work? And your skin, Mandaha! It's so beautiful! How do you make it shine like that? And your hair! It's incredible, the way it looks like ropes of red earth, and how you have woven the beads into it. But you and your mother seem to be the only two people who wear your hair that way. Why is that?"

Mandaha was smiling and giggling, clearly thrilled with Wakíŋyaŋ's questions and enthusiasm. "There's plenty of time for me to tell you all about my hair and my skin. But for now," she beamed, "I'll take you on a tour of the manyatta and the boma, and explain everything."

After the tour they met up with the family on the front patio for breakfast under the shade of a tree that challenged her idea of what a tree could even be.

"I've seen a tree like this before..." She muttered to herself.

"What was that?" asked Okuruwo.

She didn't realize that she had said the words out loud. "Oh, nothing. I was just amazed by the size of this tree," she gawked, pointing at the branches that arched high above, shading most of the family compound.

"Yes. they've always been large, but since Iworo they have grown into true giants."

"What is it called?"

"It is a baobab tree," responded EnKulupuoni. "This one's name is EnKishón, *Life* in the Maa tongue." Then, rising to his feet, "Now if you'll excuse me, I'll go get breakfast started."

As the elder disappeared into the house, Redbraids came shuffling out onto the patio, puffy-eyed and yawning. "Morning, everyone. I don't know 'bout you Wakíŋyaŋ, but I slept like a baby."

The morning conversation was light and relatively uneventful. Over a breakfast of chapatis served with a stew of gazelle meat and cassava root, the family fed her curiosity of composting toilets, bio-gas digesting systems, solar and wind electricity, and all the incredible things that the town was able to do with the power generated.

When they were done eating, Okuruwo spoke. "Son, go and prepare yourself." Redbraids dropped his head down and exhaled loudly. His mother continued, "The Council of Elders has called a special meeting today to discuss what has happened. You will have a chance to explain yourself, and then you will have to face the consequences of your actions."

"Oh boy. Si, Máma," he muttered in a somber voice. "Can Wakíŋyaŋ come along?"

"Yes, of course," his mother responded. "We will all attend."

When breakfast had been cleared and the kitchen cleaned up, everyone disappeared to their rooms to dress for the occasion.

Wakíŋyaŋ watched as Mandaha fixed a series of colorfully beaded leather strands around her neck. "Do you think he'll be punished?" she asked.

"I don't know, sista." Mandaha responded, her voice betraying a hint of concern. "But right now let's focus on you for a moment. I don't imagine you managed to squeeze a change of clothing into that leather bag that you brought with you?" Wakíŋyaŋ shook her head. "No, I didn't think so.

Here, you can borrow some of my clothing till we get yours all washed up. And remember how you were asking me about my skin? Well, would you like to find out? Come, sit here, and I'll show you." Mandaha reached under her bedside table and produced a small, round, dark brown gourd that had an oily shine to its surface. She set it on the table and lifted the top off. "This is a mixture of shea nut butter and ochre from down near the river." She dipped two fingers into the gourd and scooped out a portion of thick, red butter. "Here, you take some now. Rub it into your hands and then rub it into the skin of your arms and legs, around your neck and well, pretty much everywhere."

Sister. A warmth spread through Wakíŋyaŋ.

When they were done, the two young ladies stepped out onto the patio where the family was waiting.

"EnKare, you know it's not polite to stare." Okuruwo's words snapped the young man to attention.

Wakíŋyaŋ was wearing a long, sleeveless dress made from a patchwork of skins. Her hair was braided into a series of cornrows that laced crosshatch over her head and transitioned into thin braids that cascaded down her back and shoulders. At the end of each braid Mandaha had meticulously fastened two or three colorful glass beads that held the quill of an equally colorful feather. And all of this complimented the brilliant red coral necklace that draped across her bosom. Yes, they had overdone it just a little, but what a magnificent affair it had been.

"I'm sorry," Redbraids said, without taking his eyes off of her. "It's just…your skin...and hair. I'm not used to seeing you like this."

"OK, son, it's time to go now." EnKulupuoni's words managed to do the trick, and Redbraids finally looked away, stunned and speechless.

Wakíŋyaŋ smiled to herself.

Wenye Hekima

Sitting cross legged on the tall grass, she took a moment to look around. They were gathered outside of the entrance to a large, round hut on the outskirts of town. The hut was made of earth, with a thick thatched roof, and was surrounded by a tall hedge of thorns. A well worn path through the opening in the hedge led directly to the entrance. She sat on one side of the path, along with Mandaha, Redbraids' parents, and a handful of elders who Mandaha described as the City Council of Elders. On the other side of the path sat Redbraids, looking a little scared and confused, and beside him Jioba, Tomobo, and Jafra. Each of the four young men were in formal clothing, even Jioba, who she had only ever seen in a pair of shorts and the occasional shirt. Today the young fisherman wore a coarse button up shirt and a pair of pants that were a little too short for him.

Mandaha pointed at Jioba then nudged Wakíŋyaŋ and whispered, "He looks so silly all dressed up like that, doesn't he, sista?"

"I know. I almost didn't recognize him."

Suddenly, Okuruwo rose to her feet along with the other elders. Wakíŋyaŋ moved to get up but Mandaha tugged on her dress and motioned for her to remain seated. A new group of elders had arrived, and they walked through the opening in the thorn hedge in a single file line. Okuruwo greeted each one warmly as they passed by her and moved silently into the hut. With the arrival of this new group, Wakíŋyaŋ perceived a shift in the energy surrounding the area.

The energy these people radiated was palpable. Each of the seven newcomers appeared utterly unique, both physically and in cultural adornment. The first to enter the hut was a slender and unusually tall man. His shaved head, which had three rows of scars that ran the full circumference of his skull in parallel, was covered in a layer of white ash. Around his waist and over his shoulder he wore an off white woven cloth that covered at least half of his earthen brown skin.

The next to enter the hut was a small-boned woman with skin that looked like aged leather. The high cheekbones of her smiling face held up the white-beaded headband that she wore around the temple of her shaved head. For clothing she wore nothing more than a simple tanned skin wrap.

Next was a mysterious looking man, dressed in a light blue tunic that flowed down to the sandy pathway. A dark blue sash was tied up in a turban about his head and wound its way down around his neck and across his face like a veil. The only part of him that she could see were his obsidian eyes peering out from the rim of blue.

Following the man in blue came a woman with short-cropped curly hair and skin the color of wet garden soil. She wore a headband beaded in green, red, black, white, and yellow, and around her waist and over her shoulders she wore colorfully printed cloth.

Next to enter the hut was a man with skin the color of fire-darkened red cedar bark. He wore a dark blue robe with a beautifully woven blue and white cloth draped over one shoulder. Over his other shoulder hung a leather bag. He carried a long walking stick in one hand and a beaded fly-whisk, fashioned from the tail of a creature she could not identify, in the other. His hair was hidden, tucked up under a thick, oil-rubbed skin hat that he wore high on his forehead. His white beard was long and distinct, making his drawn, unsmiling face appear even more gaunt.

The next to step forward and greet Okuruwo with a handshake and a warm smile was the smallest woman she had ever seen. With skin the color of a moonless night, the old woman was half as tall as Redbraids' mother. She wore a skirt made of laced strands of dried grass and a simple top made from animal fur. Most striking of all was the tattoo that adorned the old woman's face, broken up only by the deep smile lines around her mouth and eyes. It had a distinct shape, or perhaps told a story, but she couldn't decipher the meaning. Okuruwo stooped down and embraced the woman, as though she where a long lost sister returning home.

The last to enter was a man dressed in a colorful, intricately woven tunic that hung loosely over his slender body. A wide-brimmed, woven reed hat sat atop his head, which had been partly covered by a white cloth, wrapped like a turban and draped under his chin. A line of dark paint ringed each eye. A single, yellow stripe was painted down his forehead, along the high, narrow bridge of his slender nose, over his painted black lips, and down his chin and neck where it disappeared into the cloth of his tunic. The hat itself was a marvel, expertly woven with different types and colors of reed, creating patterns and pictures that were only partly covered by the feathers that dangled from strips of leather tied to the center.

When the last elder entered the hut, EnKulupuoni stepped forward and greeted Okuruwo, just as the seven others had done. He wore a red shuka cloth that was held about his waist with a thin strip of leather. His ear lobes, that had been stretched over the years to support large diameter earrings, were bare, except for a narrow band of shiny metal wrapped around the flesh and pulling the lobes downward. He carried with him a spear in one hand, and around his waist a wooden club and a short sword sheathed in a leather scabbard.

After Redbraids' father stepped into the hut, his mother turned to the City Counsel Elders and motioned for them to enter. Okuruwo waited until they were all inside, then stepped through the opening and closed the wooden door behind.

"Toots! Toots! Toots! Did you see that, bwana?" Jioba was practically whisper shouting with excitement.

"I know bwana, I know! What, Baba? I don't understand how they…? Oh no, Mandaha, does this mean we…?" Redbraids was having a hard time completing a sentence. Tomobo was biting the skin of his clenched fist, and Jafra was holding his head between his hands and rocking back and forth.

"Okay, calm down everyone," Mandaha finally spoke up. "Just because they…I mean it doesn't mean anything bad…necessarily."

"And what about Baba?" Redbraids' voice was climbing in pitch. "Did you notice that he entered with the rest of them? And there were only eight others including Mom. Does that mean that he's…?"

Mandaha finished his thought. "The ninth. It'll be okay EnKare. Look, they are calling you in. Go. Go."

The door closed behind the four quaking boys, and for a moment the two young women sat silently, absorbing what had just transpired and listening to see if they could hear anything coming from inside the hut.

"Who are those people?" Wakíŋyaŋ inquired.

After a pause, Mandaha turned her head slowly and responded, "If I'm not mistaken, those are the Wenye Hekima, the founders of unified Africa."

"So they are…important?" Wakíŋyaŋ asked.

"That's putting it mildly, sista. They're kind of a big deal. After Iworo, these nine people found each other in the place where the Spirits walk. And then they physically walked from their homelands, across the entire continent, to where they all came together at a place called *Bandura Cave*, somewhere in the middle of the jungle. It is said that they didn't leave the cave until they had created the African Charter. The charter that unified the whole continent and that we all live by."

"The veil!" The word leaped from Wakíŋyaŋ's lips. "The veil, uh, where the Spirits walk. They communicated, met, there, all together?" She was bubbling over with excitement, oblivious to having fully interrupted Mandaha.

"Yes," Mandaha spouted. "That's what I've been trying to tell you this whole time. Right now, in this little hut, are the nine people who's dream we are now living here in Africa. And…" she paused for a moment to catch her breath, and appeared to be contemplating her next words. "And I think my father is one of them!"

"Wait, you think your father is one of the…?"

"Wenye Hekima! Yes! I mean I guess it makes sense, because Mother is one of them, too. We've always known that. I mean we figured that one out a long time ago. Just look at her! She knows what you are thinking before you think it and what you are going to say before you say it. She even knows what you are feeling, even when you try to hide it. And everyone comes to her for one thing or another: advice, healing, blessings, vision, you name it. But Baba? My father? I could never have imagined that he was one of them." She was holding Wakíŋyaŋ's hands and biting her lower lip.

Wakíŋyaŋ delivered her next question cautiously. "So, is that a bad thing? Your father being a Wenya Hickemup?" *I don't think I pronounced that right.*

Mandaha stopped biting her lip, and looked at Wakíŋyaŋ. Then she burst into laughter. "I'm sorry. I can't help it. I just love your accent."

"I'm so sorry if I said that wrong. I didn't mean any disrespect."

"Are you kidding? None taken. Here in Africa, we don't care how you pronounce things. There are as many different accents in Mbini as there are inhabitants. And we're proud of it."

As the meeting continued inside the hut the two young women sat together in the grass and talked. They talked about the way things were in Wakíŋyaŋ's world and compared the similarities and differences of their two homes. They talked about boys, specifically Jioba and Redbraids.

At a point in the middle of their conversation, Wakíŋyaŋ asked, "Why is it forbidden for you to travel to Khéya Wíta?"

"Well," Mandaha paused for a moment, and appeared to be looking for a respectful way to answer the question. "We were taught that during the time of the great war, what we call Iworo, most of the lands outside of Africa were physically destroyed, and then also poisoned by radiation that made it too dangerous for anyone to travel there. Africa was not a nuclear continent, so it avoided being torn to pieces when the nuclear nations of the earth attacked each other. I guess it was forbidden as a way of protecting us. But from what you've told me, things aren't all that different there, right?"

Wakíŋyaŋ thought of her homeland, her village, Uŋčí, Níškola, then looked at Mandaha and smiled. "Khéya Wíta is alive and well."

By the time the door to the hut opened again, they were fast friends. With somber looks on their faces the boys quietly emerged and closed the door.

"Well? What happened?" Mandaha was the first to speak.

Her brother answered. "We told them everything. The whole story, right from the start. Oh, and by the way, that *is* the Wenye Hekima, and yes, Baba is one of them. I guess that's how he and mom first met, somewhere out in the middle of the jungle!"

"I knew it!" Mandaha burst out. "Okay, well I didn't know it, but I knew it, you know?"

Redbraids shrugged and continued. "Oh, and by the way Wakíŋyaŋ, tomorrow it's your turn. They want to meet with you and all the others that came over from Khéya Wíta. Get your side of the story, I guess. Then tomorrow evening there's a meeting on the football field where we all get to find out our *destiny*. And by destiny, I mean punishment."

"It's okay," Mandaha consoled. "It's not as bad as it seems, Wakíŋyaŋ. I mean they are old and scary looking, but I live with two of them, right? And I'm still breathing."

Wakíŋyaŋ smiled at this remark, but Jafra retorted, "Oh, like you would know. You didn't just have to spend who knows how many hours getting grilled by all nine of them."

"Chabalangus, bwana," Jioba gasped. "I'm not sure I'm not dead already, and this," he slapped the palms of his hands into his chest, "this is just a dead man walking."

"Looking pretty good for a dead man, bwana," Mandaha teased. Then grabbing Jioba by the hand and motioning to Wakíŋyaŋ, "Come on, sista, let's get out of here. Unless you want to make a bed right here and wait for your turn tomorrow."

"No thanks," Wakíŋyaŋ grimaced.

As they left the enclosure and headed back towards town, Jioba teased, "Hey, Toots, so you think they'll have us drawn and quartered?"

Redbraids scratched his head comically. "Mmm. Maybe. But if I was in charge of the sentencing, I'd send the lot of us to the *iron maiden*!"

Face The Music

The grassy field that served as the town's football field, central market, and town hall for meetings such as this one, began to fill with the people of Mbini. Children ran amok, playing tag and spinning cartwheels while families laid out blankets and covered them with scrumptious snacks and gourds of tasty libations.

"Well, the people of Mbini sure take their entertainment seriously," commented Jafra.

Jioba chuckled. "Right, bwana. Here we are getting ready to face the guillotine, and people are settling down for a lovely afternoon picnic in the park!"

Redbraids laughed nervously, but it was Clifton who asked the question that was on most of their minds. "What's a gorilaten, or girlintine, or whatever it was you just said?"

"What? The guillotine? OK, picture something like a goat milking stand, only replace the goat with a person and the food basket with a basket to catch heads. Now imagine a razor sharp, weighted blade attached to a track and pulley system that hoists the blade high in the air. Down comes blade, *whoosh*, then *schwack*! Head is cleanly separated from body and falls neatly into handy basket, *thwunk*." He acted out the whole, gruesome event, then pantomimed picking up his own head and having a conversation with himself.

Wakíŋyaŋ's gut was starting to hurt from excessive laughter. Jioba continued, "The French found it to be a handy tool when getting rid of the noble class during one of their revolutions. It was named after the fellow who invented the thing. Can you imagine? Let's say I invent..."

"A device for cutting the heads off fishies," Mandaha cut in with a giggle. "We'd name it *The Jimmy*." She did a little pantomime of Jioba on his fishing boat trying to stuff a floundering fish head-first into a tiny guillotine. Everyone, including Jioba, was laughing so hard they were holding their stomachs and wiping the tears from their eyes.

Jioba raised a hand high overhead, still laughing, and Mandaha responded, giving him a high five, then a low five, elbow bump, and hip bump, the last of which sent him flying.

Wakíŋyaŋ realized that she must have looked concerned, because Redbraids hushed everyone. "Jimmy, you've got everyone scared now, bwana!" Then addressing Wakíŋyaŋ and the others from Khéya Wíta, "We don't have any guillotines here in Africa. At least not that I know of...no, but seriously, it couldn't be that bad, could it? Besides, you lot didn't do anything wrong. It's our heads on the chopping block! Sorry! That was the wrong analogy to use. I'll just be quiet now."

Earlier that morning the entire crew from Khéya Wíta had sat before the Wenye Hekima, answering questions and telling the story from each of their perspectives. Wakíŋyaŋ had participated as best she could, but she found herself distracted by the striking cultural differences between the Elders. She wanted to know everything about them, their rituals, languages, skills and crafts. What tools and techniques did they use to hunt and to tan skins? How did they create their fabrics that had been dyed such vivid colors and woven so masterfully?

This Africa, it seemed to her, was a land of endless wonder, mystery, and awesome beauty. From the moment she arrived, she had become aware of an intangible feeling, a lightness, like a weight had been lifted.

For the first time in her life she could... relax. Completely. This was something that she couldn't do back home. There was always something around the corner eager to snack on you, waiting for you to let down your guard.

She looked at Redbraids, who was still laughing and joking around with the others. A warmth radiated deep within.

Just as she was about to reach for the young warrior's hand, the townsfolk erupted in celebration, singing and dancing. The Elders had arrived and were making their way through the people to a small area of flat stones at the edge of the field.

These people, Wakíŋyaŋ mused, *they never miss a chance to celebrate.* In her village there was plenty of dancing and singing, though it was usually associated with one ceremony or another, like a birthday, a wedding, a successful hunt, a rite of passage, or a blessing for the rain. But here, in this place of abundance, life was easy. One could relax, feed themselves from the land and not have to constantly avoid things that wanted to eat you. At least that's how it seemed.

She thought of that night on the beach. Lost in the fire-sand and the cicadas' song, she had let the rogues get passed her defenses. She should have heard their footsteps in the sand, detected the broken rhythm of waves lapping against the wooden planks of their boats.

A hand reached down and pulled her out of her thoughts and onto her feet. It was Mandaha, and her friend was smiling and dancing. "Come on, sista," Mandaha yelled over the singing, "dance with us." Redbraids and Jioba were already hopping around. She felt a little nervous and self conscious. Then she took in a deep breath, exhaled loudly, and relaxed, even more than before—and started to dance. It felt right. It felt good. There really was so much to celebrate here.

One of the village elders stepped forward and raised a hand. A hush spread over the field and everyone sat down again. Wakíŋyaŋ's group was positioned at the front of the assembly, right in front of the Wenye Hekima and Town Council.

The Elder called out, "Adamfo, awọn ọrẹ, marafiki, amis, amigos, friends. As you can see, our little town has been graced with the presence of our nation's founding Mothers and Fathers. The Wenye Hekima have come to offer council on the recent events that have impacted our entire nation. From the sands of the Kalahari, to the pyramids of Giza, the story of the *Buganvilla* and her crew are being told around the fire, by the young and by the old. From the rain forest at the very heart of Africa, Mama Bandura will address us first."

Then the town elder sat down again, and the Mbuti Wenye Hekima popped up off of the mat with the agility of a teenager, though the lines on her face whispered that she was as old as the mountains themselves. Despite her tiny stature, Mama Bandura's presence was mighty. She spoke with a soft, powerful voice, and used her entire body to illustrate her points. Even the youngest child sat silent and motionless, so her voice could be heard across the field.

"We have sat in council with these young men and women. We have heard their story. For disregarding a major tenet of our Charter, one chosen by the people of Africa, our four native sons will do service in their hometown communities for three moons."

A hushed murmur spread through the crowd.

"For those of you who have been up-rooted from your homeland, the winds of fate have brought you to our shores, and Africa opens her arms to you. If you wish to return to your homeland, the Wenye Hekima has agreed to support you in whatever manner we are able. If, however, you choose to remain here, and to learn and live by the tenets of our Charter, then from this day forward…" she paused for dramatic effect… "you are Africans." Mama Bandura threw her arms up in the air and the field erupted in cheering.

When the crowd settled, she continued. "We have one more matter to address. Courage, bravery, selflessness. We consider these qualities to reside in the heart. With the twelve of you here among us now, the heart of Africa, and even the heart of Mother Earth, has grown larger, is stronger and more resilient. By abandoning the self and acting as one, you worked together and escaped the clutches of slavery. To recognize your selfless courage and preservation of freedom, we would like to present you with an award that we will call Timá, from the ancient Bantu word for courage." The rest of the Wenye Hekima stood and moved to either side of Mama Bandura. "We honor you now!"

The elders raised their arms up high and yelled, "Timá!" three times with the whole crowd echoing their cries.

Mama Bandura continued. "Now we are done with words. It is time for celebration. Perhaps a little music and dancing?" Then the mighty little woman threw her hands over her head and let out a series of piercing ululations, and the field exploded in celebration.

"Well, that didn't go too badly, I guess," Jioba yelled over the crowd.

Redbraids yelled back, "Ya, bwana! I was expecting much worse."

"What do you mean it didn't go *too* badly? Seriously? If I didn't know better I'd say you two had elephant droppings for heads. The Wenye Hekima created a whole award just to honor all of you! I'd say it didn't go *too* badly at all." Mandaha danced between the boys and smacked them on the backs of their heads.

"OK, OK, you're right, you're right." Redbraids protested.

Jioba grabbed Mandaha's hand. "Shall we, mi amor."

Mandaha shrieked, "MI AMOR? How can I say no to *that*?"

Wakíŋyaŋ looked up. Redbraids stood in front of her, grinning boyishly, with a hand extending down towards her.

"Now, we dance!"

The Naming

She entered the meadow and walked through the tall grass towards him. The warm glow of the late afternoon sun shined through the silky veneer of her raven-black hair as it sashayed in the wind, gently caressing her bare shoulders. Every time he saw her, she looked even more beautiful than the time before. She entered the clearing, where he sat on an embroidered blanket, walked right up and dropped to her knees in front of him.

Looking directly into his eyes, she uttered the words he longed to hear, "I love you, Redbraids," and then leaned forward, stuck her tongue out, and licked the tip of his nose three or four times.

He squirmed a little and scrunched up his face. It tickled. Then, slowly opening one sleepy eye, he found himself looking directly into Pilipili's furry little face. She was sitting on his chest and licking his nose.

"OK, Pilipili, OK. That's enough." He reached out to push her away. She jumped clear of his hand, landing on his head where she promptly burrowed herself into his braids. Wiping the sleep from his eyes, he attempted to hold on to the feeling from the dream he was having moments before he was so rudely awakened.

Then the door to his room opened part way, dashing the last of his pleasant thoughts, and Baba's face peered in.

"Son," He said in his usual, calm voice, "today we are hiking to Rhino Overlook. Wear your shuka, and bring your ancestral weapons with you. We leave before the sun crests EnKishón."

"Hóyia, Baba, I'll be ready." He sat up and scratched his head as his father left the room. Pilipili latched on to his thumb and hitched a ride from her nesting spot. "And you, you little bugga," he addressed the fur ball. "How many times have I told you not to lick my face while I'm sleeping?" She cocked her head to one side then lowered her chin and covered her face with her hands. "Stop it." Now he was starting to feel bad for hurting her feelings. "Pilipili. I'm sorry, I didn't mean to scold you. It's just, I wasn't ready to wake up yet, that's all. Come here."

She slowly pulled her hands from her face and looked up at him through two innocent, large, moist eyes.

"C'mon my little friend, looks like we're going on a trek today." He hopped out of bed and rummaged through his closet for an appropriate shuka. "Yes, you can ride on my shoulder if you like. Baba said I needed to bring along my weapons, but my rungu and simi were taken from me by the rogues. And my spear is probably still lodged in a giant's chest at the bottom of the sea off the coast of Nchi Mbaya." He paused and looked at Pilipili, who was staring at him with her head tilted to one side. "Point is, I don't have any of my weapons, and Baba is going to be furious with me when he finds out."

He dressed in his favorite red kikoi, strapped a rawhide belt around his hips and wrapped his shuka over his shoulders. Then he turned to head out the door as Pilipili jumped from the bed to the wall lamp and up onto his back. "Why walk when you can ride, hey?"

He was surprised to see everyone up, dressed, and waiting for him as he walked into the family room. "What ya doing here, bwana? Nobody invited you!" Though his words were meant as a joke, he was genuinely surprised to see Jioba standing with the rest of the family.

"I did, little brotha." Mandaha's eyebrows were raised and her lips pursed, as if to say, *what ya gonna do about it?* Then with a coy smile, she added, "Guess you're not the only one who likes having him around."

EnKare scowled at her, then, licking his lips, "I'm hungry. Is there time for breakfast before we head out?"

"Actually," his mother responded, "Wakíŋyaŋ and your sister have put together some food for us to take with us. Let's leave now. We can eat when we get there."

As the group left the manyatta, following the track that lead through the river basin, the jungle, and eventually up onto the hilly grasslands, he pondered the purpose of the outing. *Why is everyone coming with us? Baba and me, Jimmy, sure. But everyone? Maybe Mama missed me a little too much and wants some quality family time, or something.*

About an hour later the trail left the acacia forest and opened up into the grasslands. The soils on these hills, thanks in part to the return of the rhino herds, were a deep, rich humus, and in areas the grass grew to such heights that the only thing tall enough to rise above the canopy were the necks of giraffes. No matter how many times he saw it, the spectacle never failed to amaze him; gentle, swirling wind ripples transforming the savanna into a liquid realm, with giraffe necks undulating over its surface like giant water serpents plying an other-worldly sea.

The group stuck together along this portion of the trail, just in case one of the great cats was hunting in the area. After heading up the gentle incline they spilled out onto a clearing at the top of the hill.

"We call this place Rhino Overlook," he said to Wakíŋyaŋ, who stopped in her tracks and grabbed him by the arm. "And now you know why." The vegetation along the top of the hill had been cut low to the ground, allowing one to look out over the rolling hills. Just beyond the next rise a herd of black rhino lumbered, nibbling on shoots and lounging with their young.

Wide eyed and with a hint of concern in her voice, Wakíŋyaŋ stammered, "What are those?"

"Oh, those?" He chuckled under his breath. "Those are rhino, the animal we named this hill after. Baba and I come here all the time to check on the herds, play a game of bao and hang out."

He was so busy pointing out all the different plants and animals to Wakíŋyaŋ that, at first, he didn't notice the others joining them on the hill. First to show up was Auntie Naserian, then Uncle Wafula, and Cousin Olubi. This wasn't too unusual. They would frequent the overlook when helping watch the herds, or coming to scout for game. But then Sironka, Lemayian, and Koinet, along with their entire families, crested the hilltop. These young men were also Maasai Morani, young warriors-in-training in the same orporror warrior age group as EnKare. Behind them came the town elders along with Señora Concha and Clifton, Bark, Bite, Hiva, and the others from Khéya Wíta. Mrs. Msoke stepped over the rise next. And last to show up was Jioba's mom, along with his entire family, including Bimi and Bapu!

OK, something big is going on here. Either my sister, or Olubi, or one of the other boys in my orporror has done something amazing, and we're gonna have a ceremony to recognize their achievement. Now I understand why Baba wanted me to bring my ancestral weapons.

"This is fairly unusual," he whispered to Wakíŋyaŋ. "I'm guessing one of them," pointing to the group of youth clustered on the far side of the clearing, "has accomplished some milestone in their rites of passage. You know, becoming an adult? And we're going to perform a recognition ceremony for him or her."

Wakíŋyaŋ didn't respond, but just looked at him, nodded, and smiled.

EnKulupuoni signaled for everyone to form a circle so the ceremony could begin.

"Come on," he said, grabbing her by the hand.

The chitter chatter died down as everyone went about finding their places in the circle, which was organized by age, starting with EnKare's parents and the other elders, then continuing around with relative age groups clustered together. They lay out their blankets, then everyone sat down, arranging their gourds of food and water out in front of them.

A silence fell over Rhino Overlook as EnKulupuoni began to speak. His words came slowly and with great purpose. "In the time before Iworo the young warriors of our tribes went through a series of ceremonies as they transitioned from children to adults. Since that time, our world has changed. So, too, has the role of the warrior in our society. Our ceremonies have changed as well, ever adapting to the world we live in. Gathered here we have Ntumu, Okak, Kombe, Mabea, Lengi, Benga, yoruba, Igbo, Seke, Himba, Maasai, and Bube descendants. But we are one people now. One tribe with countless roots. We have chosen this day, when the equinox and the new moon align, to come together in celebration to recognize the achievements of one of our own, to bestow a name, and to acknowledge a transition.

"Told you something big was going down," he whispered to Wakíŋyaŋ. Then he looked over at Jioba and lifted the palms of his hands towards the sky and shrugged, as if to say, *who do you think it is?*

Jioba scrunched his brow, stretched his lips out and downwards, and shrugged back, *I don't know*. But he knew his friend too well. Jioba was hiding something behind those twinkling eyes.

EnKulupuoni paused for a moment and looked out over the world, then lifted a long, beaded ingri from his blanket and handed it to Okuruwo. She poured a portion into a drinking vessel and then passed it to the left around the circle. When all cups were filled, everyone took a sip together. The mixture of cow's blood and curdled goat's milk wasn't his favorite thing in the word to drink, but considering the occasion, EnKare tolerated the smokey, mucilaginous liquid.

Not as bad as I remember.

Baba had told him that for millennium this drink had not only been used in ceremony, but had sustained their people through droughts and famine.

EnKulupuoni spoke again. "For our newcomers from the west I will explain the history of this ceremony. In the time before Iworo it was a custom in my tribe that a young warrior-in-training would demonstrate an act of bravery that would mark their transition from junior, to senior warrior. Their task was to single-handedly kill a lion in order to protect our herds and our people. A junior warrior who did this was given a new name. A Lion Name. It was one of the greatest honors a Morani could be given, a moment that marked the end of childhood.

"As human populations grew, the great cat was pushed to the edge of annihilation. We saw that not only the lion, but our own people, our own culture, was fighting for survival. The lion and the Maasai both faced the same destiny. Extinction. We saw that our fates were one, so we changed our ways, knowing that if the lion could survive, then so would we. We adopted the practice of protecting the lion from poachers, instead of killing them, and we awarded a Lion Name to any warrior who demonstrated great bravery in this act.

"Today the Lion Naming Ceremony has evolved yet again. This honor is now given to any person who demonstrates the greatest act of bravery and courage; the abandonment of self in order to protect another life that is being unjustly threatened. Today, this honor goes to you, EnKare."

EnKare felt of the blood drain from his face. *There must be some mistake.* He looked up at his father, questioning, confused.

Baba looked back at him with a warm, steady gaze. "Place your shuka in the center of the circle and sit before your peers and elders, your friends and family, so that we can honor and recognize you."

Slowly rising to his feet, he stumbled slightly to one side then regained balance. He lifted his shuka from the ground and stepped out into the circle. *This can't be right.* He racked his brain to recall some action, any action that warranted such an honor. Jioba had been brave. Wakíŋyaŋ had been courageous time and time again. All of them had simply done what they had to, to survive and to get home. Maybe he could explain all of this, and the name could be given to someone more deserving.

He lay his shuka down in the middle of the circle then sat cross legged facing his parents, eager for an explanation that would justify all this.

"Son, you were born on a day, like today, when our earth is perfectly balanced on its axis. You were given the name 'EnKare,' named for that magical element from which all life comes. Water. And though you were born on land, it was Water that called to you, Water that carried you across the seas to find your destiny. And it was in Water that your Lion Name found you.

"To set one's own safety and well being aside for the protection and well being of another, is to embody the highest aspirations of our people. We have heard from all the members of the *Buganvilla,* and it is told that time and time again you risked your own freedom for the freedom of all, your own life for the lives of all. Your actions showed a quality that is rare among beings. Even more rare in human beings—that you do not separate yourself from the Life Force. Because of your actions and your choices, those who were slaves, are now free, and some of those who would be dead, are sitting among us."

As his father's words ended, one of the village elders rose to her feet, pulling a mahogany rungu from a leather satchel. She stood before EnKare and placed the rungu in front of him on his shuka, bowed her head slowly, then returned to her place. He lowered his head, overwhelmed by the gesture, still feeling undeserving. Then a second elder rose to his feet and presented him with a simi. And finally, with his spear in hand, EnKulupuoni stood, walked towards him and extended his arm.

"Take my spear, Son. Now it belongs to you."

"But, Baba," EnKare began to protest.

EnKulupuoni remained still, holding the spear at arm's length. His soft smile and kind eyes spoke to EnKare. *He already knew about my weapons. Somehow. And he's not angry. I don't understand.*

At the same time, his mother and sister came forward and motioned for him to be seated again. As they worked, his mother explained, "Son, with the shedding of your boyhood, so too must you shed your braids. Mandaha will cut them short, and I'll shave off the rest."

He sat in silence, nervously watching the braids tumble to the ground beside him. What if he had an ugly head? What if it was disfigured, or oddly shaped? He'd always either had the thick covering of curly black hair of his childhood, or the ochre-stained braids as a junior warrior. Never, in all his life, had his head been bare.

He felt the cold blade scraping over his scalp and wondered how many times his mother had done this before. Would he have any skin left when she was finished? But to his surprise, the whole thing was over in no time, without a single drop of blood dripping down his face. Mandaha pulled her shea butter and ochre gourd from a pouch on her dress, and rubbed a generous blob of the thick, reddish substance into his scalp.

Then EnKulupuoni motioned for everyone to rise, and he stood before EnKare again. "Your Lion Name found you. Now your birth name will return to the waters that have protected and guided your spirit.

"From this day forward you will be known as...Uhuru! Freedom! For that is what you represent in this world." His father then made a fist, raised it over his head, and shouted, "Uhuru!" and the gathering echoed the cry. Baba then pumped his fist again, "Uhuru," and again the cry was answered. They repeated this chant, moving the circle in until the elders were clustered around him with the others forming two larger circles just beyond them.

Then the chanting stopped, and the elders reached out with one hand and placed it on his shoulders, back, and chest. His mother was standing directly behind him, father in front, and Mandaha to one side. Then the others in the outer circles reached out and placed a hand on the shoulder of the person in front of them, linking the whole group together in a human enkarewa.

He had been standing with his head tilted, looking down at the ground, unable to fully comprehend the magnitude of what was happening, when he looked up and found himself gazing directly into his father's eyes. Eyes that were trying to tell him something. But what? Then he felt it in his chest, an understanding in his heart, and he knew that his father was saying goodbye—goodbye to EnKare, goodbye to the innocence of childhood.

The feeling rose from his rib cage until it reached his eyes, where it flowed freely, streaming down his cheeks.

"Welcome, Uhuru! Welcome to your people! Welcome to Africa!" It was his mother's voice from behind him that broke the silence. Then a sharp ululation split the air and the congregation broke into song and dance, an eruption of joy and celebration.

Jioba bounced and gyrated through the crowd until he was close enough to shout, "Don't worry, bwana. You might be Uhuru to all these old farts, but you're still just Toots to me. Tu sabes!"

Then Wakíŋyaŋ approached, staring as she ran a hand over the smooth skin of his head. "I guess I won't be able to call you Redbraids anymore."

He scrunched his face up. "Look, if you call me anything else, I won't talk to you ever again! You got it!"

She smiled. "Chabalangus, bwana. I got it."

Some part of him still questioned what he had done to deserve all this fuss. But that mood quickly dissolved as he gave himself over to the dance, the song, the celebration of life.

He locked arms with Jioba and Wakíŋyaŋ, two of his best friends in the whole world, two of his best friends that ever were, and the three of them leapt high into the air.

And So It Begins

The tree itself was tall, thorny, with sparsely leaved branches that fanned out horizontally. What really intrigued her, however, was the vining plant that used the tree as a base, twisting its way up to the highest limbs. The vine was covered with vibrant orange flowers that reflected such a rich color that the whole tree appeared to be emblazoned with fire.

"I love the color," she marveled, looking up at the tree as they walked passed.

"That's a buganvilla. You know, like the name of the ship. It comes from the French word, bougainvillea, originally named after a French navigator named Louis Bougainville. Here we use the Castilian version, but they sound pretty much the same."

"French? Castilian? What's that?" They spoke so many different languages that it was nearly impossible for her to keep up.

"French. It's a language that was spoken by the people of France. It was a people in Europe, in an area of Nchi Mbaya to the north of Africa. The same with Castilian."

Looking at the colorful vine again, "This one is orange, but the one back at your house is sky blue, and earlier we passed one that was a bright yellow! There are so many colors here. And birds..." her eyes narrowed as she tenderly caressed the feathers that hung from her ears and clothing. She had even replaced the fletching on her arrows with feathers. "The birds are just as colorful, and so magnificent. Sometimes I watch them all day."

As they walked under the tree, that Redbraids identified as an acacia, she reached up and gently caressed the orange flowers, feeling their slightly stiff, dry petals between her thumb and index finger.

Redbraids, who was walking a few paces in front of her, looked back and commented, "I can't believe that you've been here for at least three or four moons now."

"Almost six moons actually," she corrected him. And during that period she had become enamored with the land and all its inhabitants. What was there not to love? The skies were filled with great flocks of birds that rode the currents, spiraling, racing, dancing, sometimes in numbers so great that the sky would darken. The forests and grasslands were teeming with species she had never even dreamed of.

During those six moons she had spent much of her days out with Redbraids, and on her own, learning the plants and animals as she had done back home, stalking them and sitting and observing them for days at a time.

She had experimented with different woods and found the perfect one for the type of bow she preferred; a short re-curve with plenty of snap, small and light enough to carry with her no matter where she went. Africa was a vast land, so filled with life that one could spend many lives studying and learning her ways, and not come close to mastering all that there was to know.

And yet, a part of her felt empty. There was no Níškola here, no Uŋčí. She missed her village, the stretch of beach down at the water's edge, with its magical fire-sand. Redbraids called it *phosphorescence*. She missed her forests, the smell of the loamy, damp earth and the crisp scent of young fir needles in spring.

Seeing Pilipili on his shoulder made her miss Níškola all the more. "I miss Níška." She heard the words before she realized that she had said them out loud. Redbraids stopped and turned to face her. "Sorry, I was just thinking about my friend back home. I've told you about him, right?"

"Of course. How could I forget about the giant wolf-dog that you grew up with." Looking at Pilipili, he added, "It must be tough to be away from him for so long. I would have missed this little bugga, had she not found a way onto the *Mandaha*. I still don't know how she did it. I can't believe she survived Nchi... I mean, um, Khéya Wíta. Did I pronounce that right?" Wakíŋyaŋ nodded. "Khéya Wíta, Turtle Island. That sounds so much nicer than Nchi Mbaya, Bad Land!"

As they continued walking through the forest, she bantered, "I always thought it was amusing that your Pilipili is the size of a pispíza, while my Níška is bigger than most of your deer. They are opposites in so many ways."

"Ya, well you know what the say about opposites..." He gave her an odd look.

"No, I don't. What do they say about opposites?"

"*Hm*? Oh, nothing. It's just a saying."

They walked in silence for a while and her thoughts drifted to home, to Uŋčí, and to the veil. When it came to the spirit world she still had more questions than answers and longed to see Grandmother again so she could get to the bottom of the mystery. Uŋčí said that she had mastered much here in the physical world and that it was time she learned to master the veil. But how was she supposed to do that without a teacher, without someone to guide her?

She had been so immersed in her own thoughts that she had not noticed that they had stepped out of the forest and were crossing an open, grassy clearing.

They came to a halt, and she looked to one side. A large, black leopard had entered the clearing at the same moment, not thirty paces away.

It stopped and looked at them.

The three stood motionless, staring into each others' eyes.

Then the great cat broke the spell, turned its head and calmly carried on its way, disappearing into the forest on the far side of the glade.

Without a word spoken, they walked over to where the leopard had been, stepped onto the small path, and followed it into the thicket of trees.

~E~

The old soothsayers words drifted into Uhuru's mind unexpectedly, and he spoke one of the verses out loud. "On tendua's path you have chosen to be, follow her through the darkness and you will be free." The words tumbled effortlessly from his lips. "Remember the old oracle in the market in Accra that I told you about?"

"Yes. Why?"

"Well, I don't know what 'tendua's path' is. My father spoke to me of something called the Heart Path. What if tendua means heart? That could make sense. Or what if tendua means leopard or something like that, in the old man's language? What if *this* is tendua's path," he pointed to ground at their feet, "and we are literally following tendua's path right now! This isn't the first time this has happened to me, you know. Before I ever met you, I followed a chui nyeusi, a black leopard just like this one. I connected with it. This might sound a bit strange, but through its eyes, the look it gave me, I… na. Never mind. It's silly." *Follow her through the darkness and you will be free. Follow who? The leopard? Through the darkness and I'll be free. But there was no leopard around in our escape. I followed the darkness, yes. I followed the water. I followed the song. Ha, Jioba never stopped singing. And I followed Wakíŋyaŋ...*

He recalled the look in the eyes of the black leopard. He'd seen that same look when the old man's face had transformed. And then again, somewhere else, but where?

He turned towards Wakíŋyaŋ to bring up another point, but when their eyes met his heart froze mid-beat, his lips parted but uttered no words, and he stared at her as if in a trance.

"You?"

~W~

She smiled and looked away. "We should, you know, keep walking."

She had never spoken to Redbraids about Igmútȟaŋka, her Spirit Teacher. She understood that the spirit world was an important part of life in Africa, but it had never been the right moment for that conversation. Or maybe she was afraid to discuss it with him. Considering they had just followed an igmútȟaŋka into the woods, perhaps now was as good a time as any. But something he said sent her thoughts spinning out of control. *My dream. The dark tunnel with the shadow figure, wild clumps of hair drifting around, someone reaching down towards me. Bronx in the worm hole? No, it was Redbraids swimming down through the water to save my life. It was always Redbraids. And the animal I saw in the field when I was sitting with Uŋčí under the baobab! The same as this leopard that we just saw.*

Then it was clear. A knowing washed over her.

Her eyelids lowered half way and she let out a soft, guttural snarl through her nostrils as Igmúthaŋka's energy moved through her. *All along it was you, guiding us together from opposites sides of the wold. But why?*

They walked in silence. Birds of every size and color soared through the skies, flitted from branch to branch, and scurried through the bending grasses. Butterflies danced flower to flower, moving in erratic, evasive fits of flight, folding and falling, then rising again with wings spread on the slightest wind current. Tiny deer, no bigger than a maštíŋska, nibbled on tender grass shoots and fallen seed.

"Can you believe how Señora Concha has taken to Clifton?" Redbraids' voice joined the sounds of the forest. "I don't think he's ever gonna leave, you know?"

"Yes. He seems quite happy. And Bark and Bite! I'm so glad they found a family to love them. If anyone deserves to be loved, cared for by family, it's them."

"They have a home now." Redbraids' voice was warm and reassuring. "They will never have to suffer like that again."

"I know. I feel such happiness for them. And the others, too. I think most of us are still in shock to be in a land where the people welcome us with open arms and hearts, where we don't have to defend our territory or worry about being captured or killed by others. Life is...harder in Khéya Wíta, yes, but no less beautiful. I...miss my homeland." She stopped for a moment and reached out to grab hold of his hand. "I miss Uŋčí, Níškola, the village."

He looked down at their hands, then into her eyes. "I know that it was never your plan to come here. We were meant to board the ship and sail to your village. But things...happened...Bronx, Wit'é..." She saw a wave of sadness wash over his face as he spoke.

She grabbed hold of his other hand. "You saved my life," she said, looking at him straight in the eyes. "I... owe you mine." A mixture of gratitude and deep sorrow was welling up inside her. To owe her very life to another, this was an honor beyond words. But her heart longed to return to her people. She loved Africa, but something called to her, something inexplicable pulled at her. How could she honor her debt to Redbraids and return home at the same time?

"You owe me nothing. Do you understand? Nothing! I...I would never wish such a burden on anyone. Look, you feel you must return to your people, then that is what you must do. I don't know how we are going to get you there, but we'll find a way. Do you understand?"

His voice sounded so confident and reassuring. "Thank you," she praised. "So, where are you taking me?"

"Oh, just to a little spot up ahead that I like to go to. It's not much farther, come on."

They were walking along small game trails in a forest of acacia trees. After a short while they came to a clearing and on the far side the vegetation changed abruptly. The trees were unlike any she had seen before. They had perfectly round, smooth trunks, almost as wide around as the giant baobab trees, and they stretched up into the sky beyond sight. She craned her neck to look up into the distant canopy floating in the clouds.

"What type of tree are these?"

"Actually, they aren't a tree at all. They're a type of grass! Can you believe it? Grass!"

"Grass! What do you mean?"

"Grass. Like this here," he boasted, reaching down and touching some of the knee high blades at his feet. "It's called bamboo."

"Bamboo? Can we get closer to it? I want to see it." She couldn't contain the excitement rising in her voice. Then without waiting for a response she started out across the clearing.

She only got a few paces when she stopped abruptly and dropped into a half-crouch. Not fifty running paces away, standing at the base of one of the monolithic stalks of grass, was one of those armored beasts that she had seen back at the Naming. A rhino!

She stepped backwards slowly while taking careful inventory of the threat. Its whitish skin was folded like plates of armor. *Too thick for my arrows to pierce*. Two lethal horns protruded from its elongated snout, the foremost of which was the length and girth of a young tree. Its head was bowed towards the earth. *Asleep?* She took another step back and bumped into Redbraids, who was standing right behind her.

"Don't...move," he said in a staccato whisper. "If it wakes up, we're both dead."

"So what do we do now?" she whispered back.

"Well," he paused, and a mischievous smile crawled across his face, "among my people there is a rite of passage..." He reached into the leather bag at his side and produced a smooth, shiny brown seed.

Then, holding the seed up in the air, he cocked one eyebrow. "But I don't think you're up for the challenge."

~MWISHO~

Glossary

Explanation: This book is filled with words from various languages, including some made up words. Some of the words have been intentionally altered from their original form and meaning, may be pronounced differently, spelled differently, and have different accent marks than their original form. I've created my own pronunciation guide for the more challenging words. But if all else fails, feel free to pronounce the words how ever you like. That's half the fun, right?

How to use this glossary: Fist I give you the **word** in bold, followed by the *pronunciation* in italics with the accented syllables in ***bold***, then the underlined name of the language the word is derived from, and finally the meaning of the word or phrase in English.

adamfo: *ah-**dahm**-foh*; Akan; friends
akwaaba: *ah-**kwah**-bah*; Akan; welcome
amigos: *ah-**mee**-gohs*; Castilian; friends
apaka svagat hai: ***ahp**-khe **svah**-gaht heh*; Hindi; you're welcome
asante sana: *ah-**sahn**-teh **sah**-nah*; Swahili; thank you very much
a su servicio: Castilian; at your service
awọn ọrẹ: ***ah**-won oh-reh*; Yoruba; friends
Aye: ***ah**-ye*; Yoruba; life, name given to the market in Accra

baba: *bah-bah*; Swahili; father
bibi: *bee-bee*; Swahili; slang for gal
boma: ***boh**-mah*; Maa; family or village compound, cluster of homes
Bötébbá: *boh-**teh**-bah*; Bube; heart, name of Jioba's mother
bulu: ***boo**-loo*; Yoruba; the color blue

bwana: *bwah*-*nah*; <u>Swahili</u>; man, mister, used commonly, as in "hey man", "bro", "dude", "bruv"

cálmate: *kahl-mah-teh*; <u>Castilian</u>; calm down
capitán: *kah-pee-**tahn***; <u>Castilian</u>; captain
chabalangus: *chah-bah-**lahng**-guhs*; <u>Author's Creation From Childhood</u>; an expression of surprise or disbelief, like 'wow!' or 'ho dang,' sometimes used to mark an event as amazing, awesome, fantastic, terrible, horrible, etc. sometimes used as an expletive
Čhaŋšká: *chung-**shkah***; <u>Lakota</u>; hawk or falcon, name of Wakíŋyaŋ's village friend
čhekpá: *chehk-**pah***; <u>Lakota</u>; Twins
chui: ***chew**-ee*; <u>Swahili</u>; leopard, cheetah

datura inoxia: <u>Latin</u>; plant used medicinally and spiritually around the world, can be poisonous if not used properly

el fin de la calle: *ehl **feen** deh lah **kah**-yeh*; <u>Castilian</u>; the end of the road
ElKikau: *ehl-kee-**kahoo***; <u>Maa</u>; first born, name of EnKare's father (Birth Name)
EnKare: *ehn-**kah**-reh*; <u>Maa</u>; water, name of main character (Birth Name)
enkarewa: <u>Maa</u>; round, beaded wedding necklace, consisting of multiple consecutive rings fanning out from the center, warn by Maasai brides and handed down generation after generation
EnKishón: *ehn-kee-**shohn***; <u>Maa</u>; life, name of giant baobab tree
EnKulupuoni: *ehn-**koo**-loo-poo-**oh**-nee*; <u>Maa</u>; earth, name of EnKare's father (Lion Name)
Ëtulá a Ëri: *eh-too-**lah** ah **eh**-ree*; <u>Bube</u>; name of the island where Jioba and his family come from

háŋ: *hung*; <u>Lakota</u>; yes
heyókȟa: *hehy-**ohk**-hah*; <u>Lakota</u>; clown(s)
hóyia: ***hoh***-ee-yah*; <u>Maa</u>; yes

igmútȟaŋka: *eeg-moo-**thung**-kah*; <u>Lakota</u>; jaguar
inážiŋkhiya: *een-**ahzsh**-ingk-**hee**-yah*; <u>Lakota</u>; stop!
ingri: ***een***-gree*; <u>Maa</u>; container for liquids made from gourd
išnáthi: *eesh-**nah**-thee*; <u>Lakota</u>; menstrual cycle
itóhekiya: *ee-**toh**-hehk-ee-yah*; <u>Lakota</u>; to go home
Itòhí: *ee-**toh**-hee*; <u>Bube</u>; sun, name of Jioba's father
Iworo: *ee-**woh**-roh*; <u>Yoruba</u>; holocaust, name used in Africa to describe the war that destroyed the previous age on Earth

jambo: ***jahm***-boh*; <u>Swahili</u>; hello
jina langu ni: *jee-nah lahn-goo nee*; <u>Swahili</u>; my name is
Jioba: j*ee-**oh**-bah*; <u>Bube</u>; name of main character, taken from the name of a mountain spirit from the volcano above Luba village on Ëtulá a Ëri Island

kesho: *keh-shoh*; <u>Swahili</u>; tomorrow
Khéya Wíta: *keh-yah wee-tah*; <u>Lakota</u>; Turtle Island, Wakíŋyaŋ's tribe's name for the land mass formerly known as North America
kikoi: *kee-**kohee***; <u>Swahili</u>; woven piece of cloth used for clothing and multiple other uses
kizunguzungu: *kee-**zoong**-goo-**zoong**-goo*; <u>Swahili</u>; crazy
kwisha kabisa: *kwee-shah kah-**bee**-sah*; <u>Swahili</u>; completely finished

maȟpíya: *mah-**pee**-yah*; <u>Lakota</u>; sky
Mami Wata: <u>Bube / Creole</u>; mermaid or siren spirit from West African coast

Mandaha: *mahn-**dah**-hah*; <u>Himba</u>; moon, name of EnKare's sister
manyatta: *mahn-**yah**-tah*; <u>Maa</u>; house
marafiki: *mah-rah-**fee**-kee*; <u>Swahili</u>; friends
maštíŋska: *mahsh-**ting**-skah*; <u>Lakota</u>; rabbit
meda wo ase: <u>Akan</u>; thank you
Mezumo: *meh-**zoo**-moh*; <u>Himba</u>; womb, name of cave in South West Africa where Okuruwo was born during Iworo and the six winters
mi amor: <u>Castilian</u>; my love
mon ami: <u>French</u>; my friend
morani: *moh-**rah**-nee*; <u>Maa</u>; warrior(s)
mwisho: *mm-**wee**-shoh*; <u>Swahili</u>; end
mzungu: *mm-**zoong**-goo*; <u>Swahili</u>; a person of European descent

Nchi Mbaya: *nn-chee mm-**bah**-eeyah*; <u>Swahili</u>; bad lands, everywhere on Earth besides Africa
ndio: *nn-**dee**-yoh*; <u>Swahili</u>; yes
Ngabunat: *nn-**gah**-boo-naht*; <u>Maa</u>; secret, hidden, name of cave where EnKulupuoni's parents lived during Iworo
Níškola: *neesh-**koh**-lah*; <u>Lakota</u>; tiny, the name of Wakíŋyaŋ's canine companion
nyeusi: *nyeh-**oo**-si*; <u>Swahili</u>; black

O dabọ: *oh **dah**-boh*; <u>Yoruba</u>; goodbye
Oke osimiri na-eduzi gị. Oké osimiri na-echebe gị. Daalụ nwanne nwanyị maka ịkpọtara ụmụ anyị n'ụlọ. Nabata ụmụaka n'ụlọ. Nnọọ n'ụlọ: <u>Igbo</u>; The ocean guides you. The sea protects you. Thank you sister for bringing our children home. Welcome home children. Welcome home
Okuruwo: *oh-koo-**roo**-woh*; <u>Himba</u>; sacred fire, name of EnKare's mother

Oldoinyo: *ohl-**doheen**-yoh*; <u>Maa</u>; mountain, name of EnKulupuoni's friend rhino

Opanin: *oh-**pah**-neen*; <u>Akan</u>; elder, term of respect

orporror: *ohr-poh-**rohr***; <u>Maa</u>; warrior age group

p̌ahíŋ: *pah-**hing***; <u>Lakota</u>; giant porcupine

p̌ežúta: *peh-**zshoo**-tah*; <u>Lakota</u>; herb

Pilipili: *pee-lee-**pee**-lee*; <u>Swahili</u>; a spicy hot herbal blend or sauce, the name of EnKare's galago friend

pispíza: *pis-**pee**-zah*; <u>Lakota</u>; prairie dog or ground squirrel

rafiki zangu: *rah-**fee**-kee **zahn**-goo*; <u>Swahili</u>; my friends

rungu: *roon-goo*; <u>Maa</u>; wooden club

sápa: <u>Lakota</u>; black

siesta: <u>Castilian</u>; mid-afternoon nap

simi: *see-mee*; <u>Maa</u>; short, double edged sword

Sobaco: *soh-**bah**-coh*; <u>Castilian</u>; armpit, nickname the villagers give to an area of swampy lowlands by the river near Mbini

stuckmuck: *stuhk-muhk*; <u>Author's Creation From Childhood</u>; a type of coarse grass that grows in tightly clustered clumps, ranging in height from one to twelve feet tall

šuŋgmánitu: *shoong-**mah**-nee-too*; <u>Lakota</u>; coyote

tendua: <u>Hindi</u>; leopard, panther

ťȟáȟča: *thah-chah*; <u>Lakota</u>; deer or stag

the burn: <u>English</u>; casual name being used to describe the civilization-ending war by the inhabitants of Khéya Wíta

timá: tee-**mah**; <u>Old Bantu</u>; courage

tu sabes: <u>Castilian</u>; you know

twendeni: Swahili; let's go

Udo: Igbo; peace
Uhuru: *oo-**hoo**-roo*; Swahili; freedom
Uŋčí: **oong**-chee; Lakota; Grandmother
uší: *oo-**shee***; Lakota; come here

vamanos: Castilian; let's go

Wakȟáŋ Kiktá: *wah-**khung** kihk-**tah***; Lakota; awakened spirit, name of Wakíŋyaŋ's grandmother
Wakíŋyaŋ: *wah-**king**-yung*; Lakota; thunder, name of main character
wašúŋ: *wah-**shoong***; Lakota; cave
Wašúŋ Wóniya: *wah-**shoong** woh-**nee**-yah*; Lakota; Spirit Cave, Breath of Life Cave; name of cave where Wakíŋyaŋ's grandparents escape the burn and survive the six winters
Wenye Hekima: *wehn-yeh **heh**-kee-mah*; Swahili; wise ones
wewe ni: Swahili; you are
Wíŋyaŋ Wakȟáŋ: *wing-yung wah-**khung***; Lakota; holy woman or medicine woman
Wit'é: *weet-**eh***; Lakota; new moon, name Wakíŋyaŋ gives to the straw-haired girl
wóniya: *woh-**nee**-yah*; Lakota; spirit
wóphiye: *woh-**pee**-yeh*; Lakota; medicine bag

yuška: *ee-oosh-**kah***; Lakota; to free oneself

zičá: *zee-**chah***; Lakota; squirrel
zitkála: *zit-**kah**-lah*; Lokota; giant flying fox

Nine Tribes Of The Wenye Hekima:

Dogon: farmers from the Bandiagara Plateau of North West Africa
Hadza: fisher people from the Lake Eyasi region of East Africa
Himba: pastoralists from the Kunene River Basin of South West Africa
Jieng (Dinka): pastoralists from the fertile Nile River Basin of North East Africa
!KungSan: *(tongue-click)-koong-sahn*; hunters from the Kalahari Desert and surrounding forests of Southern Africa
Maasai: *mah-sahee*; pastoralists of the Great Serengeti savanna lands of East Africa
Mbuti: *mm-boo-tee*; people of the rain forests in the Heart of Africa
Tuareg: nomads from the Tenere Sands of North Africa
Wodaabe: *woh-dayb*; wanderers of the Sahel Desert of North West Africa

Acknowledgements

The following acknowledgements are not presented in order of magnitude of appreciation, importance, significance, or any other hierarchical scheme. I love, appreciate, and value all of you.

To **Lynda**, thank you for all of your positive support and encouragement throughout my book writing adventure. The way you speak of the book's success as a present reality; 'once they've made a television series out of it, we'll be on a beach celebrating,' has helped immensely to mitigate my own self doubts.

To **Caz**, your endless positive support, joyous exuberance, and care keep me nourished and inspired. If I sell a couple copies, then perhaps we'll be able to 'just get away' together, with the whole family.

To **Alan**, for blazing the trail, showing me that it is possible to write a book, and for demonstrating the patience, dedication, and fortitude required to accomplish such a monumental task. You are, in your book writing, as you are in being a father, and not a moment passes that I'm not thankful for your presence in my life.

To **Amani** and **Etana**, for giving me the opportunity in this life to learn how to love unconditionally, and for your strength and grace which continues to teach and humble me at every step along our journey together.

To **Dagny**, for igniting in me an adventurous, creative spirit that questions everything, and for giving me the strength and resolve to swim against the currents, even when that means being a tiny island in a great big world.

To **Fela**, for not only being my beta reader, but for taking the time and the care to print out the whole manuscript, sit down with blue and red pens in hand, and pour over every inch of it from start to finish. I could not have hoped for better help, direction, and advice. You are a master. You rock!

To **Molly** and **Will**, thank you for tolerating me and my unorthodox attempts at parenting. It has been such an honor to grow with you and I look forward to seeing what you have in store for us tomorrow.

To **Mija** and **Pele**, for loving me unconditionally. I see how effortless it is for you, and I strive to follow your example (without the tail wagging and forceful tongue bath kisses—(that's just not acceptable behavior in humans :)

L. D. MUSSELL

I come from the dirt floor of a converted cow shed, squatting barefoot around an open fire with friends, eating ugali and sukuma wiki with our fingers. I come from parleys with lions in the misty high mountains, and sleepy nights with elephants at the watering hole. I come from snow covered peaks at the top of the world, bucketfuls of baby sea turtles scattered on the waves, and the solemn song of the muezzin calling out through the still, early morning air. I come from skateboarding down eight lane highways hanging on to the back of jeepneys, lumpia stacked high at the charcoal grill on a busy corner, and streets that turn to rivers in the monsoon rains. I come from the flame coaxed to life in a nest of dry moss, beating drums thundering through the forest, long days of hard labor with a love song in my heart. I come from the roots of seeds planted in the rich soil of the Great Rift Valley, cries of a lone wolf drifting over the Sierra Madre, water lapping at the shore of a lowland loch, and mighty stone circles marking our planet's journey through the cosmos.

I come from peanut butter on pancakes.

This is where I come from.

This is my world.

Made in the USA
Monee, IL
17 September 2023

42877789R00236